Hans Bernsteen, July 1939

Islands of Deception

Islands of Deception

LYING WITH THE ENEMY

Constance Hood

ISLANDS OF DECEPTION
Waves Press

Author services by Pedernales Publishing, LLC.
www.pedernalespublishing.com

ISBN: 0-9993946-1-4
ISBN 13: 978-0-9993946-1-8

Library of Congress Control Number: Pending

Printed in the United States of America

Acknowledgements

In 2002 my father sent me a thick envelope. In it were several closely spaced pages of notes. He was particularly proud of work that he had done as an intelligence operative in World War II. The tasks had been classified under a long-term non-disclosure agreement, and he was releasing his account of 1943 events in the South Pacific.

His story was complex. For one thing, no one had ever heard an accurate account of how he came to leave Holland, or why he decided to reject his cultural origins as a Dutch Jew. Even his name was changed. The shadows of partial truths led loved ones into complex paths of obscure intentions and resulting misunderstandings. We disregarded his intriguing narrative until we found the parallel reports in released Army Counter Intelligence documents.

Many people shared the vision of this book. The long dead needed to be brought back to life. Adapting their story as a novel gave me the freedom to add characters that were missing from official reports. My husband, actor Chet Hood, worked daily to help me understand a little about the life of a warrior. I'm sure the neighbors wondered why we were having slow motion knife fights in the backyard. Nancy Hall and I talked for hours about how threat and fear led people into a lifetime of hiding.

Dutch relatives shed a lot of light on the subject during the same period of time. My aunt told her story piece by piece in a series of long visits to Amsterdam. I ended up with a narrative that was accurate but colorful, fascinating but heartbreaking.

Photographs needed to become scenes. Philip and Marcia Goudsmit collected hundreds of photos of the main characters and shots of Amsterdam from the 1930s and 1940s. Imagine my surprise when the collection mirrored things that I had made up to cover missing pieces of the story. Hendrina Lisiewicz and I translated Dutch maritime records that chronicled her father's years at sea. The curator at Battleship Cove, Fall River MA gave me a day to crawl around PT boats and construct key scenes. Dr. John Munholland, author of Rock of Contention offered valuable descriptions of the partitioning of France and the role of New Caledonia as an improvised Allied staging area for the War in the Pacific.

The Ventura Writer's Group read draft after draft of chapters and asked all the right questions to bring the story alive. Ross R. Olney, Francis Moss, Chris Frederic and Charlie Schwartz also read drafts and shared true stories that added authenticity to the narrative.

A story of this scope cannot be accomplished without editors. I am truly grateful for the support of Kate Breckenridge and Brenda Podagrosi-Georgi who spent countless hours with these characters. Finally, special thanks to Mary Ellen Gavin, Literary Agent who helped bring the story to you.

July 14, 2017

Table of Contents

CHAPTER 1

Amsterdam, Holland
May 1939

The Night of Broken Glass (Kristallnacht) *raged from November 9 to 10, 1938. After celebrating victories over Jewish neighborhoods, the Nazis announced a decree to remove all Jews from German economy, society and culture.*

SAM GOUDBERG'S VOICE SNAPPED LIKE a whip through the entire office. "Hans, have you completed the accounts for the shops in Rotterdam?" Hans Bernsteen wiped off the tips of his two pens and placed them in a jar on his desk. Silence announced that the bookkeeping staff had departed for midday. Tall front windows reflected spots of sunshine onto the marble floors, an uncertain promise of a sunny afternoon. The converted ballroom still had its gilded light fixtures, but its interior had been occupied with commerce for years. His desk was in a dark corner of the offices, where he counted his parents' wealth for hours on end.

He turned his head aside and muttered a quick response to his stepfather. A blotter lay across the sheet in an enormous book while he stretched his long legs and rolled back his cramped shoulders, waiting for the ink to dry. Columns of black and red numbers marched up and down the page, each entry standing for an item in a warehouse or a shop, stacks of laces here or rolls of ribbons there. The hefty volume contained more than a hundred balance sheets and Hans placed it on a shelf with a row of similar books, each dated with registers of accounts. Standing up from the stiff leather chair, he brushed off his tweed jacket and buttoned on a clean pair of spats in anticipation of mud on the streets. He checked his leather briefcase a final time and stepped out the doors of Herengracht 94. If this afternoon meeting went well he would not ever need to return to the ledgers.

Thank heavens the upstairs dining room curtains were closed. By now his stepfather, Sam, would be upstairs with his mouth full of boiled meat or potato, reporting to mother on the morning's profits and losses. Sara would ask a few questions and then serve dessert. Hans's nervous stomach cramped at the thought of food. Bicyclists bumped and rattled across cobblestones, avoiding iron stanchions and bars that lined the canal. Barges poked along the water, sloughing off their loads of merchandise. The little shops were shuttered for midday. Hans dodged into a shaded alley and another turn placed him onto the next canal. A solid wall of dark red bricks continued along the Keizersgracht. Head down, he followed the angled patterns in the brick sidewalk, avoiding stray dog droppings that lay in his path, until the scrubbed white stone steps and arched double doors of the United States Consulate came into view.

The young man introduced himself at reception, and expected to be ushered right into the office of the consul. Hans's father had been Minister of Finance for the Netherlands, and Consul Van den Arend was a family friend. The receptionist looked at Hans as if he were nobody, just one person in a herd of civilians who asked for favors. It had been necessary to wrestle his way through phone lines and calling cards to obtain an appointment. In the noisy lobby, he took a seat and read the same pamphlet over and over. After several minutes, an unsmiling secretary came toward him, heels clicking on the marble flooring. She stood over his chair, waiting for him to look up. "*Heer* van den Arend will see you now."

Recent political actions in Germany had prompted the American consulate to expedite papers for those claiming refugee status. Jews in Berlin were sweeping up the shattered glass of commerce and broken hopes. Now Dutch Nazis participated in isolated incidents throughout Holland, raiding Jewish homes and shops, vandalizing synagogues, and killing nearly 40 Jewish citizens. Instead of expressing public outrage, Dutch people quietly went about their everyday lives.

Hans took a deep breath as he stepped into the office. The consul set his reading glasses aside. "Hans, my dear boy! How have you been?"

Van den Arend extended his hand, and Hans quickly wiped sweat from his palm. He smiled nervously as he glanced around the room. "Business has been steady... people still need .... the things they need." Although he was heir to a prestigious Amsterdam mercantile enterprise, his stepfather had dismissed him from any duties that required working with customers. Hans took exception to a new business philosophy that the "customer is always the boss." A business proprietor was not a servant.

Consul Van den Arend nodded. "Are you certain you wish to go through with this?"

Hans looked boldly at the consul and nodded his head.

The consul handed the thick envelope to Hans. "Everything is in order then. Your visas were approved."

Instead of tearing the envelope open, Hans examined it, took out his penknife and carefully cut the U.S. stamps from the corner. "For my stamp collection." He pulled out two visas, one for himself and one for his sister, Esther. There were lengthy explanations and fine print in English, and he asked for help understanding the detailed instructions before placing the visas in his leather briefcase. The consul came around his desk and grasped Hans by the shoulder. "Good luck."

The morning rain had dried completely. He looked through the narrow brick buildings into a bright sun and a renewed day. Amsterdam was beautiful, with vibrant greenery filling out branches of the trees and reflecting into the canals. Flower stalls were full of fresh tulips and every window box was overflowing with colors. Freshly washed lace curtains hung in windows that had been sealed all winter. These were ordinary things that he would miss when he left Holland.

Another stone street led toward the Leidseplein and to the Café Americain. Its sparkling windows and black and white stone floors evoked jazz and fun. It was easy to spot his coquettish sister at a table for two, her auburn hair bobbing to music. He grinned, slipped through the glass doors and moved toward her table. Beautiful and headstrong, his younger sister Esther had once again fought with mother. God knows what this most recent rift was about.

Waiters hurried everywhere, rolling their carts of pastries and delicate china cups. He followed behind a large cart with a heavy silver urn and retrieved his new Leica from a coat pocket. Esther startled at the pop of the flashbulb.

"Why, it's you! I thought I was meeting Hedy Lamar. Happy Birthday!" He reached his arms out for an embrace.

Esther stiffened as he kissed her cheeks, then pushed his elbows away.

"You're dreaming again."

He took his seat, folding his long legs under the small table. "But we need to celebrate. Mother and Max both asked me to wish you a happy birthday."

Sparks flashed through her deep green eyes. "Oh, Mama. I haven't seen her for weeks. I'm sure she must be *devastated* by my absence."

Hans searched for a vague comment, something to avoid any eruption of Esther's temper. "She goes out for tea every afternoon, and still orders extra whipped cream on her pastry. The old ladies gossip about misbehaving adult children, trying to arrange our lives."

Esther's tapered fingertips pushed at her bobbed waves. She raised her penciled eyebrows and laughed. "Then she is still fat, or fatter if that is at all possible. I don't know how Sam stands her. He likes our money, but there has to be a limit to his lust."

Hans's ear twitched and he blinked. "Ah well, enough about them. Esther, we need to talk. I have something for you."

"What?"

"In my briefcase."

"Ooh la la, it must be small and lovely!"

"Esther, you're the limit. And I'm hungry. What shall we have, sandwiches, cakes, or both? My God, are those strawberries?" The gloved waiter displayed his trays proudly, and poured a fragrant dark tea into their cups.

"They're probably from Spain. They won't be ripe. Sometimes they aren't as sweet as they look."

He selected a large strawberry pastry with golden custard and whipped cream. Esther picked over the tray, and settled on dark chocolate gateau drenched with a rich orange liqueur. The noise of the busy café rang around them with the clatter of dishes and the buzz of conversations. Casting a glance about the room, Hans leaned in to comment quietly.

"You know this is just as serious for me as it is for you. My inheritance is gone – Mother signed over our business to Sam. I work in a place that I should own. A job? I don't even get a salary – Sam says there aren't enough profits. He gives me an allowance, like a spoiled child." His intense blue eyes looked at her, unblinking and seeing all.

That look frightened her. They had conspired against adults all their lives, and she knew when he was joking and when he planned to act. Helpless inaction was not part of his lexicon.

"What are you thinking?" She picked at the dense glaze on her pastry. "You make me nervous."

"Have you even been paying attention to the news reports?"

Esther pouted. "Boring. All about market prices. And I certainly don't listen to German radio. Who cares about the Germans? I like American music." Hans smiled in anticipation of delivering her surprise, and then the light left his eyes.

"What about Kristallnacht? Esther, the Nazis are not just German thugs. We have them here too. Nothing else will matter if they gain any more power, or worse, if their ideals take hold in the rest of Europe. They are not going to stop with Berlin."

"Politics! Look, I came to see you and have tea." She picked up two more sugar cubes, put one into the cup and the other into her mouth. "For God's sake, *Kristallnacht* was six months ago. There's no reason to be afraid of the Nazis. We're half German."

"*Kristallnacht* wasn't an end; it was a beginning. You really don't pay any attention to things you don't want to understand, do you?"

Esther pulled the teacup up to her face and then banged it back down, tea spilling into the saucer. "Maybe I should have ordered Genever. This is not fun. In your note you promised me something special."

He lifted the briefcase to the table and opened it. Instead of a brightly wrapped gift, he pulled out his envelope. "Esther, remember that bird in the attic?"

"Oh God, that was awful." She looked at the packet. There was no bright paper or ribbon.

"The point is, we set it free." Hans pushed the envelope to the side of his plate and covered it with his napkin.

"No, *you* got to be a hero and set it free. I had to stand on your shoulders and grab it from the rafter. It was disgusting – it screamed and it bit my hand. I almost killed it." She looked down at a tiny scar on her finger.

"But you didn't kill it. It hopped out onto the upstairs pulley and then flew up and sang from the gables."

"So what does any of that have to do with my birthday? You sometimes speak in riddles that no one understands."

He looked ahead quietly. "We need to free ourselves, and you can't tell anyone what we're going to do." He ran his fingers through his hair, pushing a stray curl off of his forehead. A waiter approached them with the teapot. "It has to be like the attic, our secret. Little birds sometimes talk, and I couldn't tell you what I was planning."

He uncovered the envelope and pulled out a letter from inside. "Would you like to see your gift now? It took weeks to prepare it. I called on everyone for these. Immigration visas to the U.S., even though there is a tight quota on Jews. We're going to New York!"

He expected her to be thrilled with his initiative. Her eyes widened, and she covered her mouth. He had gone mad.

Tea at the elegant café was an error. Everyone on the street could see into the large glass windows with their gold lettering. The pastel walls and mirrors displayed elegant clientele, but he didn't wish to be displayed. He wanted to hide. He needed to remind her of who and what they were.

Her mouth gaped, closed, and then opened again, her lipstick mask torn and distorted. "There is no 'we' in this discussion. You don't tell me what to do." He shook his head curtly, shooing the waiter away. A whisper broke across the table. Even Esther realized that this was a dangerous conversation in a public place. "Are you crazy?" A perplexed smile crossed her face. "Is this one of your imaginary conspiracies? You shouldn't worry about the Germans. Mother was born in Germany. We can apply for German citizenship if we need to."

Hans lifted his face, and lowered his voice. "And then what? What makes you think that Holland will stand up against Hitler? My God, they just elected forty Nazis to our parliament." He stared at her in disbelief.

"Why do you want to blame the Nazis?" Esther didn't listen for an answer, but instead folded her napkin. Her foot was tapping under the table as she glowered at him. "You just want to escape."

"Just how do you think you can leave Amsterdam? We don't know anyone in America!"

Hans paused to think a moment about how their parents' connections had helped them get anything they had ever wanted, including the visas.

Esther continued. "The only English I know is 'Good Afternoon' and, 'Yes please, I would like some more tea.' All you know how to do is to fill out invoices. That will not even get us a sandwich in New York."

He opened the envelope and handed her the papers to examine. "Look, I have been able to get two visas." She looked at the papers with her name and the seal of the United States, then idly smeared the chocolate on her plate, daring him to lose his temper.

"It is risky, but we can do this."

"You don't even have any money."

"I have already gone to the camera shop. I'm selling all my box cameras, the Rollei, tripods, everything. I can't carry them with me.

Even my stamp albums are with a dealer. I'm starting new ones, all American stamps."

Her gaze narrowed. "Visas! You can't be serious. How did you manage to get two visas?"

"I called on Consul van den Arend, father's old friend from the U.S. Consulate. Remember? They worked together on trade agreements for years. Anyway, everyone is nervous about the Nazis gaining too much power. Have you looked at the German films? My God, they are trying to recreate another Roman Empire. It would almost be funny to a Latin School boy if their cries of hate weren't real."

"I'm not going to America. I am Dutch and I live in Amsterdam."

Her face rested on both hands as if she were using them to keep her jaw from dropping open and her gaze from wandering throughout the entire café. Hans's blue eyes turned angry, a steely gray, like a storm brewing. "Esther, there is nothing here for us."

"I can't believe this. You don't even want to be a businessman; you want to be a photographer."

Knuckles showed white as he clenched his fist. "You are wasting time." He looked around the restaurant, which thankfully was not as full as it was an hour ago. "We must act quickly. I need to book our passage."

She shook her head. "I could never leave Peter."

"Who in the heck is Peter? I've never heard of him. You haven't introduced us." Hans scraped at the whipped cream and crumbs on his plate, his silver fork clattering along the edge. "My God, what are you doing with yourself?" The air froze around him as he searched for his breath. "This is not the right way to get a husband. How long have you known this man?"

"You're being nasty now. You've never approved of my boyfriends. Okay, I have shared some things with you that I shouldn't have, but it's not my fault that you're a prude. Anyway, Peter's an artist."

"I don't care if he's painted you in the nude, even though it's wrong."

Esther's pursed her mouth in a tiny smooch. "He has."

"Marvelous! Great! I have a sister who became an artist and ended up a courtesan. What is your next role?"

"Hans, I do not want us to part with a fight. I am not going to New York. I will order a Genever and toast to your newest endeavor. We will drink the gin, and you will leave."

Hans took his handkerchief and wiped his eyes. "Esther, Esther… I'm sorry." He took a deep breath. "No, I didn't confide in you. I couldn't. But my action is intended for the best. We can send for Peter later, but you and I must act now." He was talking to her back as she bent under the table in an effort to retrieve her shopping bags.

"You never listen. You're like mother; you only hear what you want to. Thanks a lot for your 'gift' but I'm not going without Peter. We're done here, and I have an appointment."

He sat perfectly still, cleared his throat and spoke very quietly. "I can't get a third visa. Don't be a fool. Just take this one, and we will talk again before I buy our tickets. We still have two weeks' time."

Esther took the visa in her hand, stared at it thoughtfully, and tore the papers in half.

CHAPTER 2

Ellis Island
August 01, 1939

"Each island is only a place to depart from to go to another island. You never know where you are going."

~ SIDNEY DIAMOND

HANS LOOKED AROUND THE ELLIS Island terminal with its queues of passengers winding their way through the labyrinth. The vast entry hall was full of new arrivals. Afternoon sun baked the upper windows, and the place reeked of thousands of sweating, exhausted bodies. Even though it was a hot and humid summer day, people were piled deeply into vests, jackets and coats, as if everything they owned were on their backs. Hans was dressed like a first class passenger, even though he was in the line with third class immigrants who had traveled in close spaces for days. His business suit was not in the latest style, but it fit well and he carried expensive leather luggage. This was the day to make a good impression, as long as he didn't faint in the August heat.

An immigration inspector looked up at Hans's lean figure, sweating under a black felt hat. The young man looked like a hungry bird, with a prominently hooked nose and piercing blue eyes that scattered glances all over the entry hall. They were midway through the interview, filling out line #7 in the enormous logbook – Bernsteen, Hans.

QIV 2710 Visa # - Quota Immigration Visa, status refugee
Date of issue: 5/17/39
Can read and write in Dutch
Intent to return to country of origin – NO
Are you in possession of more than $50? If so, how much?

Hans had $400.00 to begin his new life in the United States, a gift from his mother. Ellis Island doctors and nurses took over with their inspections, listening to his heart and lungs and, finally, pulling down his eyelids. His tear ducts were working. Once his vision cleared, he looked across the counter at the inspector and the notebook.

Condition of Health, Mental and Physical:
Height: 6'2"
Hair: Brn
Eyes: Blu

Hans was called aside for a separate interview. His hands went cold in spite of the muggy day. These questions were much harder to answer, and he wasn't sure that his English was good enough to satisfy the officer.

"Have you ever been an anarchist?
"Have you ever been a polygamist?"
"Are you a person who believes in or advocates for the overthrow by force or violence of the government of the United States or all forms of law?"
"Are you coming as a result of any offer, solicitation, promise or agreements expressed or implied, to labor in the United States?"

He hesitated, "I will be seeking work."

"Do you intend to become a U.S. citizen?" For the first time Hans looked up, wide eyed, and smiled at the officer with a deliberate nod. Coming from generations of service to the Royal Palace of the Netherlands, he understood citizenship and planned to do his best.

"Welcome to the United States." Hans extended his hand and a cordial handshake ended the interview.

As the ferry to Manhattan pulled away from Ellis Island, Hans saw that the building was really quite lovely, a brick palace designed to make newcomers feel that they had arrived in a special place. They sailed past Liberty Island with its green lady welcoming visitors like a friendly but imposing aunt, and people rushed to the side of the broad beamed boat to get a good look at her. At last Hans was in New York on the way to making his fortune.

The ferry landed at Battery Park where hundreds of workers were taking noontime walks in the sun, and paths were worn through the grass where people had spilled off the walkways. One lone bench stood in the sun, and he sat down to plan out his day. He still needed to find lodging and look for work. A newspaper boy passed by and called out the day's headlines.... something about a prison named "Alcatraz." A gentleman sat down on the bench next to him, dressed in a dirty shirt, jacket, tie and hat. Instead of proper trousers he wore dungarees.

"Hey buddy, you new here?"

Hans regarded the fellow, and tried to think of proper American etiquette for meeting total strangers. He didn't like strangers. "Yes." His eyes remained focused on unfamiliar words in the newspaper.

"D'ya have a cigarette?"

A disgruntled sigh escaped. "I don't smoke."

"Wanna get a beer?"

Hans did not answer.

"You some kind of foreigner? Like just off the boat? Whatsa matter? Can't ya even answer a fellow?"

"Good day." Hans began to look around at passersby. They rarely stopped to sit on benches. The crabgrass was brown and flowers had already wilted and gone to seed. Greedy gulls and pigeons snatched up crumbs dropped from lunchboxes. He stood up, brushed off his slacks and folded his jacket. This was not a good place to rest. With a heavy bag and a thin wallet, he located the subway train and made his way up to Grand Central Station.

New York City was an assault on his senses. Wide streets roared with the sounds of the cars and buses – honking, beeping, and screeching to their destinations. Even the draft of wind behind them was annoying. An occasional horse drawn wagon or open carriage would also appear on the street, with the animal's head bent down, and blinders folded in to keep it from startling, or even defending itself from a bicycle or auto. Hans could use a set of blinders. He searched for the subway stop, a dark hole in the ground. Its tunnels were decorated with bright advertising posters that jumped out from the blackness. Noise from the crowds and the rumbling of the trains was deafening. Scraps of food, urine and the smell of combustion permeated the air, or what there was of it. He watched a pair of rats scuttling between cracks in the concrete, searching for nibbles of dropped breakfast rolls or fruit pits.

Hans only knew the name of one hotel, the Hotel Empire, recommended by the Consul in Amsterdam. He stepped into the lobby of the Empire to find some lunch. The dining room with its immaculate white place settings was the first thing he had seen in two weeks that looked vaguely like home. A small room was available for $2.00 a night. It would be necessary to find work and a cheaper address. He would immediately deposit his money to use when he opened his photography studio, leaving aside $20.00 a week to live on until he was settled.

He walked back out into the streets. Above him, as far as he could see, enormous skyscrapers loomed, blocking out the sky. Not a tree or a weed would grow in this mass of concrete and steel. The windows indicated that there were workers somewhere, but to him they looked like the eyes of insects observing their prey from all directions. People in business dress strode hurriedly, eagerly entering revolving doors to be devoured and then regurgitated by the buildings. He stepped into an ornate lobby where an elevator cage captured him.

A large office with modern glass doors looked out into a fourth floor elevator lobby. Across the parquet was a flash of platinum blonde hair. She looked like a movie star. He grasped the elegant brass handle of the door and stepped confidently into the office. The blonde glanced up from her magazine and ignored him. She was also ignoring instructions from a tall lady in a tailored suit.

"Mabel, would you please type up these invoices? They need to go out today."

The blonde responded, "Aw, I have a hurt finger. See, it's all red and puffy. I can't type, but I'll put them in the mailbox."

Mabel turned and directed her attention to the handsome young man. "Can I help you, sir?"

"I am here to inquire about the job."

"I'm sorry, do we have an opening?"

"I surely hope so. I have come from Amsterdam to meet with Mr. Springhorn."

"Mr. Springhorn is out of town." The two ladies laughed and the tall one turned on her heel. She left the box of papers on the front desk.

"Say buddy, can you type?"

Hans smiled. "Yes, as a matter of fact I can." He looked at her, puzzled. "Do I have a job?"

"Nah, but I can recommend you to Springhorn this Saturday. We have a… meeting."

His hand was on the business card case in his pocket. Mabel glanced up from her magazine at the foreigner. He tugged at the leather casing and handed her his card, Hans Bernsteen, Director, Holland-America Import/Export. She looked intently at the card, and then at him.

"By the way, we don't hire kikes." Hans took a deep breath. He hadn't heard anything about American restrictions on hiring Jews. His blue eyes shifted from her face toward a picture on the wall.

By afternoon his best suit began to rumple, and his shirt was damp. A bright smile turned into a hopeful smile, and then into a mask. His slow foreign enunciation indicated that he was not qualified to do office work in New York. "Buddy, we can't use you. You could cut that accent with a knife." Apparently he wasn't going to be a bookkeeper. That was probably a good thing, but it just didn't feel very good. Tomorrow he would visit the fashion district with his cameras, and see if anyone could use a photographer.

Returning to the Empire, Hans collapsed on the narrow hotel bed, drained of sweat, his head in a whirl of doubts. For the first time in weeks, he was glad that Esther had not come to New York.

Thick clouds and drizzle heralded the new day. Hans shouldered his camera bag. Should he represent himself as a Dutch businessman or a photographer? The bustling Seventh Avenue fashion district looked much more like the New York he had envisioned. Tall brick buildings hummed with the work inside. Stock boys rolled racks of garments down the street. The Jewish names were recognizable, and dry goods shops were scattered between manufacturers and some showrooms. "Help Wanted" signs were all looking for experienced cutters or draftsmen. He didn't have the skills of a garment laborer and, after all the remarks about his accent he was not looking forward to conversations.

New York was supposed to be his golden land, a place where he would be free from his parents, free to be an artist, and free of Amsterdam's rules. The uptown hiring restrictions on hiring Jews puzzled him. Hans had never given much thought to people's beliefs. He was responsible for himself, for his thoughts and for his actions. Actions were what mattered. The stories said that Jewish people lived together in a desert thousands of years ago, that they had established a set of laws. The Gentiles said they followed the same ten laws. So what was the problem? Each fall one atoned for shortcomings and closed the book on that year.

Ah well, August was the height of summer. There was still time to make mistakes before the book closed. He had a chance to change his identity completely and irrevocably. Was it possible to be the same person if you shed the common understandings of your people? It was exhilarating and dangerous, both at once.

At the Empire he asked the front desk concierge for a listing of churches. The concierge remarked, "Excuse me, sir, but most people here go to church on Sundays."

"If you could just give me a list, I shall decide when and where I wish to go to church." The listing may as well have been in Greek. None of the names of the churches or their denominations made any sense. There seemed to be a Presbyterian church just a few blocks away, and he knew that Presbyterian was something like the Dutch Protestants, people who had simple ways.

He stood at the corner of 57th Street, staring at the massive brown stones of Fifth Avenue Presbyterian. There were at least a dozen doors to the inside, and he wasn't sure that he wanted to enter any of them. Hans looked up at the sky. The clouds were dispersing rapidly, and sunny blue shone through. Tall buildings converged on the four corners leaving a luminous cross in the middle of the sky, a panorama of movement and light. A set of broad steps led to the wide doors. They were unlocked. Inside, radiant colors streamed into the sanctuary, brighter than images from any camera. It was wonderful. He had been raised in a 17th century synagogue with plain glass windows and straightforward woodwork. The synagogue didn't even have electricity, because it was against Jewish law to run power on the Sabbath. Several large rooms lined a hallway behind the sanctuary, and eventually a kindly middle-aged lady appeared.

"How can we help you, sir?"

He struggled for the words in English. "I am looking for a church." She knew that wasn't what he was trying to say, so she stepped down a hallway and returned with a man in corduroys and a tweed jacket.

"Good afternoon, I'm Reverend Kirkland. What can we do for you, young man?" The minister shook his hand firmly.

Hans was not quite as confident about where he had landed. "I'm not sure, but I think I need to become a Presbyterian. How do I do that?"

"Where are you from?"

"Amsterdam, Holland."

"So you are Dutch Reformed?"

"No, we are not reformed, my parents were…conservative?" An embarrassed grimace crossed his face. "How do I learn about this church?"

Reverend Kirkland wrinkled his forehead, listening to the heavy accent of his visitor. "Young man, when did you arrive in New York?"

"Yesterday."

"And you feel you need to go to church? Where do you live?" The reverend led him down a dimly lit hallway to an office. The stone floor was well worn, but there was a grace and warmth to the oak paneled hallway, as if many others had come here for help and received it.

"I'm at the Hotel Empire right now, but I need to find a job. And they might not give me a job because I don't go to a church."

The reverend paused. "We have freedom of religion in the United States. You can go to any church you wish." He handed a shiny pamphlet to Hans. "Though, I will say this is an excellent church and it undoubtedly is Presbyterian. Have a seat."

Hans took the chair furthest from the minister's desk. Maybe he was making a mistake. This didn't feel like a church. The minister's office had no lighted windows and no elaborate decorations. It was a simple workplace, even a little shabby.

He certainly didn't know what questions to ask, so he let Reverend Kirkland lead the conversation. "Why do you believe you must become a Presbyterian? If your family is conservative, are you Jewish?"

"No, no. I don't know anything about those people." The lie was uncomfortable. It was true he had rarely attended synagogue after his Bar Mitzvah, but he had never been in a church either.

Reverend Kirkland swiveled his chair and tipped forward, looking directly into Hans's face. Hans did not avoid the examination. He sat impassively, holding his face still, including his eyes. "Then let me get to know you. It seems you are confused and searching. Are you ready to go where God is leading you?"

"Pardon? I don't believe in fortunetellers." This was getting very awkward.

"No one knows the future, but there is a larger plan at work. I do believe you were meant to be here at this time. Does it help to know that God has provided everything you will need?"

"Pardon?"

"God helped our Savior create miracles. Jesus could turn water into wine. He fed thousands of people from five loaves of bread and two fish. He.... provided."

Hans looked at him. The man seemed sane. He was in charge of a large institution. Millions of people believed...this?

"Let's talk about Moses. Perhaps that is more familiar to you. God was patient with him, and made sure he had what he needed to bring the people to safety. God will do the same for you. Come now, you are in the right place." Reverend Kirkland opened the large bottom drawer in his desk and began to dig around in the file folders. "Here, let me get you some information about our church. How about we talk on Sunday at noon, after church services. Where can I reach you?"

"I am staying at the Empire, but I must move to a... a..."

"A more modest place?"

"Yes, the hotel was recommended by a friend in Amsterdam, but I need some place to live."

The door opened, and the nice lady inserted herself, resolute in her sturdy shoes and dark skirt. "Reverend Kirkland, Reverend Lawson is waiting outside." She looked at Hans, expecting him to pick up his hat and leave. He made no effort to collect himself. Once he left this building, he would be on his own again.

"Good heavens, is it four o'clock already? I have an appointment. Wait a minute – young man, I would like to introduce you to Reverend James Lawson. Helen, please show the Reverend in."

"Is he Presbyterian?"

"Oh no, no. Reverend Lawson is an Episcopalian." A bald man entered the room. He seemed younger than Kirkland, and was suitably attired in a clerical collar and dark jacket. Lawson looked at Hans, trying to see how he fit into the picture. The young man did not look like a major donor; but he was too conservatively dressed to be a young person in trouble.

"Hello Jim, I'd like to introduce you to Hans Bernsteen, a recent arrival from Holland."

Hans stood and shook hands, nodding his head slightly. He couldn't remember if it was polite to bow in New York. "I am from Amsterdam." Hans didn't intend to contradict Kirkland, but he wanted to be correct.

"Amsterdam? Seems to be quite a bit of trouble brewing in Europe now. What brings you to New York?"

"I am looking for work."

Kirkland continued. "Hans and I were just discussing his future and I forgot that we are expected at the soup kitchen."

Hans looked at the two. *Did ministers have to cook?* He didn't want to show his ignorance, but decided that some curiosity would be permissible. "What is a soup kitchen?"

Lawson defaulted into his preacher demeanor. He spoke to Hans as if he were guiding a Sunday school class. "In these difficult times, we help out those brothers and sisters who have been left with nothing at all." Hans tried to be appropriately attentive. At least they weren't turning water into wine here. "So, many of us give our time and effort at establishments set up to provide a sustaining hot meal. Today we are serving at a soup kitchen on Welfare Island."

Hans had already seen enough dirty people in the last two days.

"Hans, do you like to walk?" Kirkland's friendly gaze indicated that an invitation was forthcoming.

"Yes, yes I do." Truthfully, he didn't wish to take another step today. He had already walked through the garment district and then sought out the church. Something in Kirkland's voice indicated that this was not going to be a short stroll. He might as well follow the two reverends. It sounded like it would include a free supper.

"Would you care to join us? It is a delightful walk, just 10 blocks and a bridge. We can continue our conversation."

Completely bewildered, Hans headed uptown with his two new friends. The afternoon was almost gone, and he still had not located a job. His suit was getting wrinkled and his starched collar was discolored from perspiration. At this rate, his expensive leather shoes would begin to show signs of wear, and no one hires a man whose shoes are worn.

Within two blocks they turned right, and a painted red tower rose in front of them with the biggest bridge he had ever seen. People lined up to get on an aerial tramway over to a small island in the East River, a kind of no man's land with a mental hospital, a smallpox hospital, and some simple brick buildings with no labels at all. The tram landed on the little island, and he looked back at Manhattan.

Kirkland spoke. "Hans, this decision you are contemplating is important. The choice of religion guides a lot of your life."

Hans nodded his head. His parents and rabbis had taught him rules and rituals. They were good rules. Now he needed new ones.

Lawson continued the statement, "But there is no hurry to become a Presbyterian."

Kirkland turned his head, "... or an Episcopalian." He turned quietly to Lawson. "Watch it, Jim. He came into our church for assistance."

Lawson pulled out his keys and they entered the Chapel of the Good Shepherd, a little Episcopalian refuge on the island. He changed the subject quickly. "Would you like me to make a phone call and see if the Y has any space? Do you want to share a room or to bunk alone?"

"Bunk?"

"Do you need to sleep alone or can you share a room?" He paused, and looked at Hans. "After Sunday, I can make some additional calls and introductions. Some members of our congregation rent out rooms."

Tomorrow was another day, but there seemed to be a place where he could afford to stay for a couple weeks. Standing in the soup kitchen, Hans wished that he had not been so eager to make new friends. He smelled greasy broth, edible but not appealing. The unmistakable aroma of cooked cabbages and turnips hung over the room. It mixed with the stale sweat of the vagrants and idlers, dirty and in no hurry to return to any type of afternoon work. Some were asking for food and money. Others had obviously already spent their grocery money on cheap liquor and cigarettes. On the other hand, since the men of

God were providing soup, at least no one would die from starvation tonight.

So this is what would happen if he ran out of money? He was hopelessly out of place here.

"Come, we have work to do, and we need a strong young man to help us." Hans was led into the back kitchen, and an apron was tied around his waist. "Here, bring that kettle to the long table – yes the big one." The enormous kettle must have held twenty liters of liquid with bits of meat and vegetables floating inside. At least, some of them looked like they may have been carrots once. Hans had never handled a kettle or a ladle. He did not know how to prepare or serve any type of food. His meals had always been presented to him on china plates. If he liked a food he would eat it. If he disliked it, he would ask for something different. He had never seen anything like the swill in these kettles. He could barely lift the kettle, and knew that he must not trip. People were depending on him, and he did not like the feeling.

CHAPTER 3

Amsterdam, Holland
Rosh Hashanah, September 14, 1939

September 1, 1939 – HITLER INVADES POLAND

"Danzig was and is a German city. We are obligated to protect people of German blood."

– A. Hitler, Amsterdam Courant

Esther struck a match and lit the end of her cigarette. A new ivory holder made her look elegant, like the ladies in movie magazines, "Stay slender! Reach for a cigarette instead of a sweet." The burning tip glowed in the twilight, and she took a deep drag, stifling a cough. The first ashes fell onto the open windowsill, and she pulled her sweater across her shoulders. She would rather be a little chilled than explain cigarette smoke in her mother's house. A record wafted soft jazz into the room and her fingers pressed the keys of an imaginary piano.

The peaceful Herengracht canal rippled with reflections of its red and white tour boats, and an occasional barge moving goods along to the shops. A few of the deep green leaves were beginning to turn.

She watched the late summer tourists. *Isn't it pretty? Isn't it nice? Too bad, you're just a tourist and I live here.* But she hadn't lived here for months. She had left this room and this sturdy brick house to be with Peter. *Over her mother's dead body…* except that no one was dead yet. As far as she knew, she wasn't even disinherited.

Her fifteen-year-old brother, Max, had begged her to come and join their parents for Rosh Hashanah dinner. They missed her, and Mother especially was distraught that two of her three children had left home.

The shiny cigarette case lay on her dresser, next to a photo of Hans. His white flannel trousers were pressed into perfect pleats and there was not a speck of sand on his navy blazer, even though they were at the seashore. His face smiled out from the photo, calm and resolute, his blue eyes reflecting the North Sea behind him. There was nothing calm about the North Sea. Hans was a storm in progress, willing to flail his way through life. She found comfort in the ancient city walls, heavy brick houses that were hundreds of years old, and habits that existed for a reason. She reached for another cigarette. Hans hated cigarettes. She missed his disapproval.

Where, in God's name, was he? All his remaining possessions had fit neatly into two suitcases, and he had left Amsterdam with a bank note that would be enough to support him in a new business venture. He hadn't written in nearly two months.

Mother's voice rang out. "Esther, come join us for a drink in the courtyard!" Apples and wine were laid out in the garden, a toast to a sweet new year. The quiet of the courtyard was marred by the spluttering of a radio, located in some nearby home. The broadcast was interspersed with the harsh and strident sounds of German, and Hitler's voice.

"Damn it, they don't need to play that tonight. We need a day off from this." Her stepfather, Sam Goudberg, was weary from working hurriedly through the day in order to be finished by sundown. He gazed at his wife, who brought him the wine bottle, followed by Max with the tray of glasses. The *blitzkrieg* invasion of Poland by Germany had disturbed him deeply. Hitler evidently felt that Northern Europe was his to take. The broadcast rant continued.

Sam poured the wine. "A toast to the home! Esther, we are so happy to see you." Esther smiled and sipped her wine. She had nothing to say. "So, how is your part time work at the stationers? Do you enjoy your co-workers?"

Max interjected, "Mother, they have a display of her calligraphy and drawings in the window. Haven't you seen them?"

Sarah looked at him. She had avoided the shop and thoughts of her daughter at work. It was one thing to be talented and another to have to use talent to exist.

Esther smiled. "Mr. Bolsman lets me use the most expensive pens and inks. I can't afford to actually buy one, of course, but it is nice to use a gold tipped pen. The lines just flow from your hand, no scratches, no blots, no surprises."

Max picked up a tiny silver spoon, holding it like a pen. He wiggled his nose and in a nasal falsetto asked, "Please miss, how much for a nice pen? Ten cents or twenty?"

"About two hundred guilders." Her eyes narrowed. "They also have beautiful inks, all colors. I wrote a poem on rice paper from Japan."

"Japanese imports are becoming harder and harder to get." Sam was back to business. "They open and close their harbors like the mouth of a carp. I actually like working with the Japanese, polite people who let you know exactly where you stand."

The kitchen maid stepped into the garden. "Dinner is ready, Madam. Shall I serve your soup?"

Max blurted out, "I wish Hans were here. This is his favorite dinner."

Esther turned her head sharply. "I'm sure he is enjoying his holiday with others now. He is twenty-one years old, and living his own life."

"What makes you say that? Do you know where he is?" Her mother's eyes were closed, and a deep sigh silenced the room. A brief happiness of this evening was marred. Where, in God's name, was Hans? They missed his energy and his quirks.

The table was set. Long linen cloths were perfection, and each starched napkin glowed in its silver ring. The classic silver table setting and blue patterned china looked like still-life paintings from rooms long ago. Aromas of golden chicken broth wafted through the air. A shiny egg bread lay in the center of the table. Esther was home for the first time in six months. She wouldn't be staying the night, but she was at the table.

"Tov Hashanah! To a sweet New Year!"

Amsterdam, Portuguese Synagogue

Yom Kippur

September 23, 1939

"Behind enemy powers, the Jew!"

~ Poster

Climbing up the stairs to the women's balcony, Esther and Sarah joined friends for the sundown Yom Kippur service at the Portuguese Synagogue. She pondered the ancient traditions. The building was dark, and these heavy wooden stairs were sunken with the footsteps of three hundred years. Why was this a part of her?

Esther looked out over the synagogue, fully illuminated with a thousand candles, long tapers set for a three-hour service of meditation and chant. On the floor of the building men congregated, standing in groups conversing. But once congregants were covered with their striped prayer shawls, one was reminded of the antique paintings of shepherds and prophets.

The screen obscured views of the floor and the altars. Directly in sight were magnificent brass chandeliers, massive stone pillars and the timbered vault of the ceiling. Much of the building resembled the descriptions of the temple of Solomon.

Cantors intoned their first chants, simple Phrygian melodies, repeated by the men. Waves of sound coursed down the length of the building, rolling over and over as the men repeated their pleas to God. The women observed the worship. Throughout the ancient building, both women and men held active conversations while their children were running and slamming the heavy wooden doors. The building was alive on this night.

Esther listened more closely than usual to the rabbinical sermon. God is everywhere, and this was God's house, but the rabbi was not talking about God on this, the holiest night of the year.

"We must convince the Queen to denounce the German invasion of Poland. Holland has been known for its tolerance, but we must make it clear that this will not be tolerated."

Her mother had often told the children of her childhood in Poland after pogroms had forced the family to flee westward. All she remembered about Poland were the fields of wildflowers, flowers that bloomed all over the countryside on her birthday. There she had played with her cousins... until another forced emigration, and still another. Mother had come through Germany to Holland. Thank God the Germans were moving in the other direction.

A celebrant tripped and stumbled, upsetting a large wooden torchiere. The heavy stand and its candles began to tip. Esther thought about her city, and the community she had joined at birth. Since infancy, she had been terrified of fire. A nightmare began as she sat on her bench, looking at a candelabra above her head. A set of candles burning, flames licking up the long hem of a man's coat, then lighting on the wooden furniture, draperies catching, a congregation immolated, and her community lost in the flames.

Through the screen she could see that the stand had been caught and was once again upright. Today's prayers had done their work, and tonight they were safe. Once again they were threatened, but they would survive. Her fears were groundless.

CHAPTER 4

Upstate New York September 1939

"German forces have invaded Poland and its planes have bombed Polish cities, including the capital, Warsaw. The attack comes without any warning or declaration of war."

- BBC

HANS DRAGGED HIS LUGGAGE BEHIND him. The vast lobby of Grand Central station had hundreds of signs in English and a labyrinth of hallways that tunneled under the streets. It reminded him of anthills that he had played with once on a sandy farm. Just shoving a stick into the anthill would release thousands of creatures, hurrying to their invisible destinations. Then they would form into lines and return underground with their treasures, morsels of food, and thousands of ants following. But now he was one of the ants, a nobody. He had wanted to become anonymous and in this vast train station he had found anonymity. The signs were a tangle of letters. These odd American names – Mohawk, Mohegan, Poughkeepsie, Narragansett, Massachusetts – were utterly confusing. How did people say such words?

Bums slept in corners of the station and Hans stepped carefully to avoid scattered remains of food and cigarettes. He hurried through the tunnels in order to look like a businessman, a furious race with no destination. So many people were rushing around to do important things. What would it take to be like them? After two weeks of searching for work in New York, he realized that he could end up spending a long time as a junior accounting clerk in a business that did not interest him.

Hans had come to New York to be a photographer, but he would have to settle for an entry-level position in someone else's business. Inquiries led him to Eastman Kodak in Rochester, about an eight-hour train ride away. At least a trip to Rochester would give him a breath of fresh air. Reading board after board he found a schedule of upstate trains and approached a ticket agent. The day was warm but his hands were clammy as he tugged at the bills in his wallet.

The Erie Lackawanna train pulled out of Penn Station, and headed upstate. As it left the city, Hans scrutinized his surroundings. The coach was full of travelers. Men were reading newspapers. Nobody was looking out the windows as the train pulled north. He did look. The shadows of Harlem were even darker than Manhattan's. Jazz had been born and become popular in Harlem, but he had stayed away from its intimate dark cellars. The Bernsteen teenagers had imagined that Jazz came from grand hotels and nightclubs with crystal lights and cocktails with twists of lemon. A glittering stage would separate dark skinned musicians from patrons. The letter he wished to write to Esther and Max might have been about seeing a great dance band and meeting a beautiful blonde. The realities of New York were so different from his expectations.

Harlem was bleak and dirty. Blockhouses had laundry hanging on lines from the windows, that is, when the windows were not broken out. The overall impression was of a war zone. Evidence of poverty was everywhere, not just a few bums out of work, but an entire community without homes or workplaces.

Following the river, lovely homes with broad lawns appeared. The train tracks went along back yards, but wood framed houses and gardens were neatly lined up along wider streets. The houses were painted in colors. Brick was used as trim, and the whole effect was one that seemed cheap to him. The sturdy brick houses of Amsterdam had stood for centuries, and many of these seemed to have been built quickly.

The Hudson Valley flowed into view, with broad tributaries leading away from the river. The dense hillsides and their broad trees painted a tapestry of greens and golds, reflecting an autumn sun above. Oh, if only he had color film and a day to wander these hills.

"Nice day, isn't it?" A new passenger sat down next to him, stout and sweating. He wiped his face with a handkerchief, opened his briefcase, and settled a newspaper onto his lap. For some reason, he decided to read the comics first. Here the world was imploding, and an adult man wanted to read the funnies. Well, people were strange. The man responded to his gaze. "Where you headed?"

"Rochester."

"Good God, why? It's cold up there. Damn winds blow off the lake and the whole town freezes over."

"Today?" Actually, Hans would have welcomed a blizzard at this point.

"Nah, not today. Lots of mosquitos though. Got mosquitos the size of small birds. Suck you dry." The man turned back to his paper, this time opening up the sports section. Football season was in full swing. Hans had no concept of American football, except that they dressed up in strange gladiator armor with helmets. Most of the time players seemed to be piled on the ground, in some sort of grotesque wrestling match.

"I want to work for Eastman Kodak."

The man did not look up from his paper. "What do you do?"

"I'm a photographer, but I have been processing my own film since I was eight years old."

"You mean you want to make a living taking pictures? What kind of luck do you think you're gonna have?"

"They use pictures in advertising and magazines. I can take pictures of things to sell."

"Maybe, but that work is all in New York. You're going the wrong direction."

"My boss in New York thought I would like Rochester."

The stout man shook his head. "I'll bet he did." He pulled his newspaper up over his face, and pretended to read it.

The train moved along riverbanks, rocky cliffs, and waterfalls. There was no evidence of proper cities – just simple little towns, a few factory smokestacks here and there. Where exactly had he been sent? He needed to get noticed as a talented photographer and Kodak was in Rochester. He had no idea where Rochester was. By evening, lights began to glow from a city and, eventually, the train began to slow down. Newspapers folded, and bags lifted from the racks as passengers prepared to end their long day. He had arrived, and he found his way to the local YMCA.

The following morning, Hans located a bathroom with a mirror and got out his shaving kit, put a new blade into the razor and began to lather up. He needed to look his best today. In his travel bag was one starched collar that he had carried for a special meeting. He dressed and slung his camera bag over his shoulder, looking like the photographers he had seen in magazines.

In the lobby of the Eastman Kodak company he boarded an elevator leading to the Executive Offices. At the top of the building there was yet another lobby, carpeted and even grander than the one downstairs. At the end of the lobby near tall windows sat a group of three secretaries. One seemed to be taking phone calls, a second was writing notes, and the third, a pretty brunette, looked up at him.

"May I help you?"

"Please. I am here to see Mr. Eastman."

"What is your name?"

"Bernsteen. Hans Bernsteen."

"Excuse me, sir, but what time is your appointment?"

He did not have an appointment. In Holland, his father's friends would see him whenever he was announced. The combination of telephone static and a foreign accent would not convince anyone to see him. Hopefully, a broad smile and friendly gaze would encourage her to make room for him. "He asked me to be here at 9:00, but of course I am a little early."

"It's only 8:15 and I don't see your name on the schedule. In fact, he is in meetings until 11:00. With whom did you make your appointment?"

He presented a business card. "Hans Bernsteen, Photographie, Amsterdam Holland." The address would have impressed a Dutchman, but she recognized nothing except that this young gentleman did not belong here.

"Sir, Kodak does not hire aliens."

"Excuse me?"

"We do not employ aliens. Europe is at war, and no Europeans are allowed in our facilities. Or Japanese either."

Confusion and doubt crossed his face. "There must be some mistake? I have come all the way from Holland."

"You need work, don't you?"

"Yes."

The brunette looked at him sympathetically. The other two ladies peeked up from their desks as they watched her escort the handsome young man to the door. She spoke very softly. "Why don't you go and visit the drugstores? Most of them have a photo lab. At least you can get some darkroom work. They don't care who they hire, and they will pay by the hour. It's not regular, but at least it will be something." Barely concealing his disappointment, Hans lowered his head and mumbled, "Good day."

He didn't even thank her. The idea that a pharmacy would also develop pictures was strange to him, but this was new territory.

Near the YMCA was a F.W. Woolworth Company five and dime store. Woolworth's did not have a photography department. It looked something like the shops of his family's clients in Holland: wooden bins were piled high with small items. Women threaded their way down narrow aisles to grab prizes tangled into a web of tags and string. He began to recognize the names of some items from the ledgers that he had been keeping since he was fourteen. He wandered the aisles, memorizing the names of common household items.

Along one side of the store was something like a café, a place where people were drinking coffee and eating ice cream. It certainly was far-removed from the *Café Americain* where he had enjoyed many pleasant afternoons. The black and white linoleum tiles were a poor substitute for the elegant marble block floors in Amsterdam cafes. This was clearly not for social gatherings. These people were all in a hurry, or thinking about something besides eating. The frustration of his "interview" at Eastman Kodak left him with a growling stomach and he stared at a menu on the counter, a list of items named after German cities, like Hamburgers and Frankfurters, and Italian dishes like macaroni and spaghetti. Didn't America have any food of its own? His forehead began to throb. A young waitress approached him, a real blonde, caramel and honey colored, not like the platinum blondes in New York City.

"Hello dear, what can I get you?" He looked around to see who was being addressed so familiarly. "Would you like a coffee?"

He hated coffee. "How about some tea? And maybe some bread?"

"Coming right up. Say, I haven't seen you around here before. Are you new?

"Oh, yes. Quite new."

"And you have an accent. Where are you from?"

"I am from Amsterdam." He was a little flustered at her forwardness, but taking care of customers was her job.

"Holland? Oh, my father is from Germany. So were my mother's parents."

He smiled at her friendly comments, and then responded in German. *"Meine Mutter war Deutsch."* They continued to speak a few sentences in German.

"What would you like to eat? *Was wollen sie essen?"*

He struggled with the menu. All sorts of odd words jumped out at him. A hot dog? No, he certainly wouldn't eat dog meat. A hamburger? He recognized the greasy patties, but they were adding all sorts of colored goo to them, red, yellow, some odd greenish bits, slimy fried onion. His eyes wandered off into space. He didn't know what to ask.

"What can I get you? Would you like today's special?"

"Yes, please."

The questions stopped. He was tired and very hungry, and happily settled into his plate of meatloaf and mashed potatoes served by the pretty blonde. She watched him eat until the service bell rang.

Moments later his plate was empty. He had inhaled his food, and looked up and down the counter, trying to figure out what to do next. She came back to him after a few customers left and pointed toward the glass cabinet full of desserts.

"Would you like a dessert? A sweet?"

A caramel and honey ice cream sundae, he thought, but he pointed to a piece of cherry pie. "Please." She set the coffeepot down and began a conversation in German.

"Oh, I bet your family misses you."

"No, my brother and sister do not miss me. I have my own life."

Searching his face for a clue, she asked, "Did you leave someone behind?"

"Do you mean, a girlfriend? No, I did not have a girlfriend."

"At least you're not brokenhearted then."

He appeared at Woolworth's lunch counter every day for the next week.

CHAPTER 5

Amsterdam, Holland Friday, May 17, 1940

"Holland, Belgium and Luxemburg Invaded; Britain and France Send Help"

~ The Star (London) May 10-14, 1940

Esther put her pen down and carefully capped the ink. God it was warm in here. Her light sweater itched and she didn't have a way to scratch, unless she went to the bricks out in the courtyard and rubbed herself like a cat. She hated this sweater. Her new skirt pulled on her waist. Even her breasts wanted out of their bindings. Maybe she should just take all the irritating clothes off. Not a good thought. But her chest felt sore, swollen and inflamed. She examined her arm for an allergic rash. Nothing, but who ever heard of "sweater sickness?"

Fresh tulips were appearing in sunny window boxes. She thought about her last birthday, the awful afternoon when her brother Hans had taken her to tea. Well, that was in the past. He was wrong. Amsterdam was lovely and the peaceful canals and old buildings had not faced any crisis. The thing to do with news reports was to ignore them. People made news so they could feel important. Once they had made their statement, others would make sure that the status quo would return. It was just like Hans to make too much of everything around him. He was too sensitive, but being sensitive at the wrong times and for the wrong reasons would not help him much. Good luck, wherever he was.

Enough, she had to return to the proclamation for the Lord Mayor. The Assistant to the General Manager had been very insistent that special inks on vellum would be used. It was supposed to be done in a simplified Gothic style, elaborate but legible, and God help her if she misspelled any of the Latin text. One letter at a time appeared in perfectly formed lines and serifs. Once the text was done, she could draw. Patrons requested her drawings, especially when she wove animals into the never ending curls and embellishments. She sometimes liked to add rare flowers, poisonous ones if she didn't like the message. "Oh how pretty!" And to herself she would think, "*Yes, and three centimeters of that lovely lacy hemlock will stop your heart – if you have one.*" Her lithe animals carried secret meanings – like the hidden leopards and tigers peeking out, *Do I eat him or does he eat me? Which is it?* They watched the viewer, waiting to pounce and attack. Oh well, the drawings were for customers, and father had told her "Never, ever, be rude with customers." No one said she couldn't enjoy a little joke here and there.

The shop bell rang, and a tweed-coated gentleman hurried through the door.

"*Guten Tag...ich möchte...*"

Heer Bolsman corrected him, "Sir, you are in Holland."

"Not as of two days ago. Your queen has surrendered. Heil Hitler!"

Bolsman turned to Esther, "You speak German, yes? Your mother is German. Find out what this man wants." He turned on his heels and strode to the back of the shop. Esther stared at the man, customer or imposter? She wasn't sure.

The intruder looked down at her. "We need a proclamation."

"What kind, sir? Shall I show you our style book?"

"I am not looking for artwork. We need a prominent document to post on the palace, and three large copies to post in the Damplatz. This is a very nice contract for your shop. If you can help us design the poster, we will remember you. All our artists live in Berlin. Your proprietor should be very pleased. Perhaps he is available to talk now?"

"Heer Bolsman!" She wandered slowly to the back. Bolsman looked at her, and nervously set down his freshly brewed cup of tea. He had not taken a sip from the steaming cup. He put it down on the table, littered with newspapers. His hand shook, and tea splashed into the saucer. Then he lifted the cup again and tried to drink. Beneath the saucer, a wet ring began to spread across headlines of the previous day.

> ***Rotterdam Destroyed!*** *Bombardment of the entire historic city centre. 900 killed and 85,000 homeless.*
> ***Holland surrenders*** *- Fall Gelb - Operation Yellow, invasion and occupation of the Low Countries.*

"Oh, God. Why him, why German business? Couldn't God choose someone else, just once?" He shuffled out to the front in his slippers, thinking and muttering, *Gelb – yellow – we are not cowards.* Confronting the stranger he announced, "You are in a Dutch shop.

If you have German business, you need to go to a German shop. I'm sure you will find something."

"*Gnädige Herr*, I have given you a polite offer. I can make it a command. I would suggest you treat us with courtesy and respect. We have gone to great trouble to liberate your country."

Esther looked at one man, then the other. Two strangers who had not met ten minutes before were in a standoff. Bolsman didn't even know this man – and he was nearly snarling at his customer. No wonder men loved their politics and wars. Dutch and German people had lived side by side, and shared land peacefully for centuries. How could this be a problem? What did it matter? She could see that Heer Bolsman was furious, but she had done nothing wrong. She took the announcement and dropped it on her desk. Both men kept their silence as she presented a calendar and marked a date to deliver a simple rendering. When the German left, no one said "Good day" or "Thank you." A curt nod indicated that he was done with his business.

Heer Bolsman's door was closed. She stuffed the proclamation into a drawer of papers to be forgotten. Soon she would be home with Peter to celebrate her birthday. They were not going out to a café. There was a new 20:00 curfew in place, and many cafés were hanging out signs that announced, "We do not serve Jews." With her bobbed hair and bright smile, Esther was ready to just step in, flirt with the maître dix, and order dinner, but she knew her friends would not approve. The Germans wouldn't know who was Jewish and who was not. However, Dutch boys were joining the police force and even the German army, putting on green uniforms and marching down the street. Apparently these Dutch boys were "Aryan", whatever that was, and they were dangerous because they knew the neighborhoods of the city. The Queen didn't stop them. She and her ministers had already fled to England. Holland was closing shop as quickly as it could in an effort to maintain peace.

Peter had promised to stop at the cheese shop and the bakery, and maybe splurge on a bottle of wine if one could be found. When she thought of the wine cellars at the Herengracht house she wondered how she could get a couple bottles. The cellars faced the courtyard, away from the main house. Unfortunately, there were no loyal servants left, at least no one who was loyal to her. They had been polite to her when she lived at home, but she had never exchanged a word with the girl who took care of her clothes or made her bed.

Dammit. This sweater was really bothering her. She needed to take it off. When she got home to Peter, she could take off the sweater and anything else she wanted. She would be dressed in kisses. He would kiss her neck, her arms, her….it was so hot in here. She picked up the pen and started to draw two lions rampant, one on either corner of the page. Not exactly what was on her mind, but it would have to do. Now her stomach seemed to be just a little upset.

Heer Bolsman came in and checked the proclamation. "This is lovely, but can you work a little faster? The customer wants to pick it up late this afternoon, and we need time for the inks to dry."

"Oh, certainly, *mijnheer.*" Under her breath she muttered, "Vincent, you must really paint a little faster."

"Young lady, you are a fine calligrapher. You are not an artist, and your lack of decent manners pushes me to the limit. Anyway, Van Gogh is not an artist or a painter. I would not hire him to paint my walls."

Esther smiled at him, blinked her large green eyes, and settled back to her work. At last it was time to tidy up the shop and walk down the cobbled streets to Peter's flat. It was a good job, and Heer

Bolsman did not mind that she was living with Peter, so long as Peter did not stop by the shop. He appeared to be a nice young man, but one with no prospects. Esther and Peter were enamored with the wild arts scene in Paris, but, thank God, they didn't have enough money to go there. Whenever Peter had a little cash, he would spend it on a new piece of stone or clay, anything that he could sculpt. They had no way to survive without the generosity of their parents and patrons.

As soon as Esther reached the flat, she shed her offending sweater and dropped it on the floor beside the chaise lounge. The gabardine skirt fell beside it, and she tossed her pumps on the Persian rug. Company was coming to supper, and she hadn't cleared away the coffee cups from the morning. Nobody should have to clean on a birthday. The breakfast dishes got shoved into a dishpan and hidden in the cupboard. She hadn't dusted in days, and some sculptures in the apartment looked like ancient relics.

Peter arrived at the door with the shopping bags in his arms. He looked at her quizzically. "Happy Birthday! But may I ask what you have done with your clothes?"

"Oh, they were itchy." She adjusted the strap to her slip.

He paused. Sometimes Esther acted like a twelve-year old nymph. "Well, perhaps you might like to put on your Japanese kimono and be a geisha tonight. I did invite Mark and Sasha to join us for supper." He unpacked a wrapped box. "These are for you."

She eyed the label from her favorite chocolatier, a little shop down by the Leidseplein. Her eyes filled. "Thank you. Now I will just want chocolates for supper. Are they for me to keep?"

"You're impossible. Do as you wish. But I think you would be better off eating them than keeping them."

"If I have one a week they'll last a long time and I won't get fat."

The downstairs buzzer sounded. "Can you go and put something on so I can let them in?" She jumped up and scurried into the bedroom as Mark's heavy footsteps announced their presence. Sasha was wearing high heels; she could tell by the clicking. Dammit. She didn't have anything like that, and they probably had some wonderful tales of Paris besides. Think. In her bedroom she brushed out her hair and applied some lipstick. The Japanese robe was a wonderful idea. She would put on a silk camisole, and leave the front slightly open. Instead of the wide obi binding her waist she took a braided ribbon sash and tied it high, just enough to keep the robe from falling open. She loved this robe, with its powerful birds resting in still waters. A little powder and some dramatic earrings and bracelets…voila! Oh, perfume; she needed more perfume.

Rushing out from the bedroom, she ran to Sasha, embraced her and kissed her on each cheek, then stepped back holding on to her friend's hand. "Sasha, you look absolutely chic, *tres chic*! Tell me about your shoes. Wherever did you find those?" The two ladies scurried over to the table to talk.

Meanwhile, Peter was pouring the first surprise, a shot of Dutch gin, Genever, for the gentlemen. They sipped the icy drinks slowly, savoring the rich taste of the juniper. Mark spoke in a quiet voice, serious words to be kept out of ladies' earshot.

Peter stared out the window, seeing nothing. A vague comment, "I didn't know you had an English grandfather."

A quiet force behind Mark's words forced Peter to turn and look his friend in the eye. Mark continued, "He was a British officer abroad in South America when he met my grandmother. Her father was a local liaison, and they met at one of those endless parties. I think that's all they have to do in those colonies, drink and have parties." As Mark spoke of the parties, he transformed into someone else entirely.

Peter now observed a young man frozen like an imperial officer from a time past, coiled up under pressure, prepared to strike.

Mark continued to explain, "I'm not even sure whose colony was whose. But somehow the Dutch and English are pretty friendly." He set down his shot cup. Clatter from the kitchenette broke into his thoughts.

"Esther! Here is the smoked fish. We brought herring and eel." Sasha held up the wrapped packets. "— and white bread" as she set a fresh baked loaf on a board.

Esther grabbed the baguette, inhaled the odor of the warm yeast and began rubbing it, slowly, her tongue flickering around the tip of the hard bread as she danced a striptease around the kitchenette, removed her apron and dropped the shoulder on the kimono. Then she picked up a knife and sliced the end off, shoving it in her mouth and crunching the treat. "I'd rather be in the kitchen with you, and you know I hate to cook. Look at those two, cold sober even after the Genever."

Sasha laughed. "At least there is no cooking tonight – just a little slicing, and maybe a glass of wine."

In the small sitting area, Peter poured two more polite shots of icy Dutch gin. Mark responded, "*Bedankt!* Today I need this." He tipped the shot back and followed it with a piece of bread, then exhaled, snorting like a dragon.

Peter followed with his shot. Mark asked for a third shot of the dense cold gin. "You sure? We still have a long evening ahead of us, and a bottle of wine. There is only one bed here." Mark took his third drink, and set it on the windowsill. "You thinking of going anywhere?"

Mark paused and looked out the window. "The Fascists are making a real mess of Europe."

"You're seriously thinking of going to England?"

Mark pulled a newspaper out of his pocket, opened it, and then handed it to Peter. "We don't have a country any more. Even our Queen and Cabinet have left, along with our national treasury. They asked the British for protection." He tossed the third shot back. "I am going to England." He lifted the empty Genever glass, tipped it upside down, and set it on an end table by the chaise. Then he stood at attention, unshakeable, unmovable, and sober. "I've decided to join the RAF. I know how to fly, and they're recruiting pilots."

"Does Sasha know?" Peter nodded toward the girls laughing and setting the table.

"She knows I like to fly. She's even been up with me." Evidently, Mark was more nervous about Sasha's response than he was about getting shot out of the air. "I will be telling her very soon."

"My God, Mark, they taught you how to take that thing up and bring it down! You're not a competitor or a daredevil!" Peter snorted back his shot.

"I don't know how I can continue here. Whatever we have here is lost."

"What the hell are you talking about? The girls are in the kitchen, the – you're drunk. You can't even walk, let alone fly an airplane." Peter's hands began to shake, just a slight nervousness. Anxiety always came through his hands. He saw with his hands, and now he listened to his hands.

"Our only choice is to go to England and fight," Mark continued.

"*Our* choice?"

"We can't fight from here. What do you plan to do to save Holland?"

Peter closed his eyes and exhaled. "I've been working in metals since I was a boy, and I'm not afraid to get my hands dirty. Someone is going to have to fix the planes after you guys wreck them."

Mark's eyes met his. "I hear Germany is lovely this time of year. Let's see how it looks in flames."

Peter picked up the bottle. "Now I need another drink."

Mark turned Peter's glass over. "You need to swear to this one with your wits about you."

Peter looked around his apartment, every surface adorned with a bronze, a sculpture, or a painting. A soft bed and an even softer woman waited for him at the end of each day. He had never acted on a decision in his life. Esther observed his clenched fists. "I am not drunk." Silence split the air. Then he opened the right fist and extended it for a stiff handshake, a promise that Mark would not be fighting alone.

———

"Drunk? Who's drunk? We have to catch up with you now!" Sasha had removed her high heels and stepped quietly across the room. Esther followed behind, displaying a lovely platter of thinly sliced fish, lemon, onions and cheese. She lit the candles on the table and paused. A few words of an unspoken Sabbath prayer went through her head. It was Friday night. Crunchy baguette appeared next to the black bread on the table and they poured wine to toast her birthday.

"Let's have a nice supper. No politics." The room went silent and the food was passed without comments. After several minutes with no conversation, Sasha reached into her handbag and pulled out a tiny package. In it was an ounce of French perfume. "We brought you a gift! Happy Birthday."

"Oh, it's beautiful, and I love this crystal bottle. I shall have this for the rest of my life." Esther opened it and let its fragrance waft through the small room. "Wait a moment. I have something for all of us."

Esther brought out the chocolates and offered each of them their choice of the bon-bons and wine jellies. "See, it's so much better when we are not serious. We can take care of ourselves and let others live with their own problems. As long as chocolate like this exists, who cares about the Germans?"

Peter's glass stopped in mid-air. "Well, the Queen is not having a good day."

Esther raised hers. "Let's toast the Queen."

"Let us toast the eventual defeat and removal of the Germans from Holland." Mark set his glass down with a bang.

"Oh, for heaven's sake, they're hardly even here. Soon it will be business as usual," Sasha exclaimed.

Esther took a deep breath. "I don't know. These Germans are not like our mothers. One came into the store this afternoon. Bolsman nearly lost his temper. He doesn't lose his temper at anyone, ever." Esther's uncharacteristic stillness contrasted with the flare of temper she had witnessed in the shop; reflective moments before the sunlight in a mirror ignites dry weeds. "I don't know what to think."

Mark regarded his plate, squared his shoulders and looked Peter in the eye. "I'm going to join the English. The RAF needs pilots."

Sasha started at him. "In a pig's eye!"

"We don't eat pigs," remarked Esther.

Mark steadied his gaze, first on Esther, then on Sasha, who reached up and covered her mouth with her napkin. "I sail on Monday. My application has been approved."

"You are not!" Sasha began to tear up, and wiped her face with the napkin.

"Sasha, you are my heart, but I have to do this."

Her eyes widened, incredulous. "What about us?"

"I'm doing this for us. But love is greater than just the two of us. We will want a family, and we will want to be Dutch, not German."

Esther glanced nervously at Peter. "Sasha, it's OK. Peter will take care of us."

Peter looked down at his empty plate. "Actually, I think you two girls will do fine together. You are both strong and able. This invasion is not to be tolerated." Determination crossed his face. "I will also be enlisting in the RAF." Esther got up from the table without excusing herself. The kitchen sink was the nearest basin, and she began to heave her dinner – herring, chocolate, cheese and wine. Even though she was cold and perspiring, she did not faint. Vomiting cleared her head.

Mark looked up, stunned. "How could she be that drunk? All she's had is a little wine!"

Esther's glare froze the other three at the table. "Well, my dears, I really must go to bed now. Don't mind me." She moved toward the bedroom, but Peter grabbed her arm.

"Sit down!" he commanded. Peter wet a towel and slung it across her forehead. "Your daydreams need to end. Our government collapsed into a vacuum this week. Peace is over."

Esther's tossed the towel on the floor. She headed for the basin again, but instead of vomiting once more, she began to frantically clean it. She ignited the water heater and pulled out the dishpan, scouring everything in the kitchen with scalding water. Her hands turned red, but not as red as her eyes and nose. The tears ran down her face and into the sink. Peter crossed the room, fishing out his handkerchief. His arm went across her shoulders and he steered her back into her chair. She gasped, and then spoke.

"This German who came into the shop…"

Peter looked at her puzzled. "What does that have to do with anything?"

"The Germans want posters in the Damplatz announcing the capitulation of Holland."

"Good God." Mark continued. "We aren't done yet."

"I didn't know what to think then. I just wanted to get him out of there because Heer Bolsman was furious."

Sasha had been listening closely to the heated argument and responded with gasps of frustration and her hands in the air. "We don't have to get involved in the ongoing squabbles between Germany and England. Mark has an English grandfather, but Peter, it's nothing you need to do."

"I am sober. I just haven't had the courage to make a plan yet. It's settled now."

"It may not even turn out to be anything," Sasha continued. "English and German royal families have been intermarried for two hundred years. We can make peace with this."

Esther shook her head and glared at Peter. "Are you crazy? For God's sake, we don't even know peace because all our parents talk about is the Great War."

Mark continued. "Sasha, the Royals are useless. Hitler is counting on it. They're all drinking tea together while Europe burns. Even England is at that party. And now you see why it will be necessary to fight." Mark's resolve was based on inconvenient facts about European rulers.

Esther dreaded the task waiting on her work table at the shop – her personal role in the surrender. "So, about the man in our shop…. Germany has taken Holland. He threatened Mr. Bolsman. We have to do what they say, or it could be dangerous for us." She had grown up on the shadow of the now abandoned palace. She had always been able to refuse to do unpleasant things, but she would not have Bolsman punished over some cardboard posters.

"If you leave, I'll…" Silent sobs began to rack Esther. She took a deep breath. "I see now that I should have gone to New York when Hans had my passage paid." Esther folded her arms, a frozen glare darting around the table.

Sasha countered, "We'll survive; we can live here. We are a strong people. The Germans are obnoxious, but what can they really change?"

"There is no other way — and there is no alternative to driving the Germans back home," Peter concluded.

He opened a cabinet and selected four ancient pewter shot cups that had seen Holland through many wars. He set one down in front of each of them, picked up the bottle of Genever and poured out the remaining liquor.

"We are Dutch. This is our home. You will continue to live here and we will survive this."

"To Holland!"

CHAPTER 6

Rochester, New York
June 1940

"Paris falls under German occupation."

~ *Newsreel*

Hans was a man of habits, and he appeared each afternoon at the cheery Woolworths lunch counter. He would have preferred a solid wood table and chair, but a big grin crossed his face when he took his place on a slippery red stool. He looked expectantly at Greta, like a puppy waiting for a pat or a treat.

Greta's casual banter with customers made everything right in his world. She greeted him in German, and gave him a break from the torrents of English that he heard in the camera shop. Their German conversation always began with a discussion of the menu and the specials, even though he ordered the same meal each afternoon. Hans stumbled over long English words, and her furrowed brow and blue eyes took in every word from the smiling friendly newcomer. Greta was not bothered by his European manners, including his insistence on eating a sandwich with a knife and fork.

On a nasty November afternoon, they sat at the counter and talked for hours. Woolworths was empty as the black storm clouds blew down into the streets. "It's hard being an immigrant," she offered. "My parents are German. Papa's family moved to Wisconsin when he was a little boy, just before the Great War. They picked on him in school because he sounded German. It was easier once he learned to speak like an American." She smiled, "Actually, he still has an accent, but he doesn't hear it. Papa likes to go to the movies. Then he copies what the actors say. Sometimes it's really funny, but a lot of the time it works pretty well."

Hans laughed. "My sister loves acting. She wanted to be a movie star." He reflected for a moment on Esther's startling decision to remain in Holland.

"What's she like? Your sister."

"For one thing … very pretty, but not like you. She has dark hair and green eyes." He closed his eyes and took a deep breath. Esther would have regarded Greta as a servant, someone whose job was to take care of others.

A large piece of Hans Bernsteen had been left in Amsterdam. His refugee status was now just a mark on his visa. He was in the process of creating an American.

Greta noted his pensive mood.

"Do you miss her?"

"Of course I do, but – " and he realized that he could not discuss any circumstances of his leaving Holland. He certainly didn't want Greta to know about Esther's liaisons. She might think that he would approve of these illicit behaviors. He tolerated them, but he couldn't convince Esther to think beyond her next adventure.

"So, she is a green-eyed beauty and self-centered? Like Vivien Leigh? The movie star?"

He was completely bewildered. "Most of Esther's acting takes place at home. I actually never knew what movie she lived in from one day to the next."

"Vivien Leigh is in *Gone with the Wind*, the new hit movie. Have you seen it?"

"No, but I would like to take you to see it, if you would like to go."

"Certainly!"

He couldn't believe his luck, a date with Greta. What a thrill to be seen with his blonde beauty on his arm. *Gone with the Wind* was difficult to understand. He was looking for the hero, but instead the predatory green-eyed Scarlett O'Hara manipulated men who were not strong enough to control her. Greta was more intrigued by the kindnesses that prevailed though the story, the loyalties, and the sacrifices that were made for home. It was almost as if they looked at two different stories in the same movie.

They went to more movies. Greta loved romances and musicals, and he tolerated the fluffy pictures to be with her. His favorites were the crime stories, black and white palettes of morality and justice captured though the photography. Greta was afraid of the bad guys and worried about the victims even after the story was over. When she looked down to her lap his arm went around her, and she buried her face into his shoulder while he solved the puzzles. Many, many movie dates followed as he held Greta's hand and studied how the actors spoke.

They spent frozen winter evenings at her boarding house, and he brought albums of photos he had taken. An uncomfortable black horsehair couch with white antimacassars had stood in that living room for more than 50 years. It was an excellent choice for a girls' boarding house. If a man tried to lean over and kiss, one or both people would slide off its hard seat. The long conversations continued.

"I am so glad you enjoy photography. I like the way you see things." Greta was admiring a close-up of a Queen Anne's lace flower.

Hans blushed, desperately in love with Greta. "I had hoped to go to work for Kodak but— I guess they can't hire me."

Greta continued his sentence, "I don't think they can hire aliens. None of the defense contractors can. I'm not sure why, because we aren't in the war." She paused, and then smiled at him. "After you earn your U.S. Citizenship you can work anywhere. My Papa has done very well. He works in optics, over at Bausch and Lomb."

During the spring thaw they began to go dancing. The Four Aces club had a low cover charge on Thursdays, and they only had to buy one drink. Greta loved jazz, and the club reminded him of the Café Americain with its snappy black and white décor. It was much louder, though. Blasts of the trumpet split the air. On the dance floor men strutted and kicked, lifting partners into the air, petticoats flung high and panties and garters exposed. Hans took Greta into his arms and walked her across the floor, taking care to hold her firmly by the waist. Once in a while she would wriggle out from underneath and persuade him to let her spin.

They began to discuss their dreams. He hoped to own his own photography business one day. She had another few months of nursing school ahead. In the late June evenings, dates would end on a park bench by the river, looking at stars rising in the night sky. They kissed in the dark of the lilac bushes next to the rooming house, and at last she would step up onto the porch and wave goodnight.

CHAPTER 7

Amsterdam, Holland
July 1940

"Where has your lover gone, O beautiful one?
Say where he is and we will seek him with you."

~ *Song of Songs*

Esther lay on the extended dining table and listened to the instructions. "You cannot turn, you cannot move your legs, and you cannot push back. If you do, you will never have children, and you might bleed to death." Dr. Hemelrijk had come. The tears slid back across Esther's temples, dripping onto the white feather pillow. She lifted herself and reached for a handkerchief to blow her nose. More tears fell, heavier ones, a storm opening through threatening clouds.

"Where is that bastard now?"

Sasha wiped Esther's face. "This isn't a good time to think about Peter. Let's talk about going to the seaside next week, when you are feeling better. The sunshine, birds swooping to steal our bread…."

A week ago, while getting dressed for work, Esther discovered that the waistline on her favorite skirt was too tight. She couldn't button it. She hadn't been overeating. In fact, she had been eating very little because of the stomach upsets. Nerves. Dammit. Now she would need to go on a diet, as if throwing up every day weren't enough. There was no money to go and see a doctor.

Sasha had quipped, "Eating well, aren't you?" Esther's glare cut off the rest of the joke. Their larder was nearly empty.

"Esther, are you pregnant?" Sasha began to mull over Esther's complaints of the last two weeks.

"Peter's gone."

"Yes, but he has only been gone a month. When did you have your last menstruation?"

"Before Peter left … let me think." She lowered her head and began to count on her fingers – count what? Events? Days? Nights with Peter? Nights without him? "My God, I couldn't be … he's not even here… we can't even get married." Tears started. "I hate him."

Sasha frowned and shook her head. "That's not true. You don't hate Peter. You miss him. Why do you get so angry before you think about how you really feel?" Esther really tried her patience. "He probably misses you too."

"He hasn't written."

"He's put his life on the line for us. You should be hoping that he is safe."

"Who is 'us'? If he loved me, he wouldn't have left. I need to go for a walk." Esther pulled on her shoes.

"You are not going to escape this one. Sit down. Now. We need to make a plan."

"I can't be pregnant!"

"Esther, when two people live together someone gets pregnant, usually the woman."

"You and Mark don't have any children. Obviously this doesn't happen to everyone."

"But we want them." Her eyes met Esther's face. She sighed, and then asked, "If Peter did know, what would he want to do?"

"He does not believe in conventional marriages – he says people are too unhappy. I don't have any evidence to the contrary. I haven't had a letter from him. My God, he may not even be alive. I can't have some bastard child."

"Oh, yes you can. It's not having one that is the problem."

"Who would take care of it? My mother? She can't stand children. She hated us, and we hated our governesses." Esther began to gag. "I think I'm going to throw up again."

"No, you're not. I'll make us some tea. You need to get your wits about you."

"Can we get rid of it?"

"Get rid of what?"

"You know, 'it.'"

A very sad expression crossed Sasha's face, one of regret and confusion. "My mother did not plan on having me, but we managed very nicely. I can write Mark. Maybe he is able to get a message to Peter."

"And then what? Peter should have written me. Obviously he doesn't wish to. Anyway, I don't want to manage…this. Leave me alone."

Sasha stood up from the chair. "What, do you think you are just going to lay an egg and fly away? It doesn't work that way." That settled it. She would call on Esther's mother and ask for help, living expenses or doctor's fees at least. It was a family problem, not her problem. Sarah Goudberg would understand this. As she stormed through the door she called out, "Oh, and by the way, you are not alone any more. In fact, you will not ever be alone again."

Sarah had listened intently to Sasha's account. "Of course Esther is in trouble, we expected no less. The question is, 'What do we do now that her lover is somewhere in England?'" She paused and looked around the parlor. "And no, we are not taking her in. However, I will call on our private doctor tomorrow and learn what our options are."

It was nearly dark when Sasha returned to her sulking roommate. Esther looked up from her book. "Did you have a nice walk?"

"Oh, it was lovely." Sasha pulled off her sweater and hung it on the hall tree. "It's beginning to sprinkle though, and I didn't have an umbrella with me." Then she plopped down on the couch and picked up her tatting shuttle and cotton. A new lace collar was beginning to appear under the repetitive motions of her busy hands.

"I'm starving. What are we having for dinner?" Esther had not moved.

"Boiled babies," Sasha retorted and then left the room.

Three days later Esther lay on the sheets and pillows listening to Dr. Hemelrijk's clinical babble, talk that was about her but not directed at her.

"Sasha, please keep her knees bent. Let me know if she starts to shake. I'm going to give her a little something to relax her." He squirted a little clear liquid out of the end of a sharp needle to make sure there was no air bubble, then took Esther's wrist and punctured her upper arm. She winced and yelped. "You also must be quiet." A tray of sterile instruments lay next to the dining table. Sasha and Esther had boiled every sheet and pillowcase in the house for twenty minutes, as directed by the doctor. Her white summer nightgown was already drenched in sweat, the animal smell of fear rising from her pores. Dr. Hemelrijk was about to perform a secret and highly illegal procedure. It was time.

Esther began to breathe slowly, her eyes closed. Slipping into the twilight sleep, she saw clouded images and heard voices from her final week with Peter. In the first days after Peter and Mark announced their intentions to fight, she remained silent. Peter had never spoken strongly of home or a homeland in the past. Commitments were for the bourgeois. He would get over it.

The image of his canvas bag on the floor haunted her. The familiar bag looked like it was packed for a sketching trip. All his possessions and his artwork were still in place on the walls and shelves. His tweed suits still hung in the closet. "I've paid three months' rent, so that you have plenty of time to figure out what you want to do." Peter's comment had been matter of fact. "Either this will be over quickly and I'll be back, or you will have to make a decision - whether to house with Sasha or your mother."

Bewilderment turned to fear and fear turned to rage. Her teeth clenched as the tears started. "I stayed in Holland because of you. I had a visa to New York!" Peter said nothing. He knew. "You have no right to do this to me!"

"You made a choice. Now I am making one."

She picked up her glass and threw it at him.

Peter caught the glass. "I don't want to fight."

"If you're going to join the bloody English war, you had better learn how to fight!" A heavy bronze sculpture followed the path of the wineglass.

"If you make more noise, you will be thrown out of the flat, whether or not it is paid for." He did not make any attempt to soothe her, to take her in his arms, or to restrain her.

Esther ran to the bedroom, slammed the door and turned the key. Peter left the apartment for the evening. When she opened the door in the morning, both he and the pack were gone.

She was no longer in the present. Sasha and the doctor took over.

"Sasha, did she bathe and douche with the hot soapy water as I asked?"

"Yes, the bag is still hanging over the bathtub."

"Good. Now we need to shave her. Please hold her legs open, and I will take care of it." He pulled a straight razor out of his bag and lathered her pudenda, then cleanly shaved off all the dark hair. Sasha removed the towel. A speculum was inserted and the doctor pulled the living room reading lamp over for additional light. "She's healthy. This should not be too difficult. There is no evidence of disease."

"Disease!"

"Well, you know, women like this…"

"Like what? She has been faithful to one man for nearly two years, living as husband and wife."

"Where is he?"

"He joined the RAF to help the Dutch resistance."

Sasha went silent as the doctor picked up a curette, and began his work. Blood began pouring out onto the pillows, along with mucus and a tiny glob of flesh. Esther moaned but did not move. The doctor saved all the excavated tissue in a glass dish. Then he pulled out a magnifying glass and examined what had been the contents of Esther's womb. "Now we need to clean her up." Sasha was sitting on a chair in the corner of the room, dizzy and faint. The doctor looked at her and then said, "I'm sorry you feel unwell, but she needs you right now. Esther will be fine. Please write down these instructions. She needs to douche every day for two weeks. There must be absolutely no man for at least six weeks, and then only after she has had a problem free menses."

"That's highly unlikely isn't it?"

"What do you mean, unlikely? Unlikely that she will have a man, or unlikely that she will not?"

Sasha snapped, "Esther is faithful to a man who is now flying airplanes, trying to save our country."

Dr. Hemelrijk began to wash off his instruments and pack his black bag. He would report to Sarah Goudberg once he knew that Esther was going to be in good health. Sasha sat down on a chair next to the table and took Esther's hand. As Esther regained consciousness, she looked at her friend and began to stroke her hair. A torrent of loss overtook the two young women and they began to sob quietly from pain of the heart, pain of the body, and pain of the world. Sasha collected the bloody sheets. She set the kettles of soapy water and bleach on the stove and turned on the burners. Then she lay down on the couch and sobbed into a thick pillow.

———

Hours later, Esther struggled to the door to answer the persistent buzzer. She had been in a blackout sleep, somewhere warm, a place where large brightly colored birds flew through the air or landed on branches to take a rest and a treat. They did as they wished. Many of them had partners, and spent their days feeding and grooming each other. Her feather comforter was a safe place, and she didn't want to get up from her nest in the reading alcove. Where was Sasha?

Sasha was sound asleep on the couch, her head lifted uncomfortably onto one rounded arm, and her knees bent to fit into the cushions. She had stayed up all night to check on Esther. Linens were piled on the kitchen table, wrung out but still wet. Of course. There was no way to hang them out overnight, and late night laundry activity would have attracted the attention of neighbors.

Max, Esther's sweet younger brother, was at the door. At fifteen, he was still small for his age, a mother's boy. He carried Sarah's leather market bag and a bunch of yellow sunflowers. "Mama said you have been sick. She wanted me to bring you these."

Esther looked over at the sofa. "Sasha, you have to get up. We have company." Sasha pulled the crocheted afghan around her. "Morning, Max" and staggered into her bedroom. Max looked around at the disarray and the wet laundry, and Esther offered, "I have had the grippe.., a lot of … well, you know, both ends, but I am getting better." She felt faint.

Her little brother looked at her pale face and stringy hair. "Hey Esther, why don't you sit on the sofa and I'll put these flowers in some water for you." She dropped into the pillows, and Max located a tall coffeepot for the sunflowers and brought them to the side table near her. "Oh, you have a phonograph! Can we play some music? Look at these records!"

Esther laughed at his excitement. Instead of offering one of his favorite romantic composers she suggested, "Would you like to hear Duke Ellington? I heard him when he came to Amsterdam. When he comes again, I promise to take you."

Her brother smiled and commented, "Actually, I really like jazz ballads. "Around Midnight" is one of my very favorites—it has the feel of—of longing. The same things Schubert wrote about, but different. I love how music comes in all languages." He sat quietly as the muted horns of mourning filled the room.

"Why are you so angry with Mother? You know she really cares about us." Esther bristled at the mention of Sarah and her constant criticism of Esther's behavior.

"Why?" She was wondering if Sarah expected her to confide in her little brother.

"She worries that, with Peter gone, you may not have the life you wished for. Maybe you could come by now and then for a nice meal? Oh, she fixed you some really nice chopped liver pate, cornichons, and a wonderful loaf of *roggebrot*, the dark rye straight from the farms. She said it would restore you. Shall I make you a sandwich?"

Esther watched her little brother take charge. "That would be very nice, and a cup of tea as well? Do you know how?"

"I think so. I have asked cook to show me a couple things. I like food."

He brought her an open-faced sandwich, with two cornichons as garnish. Then he sat down at the table in the corner with his. On the shelf was her camera. "Do you ever hear from Hans?"

"No, I don't even know where he is. I thought he would have written us months ago from New York. If he becomes a famous photographer, we will learn about it in the papers. Otherwise, we'll just have to guess."

Max lifted the camera, pointed it northward up the Amstel river, and shot a picture of the city skyline with its intricate rooftops and church steeples. "Here, there is a picture of home for you. You can go there whenever you look at my photo. Or, you can come home whenever you wish."

Surrender brings its own kind of peace. Esther did not laugh and she did not cry. She could continue to fight alone, or she could accept the idea that she did not always need to win. Maybe others needed a chance as well.

"Tell mother, this pate is delicious! I always adored her chopped liver." She chewed the sandwich carefully, savoring the fat.

"She is welcome to visit me as well. She knows the shop where I work. Perhaps she would like to come by for tea one afternoon."

CHAPTER 8

Upstate New York July 1940

Warning from the FBI

The war against spies and saboteurs demands the aid of every American. When you see evidence of sabotage, notify the Federal Bureau of Investigation at once. When you suspect the presence of enemy agents, tell it to the FBI. Beware of those who spread enemy propaganda! Don't repeat vicious rumors or vicious whispers. Tell it to the FBI!

J. Edgar Hoover, *Director Federal Bureau of Investigation*

Hans opened the little velvet-covered box just once more and scrutinized the tiny solitaire before placing it securely in a pocket in his camera bag. All his dreams were coming true, and he continued packing for the long holiday weekend.

He shivered at the thought of Greta's honey colored hair falling in long waves, like a river at sunset. It was all he could do to keep his hands out of it. He wanted to walk in the woods with her forever, stopping now and then to kiss by the river. They exchanged endearments in German – *Herzchen* – sweetheart, *Liebling* – lover, the affectionate words of their mothers. It was their secret language, a way to talk of dreams that no one else could understand.

They would pursue those dreams together. Greta's nursing school graduation was coming up, and he liked the idea of being married to a nurse, a pretty heroine in a white cap. Once again, he patted his pocket with the ring box.

Hans enjoyed his work at the camera store. One afternoon he had walked into Rosenbaum's Photography to window shop the newest American equipment. As he examined a high quality lens, the elderly gentleman at the counter got up from his stool, and asked where he had studied optics. "Young man, you seem to know a lot about cameras and lenses," Mr. Rosenbaum commented.

"I'm a photographer, but no one is looking for pictures right now. I just process film until I find work."

"You know how to process film? Can you do different formats?"

Rosenbaum led him to a darkroom in the back, a messy area that was used for storage. Stacks of paper and rolls of supplies were piled onto wooden shelving, and cans of developing fluids were covered in dust. Several of the lamps were burned out.

"I have a backlog of photo processing, but the chemicals bother my eyes and make me sneeze." Hans looked around the room and didn't suggest that a clean room would help Mr. Rosenbaum's sensitivities to chemicals. Instead he offered to help out and accepted a part-time job. He showed up early the next day and asked for a mop and some cleaning rags.

Hans did beautiful work in the darkroom, producing precise images and nuanced shadings. The whole process of taking a completely blank 8x10 sheet of photo paper and gently coaxing images out of the liquid and chemicals gave him a peace and serenity like no other activity. Photography made him a modern day alchemist and provided a nice salary of nearly thirty dollars a week, $28.75 after taxes.

This week marked ten months since he had met Greta. She had invited him for the July Fourth holiday weekend with her family. If her father liked him, he would ask for her hand. He packed a starched white shirt, a sport coat and a conservative striped tie. He needed to look as if he were a gentleman of consequence.

The Fischers lived outside of town, at the edge of a state park. Dense green woodlands darkened until they edged the rocks in the Genesee River. Then the water plunged down a canyon. A New York skyscraper could easily fit into the gorge, and be swallowed as if it had never existed. This was not a place of peace. Instead it offered the roughest challenges of each season – iced waterfalls, thunderstorms, and the stinging insects of midsummer.

His bus arrived on Sunday at noon. As he walked toward the address in the note, he spotted a marvelous house, its foundation rising from the boulders of the glen. This fairytale castle was an old Victorian, studded with gables and turrets, and a confection of white lacy wood trim along all the edges. It was evident that the Fischers were also people of substance. He stopped, opened his camera bag, screwed the wide-angle lens onto his camera, and then captured everything in the scene except the sound of the waterfall.

The Fischers seemed solid as the rock foundation of their home. He liked them right away – calm placid folk, not any trouble to anyone. Mr. Fischer shook his hand heartily. "Johann Fischer. Our Greta has told us so much about you – that she had found a handsome German boy. Welcome!"

Hans's eyes wandered around the room. A spectacular mantel loomed over one entire wall, its base of river rocks topped by the carved oak. Figures of vines and flowers emerged in nearly full relief, along with birds and smaller animals climbing what had to have been a tree trunk at one time. At the top of the columns were two deer and then a set of antlers was mounted above the fireplace. He turned to Mr. Fischer, gaping.

His host smiled. "Do you like it?"

"It's absolutely marvelous."

Fischer grinned. "I carved it myself. I like to work with wood."

By now Greta had entered the room, dressed in a light blue dirndl, showing off not her long legs, but a wonderfully proportioned bosom. "Papa is an artist, like you." This moment in time was one of pure contentment, friends well met. Hans looked forward to learning Mr. Fischer's vision, how he saw things, and how he crafted beauty.

A third man entered the room, Hans's age but tall and blonde like Greta. He extended his hand and nearly crushed Hans's knuckles. Apparently he was not an artist. Both her brothers had come home for the long holiday weekend, driving their old jalopy for ten hours from Long Island. The brothers were in plaid sport shirts and well-worn slacks, a little frayed around the pockets and cuffs.

"Hans, these are my two brothers—Frank and Joe."

"Yeah, but for Hans, we will be Franz and Josef!"

Hans looked at the two warily. Was this some kind of a joke? "It's not necessary—I go by Hank nowadays. I'm American now."

"Hank the Yank!" They looked at each other. "Good one. Greta says she met you at Kresge's. Does she do a nice job?"

"It was Woolworth's." Hans was immediately aware that this small talk was going to be uncomfortable. The starched collar around his neck began to chafe.

Josef glanced sideways at Franz and rolled his eyes. "Yeah, OK." Neither cared where Greta worked, and they didn't care how Greta met Hans. Her two brothers had some sort of unspoken language. They had predicted the answer to their inane questions, and now they came in for their punch line. "So what are you doing with our Greta?"

"I beg your pardon?" He felt like he was lost in a children's guessing game.

Gertrude strode into the living room. Their mother was also tall, actually very tall, with her hair pulled back tightly into a bun. Her navy blue dress peeked out from under a pinafore apron, tied and strapped securely around her bulky figure.

"I can cook it, but I can't eat it! Are you boys hungry?" She paused. "Hans, would you like a beer?" He deliberated. What if he was not supposed to drink? He had already failed one test.

"Yeah, Hans, what kind do you drink?"

Hans hesitated. He didn't really like beer, and it was unlikely that they would have Amstel or Orangeboom, the two that he knew.

"American beer?"

"Are you kidding? That's like drinking piss. There's nothing in it."

Gertrude laughed. "You need a good stout German beer. We will need to fatten you up a little. Put some muscle on. I'll bring you a Löwenbrau."

Josef laughed. "You going to try to make this guy into a lion?"

Gertrude brought out an enormous platter of food – the largest Hans had ever seen. The sauerkraut had been marinated in wine and cooked with apples and spices, and the heaping fragrant vegetables were covered with sliced pork roast, sausages, meatballs and cutlets. It was a feast, but he was nervous. How could he eat this neatly? He did not like unfamiliar meats, or even meats that were cooked with other things. God, he hoped he would not be asked to say grace. Reverend

Kirkland warned him that sometimes the guest is asked to say grace, and he had learned one. But what if he got the words wrong? Instead, Mr. Fischer, Franz and Josef stood and pushed back their chairs. Gertrude and Greta followed them and Hans quickly stood up. The men raised their right arms straight out, and the women stood at attention with their arms to their side. They began to sing:

"*Die Fahne hoch! Die Reihe fest geschlossen*!
The flag on high, the ranks tightly closed."

Good God, it was the new German anthem, the Horst Wessel song, the anthem of the Nazi party. He had to sing, and he had better put his arm up. He had heard this on the radio as a boy, and only knew some words from the first verse.

"March in spirit within our ranks."

His blood ran cold. The back of his neck grew numb and the top of his head felt like it was going to detach. Hopefully his hair had not begun to stand on end. He had washed it and used a lot of tonic to get it smoothed down. At the end of this "grace" they sat, and Trudy turned to her husband. "I don't know why we can't just say grace the way we used to. I don't think we should be singing about marching instead of thanking God for what we have." Greta fidgeted with her ponytail and said nothing.

Franz looked at his mother impatiently. "Hitler is the hope of Germany and the world."

Hans's stomach began to cramp and rumble. He had tried to ignore the news that Holland, Belgium and France had surrendered to the Nazis. A light sweat poured across his forehead as he thought about the consequences for his mother, sister and little brother. Hopefully they would keep their mouths shut and go about their daily business. A year is a long time in the life of a young man, but it seemed just days since he had feared the Nazis and fled to America. Esther may have torn up her visa, but she also probably made up with mother and stayed comfortably at home, sneaking out at night here and there for a tryst.

"Hans, you seem quiet. You are half German and even Holland is German now. Are you not proud? We will save the world." Josef had noticed that Hans was looking away from the group, eyes fixed on a bush outside the dining room window.

"Pardon?"

Franz calculated his explanation. "Those red front commies threaten everything everywhere. We have to organize against them. Not only in Germany, but can you imagine what will happen to U.S. businesses if the commies take over?"

Mr. Fischer observed his sons and prospective son-in-law carefully.

Hans's response was satisfactory. "Yes, I know. The Communist trade unions almost ruined my father."

Josef continued, "Right. Even the great Charles Lindbergh recognizes that Hitler is the solution."

Mr. Fischer still stood at the table, carving fork and knife in hand. The leg of pork was now dismembered, and Gretchen placed a plate of roast meat, sausage, potatoes and sauerkraut in front of him.

"My Hans has a wonderful appetite and this is a true feast."

At this moment Hans had no appetite at all. He looked down at his plate of food, now an enemy to vanquish. He lifted his knife and fork, took a small bite of his potato and offered "*Mahlzeit! Guten Appetit!*"

"Lindbergh–yeah we're going to need some real flyers all right. Maybe he needs to go talk with the English. They don't seem to know what's what. Windsor needs to get the Royals lined up. They're half German, but George is a pain in the ass."

Hans decided to let curiosity replace his anxiety. "So, Franz, what do you do?"

"Do?"

"For your job."

"Oh yeah. We work for Sperry in Long Island. It's some Dutchman's project. You ever hear of Carl Norden?" Hans smiled. Apparently Johann Fischer and both of Greta's brothers worked for optics companies. He began to breathe more easily hoping they would find common ground, maybe in a nice discussion of how we look at things. He would fit in just fine. But he did not know Carl Norden.

"Actually I do not. But a lot of Dutch work with optics." He decided not to try to bluff his potential brothers-in-law. "Who is Mr. Norden?"

"Some important Dutchman."

Josef explained, "Yeah, we're his bodyguards. Norden can't even go to the john without two guys at his back. But we can get the keys."

Greta was looking down into her lap.

Franz took a piece of sausage, began to chew and commented, "You know she's in nursing school right?"

"Well, sure." He couldn't stand to look at Franz, who now wiped a bit of grease from his lip and smiled.

Hans was confused. Why in the world would their work and Greta's schooling be connected? Greta squeezed his hand under the table. He needed to keep quiet during this curious conversation. Obviously Greta and her brothers knew something about a Dutchman who he had never heard of. He carefully cut apart the sausage and took a small bite to see what it was. The sausage was fresh, and he began to eat it with some sauerkraut, threading the fermented cabbage onto the tines of his fork. He pushed the roast pork to the side of his plate.

"Aren't you going to eat mother's roast pork? It's our favorite." Josef's fork was raised in mid-air as he impaled a boiled potato. He shoved the entire thing into his mouth.

"Oh yes, but I save the best for last."

Greta looked at her mother. "Hans is a very patient man."

Trudy nodded her approval at Hans's restraint. Clearly he would exert the same patience with Greta, and that was a good thing for the girl. He continued to listen to the conversation between the men. Josef was speaking. "Yeah, they got planes, but their bombers can't hit anything. I'll be working nightshifts in August."

Franz's fists thumped into tabletop. Josef winced. The kick had hit a bruise on his ankle. "Do you know what a Norden bombsight is?"

"Not really." Hans wondered why this was important to them.

"Norden's new bombsight could change everything."

"Like what? No one is bombing anybody."

"Europe is at war."

Hans looked down, shocked, then faced Josef. "But America isn't in a war. And Europe has not recovered from 1918."

Mr. Fischer spoke up. "And what, young man, is the lesson we have learned? If Germany had won, there would have been no Communists, no Great Depression. Europe is just beginning to recover. Hitler will bring us back to glory that has not been seen in a thousand years." He wiped his mustache, folded his napkin and placed it into the silver ring. Leaning back into his chair, he said, "I only wish Norden had come to work at Bausch and Lomb. That would have made this so much easier."

Hans was now very interested in the conversation.

Josef peered into his face, straight into his eyes. He didn't dare look down, and was unsure how he should meet Josef's gaze. He settled on a spot on the wall, right above his challenger's forehead.

Franz broke into the discussion. "Here is the deal. This Norden guy has developed a bombsight that you can aim, and it'll stay stable in a moving aircraft. Blam! You can actually hit your target."

"Precisely." Josef played off his brother.

Franz continued, "You can hit a moving boat, even a submarine if you can find it." Their bragging was getting on Hans's nerves. This was not the time for a conversation of the relative advantages of war versus peace. Peace in their minds meant Nazi domination. War was unthinkable. Hans's stomach felt like a cement mixer.

"Yeah, the RAF is going to outfit Canadian planes with it."

Hans deliberated. He had to make sure he was hearing things correctly. "So you don't want the Canadians to have it?"

Franz laughed. Han's ignorance would be useful to them. "We can't stop the Canadian order. The sights will be installed in RAF planes. But Germany needs them so that we can bomb the dog shit out of England. Norden should have stayed home. If he had remained in Holland, he could be a German citizen now."

"We Germans need to stick together. We're going to celebrate Greta's graduation from her nurses training in another few months. Papa hopes to pull some strings so she can get posted to the Red Cross in Geneva. Beautiful neutral country. Nice place for a honeymoon. She's gonna carry a book to Geneva for our 'uncle'."

Hans stiffened. There were no buddies in this room. He had stepped into a den of wolves.

"I have no plans to return to Europe." Apparently Greta had been talking openly with her family about marrying him, which meant that, if he proposed, the answer would be "yes." Dammit. Why were women so naive about political consequences? She had never said her brothers were Nazis. They were born in America.

Greta's brow furrowed and her eyes met her brother's. "I have no plans at all." Her face was crimson.

Hans turned and addressed her mother, a quiet woman who had worked for hours to prepare this debacle of a dinner party. "Frau Fischer, this is a wonderful feast, one I will remember for a long time." His broad smile and wide eyes charmed the hostess nearly as much as they had charmed Greta. He needed to think. Greta and her mother began to clear the dinner dishes, and he didn't want to talk with her brothers any more. He followed Mr. Fischer to the living room. "So, what I would like to know is, what do you see in a piece of wood? Or is it something about the grain and the light that tells you its story?"

Johann Fischer beamed, "Sometimes when I walk in the forest, I hear a story, and then I see the tree that will tell the story. That's how I found the big pieces for the columns." The conversation lulled as they both shied away from discussing Hans's plans with Greta. Greta peeked out from the swinging kitchen door, and the women joined them.

Hans smiled broadly at his prospective father-in-law. "I'm not an artist like you, but maybe your family would enjoy a professional portrait?" Trudy began to tuck in a few loose ends of her hair, beaming. She removed her apron. "I can enlarge the photos at the shop, and make you something that would be nice to frame. A remembrance for all of us."

Greta added, "Yes, mama, let's do! He takes pictures of regular people and makes them into movie stars."

Hans armed himself, implementing a plan on the fly. He picked up his leather camera case, unsnapped the lens cover and fiddled with some dials. "Let me get all of you in front of the mantel."

Mr. Fischer took his place at the end of the mantel, his hand resting on the head of a carved deer. Greta eagerly lined up her parents and brothers in front of the fireplace, and Hans took photo after photo, of the whole group, the parents, the siblings, and of individuals, both full face and in various profiles. "Young man, you truly are an artist." Hans smiled graciously, appreciative of the attention and the compliment.

After dinner Greta suggested an evening walk. A setting sun hit spray from the waterfall so that the early evening drops of water looked like a scattering of diamonds. Diamonds. He felt the little box in his pocket. The air cooled as they approached the water. Looking down into the cataract of the river, he envisioned an endless whirlpool straight into the underworld. The river was not pleasant; it was treacherous. Greta's brothers were thugs and her father was fighting a war that had been lost more than twenty years ago. She could probably be changed, but he could feel his dreams sliding down a cliff and crashing into the river.

Her voice interrupted his reverie. "It's a chilly evening – my hands are cold."

"Sorry, I was just thinking. Here, I have some gloves with me. They're not very thick, but they'll help." Slipping them on, she took a deep breath and turned toward him with worry in her eyes. Her gloved hands reached across the distance between them, but he did not take her hand.

Shivering, she pulled her arms across her chest into a self-embrace. "I'm so cold."

"Do you want to go inside?"

Her hair began to glow in the evening sun. He would give anything to remove just a few hairpins and let it fall. But what would her mother think?

"– No, it's beautiful out here, I want to.... I'm just cold. Besides, I can only handle my brothers in small doses."

He removed his tweed jacket and set it about her shoulders. "They certainly are.... interesting."

"My brothers are bullies. The German Bund is just a boys club with good beer. Those guys threaten all sorts of things, but they are cowards."

"Even cowards can do dangerous things."

"Thank God the U.S. will not get into Germany's wars ever again."

"Greta, Canada is only thirty miles away from us, and they have joined the war with Britain. Holland, Belgium, and France have fallen. London is under attack, and God only knows what is going on in Eastern Europe." He began to narrate the headlines of the past two weeks. "You're right. Let's not talk about that." Her ears were open, but she wasn't listening.

"Listen *Herzchen*, I'm going to have to take the late evening bus back to Rochester. It turns out I cannot stay through the holiday. They want me to come to work in the morning, an important order of photographs that must be delivered by 4:00 p.m. tomorrow. I wouldn't have taken the overtime, but ... they are for a famous star."

She looked at him, completely stunned. This was not the weekend she had planned, or the future she imagined. "Who is the star? Why are they coming to Rosenbaum's?"

A guilty flush moved from the back of his neck, up over his ears, and across his wide forehead. His eyes focused on a tree that stood across the yard, and over her head. "I'm sorry, but I'm not allowed to mention the name. The director is an old friend of his, and these are private photos, more like art photography. I haven't even opened the roll yet, so I don't really know anything else."

"So, you're going to be looking at photos of some scantily dressed movie star all day?" She strangled her words to avoid drowning in her own spit.

"Greta, I wanted to see the fireworks with you, too. I even bought a roll of color film. I didn't want to tell you before dinner, but I've got to go in about 40 minutes."

"Shall I have my brother drive you?" He stiffened. "I guess not, huh?"

"Sweetheart—*Herzchen*—you are too kind. It's a ten-minute walk to the bus station. Let me just pick up my camera and say good night to your parents." He took her hand to walk back to the house. "We will see each other in just a few days." Now he was the one with cold hands.

The dark evening on the bus was not what he had planned. By now he should be holding his girl in his arms and making plans for a bright future. As the bus approached Rochester, he couldn't think of what to say or do. Maybe Greta was right, and her brothers were harmless bullies trying to make an impression on him. This would not be the first time he overreacted when he sensed danger. Fear is an odd emotion. You can't see it, hear it or touch it. Sometimes the fear sets in before there is evidence of a real threat. He tried to clear his head and identify a little evidence before he condemned them. Why did he think that the Fischer brothers were malevolent?

He needed to find out if it was even wrong for them to be Nazis. America had freedom of speech, so maybe it was acceptable to admire the Germans. Canada was committed to fight with Britain, but the U.S. was not in the war. However, it was wrong for them to plan a theft and to involve their innocent sister. Where does one go with rumors of a crime that hasn't been committed yet? He wandered out into the bus terminal, staring blankly at the walls with their transportation schedules and posters. The posters had not changed in months, but he had never really paid attention to them. The FBI "Warning" Poster caught his eye. He had probably read it before while he was waiting for a bus, but tonight it had new significance. He wasn't quite sure what a Federal Bureau of Investigation was, but maybe he should speak with someone at the FBI if he could find an office.

Late into the night, he sat at the desk in his upstairs room and wrote down as many details as he could possibly remember. If he reported the Fischers, he would lose Greta. If he married her, they would be his brothers as well. He had time to make a decision. The gangsters on the wall of the post office were accused of every type of murder and mayhem. Those losses of life would pale if the Germans got hold of the bombsight plans. Over and over he woke to the nightmare of a world in flames.

In the morning, he went straight to the Post Office on West Main Street, near City Hall. They had directories of Rochester, and perhaps he could find out about the FBI there. He still wasn't sure whether his concerns regarding the Fischer brothers were urgent, or even true. Franz and Josef had not even committed a crime, at least not yet.

CHAPTER 9

Rochester N.Y. July 1940

"Gentlemen don't read other gentlemen's mail."

- U.S. Secretary of State Henry Stimson, 1929

AGENT MIKE HICKS SHOVED A stack of papers into a file. Memos were piled all over his desk, and he had to conduct a briefing about a slew of new tasks to be dumped on the FBI. He hated wasting staff time on this. Goddamn FBI didn't seem to know what they were supposed to be doing any more. For 10 years he had been kicking down doors and shoving criminals through the walls. Mike stood five feet eight inches and tipped the scales at 220; he never met a door that could hold him back. The reward for his work of cleaning up gangsters was a desk job, wearing suit jackets that strained at the shoulders and collars that tugged at his short neck. He was pushing forty, and some silver hairs peppered his short sideburns.

This morning he was skimming a printed document from President Roosevelt asking that he drop everything and focus his attention on "Silver Shirts." For God's sake, didn't the President have anything better to do than snoop into a bunch of social clubs throughout upstate New York and into the Midwest? What the hell was the German American Bund? Some friendship organization of mechanics and sausage makers. He had once gone out for a swell Oktoberfest evening at a beer hall, gotten drunk and groped a chunky girl in a dirndl. Couldn't help it. Her tits popped out of the top of the blouse, and they looked good enough to eat. Dammit.

So the gist of the memo was that some friendship organizations in the U.S. were getting political, but not U.S. political. They were getting involved with the commies and some were getting involved with the fascists and Nazis. Happy Independence Day. God, what a mess. Who cares as long as they don't break the law? Just a bunch of goddam loudmouths. But, laws were being broken. There had been several cases of assault and battery and disturbing the peace, but nothing serious. This should be local police stuff. People were jittery enough about all the crap in Europe and Asia. The last thing he needed was every nutcase for miles around pounding down the doors and accusing their neighbors of treason.

A postal clerk entered the small room, an interruption to his interruptions. "Mike, there is a gentleman here to see you. He's waiting at the service counter and says he has an urgent message for the FBI."

"What does he want?"

"He says it is a matter of National Security, and that he has been advised to speak only to you." The clerk peered curiously through his wire-rimmed glasses at the pile of papers on the desk and noted the U.S. executive office seal. "He has an accent."

Oh good grief, a foreigner. Why the hell was the FBI assigned to deal with foreigners? Couldn't we find enough American crooks? "Who is he?"

"Dunno. Says his name is Hank Burns."

"Show him in. But do me a favor, will you? In five minutes I want you to ring this number to the second phone on my desk and say that the Governor is on the line. I'll get him out of here."

Mike stacked the memos, looked up and smiled at the skinny young man who entered the office. The guy had deep blue eyes that skittered around the room. He also had not had a lot of sleep lately; the violet rings under his eyes attested to that. "Good Morning, Mr. Burns, isn't it?"

Hank looked around the dimly lit, windowless office. There was no glass, there were no pretty receptionists. What a queer place for someone who was supposed to be important. "Yes, it is."

"Agent Michael Hicks, Federal Bureau of Investigation. So you have something to report on one of our posters?"

"Actually, I do not. But I have information that may be a matter of national security for the U.S. I don't know exactly where to report it. There does not seem to be an office for intelligence."

Hicks began to laugh. "Nah, our offices aren't set up for intelligence." He rubbed his right eye, and pushed back a stray hair from his forehead. Today was his day for irritation. "So, what is it that I need to know?"

"I was at a home down the river yesterday. They're Germans."

"We have Germans all over upstate New York."

"Yes, but these Germans are planning to steal something that I believe is U.S. property."

Michael sat up and pushed his chair closer to the desk, elbow on the stack of papers, and propped his chin in his hand, mouth set somewhere between neutral and stern. "So what is this U.S. property?"

"It's a set of plans – are you familiar with the Norden bombsight?"

"What?"

"The Norden bombsight is an invention of a Dutchman – you know the Dutch have been developing lenses for more than 300 years…"

"Mr. Burns, please come to the point."

"The plans for a bombsight with a new stabilizing system are being prepared at Sperry on Long Island. I met a couple men who are planning to steal them and get them to the Germans."

The second phone on the desk rang. "I have to take this. It's the Governor's office." He snatched the phone from its cradle. "Hello, I have someone in my office right now. Could you ring back in ten more minutes?" He lit a cigarette.

"So how in heck did you meet a couple thugs from Long Island?"

"I'm not sure they are thugs. I have been dating their sister for almost a year. She invited me to meet the family this weekend, and when we sat down to dinner, they raised their arms in the Nazi salute and sang the party anthem. I was shocked at the display. They're Nazis." He paused. "She never spoke of it. My mother was born in Germany, but I was raised in Amsterdam."

Mike looked at his visitor closely. "That explains the accent. So, you're Dutch." He looked at the papers on his desk. "And Holland is being occupied by Germany. How do your folks like that?"

Hank stiffened, "I am not in touch with them."

Hicks caught the discomfort at the mention of Hank's family. *Hmm, he's a lone wolf, good and bad— good because he makes independent judgments, bad because he may not follow directions. We will need to control this guy to get things right.* "Okay, so why don't you just tell me what happened?" *The whole FBI was a pack of lone wolves, so this guy might fit right in.*

Hank recounted every detail of the Sunday dinner, including exactly what had been served and eaten. "When Greta and I went for a walk she said her brothers were just a pair of bullies. But the plan is for her to carry the plans to Geneva. She has applied for a post at the American Red Cross and wants to serve as soon as she finishes nursing school."

"So, you have a girl mixed up in this?"

"I was planning to propose to her." A frown deepened the bruised shadows under his eyes. "But I refuse to have anything to do with Nazis. The ring is still in my camera bag. I guess now I have to break it off and not see her again."

"Not so fast Hank, let me think on this one." Pulling his chair back from the desk, he faced Hank again. "For the time being, do not break it off. Does she think you're coming to Geneva with her?"

Hank stiffened, remembering the comment about 'a nice place to honeymoon.' "No, I said that I would not go back to Europe, and she didn't seem to be wild about the idea either. I think if she were married she would forget nursing. She is so dear. She just needs someone to take care of."

"Maybe you should get her a kitten."

Hank stared at Hicks. Was he serious? Anyway, he hated cats. If the agent was joking, that was—rude.

"Hank—just give me a moment. I need to get another guy in here. Can you stick around a little longer? You might be able to help us." Hicks picked up another phone and buzzed, "Tom, can you come in here a minute?" A moment later the door opened and the frame of a very large man filled the space. "Hank, this is Tom O'Brien, Special Agent. Tom, Hank has brought us some very interesting information." He recapped the story from his notes, and then asked Hank if he had anything to add. Hank was astonished. Michael had recounted all the details precisely, even the explanations. It was almost as if he were reading everything on the surface, and digging a level deeper.

"That is accurate. But I don't know what to do now. I usually see Greta when I eat lunch over at Woolworth's. I don't even know if I should do that anymore."

O'Brien smiled, "Oh, we'll be seeing lots of Greta. Maybe even her brothers if we do our job right. Hank, want some coffee?"

Hank started to explain that he did not like coffee, but then decided that it was more important to fit in. "Yes, please, with two cubes of sugar." He needed something sweet today.

"So, let's start with the brothers, Frank and Joe Fischer."

Hank interrupted. "At the house they called themselves Franz and Josef Fischer. "

"Okay, we need to dig out birth certificates on both sets of names, plus any records of name changes, naturalization certificates, passports, etc. I sure hope they were born in the U.S. If we don't find it in U.S. records, we can assume they were born somewhere else. We also need to verify their employment with Sperry on Long Island. Are they actually Norden's bodyguards, or just a couple security goons? What are their shifts, who supervises them? And we don't want Sperry to think anything might be wrong. Otherwise they will change their plans." Once he got going, O'Brien's delivery was like a machine gun.

"Dig out German American friendship clubs and find out what they are up to. I heard they actually had a group marching in the Chicago May Day parade. Boy, that must have been a swell parade. The commies were there too."

Michael pushed all the briefing memos aside. He had pulled out a yellow legal pad and was writing furiously. "Hank, where do the Fischers live? We need to start tracking their actions as well."

"Oh no, do you need to spy on the whole family? On Greta?"

"Nah, we're not gonna spy on Greta." Hicks looked across his desk at O'Brien, then they both shifted in their seats. "You're going to spy on Greta." Hank clamped his mouth shut. "And we call this an investigation. We are the Federal Bureau of Investigation. The United States doesn't spy."

"Excuse me?" Hank's brows knit into total confusion.

"Hoover shut down intelligence activities in the Department of State because we would never have any more wars, and the embassies were just having cocktail parties – great place to go during Prohibition." Tom continued, "But we do investigate."

"How is investigation different?"

"Beats me. We get paid less, and we don't get to go to cocktail parties?"

Hank couldn't imagine these two rumpled bureaucrats being invited to embassy cocktail parties. He remembered the stiff suits and slick shoes they wore to glittering palace events in Amsterdam. Okay, he personally had been in uniform, but he knew that these guys would not fit in.

"Okay, Hank, when do you see Greta next?"

"Well, she is away for the holiday, so I would be having lunch there on Wednesday."

"Great. And when do you two date?"

"We usually go dancing on Saturdays."

"Where?"

"We like to go to the Four Aces. They have a great big band. Gosh, I hope she's not mad at me."

"Why would she be?"

"I didn't even kiss her good night. I was supposed to stay the weekend, and instead I said I had to work today. I just caught the late night train." He began to fish around in his pocket, and pulled out a roll of film. "I'm not sure, but do you want this? I have a roll of film."

Hicks startled, snapping his head away from O'Brien. "Excuse me?"

"Well, I thought I should take a family portrait—you know, as a thank you gift? But I did get good full face and profiles of everyone." A twinkle of blue, and then a fixed gaze. "Would you like me to develop it?"

Hicks picked up the roll and set it on top of his notepad. "We can send it to our lab. You look like you didn't have much sleep. Buddy, you go take a walk and maybe a nap. Let's surprise your girl with entrance to the Arcadia Club."

Hank took a deep breath. The Arcadia was the most exclusive club in Rochester, a place where owners of big businesses met for golf and confidential talks. No Italians, no Irish, and no Jews were allowed to join. Hicks broke in on his daydream. "And don't be surprised if one of us turns up at the Arcadia with a date. I'll see if the wife would like to go. If you see me, please do not greet us. Don't even look at us. We will do all the watching. You need to keep dating this girl and treat her like the princess that she undoubtedly is. Don't pull back, and for heaven's sake don't make promises. Act as if there are no concerns. And if she invites you to visit the family again, by all means go."

Tom O'Brien breathed a sigh of relief. At 6'4" and with his red hair he was not an ideal candidate for undercover work in a ballroom. But he would get to the bottom of the questions about the brothers. He also needed to set up undetectable surveillance for Hank Burns or whatever his real name was.

CHAPTER 10

Upstate New York July 1940

"Auf wiedersehen – until we meet again"

~ *German folk song*

Greta sat on the front porch, the muggy evening closing in around her while fireflies appeared in the bushes and disappeared again. Hans had vanished into the night. She planned to stay outside until her brothers left the front room, but Franz's voice cut the night air. "Hey Gretel, where did your Dutchman disappear to?

"Yeah, what happened to Hänsel?"

Greta looked at her brothers, puzzled. In the first place, it was none of their business and she didn't like the contempt she heard in their comments. Their beer glasses were empty and the ashtrays were full. Foul air filled the tidy house. No wonder Hans had left. He didn't drink or smoke.

There were only two emotions that she could express safely. One was to lash out in anger. The other was cold silence.

Franz persisted with his line of questions. "I thought you said Dutchman had a German mother. What did he say when we took over Holland? Did he ever express any gratitude for our protection of his precious 'Motherland'?"

Greta glared at him.

Josef laughed, "We all know there is only one Fatherland and it's not that stupid swamp full of cheese-heads."

A heavy glass ashtray was in her hand, but she set it back down on the coffee table. The last thing she needed was to attract Gertrude's concern by throwing it at her brother. Her mother had done everything to make her a good wife, but now she was about to lose her temper. She folded her arms and straightened up to her full height.

"Hank is not stupid! He has a good job and he was smart enough to leave that swamp and move here. He speaks, reads and writes German, which is more than you two know how to do. He even knew the words to your dumb song."

Franz put down his beer, and lit a new cigarette. He blew the smoke toward her and asked, "So, how was your walk by the river? Seems like the two of you weren't out long enough to have any meaningful 'talk.'"

Greta started to move toward the kitchen. Josef ordered, "You need to answer us."

"He received a late order from a very important client. He got up early, took the bus here, and didn't tell me until after dinner that he needed to return to Rochester. He didn't want to spoil our day together."

"Boy oh boy, that must have been some good night kiss. So what kind of order was it?"

"He runs the darkroom at Rosenbaum's Photo."

"Goddammit, they're not even proper Germans, they're Jews. Your boyfriend works for Jews?"

"He's a Presbyterian."

Franz stabbed out his cigarette near the clean ashtray and blew the ashes around the tabletop. "For crying out loud, you never realized that he wasn't a Lutheran? How in God's name did you miss that? That guy isn't German. You dumb bitch, you are going to have to clean this up." His beer sloshed as he slammed the glass down.

Josef's grinning mouth closed and he sat back in his father's easy chair as Greta retorted. "I don't need to clear anything up except your filthy ashtrays and beer glasses. When I'm married, I won't even need to do that anymore."

"You rotten cunt!"

"This stinks! I don't have to follow orders from you."

"Well, actually you do. So let's think about what they will be."

Greta began to fold the heavy sections of the newspapers. She drew the flowered chintz drapes. The outside door was left open in hopes that a river breeze would help clear the air. Her brothers were used to treating her like a dummy, but her ears were wide open as they conspired.

"She needs to dump him."

Josef leered at his sister. "Nah, actually, she needs to get to know him better. He pop your cherry yet?"

Gretchen spun around, mortified. "Good God, no!"

"It's time for some fireworks then."

"Not until after I'm married."

"Well, you are going to have to spend time in his apartment – where do you go to snuggle?"

"This really isn't your business." She turned back toward the kitchen door. Josef grabbed her arm, pressing hard enough to leave a mark.

"Let's try this again."

Her eyes filled. "We kiss on a park bench. Sometimes we walk by the lake."

"Bitch, where do you two go after dark?" Franz smirked. "Just tell him you are cold or uncomfortable on the park bench. He'll find a warm soft place for you. That's his duty."

"He lives in a rooming house, and they can't take girls to their rooms. I live in a rooming house, and I can't take young men upstairs." She paused, assessing the two men, rumpled and smelling of tobacco and beer. "We go out on dates. Maybe you should try an evening with a nice girl sometime."

"What else don't you know about this guy? How do you know if he doesn't have a girlfriend in Holland?"

"Or a wife?" Franz lowered his head, like a bull planning to charge. "Dutchman might have run away."

Josef stretched out his arm and reached for another cigarette, lit it and pulled on the tobacco until it glowed bright red. "Nah, I don't think there is a wife, or he would have tried to pop her cherry."

Outside a thunderstorm started. A light sprinkle began to fall from the pink sky. Toward the west the sky had already turned violet with black clouds forming in the remains of the sunset. A low rumble threatened. "Crap, that's all we need. A perfect evening. Well, hopefully your boyfriend got on the bus OK. Be a shame to get him all wet."

"Yeah, or his snazzy camera. At least he has a German camera. That little Leica cost more than our salaries for a week. He better be rich, or I hope you enjoy eating film. Oh wait, he works in a darkroom – he can steal all that stuff."

"Stealing." Franz scratched a pimple on his chin, "We need to get back to our plan. So, you will keep on dancing with Hans, or Hank or whatever he calls himself. You need to get into his room – you're a woman, figure it out. He just needs to see that we are doing the right thing. If he's with us, we're OK. If he's not, we'll make other plans."

CHAPTER 11

Rochester, N.Y. July 1940

---

*"**NORTHERN EUROPE**: Most of Europe is now under Nazi rule. France surrenders. The French Vichy Government will cooperate with the Nazis. Britain is given the choice to surrender or die."*

- N.Y. Times

Hank pulled a strip of negatives from the tank. The shop was silent, closed for the holiday. Just before leaving work on two days before he had met a new customer. Rosenbaum greeted the man. "Hi Shel! Hey Hank, I want you to meet Shel. He is a big agent–he finds actresses and models for Broadway producers. You know those gorgeous gals at Radio City Music Hall? They come from all over the country, some even from here. Pretty and talented."

Hank thought of his sister and how he could have helped Esther live her dream of being a beauty on film.

Shel laughed, "Yeah, very talented. I got a rush order here."

"Hank, can you do it?"

"I'm going to Greta's house for the long weekend."

Rosenbaum laughed, "Aah Greta, now there's a sweetheart–not talented, but a great cook. Good wife material. When are you going to ask her to marry you?" Hank began to fiddle with envelopes of photos, sorting and resorting them. "Seriously, Hank, have your weekend, but can you figure out how you can get these contact sheets to Shel right after the holiday?"

Hank did not like lying, so now he was going to make good on the excuse he had made to Greta. He shut the darkroom door and turned on the red light. In the darkroom he was alone and he could think, and right now he needed to think. The darkroom solitude helped reveal clarity in his thoughts and, like pictures, they were allowed to develop. *How could such a sweet girl be mixed in with a crime against the United States? Was she going to carry the documents to Switzerland, or were her brothers playing with him? Good God, they were security guards at a classified facility. They could get him deported as a spy. If they were truly stealing technical plans, joining them was unthinkable. Or was it all a trap to see if he was a Nazi? He sang their damned song at dinner, and they could use that as circumstantial evidence. Most important of all, what were they going to do to him?* Those guys were a real pair of goons.

There were no threats in the darkroom. Hank found Shel's envelope and pried open the first cassette. There were five rolls of film to load onto the reels. He felt the film load neatly onto the spokes, and dropped the reels into the tanks. Once the negatives were hung out to dry, he made himself a cup of tea.

O'Brien and Hicks had suggested that he continue seeing Greta, and they hinted that there would be protection available. Easy for them to say. *What was there in this for him, other than every opportunity for a disaster? If he were implicated with her and her family, he would lose his visa, and if he didn't cooperate with his newfound friends in the FBI he would lose his visa.* The Feds could pull it at any time and now they were pulling him like salt water taffy. He set up the photo enlarger. Time to work. *Good grief, did Shel want prints or did he just want a contact sheet? Darn it. He didn't say.* Hank decided to run a contact sheet. Images of girls popped into view.

What in heck were they wearing? Oh right, Shel certainly needed to see if they had nice legs. Apparently when the girl stood straight, her thighs, knees and ankles had to all match up evenly, and all the girls needed to be about the same proportions. Gorgeous, but no one had ever mentioned anything about exposed breasts. Two ladies were not covered up, they were in their tap pants with boas, but no blouses, not even camisoles. Hank whistled. That's what men do, right? He practiced his American wolf-whistle again.

A pretty Spanish shawl appeared, but the brunette was wearing nothing else. Wait a minute – Rosenbaum's didn't do this kind of thing. And obviously Rosenbaum trusted him implicitly – even with the accounting and inventory for all the materials. As nice as these girls looked, this was lewd and immoral. Now the censors would be in line to deport him for moral turpitude. *What was old Rosenbaum thinking?* He shut his eyes and took a deep breath wondering what Greta would look like without her blouse. There might not be a wedding night to find out. Thoughts about Greta did not belong in this room, not with these women who had stripped for Shel's camera. He needed air.

Outside, newsboys were yelling on the corner and he picked up a paper to hide behind at lunch. A black headache was forming. The Woolworth's lunch counter reeked of fried food, burgers on the grill and the slightly rancid odor of hot dogs. A sandwich plate arrived in front of him. *What made him think he wanted egg salad?* At least the egg salad should be easy to digest if he could gag down the mayonnaise.

Digesting the news was something else. Events of the past two days whirled around him: lovely Greta, an awkward walk by the river, and two brothers who expected that he would join them as Nazi sympathizers. They assumed that it was only a matter of time until the U.S. joined their glamorous nationalist vision. Hank blinked back tears of rage.

Why was the United States remaining neutral in the face of all this? God knows what had happened to the Amsterdam dry goods business. He really should write his mother with an update on all his successes in the U.S. Maybe she would like to see a photo of him with his fiancée, once the problems with Greta's brothers were behind them, or a special art photo of his American beauty. Oh! Those photos. The negatives and contact sheets were hanging in the dark room at Rosenbaum's and he needed to get back to work.

Hank filled the tanks of the enlarger and began to print. The contact sheets full of nude women weren't as disturbing as they had been earlier. Now they were just black and white celluloid images. Each frame revealed positive and negative space and maybe a lighting pattern here or there. He was an artist, and the images were now an abstraction.

If only life would come into focus like photos. *Is a marriage doomed if there is no brotherly love? Or do you just marry the girl and ask her to stay away from her family?* If he married Greta right away, then worries about his visa would be over. He would be on the track to becoming a naturalized citizen. What an irony to have his ticket to citizenship in the hands of Nazi sympathizers.

By lunchtime Wednesday Greta was back at her station at Woolworth's. Her friend Emily commented, "Hey, I thought Hank was going with you to your folks last weekend. Instead he was in here on Monday, reading a newspaper and nibbling at a little egg salad sandwich. You need to take better care of that boy. He looked exhausted." Instead of worrying, Greta took a breath of relief. Apparently Hank really did have a huge client order. He must have been preoccupied with the work. Now she could tell her brothers to lay off.

She carried the coffeepot to Hank. "I bet you would like some tea?"

"No, it's OK, coffee is fine."

"Since when did you start drinking coffee?"

"Since I started dating a real American girl. I know you like coffee, so I'm willing to drink it." He smiled at her, a luminous engaging smile with the twinkling blue eyes that she had come to love. "I'm awfully sorry about the extra work." He eyed at the top buttons of her blouse, and the outline of her camisole underneath. "Um, Greta, the client gave us an entrance card for the Arcadia Club. Would you like to go dancing Saturday? I know it's short notice."

Greta stared at him, then smiled. "But that's really high society. Are you sure?"

"Well, he's an important client and he liked the work." Hank paused, "Look, I need to make this up to you. And it'll be a chance for me to get out of the darkroom. How about you put on a snazzy dress and I'll pick you up at 7:00 for dinner and dancing? Let's celebrate just a little bit."

"What's your idea of a snazzy dress?"

"Oh, I don't know, maybe a little daring, something your mother would not want you to wear?"

"Do I look like my mother to you?" She pursed her lips into a little pout.

"Oh good heavens, I just was thinking, you're prettier than any of those showgirls."

"So you just want to show me?"

He wanted her to flirt, but teasing confused him. "No, no— Please, I'm just hungry. Is there any meatloaf today?"

The parlor of Mrs. Foster's rooming house was centered around the large uncomfortable Victorian sofa, covered in black horsehair. A baby grand piano stood in the corner, but Hank had never paid any attention during his seven years of weekly lessons at the conservatory. He couldn't play. Two overstuffed chairs with down cushions were separated, one under each window, probably because the high windows offered enough light to read by during the day. A jungle of small tables with doilies and plants were scattered through the room.

A hall ran past Mrs. Foster's room, leading to the creaking stairs that led up to the four young women's rooms on the second story. Mrs. Foster greeted all young men in her parlor, and left her own door ajar late at night until she heard each of the four girls enter the house, and a single set of footsteps ascend the stairs. Young men were only allowed into the parlor, and no visitor was to spend more than half an hour there. Hank walked down Maplewood Drive at 6:55, because he knew that Greta would take a few moments before coming downstairs. It wasn't proper to be too eager to meet with a young man.

She came down the stairs in a lovely wine red dress, draping softly against her figure, and pulled low on her shoulders. With it was a black shawl, covered with a field of spring blooms and long fringe. A new lipstick brightened her blonde features. He practiced his wolf whistle and grinned. "You look absolutely beautiful, like a rose in full bloom!" He also wondered what she would look like without the dress.

"One of the gals helped me. She even lent me her shawl. Is it too much?"

Thinking of the pictures he had developed over the past weekend, he gazed at her. "Just right." Her new high-heels had open toes, so he decided to splurge on a cab. The dainty straps were just the thing for kicking up her heels and she had been admiring those shoes in the shop window for weeks. His pleasure at her happiness was tinged with worry. Her brothers appeared to be very serious about their intention to steal the bombsight plans. Obviously they planned to control her, and he didn't want a wife who would be controlled by her brothers. Then again, who wants a wife who rebels against her father and brothers? Either way, he didn't see how he could spend his life with a family of Nazis. Greta chattered away about the pretty summer evening. His mind whirled as the cab meandered through streets toward downtown.

Hank had planned an evening of dinner and dancing to remember. No matter what happened, he desperately wanted to do things right. The exclusive Arcadia dinner club had awnings across the front. Candlelight glinted in the dark room illuminating white shirtfronts, and sparkles of jewelry. He had never been in there. When he ordered the Chateaubriand from an expensive club menu, Greta looked at him, puzzled. Her Hans had always been frugal, if not downright stingy. Tom O'Brien had told him that the FBI would be picking up the tab. "My God, Hank, what is the occasion?"

His hands shook imperceptibly as he unfolded the napkin, but a hawk-like glance was circling the room to either protect her or to claim her. He wasn't sure how he felt about involving the FBI in his personal affairs. Then he grinned, gazing at her. "Oh, I just wanted to treat us to a special evening. I'm so sorry I had to work overtime last weekend. The least I can do is spend the bonus on you."

He wasn't sure he had been convincing.

So, once again he was not going to propose. Greta had her own silent dialogue, the one where Hank would take her away from her family. She kept waiting for the proposal. School would be ending in three months, and she would be sent to Geneva if she didn't have a wedding to plan. Oh, dear God.

He tried small talk. "So how is your family? I'm so sorry I had to leave them. I'd really looked forward to going fishing with your brothers."

She fiddled with her napkin, picked up her glass of Cabernet and gulped, hissing out the words. "The last people I want to talk about right now are those two stupid brothers of mine." A quick swipe with the napkin removed the droplet of wine hanging from her lip.

This was one heck of a mixed message. She took him home to meet the family, and now she didn't want to talk about them. Was she a Nazi or were they assuming she was just along for their ride, like they had assumed about him? It was a little late for him to investigate the options.

"Well, at least I didn't take you out for spaghetti. It looks like Italy is joining the war. Or, maybe we should have. We may not be able to get spaghetti after they do. They can keep their tomatoes and eggplants, but I do really like a great Fettucini Alfredo."

"Hank, are you talking about food or politics?"

"Um, food, I guess."

She wiped her mouth and stifled a sigh. "Do you mind leaving the war out of it?"

"Well, may I ask you just one question and then drop the subject?"

Hank looked around the room then twisted in his seat, visibly uncomfortable. Greta interrupted his internal commentary. "Look Hank I really can't answer any questions about politics. I don't know and I don't care. Hitler and Mussolini just want to be movie stars, and put on pageants. You are a cameraman. Certainly you can see that."

"Let's kick up these new heels. I didn't put them on to hide them under a tablecloth."

He grabbed her arm, and led her onto the dance floor, holding her tightly around the waist. Other couples were swaying back and forth, ebbing and flowing with the music. The big band was playing a Duke Ellington favorite, "Don't Get Around Much Any More," and a sax solo echoed the sadness that he was studiously avoiding. Across the floor he spotted Mike Hicks seated with a plain brunette, and turned away from them. They had a pair of martini glasses on the table already and didn't look particularly worried.

There was a sudden tap on his shoulder. A tall red-headed man reeking of gin bumped into them. "Can I cut in?" He tried to grab Greta's hand.

Greta shook her head and placed her arms around Hank's neck. "No, thank you!" A moment later the same hand tapped him. O'Brien was not a person to hide on a dance floor.

"Buddy, I said I want to cut in. I'll give you the dame back in one piece."

"She is not a 'dame,' she's my...." O' Brien practically lifted Greta out of Hank's arms.

"And I don't want to ..."

"That's a sweet dress, honey." O'Brien grabbed her hands and began to spin her around. She gasped in panic, looking as if she were about to cry. O'Brien snapped his head toward the men's room, and Hank followed his eyes in that direction while O'Brien tried not to step on Greta's new shoes.

Mike Hicks was in the lavatory, washing his hands with a sink turned on full blast. "So what have you learned?"

"She doesn't care for politics. She thinks it is all posturing and show."

"I'm not sure we care what she thinks. We are investigating her brothers. And if she's neutral she is more of a threat than they are."

"That can't be right. The United States is not at war. We have businesses all over the world that would be lost if we entered a war."

"You mean like your family business in Holland?"

"What?"

"Come on Hank, we had to do a full background check on you. It came out clean. You are the real McCoy."

"The what?"

"You're okay, Mr. Bernsteen. Not sure why you changed your name. We have to get you back out on that dance floor. This is the last refrain on that song and your girl will be waiting. O'Brien hates to dance. We will talk more, Ontario Beach Park, near the carousel, tomorrow morning at 11:00. Skip church."

"But …"

"Tell her you have a headache. Women use that one all the time."

Hank put his arm around Greta and led her to the standing taxis. She smiled appreciatively, knowing that he was not going to risk being accosted by the red headed man again. Her feet hurt, and soon they would be in a softly lit parlor saying good night. But somehow, she needed to get into his rooms, and quickly. She wasn't even quite sure of the address. She snuggled into him. "If only these evenings did not end." Her face tilted up to his, and he kissed her nose. She grabbed his collar and pulled his mouth to hers, a buttery soft kiss full of intent.

He opened his eyes, astonished. "Do you want to stay out a little longer?"

"Well, if only we had somewhere to go, somewhere a little more comfortable. I can't have men into Mrs. Foster's parlor after 11:00 and it's almost that now. Do you have the same rules where you live?"

He laughed softly. "No, not really, just more of a gentleman's understanding. We don't bring immoral women into the house. The family lives downstairs, and another gentleman and I live in the two wings of the house upstairs. It's very pleasant, I have a porch overlooking the river, and there was a closet that I made into a darkroom. I plan to stay there until…"

"Until you get married?"

"Um, I haven't given much thought to marriage yet. I would want to buy a house of my own for that."

"You don't have to own a house to be a husband!"

"Well, it would be best, don't you think? I would want my wife to be comfortable."

"Any candidates?"

Hank bit his lip. The taxi pulled up and Hank quickly unlocked the right side of the duplex. A narrow staircase went up to a dark sitting room and a brightly lit kitchen area. The two gentleman's rooms were down a dark hallway. "I can make a pot of tea. Would you like that? The kitchen is away from the family bedrooms." Hank started the teakettle and pulled some bread and cheese out of a cabinet. "May I make you a toasted cheese sandwich?"

Dear God, he was hungry again. Did the man have no interests other than food and cameras? She was stuffed from dinner, but she had to report to her brothers.

"Could I just have a bite of yours? It sounds tasty, but I'm full." He made two sandwiches and dove into his with a knife and fork, fastidiously peeling the drips of melted cheese away from the edges. She picked hers up, took a bite out of the center, and set it back down on the plate.

"Hank, you don't really talk about your family. You've met mine. Will I ever be able to meet any of yours?"

Hank tried to think of a response. He had not written a letter since he arrived in New York nearly two years ago. "I am writing a letter to my mother and sister. In fact, I want to take a special photo of us together to send them."

"You have taken hundreds of photos of me."

"Yes, but I want one of us so that..."

"So that they know you are not alone?"

"Yes, that's it."

"Which is your room?"

He looked at her, quite puzzled. "You don't want to go into my bedroom, do you?"

She looked down, embarrassed, "Oh no, I just wanted to think about you in your home sometimes when we are not together."

He smiled, "It's the second one down on the left, the one with the porch."

Greta joined her parents for Saturday lunch, aware that she was facing an inquisition. Her father sliced the foam off his beer, emphatic about the news in his German papers. Italy had joined the war, and Hitler and Mussolini were going to revive the world order of antiquity, great empires cutting away at bankrupt nations and little people without substance. She couldn't even begin to think of how Hank would feel about this. He didn't talk about Holland. But when she was asked to deliver the information that papa requested, she did her duty. "Hank lives at 88 Augustine Street, and his room is on the second story on the west side of the building. There is a porch facing the street."

"I tried to get into his room, but instead he made me a cheese sandwich. It wasn't even European cheese, it was some gooey thing called 'Old English.'" Her father did not appear to be particularly disappointed in her. Her virtue was still something to be negotiated to the highest bidder. She continued, "So I don't have a way to look through his things. Besides, he is crazy about locks. He has keys to everything, his doors, his work, his boxes and his bureau drawers."

She wanted to spend the rest of her life with Hank and not with her father and brothers. "Papa, Hank is a decent man who wants to become a good American." The tears were starting. "You have ruined enough of my life. I'm not going to ruin his."

"Are you marrying him?"

"He wants to buy a house first."

"Oh, so you will go to Geneva in October. Everyone will be happy then. Your brothers will be able to celebrate your wedding, whenever that is."

Greta blinked back the tears and began to gasp as sobs choked her. "Papa, they have ruined everything I ever wanted. I don't know why I have to do this. I only know how miserable they will make me if I don't."

Her father handed her a handkerchief.

CHAPTER 12

Rochester, N.Y. Labor Day 1940

"Let's Go... Canada!"

~ *Recruitment poster*

Clouds were thickening, and a breeze picked up along the shore of Lake Ontario. Picnics were repacked into baskets and people began huddling under towels and blankets waiting for the sun to come back out. This was real Dutch weather. Hank located the merry-go-round and began snapping pictures of children playing, walking with balloons, and putting their little faces into wads of cotton candy. It reminded him of summer days at the North Sea. No one was going swimming in the whitecapped waves. One intrepid sailor was out, but the rest of the boats were lined up neatly in their moorings, masts tipping into the wind.

Hank's tweed jacket flapped in the breeze. His lean physique didn't fill out the pleated slacks and shirt. He had been avoiding his lunches at the dime store. For two months now he had been seeing Greta for movies and small talk, with a couple dry kisses ending their evenings. Mike Hicks strolled across the lawn, camera in hand. His gait was the same, but steel rimmed glasses and a new mustache made him look like an intellectual or artist of sorts, maybe someone who travels with Socialists.

Mike shot an oblique look toward Hank, and quipped. "Is this the meeting of the Blue Ribbon Photo Club?" Hank didn't understand the humor. He steadied his gaze and his eyes did not smile. What was the purpose of this meeting, if it was a meeting at all? There was no gentlemen's handshake. He slid his hands into his pockets.

"Good morning, Mike. I didn't even know you wore glasses." Mike opened up his new Kodak camera and inserted the lead from a roll of film. He closed the back and wound it into position, then began to walk toward the water. Hank followed him, wondering when Mike would stop to at least snap the shutter. Cobbles at the shore of the lake rolled as wind licked the water into waves.

Mike laughed, "When are you gonna see your blonde dish again?"

"Actually, her birthday is next weekend and I guess I'm going out again. They invited me back. It's going to take a while before they trust me, I'm afraid."

Mike stopped on the path, adjusted his spectacles and looked at Hank full in the face. "Where are her brothers going to be?"

"I don't know, why?"

"We picked them up last night."

"Picked up who?"

"Franz and Josef Fischer. We had to wait until we could catch them red-handed."

"Red handed? They aren't Communists."

Mike related a few details of the surveillance operation that had trapped Greta's brothers. There was no gangland style manhunt, there were no machine guns. Two additional men had been added on staff at Sperry. One was a personal assistant to Mr. Norden, a real engineering whiz. The other was a file clerk. The two FBI agents had been watching the guards who were assigned to watch the offices.

"We even had a camera hidden in the old man's desk. It tripped when they opened the file cabinet, which we conveniently left accessible."

"Left it unlocked?"

"Don, the assistant, made sure that Franz saw him work the combination."

Hank found a nearby park bench and sat down. He pulled out a handkerchief, and wiped his eyes and nose. The nightmare had come to an end. Unfortunately, tension in his body had racked him so that his neck cracked and his stomach hurt.

"So it's over? Thank God!"

"What's over?"

"All this hiding, all the secrets? It's all over. Greta is not implicated. We can go on like — before."

Mike's face froze, and the steel-rimmed glasses only reflected the harshness of his gaze. There was no expression at all.

"No you can't." He pulled out a cigarette and lit it, offering one to Hank. Hank shook his head. Mike continued, "This thing's about to blow like the Hindenburg. We're one spark away." He blew out the paper match and tossed it on the grass.

Hank stopped in his tracks, completely bewildered. "I don't understand."

"We have due process in this country. You are innocent until proven guilty. So those two clowns could get off with a lawyer. There are lots of other Nazi sympathizers. Someone at Sperry might notice that they have not shown up for work. A few calls into the German Bund could be very dangerous for all of us."

Hank hated being treated as if he were stupid or naïve. His nervousness was turning into anger. "But what about Greta? She doesn't want to be involved with them."

Mike's disguise glasses obscured just enough of his appearance to confuse Hank. "Greta is a big girl." He paused to rub his chin. "Nothing will happen to her." The comment didn't sound as if Greta's innocence had been considered. "Hank, you need to get out of town. We're going to be taking you into protective custody."

Hans was furious. He would have hit the FBI officer if he hadn't been aware that Hicks was armed and carrying a badge. There could still be more to lose. "I don't need to go anywhere. I'm not the criminal. Since when do citizens have to leave?"

"You're not a citizen. But O'Brien and I have a plan." He paused and looked off into the distance. "Nice day at the lake."

Hicks was right. The deep green of the dense maple trees was peaceful, and a real affirmation of life. In another month, leaves would be starting to die. So much for affirmations. Pebbles on the shore of the water shone all shades of gray, milky white to charcoal. Hicks picked up a flat stone and skipped it across the water. Hank had no idea why they were supposed to be throwing stones into the water, although the skipping was rather impressive. Why did Hicks want to talk about the lake?

"Yeah, you can see clear across."

"It's cloudy."

Hicks paused. This guy was dense. The clouds were nothing compared to the fog in Hank Burns' psyche.

"That— is Canada."

"I know that. Canada is a British colony, and it is not part of the United States."

"We have your paperwork ready. A full commendation from the FBI has been couriered to MacMillan in Ottawa, eyes only. You have been granted an extension of your American visa, and a new Dutch passport with permission to enter the Dominion of Canada."

"Who's MacMillan?"

"He is a Lieutenant Colonel in the Canadian Army. You do know there is a war going on right? They need help in combat photography. MacMillan will be assigning you."

"My God, how do I tell Greta? What do I tell Rosenbaum?"

"You don't. Two hours from now a 'friend' will be picking you up to take you to dinner. An unmarked FBI car will arrive at your rooming house. Don't take a suitcase. You can bring a camera bag with your valuables and your travel documents. The Canadian Army will give you everything else you need."

CHAPTER 13

Ontario Canada Fall-Winter 1940-41

"We shall defend our island, whatever the cost may be. We shall fight on the beaches.... we shall fight in the fields and in the streets....we shall never surrender!"

- W. Churchill, BBC

HANK SAT ON HIS BED rubbing his forehead. There was less than an hour to pack and to once again leave his life behind, a refugee with no idea what was ahead. He couldn't even take his new American clothes unless they fit on his back. Hans Bernsteen's Dutch passport, bankbook, and cameras fit neatly into the pockets of his bag.

He left out of the side door. A driver greeted him. They rode in silence for two hours.

The Toronto skyline began to rise over the lake. Reds and blues from the late afternoon sun streaked the sky as the car crossed a bridge into an old fort. Jeeps bumped along stone streets, honking at each other and watching out for pedestrians. Berets, tam o'shanters, and garrison caps hurried across the paths. They pulled up at a large limestone building where a burly captain with brush cut hair and a mustache was expecting him, and handed him a kit and new ID Tags, "Hank Burns."

"Glad to see you made it in one piece. You'll find we have plenty of Yanks here. I'm going to have Eckstrom walk you over to your barracks. Mess is at 18:00 sharp. Don't be late. They'll eat everything."

Eckstrom was a big Swede, even taller than Hank. Had to be 6'5" or so. God only knows what he was doing in the Canadian Army. The soldiers were from all over Western Europe, far away from action on the European fronts. These young men had chosen to join the fight after their homelands had surrendered. Vanquished nations had no armies, and they didn't plan to lie down to die in front of German tanks. Young Dutch farmers had fled lost homes. Immense blonde Norwegians carried bayonets that added nearly two feet to their height. They would be able to stand up against a bunch of German porkers. Energy and determination boiled in every pocket of the fort, along with pots of strong black tea.

Along with the tea came a supper of potatoes, vegetables and some sort of meatloaf. Hank looked at his plate, wondering how he would be able to fill up.

"You new here? If you don't like your dinner, we can eat it for you." Hank picked up his fork and began to wolf his food. "No American steaks here. They're trying to run us on 20 ounces of meat a week." Hank could easily eat 20 ounces of meat in a day.

When Hank reported for roll call in the morning, he heard foreign voices calling out across the grounds as sergeants lined Dutch, Norwegian and Quebecois up for training. Orders were in English, but not all the guys understood English. God help those who got a Scottish trainer. The Scots were fierce but nobody understood them, not even the English or the Yanks.

———

Within weeks the mornings were dark and chilly. Photo processing was in a quiet building far from the training grounds. Over the next months, daily courier packets arrived at a maze of partitions and standing closets in an unmarked warehouse. British Intelligence was making up for lost time in evaluating Fascist threats. Hank dipped the films into chemical baths, examining proofs for neat outlines, and clear gradations of black, white and gray. Complex images appeared in the enlarger, and he tried to make some sense of air and ground reconnaissance photos. It looked like the photographers couldn't shoot fast enough – blurs and clouds cut through pictures taken while a plane stormed through turbulent skies. He wished he were up there with them, just to see what they were looking at.

He opened up the lab on a frozen February morning. Several packets had come in a late afternoon delivery. Within minutes the red lights were on and his baths were ready. In the basin a series of tidy gables appeared, some sort of roofline. Could it be Amsterdam? Was it Copenhagen? Not possible. The Canadian Forces didn't have any men on the ground in Europe, but someone had taken these pictures. They sure weren't tourist postcards. Police were wearing Nazi uniforms and seemed to be herding long lines of men through snow dusted streets. Solemn faces peered into cameras, an occasional glint of eyeglasses, or a dark hat. They wore overcoats and many were carrying battered suitcases. They were too old to be volunteers. Who were these men, and why were they being moved? Not sure.

Sometimes the photos ended up in newspapers. More often, they went into file folders.

The next roll was a different format, a narrow strip on a spool. It was not to be enlarged. The stripfilm could be wound into projectors to roll from one picture to the next, almost like a film, but with time for someone to narrate the story. The filmstrip demonstrated what looked like a slow motion wrestling match, some sort of hand to hand combat. In the shadows he loaded the developed films, and began to imitate the body poses of the soldiers, making a fists and aiming punches toward the red light.

A banging on the outside door of the dark room disturbed his private war. His supervisor was calling. "Hank, buddy, you still in there?"

Hank opened the door and squinted at Spencer. "Sorry, I was just hanging this spool."

"What bag are you on?"

"The one with all the film strips. "

"Take a break for a few minutes. We need to talk."

"Yes, sir."

He followed Spencer to a very messy desk, covered with yellow envelopes, photos, notes, and a couple ashtrays. Spencer pulled out a pack of cigarettes and offered one to Hank. He declined. Actually he was hungry. What he would give for a juicy roast beef sandwich... but instead lunch had consisted of a cheese sandwich on white bread, mustard, no butter. He didn't like the greasy stuff they passed off as butter. After a couple drags on the cigarette, Spencer asked, "What is your citizenship status?"

Hank stared at him. Spencer knew darn well that Hank was on a U.S. visitor's visa. Hicks had handed him the papers on that afternoon when he was driven from Rochester to Toronto. Confused, Hank responded, "I am on a U.S. Visa."

"But it's clear from your accent that you are an alien. I have to file a report on who's working here. Some of the photos that are coming in are classified."

"Well, I can help you classify things. I'm good at organizing."

Spencer laughed. "Classified means that they are government information, proprietary. You're not a U.S. Citizen, are you?" The matter of fact statement unnerved Hank.

"I was born in Holland, and I have legal immigration papers."

"Yes, but if you were born in Holland, you are a Dutch citizen."

"So?"

"So we need to register you as an alien. Were both your parents born in Holland?"

Hans looked straight at Spencer frozen, unblinking, barely breathing.

"My mother was born in Russia, but…"

"But what?"

Hank realized what he could not say. Officially his mother was German. The information had to stop here. "But she was raised on a farm at the border, she never had a passport." He didn't mention which border. The lie didn't sound too bad, never mind that his mother had been born in the shifting borders of Eastern Europe, and had resettled three times in three decades. The Americans would never figure that one out. Good God, he had an entire world war just in his own family.

"Don't worry buddy. You're a good guy with excellent references. I just need to figure out what to do. We have to notify the English authorities. I'm going to give Mike Hicks a call as well. It may be time to get you home to Rochester."

"English? But we are in Canada."

"Canada is fighting for England. You know your Dutch royal family lives in Ottawa now, right?" Hank's ears drew back and his eyes widened as Spencer continued. "No, they're not planning to make Holland another English colony. We're protecting them." Spencer paused and contemplated Hank, his brow a little furrowed. "Hank, have you even looked at what is in those pictures? Young Dutch boys in Nazi uniforms are marching prisoners down the street."

"Who are the prisoners?"

"Other Dutchmen. Jews, I think."

Hank did not raise his eyes immediately. When he did, he had a handkerchief with him and blew his nose, then said, "You're right, it's stuffy in here. All those chemicals. I think I'll go for a walk, okay?" He kept his head down.

Spencer looked at him. The younger man was deeply upset about something in the interview. "Sure. Sometimes we all need fresh air."

Away from the building, Hank headed to the shorefront and began to run, his leather shoes slipping on patches of ice. The frantic pace slowed into long strides as he began to formulate a plan.

Breathless, he entered the barracks. His self-absorbed mother, sister and little brother were on his mind. A desktop lay almost bare, and in a drawer he found a pen and some thin blue writing paper. In the eighteen months since leaving Holland, he had never written. Other soldiers wrote letters constantly, notes of comfort to their mothers and fantasies to please their sweethearts. He had planned to write of his successes, but there were no photos of movie stars. The photos of Greta would never see daylight again. Boys imagined heroes, but there were none on this base, at least not yet.

No doubt the Bernsteens were captive in their own home, in their own city. Esther had accused him of not facing challenges. Now the challenge was theirs. It was time for them to flee Holland. Anti-Semitism had a Dutch voice and new legitimacy. A vision of disaster burned through him, of events that portended an unknown fate. He had left his family, but they still mattered to him.

February 24, 1941
Dear Moeder,

I really apologize for not writing sooner. I thought of you in September, the weekend that Holland would be having the Flower Parade – how you love the colors and the costumes.

You can't believe the size of New York and how busy everything is. They never rest. Max would love to visit all the skyscrapers. Some are so tall that you can't actually see where they end. Esther, I think of you often when I see little birds perched under the eaves of the tallest buildings. Even in the snow they find seeds and crumbs that people leave for them.

Some American food is delicious, and I have gained 6 kilos. Other tastes are just odd. The cheese is awful and their chocolate tastes like wax. Even the birds don't eat it.

All of you would like the movies. I have met some very nice friends and we go to the movies a lot. I have been learning to speak English like the actors.

We hear some news from Amsterdam, and I wonder how you are doing. Hopefully the German occupation isn't too difficult for you and Max. The papers here are reporting an influenza epidemic, and I know Max really suffers in the damp. How are your cousins in Portugal? Uncle Alex in Switzerland? Thank God they at least are far from the problems.

I do think of you often, and I promise to write again when I am able to. With best wishes for your health,
Yours,
Hans

There could be no answers to the letter. Esther was the one most likely to understand his message about the need to flee Holland. Her rejection of the visa had stung him deeply, but she was the one who needed to take responsibility for Max. Esther would have to step in and explain to mother that the comments about moving for Max's health were directed at all of them for safety. They didn't have family in Portugal or Switzerland, and Esther hated birds.

It was imperative that Hank's words were like the flight of an owl at night, seen but not heard.

CHAPTER 14

Amsterdam, Holland March 1941

"The simple greeting "hallo" became an acronym for "Hang alle landverraders op" (hang all traitors)."

- DUTCH RESISTANCE

A HEAVY SKY GAVE THE promise of still more sleet to come. Esther hated sleet; it didn't have the quiet beauty of a snowfall or the nourishing quality of rain. Dampness left a chill in her bones. She lived for colors, and this morning there were none, just black outlines of buildings against a gray sky. Her ugly beige sweater was pulled comfortably around her as she opened her book, read a few pages, closed it and then repeated the act over and over. Muddy prose didn't interest her. She needed something livelier, perhaps a romance, or a warm Italian setting.

Italy wasn't an option either. By now they had joined the Nazis. Jews had no reason to travel to Germany, France, or Italy. She couldn't visit a sunnier place even if she wanted to. Hell was supposed to be warm. Maybe that was the answer. The question nagged her. What had Holland become?

It was too late to care about politics now. Shouting from still another Liberation Demonstration disturbed her thought, a bunch of men and boys marching through the streets with their banners. Dutchmen were wearing Nazi uniforms and saluting Hitler. The steps of the marchers were purposeful, but they stomped through the concentric Amsterdam streets going nowhere. She didn't even bother to look out the window. It was probably a good thing that Hans had been gone for nearly two years. He would never go marching. Anyway, Jews were not invited to march.

No one had ever heard from Hans again. She would write him if she had an address. It was time to forgive him for leaving. Ah well, he knew her address, so maybe he didn't feel guilty enough to write.

Esther didn't like to be idle, even if she felt paralyzed. There were chores to do if she or Sasha wanted to go out. She opened their small closet, a jumble of clothing, art supplies and baskets of interminable laundry and mending. The mending load increased week by week. Her stylish wardrobe was outdated. Long silky scarves were fraying around the edges and dresses for going out had stains and odors. Hemlines were going up, and she could take care of that, but not the dowdy silhouettes. She was down to only a couple of Belgian lace collars to fix onto her blouses or sweaters, and there was no way to emulate the fashions from America. The fine gloves and hats from French designers were a thing of the past, and she was only twenty years old. *Merde*!

The boredom was stifling. Sasha didn't care about fashion and coffee clubs any more. Sasha's new friends had deepened their commitment to Jewish identity, and were now attending lectures on religion and culture. Their only relief from boredom was an occasional sense of doom. There had been raids recently. Dutch police had marched into Amsterdam neighborhoods, taking men from their beds in the middle of the night. Little market streets were sealed off, and signs were posted on raised bridges. The traps were everywhere.

Still, Esther did not regret her decision to stay in Amsterdam. Who knew where Hans was, or if he had even had a safe landing in America? There were reports of ships that arrived at New York shores, and sat in the Atlantic until it was determined who was aboard. Jews were not welcome in America. President Roosevelt didn't want them. What a coward, a ruler who is afraid of what his people might say. And the Dutch Queen was worse. She and her ministers had left for England months ago. Holland had no ruler.

Neither did Esther. She did not have to follow directions from a lover, her mother, or anyone else. She liked it that way. There were nights when she and Sasha ate potato soup, but they were managing. She retrieved the sewing basket. A slip had a broken strap that needed repair. Every stocking in the house needed mending once again. It would look better to go without, but the days were still too cool for bare legs. Could she use ink to dye this old white scarf a cheerful red? Maybe there was a way to paint it without making the colors run?

She needed to get outside, maybe some morning shopping on the Beethovenstraat, but she had no money. Besides, there was nothing she desired in the sparse displays of Jewish shops. Some days the bakery only offered black roasted grains to fill coffee cups, and on other days breads. There was no cream and there were no sweets. She really wished for a coffee and a real croissant, buttery and flaky, with good marmalade. Not in her neighborhood. Was everyone living like this? Most likely not. Police and soldiers in the streets appeared rosy and well fed. What if she went to a café in a different neighborhood, where she was not known? Perhaps a trolley downtown? With her green eyes and a pretty hat, she might get served. She removed her coat from the hook and brushed off her green felt cloche with its silky bow. A floral scarf around her neck and, *voila*, she still looked like a young city woman. Then she looked into the mirror. There were shadows around her eyes and her high cheekbones were exaggerated as a result of thin pale cheeks. Where was her lipstick? Did she have rouge or powder? Even going out for a walk was going to be too much of an effort. Luckily, she did not need to make a decision. It began to drizzle and she couldn't find her umbrella.

The downstairs door banged open, accompanied by a blast of wind and, of course, Sasha, who came bounding up the stairs. "Guess who I saw!"

"I can't imagine."

"Your mother! She was out shopping. She was buying cheese and … oh here, I need to give you these!" Sasha pulled packets out of her bag, and unwrapped the papers from fresh herring, cheese, bread, and butter. "And this! Real tea! Not some concoction of herbs from a flowerpot."

Esther wondered where Sasha got her energy. She felt like a rabbit in a hutch, only without a fur coat. Her friend got excited over the smallest favors.

"So, you saw mother, and—did she have anything to say?"

"Your mother got letters from Hans!" Sasha handed over two thin papers covered with Hans's neat handwriting.

Esther grabbed the papers, started to read her letter, and then lost patience. "Oh, my God, where is he?"

"We couldn't figure it out. There was no return address on the envelope. The postmark was blurred, and the stamps were from.... Canada? But he went to New York, yes?"

Esther screwed up her face into a puzzled frown. Her brows knitted themselves around each other as she thought about this. "Aren't New York and Canada next to each other? I wonder if he went to work for the British." She shook her head. "With no return address, how can I write him back? Perhaps he is waiting to see our pictures in the newspapers. 'Sunny Day In Amsterdam: Hell Freezes Over.'" She moved to the chaise and began to read again. "He's not even talking about me. He's talking about Max."

Sasha interjected, "He was very concerned about Max. Hans wanted your mother to take him to Switzerland. Of course she's not going to do it."

"How lovely. We really need a nice family vacation, all of us." She frowned, and stared at the pages. "I wonder why he wrote this?"

"Doesn't he think that Max should go to Switzerland to live? It's neutral and you can still get a visa." Sasha was trying to put the messages together.

"No, you can't. The Swiss are taking political refugees but they have banned racial refugees – which is what they are calling us this month." One doubt did cross her mind. "Although mother is putting some of our money in Switzerland, in case of another crash. Sam had her put it with a banker he knows." She set the packet of tea aside and opened up the package of cheese and bread. "Sure, we might as well all get visas and go to New York for a nice visit. Maybe we can all stand in the street and call until Hans finds us. Sasha, even the U.S. isn't taking any more of us."

Sasha bowed her head. "I know."

"Esther, there are rumors. I heard at a meeting, that they have set up special camps for Jews who are mentally disabled or sick. The Germans have posters saying that the cost of one sick person for a month would feed a healthy family of four. People have not come back from those camps."

Esther turned to the mending basket, and picked out a silk stocking. She pulled a needle out of the packet and began threading it. The thread knotted and stuck just a few centimeters after she had finally gotten the end of it through the eye of the needle.

"Damn it! How can you live like this? Going to meetings with a bunch of Jews living their parents' last pogrom. My God, you could go insane listening to those people. I can't imagine what is in it for you." A balled-up stocking flew across the room. "We need to find new stockings, any way we can. I'll get a new boyfriend with a shop pass if necessary. Take a train to France, I don't know. How in God's name will we wear shorter skirts with no stockings?" She paid no attention to Sasha and the ominous message in Hans's letter.

"Anyway, your mother is not going to move to Switzerland. But Hans is well, and she asked after you. Aren't you going to fry that herring?"

"Fry him! You are so proud of your 'catch' that I think we should crown him." Esther picked up the fish, secured his dorsal fin between her fingers and held him to her face.

"*The herring he is the king of the sea! The herring he is the fish for me.*" A brief kiss, and then the nonsense song continued.

"*What'll we do with the herring's head? We'll make it into loaves of bread!*

What'll we do with the herring's fins? We'll make them into needles and pins!"

The stockings went back into the basket and a skillet came out from the cupboard.

Just before sundown the two women walked down the street carrying their bundles of laundry. An old washerwoman greeted customers at the counter. Sasha spoke. "Hallo! Would you please mend this coat? The moths have gotten to it." Their bundles were placed behind the counter, and they were ushered into a large parlor at the back. It was time to light the Sabbath candles.

Sasha's friends had a dream to found a Jewish fatherland for themselves. Great, just what they needed, another "Fatherland." A letter from Mark had affirmed her trust in her new friends. He had now flown several successful missions into Germany and returned to England safely night after night, inflicting what damage he could on the Krauts. However, according to the newspapers, the Germans had placed England under siege. Who could be believed? Esther didn't believe any of the news, and refused to read the papers with their accounts of political mastery accompanied by pictures of people fleeing their homes.

The walk from the laundry to the apartment was not far, but the discussions had taken a long time. Sasha moved very quickly, with her dark coat and scarf and her face held either toward shop windows or toward the ground. She did not look at anyone. "Esther, you must walk more quickly, we have to be home at 8:00 sharp. The patrol will check our cards after that."

Esther met her eyes with a bold stare. "You can't be serious. Friends can't meet? Young women can't join with friends for a little fun? The Dutch police would not turn in a couple of girls!"

Sasha's sigh and sideways glare indicated otherwise. Esther sometimes was a spoiled child. "Germans make the laws now. We're not liberated by Germany, we're prisoners of Germany."

Esther stopped. "Oh nonsense! My mother was born in Germany. She is a royal pain in the neck, but she's not going to take anyone prisoner."

"In case you hadn't noticed, we've got royal nothing going on around here. Step it up."

CHAPTER 15

Rochester, N.Y.
October 1941

"Uncle Sam Wants You! *We must guard against complacency. We must not underrate the enemy."*

~ Army Recruitment poster

Hank stood behind the steel railing, listening to the roar from Niagara Falls, a force of nature so immense that it impels some visitors toward a rushing river and a violent end. The Canadian side of the falls offers a spectacular view of the horseshoe, shaped by millennia of raging waters hurtling between Lake Erie and Lake Ontario.

Shouldering his heavy camera bag, he turned toward the bridge over the Niagara River and walked across. Glimpsing his watch, he saw that it was nearly 3:00. The park was still full, but Hank was looking for something in particular. The distinctive outline of a burly man with a camera came into view.

Mike Hicks looked up with a grin. "How's things at the Blue Ribbon Photo Club?"

This time Hank knew how to answer, "I think we've won a prize, yes?"

Things at the open border had changed. For years all travelers needed to do was to state that they were American or Canadian. Now serious young guards examined vehicles and pored over the documents of foreign nationals. Drivers stated a purpose for transit and guards requested the details of their stay in the United States. Mike Hicks didn't want to share a lot of information with anonymous officers. He suggested that Hank just walk across as a day tourist, no luggage, a camera around his neck. They pulled the unmarked Packard sedan away from the parking lot and were on their way into Rochester.

Hicks delivered instructions at rapid fire. "We rented a room for you down by the University. Thought you should be with a bunch of other young people. You'll need to make some new friends." Hank wondered if some type of employment would be offered. "Also, we will be providing a per diem allowance for three months, until you find yourself a job." Hank nodded his head to each of Hicks' comments. "When we get into town, I'm going to be giving you a statement to sign. There will be some conditions to all this – the usual non-disclosure stuff. You can't brag, you can't tell about why you went to Canada, you can't talk about the FBI at all." Hicks squared his shoulders and kept his eyes on the road. "We've picked up eight Nazi agents this year, and six are on death row. They're gonna swing." Hank flinched.

For two months Hank walked into one office after another, only to hear, "We don't hire foreigners." Tension was mounting throughout this city near the Canadian border. People were on guard. Mothers held children tightly to their sides. Friendly welcomes toward strangers' questions dissolved into terse exchanges. In the shadows of the morning, Rochester's buildings and people revealed closed doors and closed minds. He felt more foreign than he had a year ago.

Sunlight struck the glass window of a broad storefront.

"Uncle Sam Needs You!" The recruiting office image pointed directly at him.

The open door invited the public, and he was public, no matter what his accent signaled. There was nothing to lose by walking in, though it was doubtful that the U.S. Army would want a foreigner either. The counter area was covered with framed posters, racks of brochures, and photos of important looking men with gold braid hanging from their shoulders and colorful ribbons on their chests. A young man at the counter looked him in the eye and held out his hand for a proper greeting.

The American radiated pride.

"Good morning, sir. I'm Sergeant McIntyre, U.S. Army. What can I do for you?"

"Mr. Burns, Hank Burns." Then he stopped. He could not disclose his experience in Canada or his commendation from the FBI. "I am looking for work."

"You've come to the right place. Where are you from?"

"Amsterdam, Holland, but I live here now. I did serve in the Queen's guard in Holland."

"So, how would you like to go back? We're recruiting foreign nationals. Can't go barging into a country with thousands of guys unless someone speaks the language. You a U.S. citizen yet?"

Hank blanched.

"I didn't think we were at war."

"Wait until after the election. Roosevelt just doesn't want it on his watch." The recruiting sergeant paused. "You know, if you do six months active duty, we can expedite your citizenship."

Although the vision of a Nazi Europe haunted him, Hank had very mixed feelings about re-crossing the Atlantic. Nazis had obliterated his future, and now they were coming after the men and boys from his neighborhood. Hank was one of a very few who had seen the hard evidence. There was a chance that, as an American soldier, he could locate his family and bring them to safety. He signed up for the official interview and marched out the door.

Walking back to the rooming house, he wondered what he had just done. The afternoon sun and the brilliant fall leaves went by unnoticed as he mulled through the possibility of military service.

There was no obligation for Hank to participate in this conflict. He paused on the steps to the brownstone, turned his key and entered a darkened hallway. The small writing table at the end of the hall held a telephone, pencils and notepads. Someone had forgotten to turn the green desk lamp off, and Hank sat down. He folded a sheet of paper, lining up the corners and drawing a neat line down the middle. His question was, "How can I help the war effort?"

In the right hand column he wrote down the risks that would be involved for the young man who had arrived in the United States. Holland had been crushed like a beetle under German boots. He did not have the physique of a combatant. He couldn't run quickly and he had never learned to fight. He could lose his life, and no one would ever know he had existed.

Or he could pursue this unlikely future. For some inexplicable reason, Hank did not respond to fear with panic. Instead an absolute clarity unfolded through his mind when others worried. He could remember facts by the thousands, and he could keep his mouth shut when he needed to. Order prevailed in the most unlikely situations. In a box with his cufflinks was a gold crossbow, the sharpshooter award given to him by Queen Wilhelmina. It wasn't for marksmanship.

In 1937 he had posed as a skinny German hiker walking along the Dutch border. His photographs of the concrete Siegfried Linie convinced the Dutch palace that Germans were preparing for a war. Hank could definitely do battle with a camera in his hand.

He decided to keep his appointment.

It was a one-way trip behind the glare of glass doors and shining windows. The recruiting sergeant walked him into offices behind the counter. A single Stars and Stripes hung in the corner of the vast beige box, which was partitioned into more and more beige boxes. Each little office was only a few meters square, with enough room for a heavy oak desk and a chair on either side. There were no decorations of any kind, no colorful collections of flags, no heroes on posters.

The recruiting sergeant offered him a seat and began to ask questions, attempting to size up the young man with the information on the paperwork. Hank sat quietly in the muffled noise of busy offices and looked straight ahead.

Name: Hank Burns, aka. (Hans Bernsteen)
Birthplace: Amsterdam, Holland
DOB: 13 FEB 1918
Occupation: Photographer
Height: 6'2"
Weight: 147

He pulled out his green card and proudly showed the personal letter of recommendation from Mike Hicks to the recruiter, who noted it in his file under "previous service." The photo showed a pale young man with a big grin, hair slicked back, and ready for business. Finally the sergeant spoke. "Buddy, do you think you can gain five pounds by next week? You are right on the line for physical fitness. Actually, you're one pound underweight. You will have an extensive medical exam before we induct you into the U.S. Army."

A year of Canadian food rations had simply not been enough. He knew he was thin. His older clothes were loose, and he didn't dare put on slacks without a tight belt.

"Well, I love to eat. I just hate to cook." The only thing Hank had learned to make was a sandwich. He didn't even ask to use the stove at the rooming house unless he wanted a pot of tea. "... and you know, restaurants are expensive." Solitude had its consequences, and one result of it was that Hank did not enjoy going out alone.

The sergeant slowed his speech and looked directly at his recruit. "Can you make it a point to get a good dinner each night? Starches will really fill you out. You might try spaghetti with extra meatballs. It's not too pricey. And eat dessert, that'll pack on the weight. We need to get a little more meat on your bones."

Hank shifted in the hard chair while the sergeant paused and examined the next part of the form.

"I see here you speak Dutch, German and French."

"Oh, yes...and some Malay."

"Malay?"

"My father was in the import-export trade. We did a lot of business with China, Japan and Singapore. When I was a kid, I went on some of the trips."

The recruiter squinted at the young man and marked something on his checklist. "Look, we need you to take a basic test to determine your mental fitness. It's the office down the hall, and they will take care of that. Good luck."

The questions on the mental fitness test were not what Hank expected. He figured they would be determining his aptitudes, how well he could process information, read, write, and maybe show off his mathematical skills. He had an extraordinary memory. Instead there were a lot of questions that had no answers. They gave him several little stories to read, and then choose from four ideas of what he would do next. Even stranger were little pictures like puzzles. This was childish. There was nothing on the test that showed off his talents. He did notice that several questions required the ability to follow directions, and then put pieces in the correct order. He hadn't thought about what a soldier should do and he was pretty sure it wasn't about puzzles. Maybe the soldier's life was not for him. He had better continue job hunting.

The examiner asked, "Do you like to take long walks?"

Sure, if I'm alone… "Yes, I take walks to think." *What the heck was that about?*

Ten days later instructions arrived to report to the Military Entrance Processing station in Buffalo. Nervous young men gathered, bragging about fights they had been in. There were no friendly greetings or welcomes here. The sergeant took his clothes, along with his bag of personal belongings, and issued him a set of boxer shorts. Nearly naked teenage boys and young men lined up, flexing arm muscles and teasing each other about slight paunches, acne, and freckles. His thin white legs, and his narrow chest were conspicuous as the line advanced to a corps of doctors and nurses. At the first needle jab, some of the bolder young men winced or swore. The needle jabs continued down the line, with nameless injections entering the bloodstream followed by a tourniquet and extraction of a vial of blood to go who knows where? What the heck is Blood Type B? And why was that important?

Still in their underwear, the men performed physical tasks. Yelling surrounded them. "Move it on!" Sergeants noted each gasping breath, red face, and straining muscle. "At ease!" Twelve at a time the recruits pushed into a closed room. "Congratulations! You are now all members of the U.S. Army. Ten-hut!" The lieutenant did not look at any of the men. They were invisible. "Please raise your right hand and repeat after me:"

> *I, (Hank Burns), do solemnly swear that I will support and defend the Constitution of the United States against all enemies, foreign and domestic; that I will bear true faith and allegiance to the same; and that I will obey the orders of the President of the United States and the orders of the officers appointed over me, according to regulations and the Uniform Code of Military Justice. So help me God.*

Hank's name was now "private."

Six weeks later, Hank admired his physique in the mirror. His trim waist was now defined by lean shoulders and visible muscles. He was glad he had gained 14 pounds since his enlistment, but he had to get serious about building some strength. A 10-mile hike through the woods with a 40-pound pack and weapons had nearly done him in. He had requested assignment to combat photography. Where the heck was he supposed to put his camera bags? Surely the photographers didn't carry cameras and rifles klunking against each other. It was hard to know.

As the men learned to fight, they began to brag about how they could win by defeating enemies man to man. As a teenager, Hank had seen the odd Japanese wrestling rituals. They didn't fight the same way as the American boys. The drill sergeant drew a big circle on the dirt, one that would hold all thirty-six men of the platoon. "Stand in, and when I blow the whistle, you guys start shoving men out. Let's see who can really take it on." Large farm boys began to push. One lost his footing, and tried to step back in. "Out!" "Once a foot is out of the circle, you are a dead soldier."

No one bothered to go after the tall skinny guy. Anyone could take him out, so he stayed in the circle while combatants screamed and snarled at one another. Suddenly, he looked at the two largest men. They were going to come after him and then duke it out for top position. He backed up as if to retreat, then ran at them, head down, right into the solar plexus of one, grabbing the second man by the shoulder and flipping him like a fish. "Sarge! He's fighting dirty!" The crowd stood around dumbfounded, as the sergeant stated,

"We're going to need guys who can fight dirty. Burns seems to have picked up jujitsu along the way."

The next morning, Lieutenant Steiner stood at attention reporting to Captain Olney. "Company C is finished and ready for deployment."

"Everybody except your boy Burns." Olney tossed the file onto the desk. "I'm going to put through his request for combat photography after I send him to the stockade at Fort Dix for a month."

Lieutenant Steiner stared at him. Olney was a patient man. Burns was kind of a jerk, but he had followed his orders. "The stockade? What did he do?"

Olney began to laugh. "Not as a prisoner. I'm just not sure what we've got there. Weren't you a little surprised by that fight? He didn't confront anyone, they all ignored him." The Captain took a deep breath and placed his hands on the desk, forearms straight and fingers curved like lion's paws. "But he didn't run – he stood there in that battle with 36 guys beating each other up, and he came in like a mongoose at the very end."

Steiner didn't comment. He had seen the teasing, and he had seen Hank's wary responses.

The captain paused and lit a cigarette. His brow tightened, and then he flicked the ash and looked at Steiner. "The guys don't like photographers. These damn journalists are extra men in companies where every fist counts. Burns will have to deal with real threats and real situations. I'm going to make him an MP."

Steiner stared at the captain. "Are you kidding me? He has more nervous ticks than a clock museum. Burns won't last two days in there."

CHAPTER 16

Fort Dix, New Jersey
January 1942

"A date which will live in infamy"

~ President Franklin D. Roosevelt, December 7, 1941

Sergeant Hood was unlike anyone Hank had ever met. The prison guard had a huge grin that didn't match his squinting eyes. As a teenager visiting Java, Hank had seen monkeys grin during play, and then bite a friend viciously. He politely shook hands and then followed the sergeant. The guy didn't seem real bright. He spoke very slowly searching for words. Hank was stunned. Hood was born in the U.S., but his English wasn't as fluid as Hank's. Hood seemed to cut through in a very different way. He looked straight into Hank's face.

"So Hank, tell me a little bit about yourself."

"Well, I am from Amsterdam..."

"No, not the file, I already read that. Tell me something about you."

"What do you mean?"

"Something you enjoy doing, sports, a best friend, something funny about your sister – whatever."

Hank blanched at the odd interrogation, searching for the right answer. "I like to take photographs."

Hood started to correct him with "we know that" but instead asked, "What is it about photography that rings your bell?"

"Rings my bell? "

"You know, gets under your skin – gets to you."

"Sometimes I see something, and I want to remember it. I like to remember things. You mean like that?" Hank looked across at Hood, doubting that he had the right answer.

"Sure, so tell me about a memorable photo."

Hank flinched. He had taken pictures of Greta at the waterfalls just before the awful dinner with her brothers. Her hair was thrown back, and she was laughing. He had wanted this image of his future bride. He reached for a handkerchief. This was not going well.

Hood looked at him, "So memory really touches your soul, does it? You're the soldier who will see the poppies in the field after the bodies have been buried." Hank had never thought of such things. He wasn't a poet. Hood was deeper than he looked.

"We are going to put you on the front gate. What I want you to do is to observe people as they come in. How do they act? What is their business?" Hank's ears pulled back tightly against his head. In the months at the photography store, he had spent as much time in the darkroom as possible, preferring to remain in shadows, seeing and unseen.

After five days, Hood put him on duty in the prisoner recreation area. Hank was terrified of the prisoners. He didn't know them, but he imagined a room full of cutthroats, thieves, and cold-blooded killers. Hood showed him how to walk slowly along the blocks. He mimicked Hood's facial expressions: eyes forward, listening and no movement in the lower half of his face. "Obviously this block is minimum security. Petty thieves, guys who have disobeyed orders, that sort of thing. Some of them really have balls, most have just done something inappropriate. They are motivated to behave because they will get out someday." Hank nodded. Thank God he wasn't going to get murdered tonight.

Hood stopped and faced Hank. "So, tonight you have a two hour shift in the rec room. Three things: don't sit down, do not read, and never let prisoners get between you and emergency phone on this wall. Is that clear?"

Hank watched as Hood strolled away to the front desk. He was on his own now, and this didn't look too hard. In the corner, a small group was playing cards. He watched them, and they watched him. The prisoners had a table and three chairs. Five guys stood and sat around the table. Hank quickly became bored and wandered around the large open room, counting floor tiles. There were 33 tan and beige squares going lengthwise and 25 crosswise. So this room was a total of 825 square feet? Boring. What else was there? He couldn't just watch the guys. They weren't goldfish in some little bowl. Well, actually they were, and that made him even more uncomfortable. He picked up a spare newspaper and glanced through the headlines. Lots of war news, and here he was in the stockade. Hank sat down to finish the paper and before he was finished he found himself surrounded by the biggest and ugliest prisoners in the barracks.

An angry bull of a man stepped forward. "We need the chair," said the group's leader. The tattoos on his forearms moved as he clenched his fist. Three of his comrades stared at Hank.

Hank looked up at the group and a sideways glance showed him the prisoners were between him and the phone. He couldn't shake, he couldn't act nervous. Frozen in place, he remembered a game that he used to play with his brother and sister in Holland, sort of a bullying version of musical chairs. Hank turned toward the man. "Take it." And he kept sitting, reading. The prisoner looked at him, fixed in place. Assaulting a guard would extend all their sentences. Then the leader said, "He's all right" and walked away. Hank waited exactly two minutes and pretended to read, while he looked around the room from behind his paper, keeping his eyes on the goldfish.

Hank learned the routines of prison life. Roll call, watch, roll call, watch. There were a number of jobs for well-behaved prisoners. Food was prepared and served by prisoners, and prisoners cleaned the facilities. Rainwater was a big Indian who kept the stainless steel kitchen of the mess hall absolutely sparkling. His auntie had owned a Barbeque joint in Texas, and he had been cleaning his whole life. Hank appreciated Rainwater's work. The man treated him with respect, called him "Sir" and was as busy as a Dutch housewife. Rainwater often stayed in the kitchen after everyone was gone, polishing the pots and the stoves over and over. They left him alone. He would be released any day now.

On a quiet Friday afternoon, Hank went into the kitchen to inspect the area. The knife drawers especially needed to be secured, all knives and implements accounted for. Everything seemed to be in order, but he heard an annoying drip. Someone had left a little water on, and he wanted to find the leaking faucet and put in the call for maintenance. In the corner of the kitchen, next to the shelving for bags of flour, sugar and potatoes, one utility door seemed to have a broken lock. Better have maintenance fix that too. He looked inside at the cooking equipment. The giant soup kettles were shelved carefully, but in a dark corner he saw cooking utensils that had never been out on the mess hall line. A milk can was on a shelf, and attached to it was a hose, a large pipe at the top, and a slanted pipe that didn't seem to be hooked up into anything. A thermostat indicated that the contents were warm, and some sort of liquid seemed to be dripping out of the slanted pipe. On the floor were five one-gallon pickle jars full of water. The place smelled like rubbing alcohol, so they must have cleaning supplies in there along with the big pots.

He left the area and notified the desk sergeant that a lock needed to be repaired, and that a big pot of something was cooking unattended. The platoon sergeant came in.

"Sergeant?"

Hood looked at Hank. "What seems to be the problem?"

"Can you look at something? I'm not sure what this thing is. I really don't know how to cook, but this thing has been left on. Is it part of the plumbing?"

Hood looked at the contraption of cooking kettles and piping. "Well, I'll be damned." He reached over to the end of the pipe. Wetting his finger, he moistened his tongue with the liquid. "We need to test this." Looking around the storeroom, he saw what he wanted. He pulled a measuring cup off the shelf, opened one of the bottles on the floor and filled the cup. Then he sipped the liquid, shaking his head like a dog and exhaling sharply. "You need to drink some. I'll need a corroborating witness on this."

"What is it?" Unfortunately, Hank thought he knew. It smelled a little like *Genever*, Dutch gin, but without the herbal scent of the juniper berries.

"I'll be back in a minute. You stay here. Lock the kitchen doors. No one comes in." Hood disappeared and returned with a canteen.

"We need to save this for evidence." He opened the jug again and filled the canteen. "Good work, Burns."

Hank stood there a little confused. He wasn't sure what he had done right, but apparently he had found something important. It was best to let others decide how this was significant. "So what happens now? What is it?"

Hood looked at the still. "It's good, but it's not exactly legal. We have to go see the boss. After we report this contraption, they'll dismantle it. I'm afraid Rainwater's kitchen duty is over."

A week later Captain Olney was shuffling through his interoffice memos, and the title of "RE: Hank Burns" caught his eye. He had seen a couple hundred guys since Burns had left, but the curious Dutchman had piqued his interest. A letter of commendation had been written up, detailing Burns's responsibilities and attention to details at Fort Dix. He had discovered an illicit alcohol brewing operation and reported it up the chain of command, responding to orders effectively. The soldier was ready. He was finally going to join the combat photography unit. At last he would do his part to beat up Italians and Germans, or at least record the events. He was going in as part of a machine, with every pipe and tube doing its job. He was the thermostat, the one to monitor the results and let the world know what was brewing.

CHAPTER 17

Amsterdam, Holland May 1942

"A woman is like a teabag – you can't tell how strong she is until you put her in hot water."

~ Eleanor Roosevelt

Esther put down her book, and picked up a pencil to sketch. Sasha's head was bent intently over her sewing, and she resembled the women in Rembrandt portraits, the ones he did of mothers, beggars, even Jews. Her curls were loosened, and the deep brown eyes were focused on her lap. The dim light made her work difficult, and she sometimes squinted. Esther worked to capture the illumination on her friend's cheekbones, light playing through her auburn curls. Sweaters and jackets were piled onto the table, and next to them a neatly stacked pile of yellow stars, inscribed with the word "Jood – Jew."

Why in God's name would she obey this order, this additional insult? Was she being proud and defiant because she was a Jew, or was she trying to be conciliatory to the authorities? Or was she trying to stay out of trouble because neighborhood police were well aware that she was a Jew? Sasha picked up still one more star, centered it neatly onto the jacket in an exact match to the diagram, and began making tiny even stitches around it.

By now, even a trip for basic provisions was a journey of harassment. Dutch police in Nazi green uniforms treated young women as if they were streetwalkers. Sometimes the men would grab their bags and take things from them, things that they needed to get by – bread, a wedge of cheese. One policeman put his cigarette to the side, and reached into his pocket for a bar of chocolate, which he would be willing to exchange for "a kiss." Esther bent her neck in close enough for the policeman to smell her perfume and asked him to close his eyes for a proper kiss. Then she grabbed the chocolate and ran down the street, while he was waiting for her lips to brush his. His comrades laughed and let her go.

The restrictions were becoming unbearable. The two women were imprisoned in their own apartment. Curfews were so strictly enforced that they did not dare to go out with friends. In fact, Jews were not allowed to congregate with other Jews at all, in public or in private. The neighborhood was deserted, absent of its life.

Sasha looked up from her work. "You had better get busy if you ever intend to go outside again."

Esther glared at her, and then looked out the window. "I don't need to go outside. I'll just read and draw in here."

"You need to start your sewing."

"Maybe I'll just put them on my chemises. That way they have to look more closely." Esther went to the sink with her teacup and turned on the water.

Sasha dropped her work, shocked. "How can you even talk of bedding those pigs? They hate us. Your pretty face and tight sweaters won't get you out of this one." She picked up her spool of thread and held the needle steady, pushing the dampened end of the thread through the eye. Her hand trembled at little at the last minute. "Dammit." She moved the needle into position again. "Esther, this is not a joke. You can go to jail for not wearing your star or carrying your Identification Card."

The water ran louder, and soap began to foam as Esther scrubbed harder at an imaginary brown stain on the cup. "I don't plan to identify myself. It's nobody's business. And I'm not going to wear those bloody yellow stars. It's not very stylish. Anyway, what can they do to us that they have not already tried?" She stood up, walked over to the table and stood over Sasha, blocking the light. "You know what's wrong with you? You are afraid. You're afraid of them. You are even afraid of your own actions. And if that weren't enough, you are afraid for everyone else too. 'Will Mark fly safely? Will the printer get caught?' Good God, I left my mother, and now you are acting like her! Don't you order me around. I do not take orders."

Sasha blinked her eyes and ignored Esther's diatribe. Instead, she commented, "Actually, they're very stylish right now. The Royals are all wearing them in solidarity with us. The Danish king has been wearing one too. If everyone wears them, we will all be Dutch and Jews can no longer be singled out. They even stitched a yellow star onto the princess' bridal gown." She turned back to her sewing and ignored Esther's stance. "You're blocking the light."

Esther continued, "Who would want to go out anyway? We have everything we need right in this apartment. We don't eat much, no one in here cares if our clothes are old, and we don't have to work. It's perfectly safe here, and even sane. We have a phonograph and can play music and dance if we wish."

"That's it. I'm going out and spend time with some friends, real friends who live in a real world. Maybe I'll ask Jaap downstairs to accompany me."

Esther's eyes widened, "And what will Mark say to that?"

"He'll be pleased that I am escorted safely to and from the coffeehouse." Sasha nipped off the yellow thread, and checked the alignment of the star on her brown tweed jacket, one with a velvet collar that highlighted her hair. In the hallway she brushed out her hair and set her hat at a coquettish angle.

The apartment door slammed, reverberating in the concrete hallway. Let Sasha and Jaap enjoy their evening out. They didn't really matter to her. Maybe friendships weren't important any more. Society wasn't worth the effort.

Hours later Esther looked out the window into the Dutch mist, reddened by moisture in the air and reflections off the clouds. Smoky streaks were a warning that the sun had set, and curfew passed. By eleven o'clock the streets were dark. Why in God's name had Sasha gone to the coffeehouse with Jaap?

Perhaps Sasha had stayed with a friend to avoid being seen after curfew. That yellow star might as well have a target printed onto it. Esther cared deeply for Sasha and regretted some of her nasty childish comments. Tomorrow she would try to make amends in some way, perhaps pretty up the apartment or try to locate a treat in the shops.

Two days later she left the apartment to seek out Sasha's mother and inform her of Sasha's disappearance. She had an address near the Apollolaan, and hoped that it was accurate. The street was intimidating, full of Germans and of Green police. Luckily she was not wearing her "labels" but if they asked for her identity card, she would be in big trouble. She made a mental note to stop by a stationer's and see if she could locate some ink eradicator. She knew how to use it to erase small mistakes in her calligraphy. She would try to correct the "J" on her identity card.

As she turned onto the street, and walked near the house where Sasha had taken her for tea now and then, she noted the silence everywhere. It was not a good silence. No one was shopping, no children were playing in the park; the bakery was empty. She knocked on the familiar door, this had to be the correct address, but no one answered. The front stoop was unkempt, and there was no sign of life in the building. Where was Sasha's mother? My God, what was happening here? Such things only happened in stories, ancient German fairy tales of disappearances, trolls and magic pipers living in mountain crags. She had better get back to the flat immediately.

The flat…. Sasha's mother had been paying the rent. There were less than two weeks until the first of the month. If Sasha did not return, she would have to, to what? To move? Where? With whom? She turned in her steps, and headed toward a tram stop. Hopefully it would be very busy and she wouldn't be noticed. She mustn't look afraid. Head up, look at people, be bold but not noticed. Don't talk – use your eyes to acknowledge others. And, above all, don't be rude to anyone. From the Dam Platz, she carefully negotiated a path through canals behind the palace, eventually able to walk along the Herengracht and toward the Bernsteen home. She had better make up with her mother, just in case.

Sophia the housekeeper answered the door. Thank god, the servants were still there. It wasn't so bad. But, the ground floor offices were empty. Typewriters and adding machines sat on empty desks. The office furniture was dusty. Sam had been ordered to cease doing business. The first floor sitting and dining rooms had not been aired, and windows were tightly closed. "My God, Esther! Max! Your sister's here."

Max strolled down the marble stairs, a serious young man, pushing his long hair aside from his thick glasses. He had not seen a barber in a while. She put her hand on the banister with its heavy carved balusters. His asthma had caused him to lose weight, and there were blue circles around his eyes. At sixteen he looked like an old man. He peered at her. "Well, if it isn't the prodigal daughter, returned home!"

"What?"

"So are we supposed to prepare a feast for you? What will it be, dry bread and blackened grain in a coffee cup?" His anger was not really directed at her, it seemed to emanate from every direction.

She looked at him sadly, then put her arms around him tightly. "I'm full. I don't need anything."

Sophia then mentioned, "Your mother is still in her bedroom. I'll let her know you are here. Did you want to see her?"

Esther's smile lit the stone hallway, now emptied of paintings and Chinese vases. "Oh, that would be wonderful. But only if it's not too much trouble."

"So, are we going to stand all day?" her brother inquired.

"Oh no, I was just in the area and thought I would come by. It's so pretty here, and I thought it would be nice to be near the water."

"You hate water." He pulled out a handkerchief, and began to cough into it, then wadded up the soggy linen and pushed it into a pocket. Her eyes widened; she was not going to tease a sick boy who had not been outdoors in weeks.

"Maybe I like it now. It's nice to see the swans and ducks swimming and flying around." She looked closely at his pale face, marked with acne and the stray dark hairs that signaled a young beard. "I don't really get out to the park as much as I would like."

"Nobody gets out to anything as much as they would like any more."

"Well, we aren't in cages yet."

"I hear caged birds die."

Sarah's ponderous steps announced her arrival. In addition to her weight, her chins had sagged, and her beautiful large eyes now squinted out of the folds in her brow. She looked worn.

"Mother, how are you doing?"

"Esther, you didn't come here to inquire about my health. Obviously, things are not going well. Sam's business is closed, and we have had to let go of our entire house staff, except Sophia. We don't go out and we don't have enough to eat. Why are you here?"

"I actually wanted to see you."

"Where's Sasha?"

Esther's eyes filled. She honestly had no idea where Sasha was, and there was no use to pretend or to make a show any more. "Sasha went to a coffeehouse on Wednesday, and never returned."

Sarah's first thoughts were that Sasha had had enough of Esther's rude behavior, but that made no sense. The flat was Sasha's. "Come, let's prepare a small dinner for tonight, light candles and thank God we have each other."

Esther followed her mother toward the unfamiliar kitchen. The copper pots were hanging, some of the large ones covered with dust. Only two servants' aprons remained on the rack that used to hold six. Sarah handed one to her. Esther looked at her mother and understood the circles under her eyes, the sagging of her jowls. She offered, "I have actually learned to cook a little. May I peel the vegetables?" The two women went to the cellar, and they filled their apron pockets with potatoes, parsnips and a leek. Esther inhaled deeply as she looked at the basket of roots. "I suppose we don't have any butter or mustard for these?" Her mother's face twisted into an odd frown. "Hans always liked his vegetables with brown butter and mustard. The way you fix them."

Sarah sighed. "I'm sure Hans is getting dinner somewhere tonight. We just won't know where for a while."

Esther opened a nearly empty closet in the dining room. The sets of silver and dishes were no longer there. The Sabbath candlesticks were pushed to the back of the shelf, tarnished. She took a soft rag and rubbed them until they reflected the soft glow of the sunset. "I think we had better pray for peace." The two women bowed their heads over the table.

Blessed are you, L-rd our G-d, King of the universe, who has sanctified us with His commandments, and commanded us to kindle the light of the Holy Shabbat.

Four people shared the soup. Sam and Sarah were silent as Esther chattered about her friends. Then she looked at her watch.

"Oh no! It's past eight o'clock. There will be police everywhere looking for violators. I don't even have stars on all my clothes yet.

Max, when you go out, do you travel a favorite route to avoid the police?"

Sarah swallowed her words. Her disapproval was palpable and her silence indicated that Max never went out.

Max broke the silence. "Why don't you stay in your old room? There are some extra books in there now, but we still have your bed."

Esther regarded her mother, and then said, "Let me clean up the dishes."

Outside the deep blue twilight announced the first Sabbath stars.

CHAPTER 18

June 1942
Sharpshooters

"Our own objectives are clear; the objective of smashing the militarism imposed by war lords upon their enslaved peoples, the objective of liberating the subjugated Nations—the objective of establishing and securing freedom of speech, freedom of religion, freedom from want, and freedom from fear everywhere in the world."

~ President Franklin D. Roosevelt, January 1942

Hank sat on his bunk, looking at his orders again. He had done everything they asked, he had taken on extra work, and he had commendations. He couldn't wait to get to Europe. These orders said, "CONFIDENTIAL – Eyes only. Report to the CO immediately for further instructions." Maybe they weren't going to take him after all.

When Hank completed his training for combat photography he was pretty sure he had passed his fitness tests. The training exercises in photography were dangerous, but thoughts of boyhood adventures kept him at ease. For days his unit had climbed towers with bulky movie cameras and squeezed into impossibly small spaces to shoot.

When they rappelled down the 50 foot wall, he looked at the distance. Men were afraid to jump off. Then he smiled. He had done worse. He had grinned like a twelve year-old imp, grabbed the rope and jumped over the edge.

As a boy he talked his little sister and brother into climbing out on the snowy gables of the four-story Herengracht house. It was icy and some tiles were loose. He had photographed the entire expedition. Esther had been in a little dress and coat, with patent leather shoes, and Max was also dressed up in tweed knickers and shiny boots. Hans had developed the photos in his bedroom closet. Enemy bullets couldn't do as much damage as the wrath of Sarah Bernsteen.

Now he measured his paces as he walked toward the brick building. The CO must not see him sweat. He had learned to keep his hands still, and his eyes steady. His Adams apple was still as he waited for the officer to speak first. "Burns, Hank Burns, is it?"

"Yes, sir."

"Tell me about your accent."

"My accent? I am a legal resident of the United States, sir. I want to earn my citizenship."

"Where are you from?"

"Amsterdam, Holland, sir." As he stood at attention a chill ran through him, and a shock ran through his feet. He regained his balance without moving. "Is there a problem?"

"At ease, Burns. We need to talk."

Hank immediately moved with his legs spread apart, and hands clasped behind his back. "Sir?"

"What other languages do you speak?"

"I was born in Holland, and I speak German." He began to rattle on. "It's because my mother was German, but she has been Dutch for many years now." Maybe he had said too much. How dumb could he be to say his mother was German? He tried not to fidget. A slight creasing around his eyes indicated that he was thinking in questions.

"And French, I speak French too."

The Captain raised his eyebrows and looked up waiting to hear more. He was visibly impressed, and Hank loved making a good impression. "My father was a merchant, sir. I also speak some Malay."

"Burns, we're reassigning you."

"Is there something wrong, sir?"

"I don't think so. The combat photographers are all in a unit from Washington. There are only a few hundred of you guys, and only a couple of you speak foreign languages. Apparently, you have been recommended for Counter Intelligence. You're good at finding things?"

Hank couldn't figure out what the CO meant. But he saw now that two letters had been pulled from his file.

"Yes, sir!"

The CO continued, "Your commendation from the FBI – says you participated in uncovering a matter of national security." He paused to read the other letter. "And this other one, a still? … Was it any good?"

"Sir, I don't know. I don't drink much."

"We're going to have you go out to the South Pacific, but your identity will be as a Dutchman. You'll be part of the U.S. Army, but they want you to be part of a team of college boys and foreigners who can figure out what is going on out there. You guys are going to some French Island, and we are in the middle of building a U.S. base out there. Only problem is, the French are a damned mess. They've got all the loyalties of a weathervane. Half are Vichy Nazi bastards and the occupied Free French are lost somewhere in their 18th century *frou-frou*."

"So who else is going from here?"

"Nobody. Oh, and by the way, you won't be meeting with other operatives. You're all reporting up different lines."

"So what kind of training–"

"There isn't any." Hank saw the CO shake his head in disbelief. The officer couldn't even look at him.

"No training, and incidentally there are 3,600 islands in the Pacific, each with a different chief, tribes of cannibals, and God knows how many settlements full of deported criminals. Beats me why the Japs want it. You'll need to be careful, and very discreet."

Hank nodded, eyes wide and ears pulled back. He was a dead man.

The CO opened up a second set of files and read some orders. "So here's the deal. There are Dutch ships harbored in South Africa right now, and we're going to fly you out to join a merchant marine cargo ship."

Hank had six hours to pack and store his civilian life. Within a day he was in the air. The assignment was still a mystery.

CHAPTER 19

July 1942
Son of Neptune

"Loose lips might sink ships!"

~ *Poster*

Pan Am clippers flew daily from New York to England. Beyond that they avoided any territories patrolled by German or Italian units. From New York the men had flown to Southampton, then been whisked to Cairo, and were now on the approach to Timbuktu. The Congo was still a Belgian colony and the new Boeing 314 could travel 2,000 miles on a single fueling. The flying elephant of a plane bounced every which way and, after the first few hours, flight was no longer a novelty.

This advance group of operatives would be in the Pacific in less than two weeks, moving ahead of the troop ships that took five weeks or more. Hank sat in the dark. He had signed up to serve, but he didn't understand his directive. Incomprehensible plans linked the fates of these men. They all spoke more than one language. All had signed documents to keep secrets, but no one knew any. There was no bravado. These men were not boasting about fistfights they had won.

Playing cards and pennies appeared on a tray. Josh, a soldier from the Midwest, pulled the bill of his cap over so it shaded his face.

"What is that, your green eyeshade? You a CPA?" A second player kept a stony silence throughout the game as men tried to mislead each other on the odds.

Josh smiled. "Yep. MBA, University of Michigan."

A lawyer from Minnesota took his glasses off – apparently he was afraid someone could see the reflection of his cards.

Hank didn't know poker, so he sat to the side, learning how to evaluate the hands. "Come on buddy, let's deal you in."

He stalled. "I'm not really good at games of chance. I don't want to make mistakes."

The lawyer commented, "You know, I've made my entire living off of people's mistakes. It happens. Are you afraid of mistakes, or of taking risks?" He put his glasses back on, and turned toward Hank.

An abrupt response, "I'm not afraid. I volunteered."

"You better be scared. We've got an entire planeload of guys who aren't a unit. I don't think anyone here knows what he's supposed to be doing. The risk is already there, so the question is, did anyone make a mistake planning this caper? That's a fatal combination."

The engines droned through that extended night, darkness of the sky concealing an even darker land. Men shifted positions on the benches, their fatigued bodies fighting for sleep that did not come. As the sky reddened with a morning sun the plane landed at Durban, South Africa. The passengers were in plain khaki shirts, stripped of all insignia. There were no ranks and no units. They had new identities, and they were walking into a nest of layered U.S. and British Army and Navy commanders. Their job was to ferret out bits of information and feed them to the hawks that were making the plans.

Hank pulled out his penknife and opened his envelope of instructions. A well- worn Dutch passport fell out of the envelope, bent, grimy and filled with pages full of foreign stamps. His photo and the name of Hans Steen appeared on the first pages. He examined the next paper.

"*AR 380-115, pertaining to handling of secret documents will be complied with in the handling of this manual.*" He was to proceed to the harbor in Durban and board a Dutch merchant marine ship, commanded by a Captain Schoonover. No other person on the ship would know that he was working for the United States. At last he was part of the war, resolutely moving toward a theater of combat. He was simultaneously being propelled backward. He had spent three years erasing his lifetime as a Dutchman. Now he had to reconstitute a Dutch identity in short order, and he hadn't even seen a Dutch newspaper since leaving Amsterdam. He hailed a taxi, and asked for a ride to the merchant marine docks.

The VNS Westerveldt was an immaculate small ship. Some twenty or more cranes were perched and chained on the deck. Thousands of meters of massive ropes and cables were wound into spools. A 50mm machine gun perched over the wheelhouse, its belt of ammunition ready to roll. Clearly this boat was not going to be carrying tea and chocolate.

Hank, once again Hans, picked up his duffel bag and walked up the gangplank, asking for the Captain. "Are you a seaman?"

"Something like that. He's expecting me."

A navy blue jacket with gold stripes came into view. Schoonover was a classic Dutchman, sturdy, somewhere in his early forties with a little grizzle around the ears and hairline. Permanent sunburn creased his face. Deep crows' feet lined blue eyes that had squinted into horizons throughout much of his life.

The Westerveldt was headed out to sea, a loaded ship tightly secured into its placement within a large convoy. There was no open view of the ocean, and not much of an unobstructed view of the sky. One boat was positioned behind the other with little room to move except forward within the entire formation. Destroyers and mine sweepers escorted the entire fleet, prepared to attack any intruders. Most of the boats were Merchant marine cargo, like the Westerveldt. The miles long fleet could be outmaneuvered by every living creature in the sea, let alone airplanes or submarines. Schoonover's job was to keep the boat moving, not get shot, and not bump into anyone else.

As twilight fell, so did the command to darken ship. No one knew what monsters lay beneath the waves, but curtains were drawn so that no glimmer of light would show. A few silvery ghosts appeared on the horizon, blending in with the night.

A couple of sailors kept watch, and the company came to life when the dinner bell rang.

The Officers' Mess was the only part of the ship that looked remotely Dutch to Hans, and the few passengers were invited to join the group. Hans Steen sat down at the officers' table and greeted the captain in Dutch. Schoonover presided over dinner. Oak chairs were upholstered in leather, and the heavy wooden tables were bolted to the floor in case of rough seas. Each meal was served on thick porcelain plates, the kind that wouldn't shatter if they slid off of a table. Cook had put together fragrant dishes from preserved foods, and served them in hotel silver. Today the crew had set a trawl, and they had a delicious meal of fresh tuna, served up with pickled vegetables and rice. Candied ginger was laid out in small dishes to aid digestion. *Heerlijk! Heavenly.*

Hans looked around the dining room space, empty of men except him and the captain. He was dressed in his tweeds, but Schoonover was still in his Navy Blue woolen suit with bars, ribbons, and stripes.

"So, you are with us as a tourist? What would make someone want to tour these days?" The captain opened a wooden box, pulled out a bottle of cognac and two small snifters. He poured some of the amber liquid into one. He would not be on deck again until eight the next morning. "Hans, would you care for a little snort? *Lekker* – it's delicious."

"I'm not sure; I don't really drink."

Schoonover poured a couple ounces into the bottom of a second snifter and handed it across the table.

"Yes, I'll try it. *Bedankt* – Thank you." The glass glowed against the lamps in the dining room.

Hans's eyes shifted toward the liquid in the glass. His prepared story now seemed phony, but he went ahead. "I need to stop by and look at some land. We haven't heard from my aunt and uncle in some time. I hear that the Japanese are all over the colonies like bees." He waited for Schoonover to complete the idea.

Instead, Schoonover pulled out two short pieces of rope from his pockets, and began tying them into knots. His fingers whipped through the line, forming a large loop, and then securing it. He studied the figure 8 that he had formed, then pulled it apart and started over, commenting.

"Ah, the Japanese have an idea that the natives will be better off under Japanese Pan-Asian rule." Hans nodded in agreement, but he actually didn't quite understand. This comment did not fit with the distinctive cultures he had seen as a teenager. He began to run his finger around the edge of the snifter. An inquiring look led the captain to continue. "Never mind that most of the natives are mixed races and nobody fits the description of the master race." Schoonover swallowed about half of his cognac and set the glass down. His steady gaze never left Hans's face. "Where do your people live?"

Hans twirled the glass in his hands, looking at the room through the rounded bowl. He didn't want to talk about the islands any more. "I am from Amsterdam."

Schoonover handed Hans a piece of rope. "Here."

Hans looked at the rope, puzzled.

"Young man, you are far too nervous, and I don't see calm days ahead. You need to busy those hands." The captain picked up his rope and lifted an end. "Do you like to tie knots?"

Hans watched intently and followed the captain's movements as they tied slipknots. Of course. Sailors used ropes for everything. While he was concentrating on the rope, Schoonover asked, "Have you heard from them recently?"

Hans spoke immediately, still not quite paying attention to the captain. "As a matter of fact, I haven't. I wrote a letter to my mother some months ago." He observed Schoonover, then tied a loop in the piece of rope.

"Things are terrible in Holland." Schoonover tied a second loop, and slipped the two lines together. "Fisherman's knot – strongest way to splice two ropes together. Won't slip." He yanked the ends, the ropes slid out to their full length, but wouldn't go beyond the knots. Two opposing forces balanced each other and acted as one.

"Even the letters from my wife are censored, but I gather that Holland has agreed to Nazi rule."

Hans dropped his rope and looked intently at the captain. "What do you think that's like?"

"Most of the food has been shipped from Dutch farms into Germany. There is very little in Holland. And, of course, the Germans now have lots of Dutch labor. Dutch police are gathering up the Jews and they are going off to work in the East." Schoonover pulled the next line tight, into a snare.

The captain's guest went completely pale, then took the snifter and finished his drink. His strength needed to be reserved for fighting, not worrying. He couldn't imagine his mother or his sister working, and Max was too young.

Schoonover's voice broke into his nervous vision of Esther in a work camp. "So I gather you will be leaving us in Noumea? I will be dropping some cargo there as well."

"Do you know New Caledonia?"

"Lots of French planters. And a big nickel mine." Schoonover looked at him and watched the reflection in his eyes. There was no indication that Hans understood that nickel and steel could be combined into tough stainless steel that would not corrode.

Hans looked up. "So Holland is once again in the business of international freight?"

Schoonover put down his glass. The captain smiled. "There are all kinds of freight. If it fits in the hold we will carry it."

He didn't disclose that the entire hold was now full of rusty iron bars and old barbed wire and had been dodging fights on its way to meet up with the convoy in the Indian Ocean. The Dutch fleet had sailed from England and the Westerveldt, along with many others, was loaded with scrap metal from South Africa. Iron and steel could make guns and bullets. Combined with nickel, the steel would not rust or lose its edge. Old scrap would fuel the Allied crucible.

"My friend, it's already near midnight, and I have to be on watch again in the early morning. Good night." Schoonover replaced his cognac in the cushioned box, protecting it from a rolling sea.

CHAPTER 20

July 1942
Indian Ocean

Damn the torpedoes, full speed ahead!

U.S. Admiral D. Farragut

Mickey, the ship's cat, ran by with a kitten in her mouth and placed it under the bar before running back outside to grab another. Hans was spreading marmalade on his roll when sirens in the dining room shrieked so loudly that he dropped the butter knife. He clapped his hands over his ears, stunned by the noise. Men shoved their chairs under tables and ran for positions. Completely paralyzed, Hans froze not knowing what to do except that he wasn't supposed to finish his breakfast. Plates and cups rattled as he jumped up from the table and ran, following the others.

Almost immediately he stumbled over the maze of various hatch covers as a swell rolled under the ship. *Hochtverdommung!* Goddammit! Picking himself up, he bumped into one of the Aussie crew. "What's happened?"

A pockmarked and unshaven face appeared at his side. "It's sure not a fish fart." The sailor looked into Hans's pale face. "Torpedoes, mate. We got Jap visitors."

"Are we hit?"

"Not yet, but someone is. They're gonna be after the rest of us. Sons of bitches. The Japs kill their wounded and chop 'em up for dinner."

The VNS Westerveldt #41 was now locked into a convoy of battleships, destroyers and merchant ships that stretched out for miles through unknown waters. The fleet was not near enemy territories but the Japanese submarines roamed where they wished, devouring ships like some monstrous leviathan. Then they would disappear, waiting for their next meal. Through the loudspeaker static came the voice of the first mate addressing the crew in English, French and Dutch. A confirmed strike on Ship #81, Visser.

Hans clung to the halyard, trying to maintain his balance. Curiosity overtook any sense of terror. "What are we supposed to do?"

The Aussie looked at Hans, white knuckles clasping the cable, and shoved past him. "You better start praying." The man began to unlash one of the big spools of rope. Hans ran to his side. "Here mate, you can help me feed this astern." The hemp cable unwound, snaking its way across the deck and Hans fed it to another seaman.

Invisible pathways joined the fleet together to move as a single unit, an imposing force too large to destroy. Each captain worked within his piece of the puzzle, making progress without getting hit by the enemy or colliding with another ship. The Visser #81 was a couple miles behind the Westerveldt #41, but once the submarines located a convoy all the ships were vulnerable. When a ship was hit, the entire convoy was forced to halt.

The loudspeaker sounded. "All in place for rescue operations."

Hans's training as a combat photographer had not prepared him for how people would react in the face of danger. The deck was a frenzy of activity. Life-rafts were inspected for leaks and supplies. Benches opened up to reveal neatly packed life preservers and inflatable canvas belts. Ropes were readied in case any of the Visser survivors ended up near the Westerveldt. That was unlikely, but it was more than likely that another ship would be hit. Once the subs found a convoy, they picked off ships until they reached open waters. They might be moving from the Visser toward the back of the fleet, or they might move forward into the center, throwing everything into confusion.

As soon as Hans finished assisting the Australian sailor, he climbed the ladder above the wheelhouse and looked back into the convoy. He was a photojournalist, and his job was to photograph action. In the distance he spotted the black plume of smoke rising into the air from the crippled ship. His lens could not capture the chaos around it.

A searing white sun hung over the Indian Ocean, but even in clear waters the submarine could not be spotted. Hans had never been fond of fishing, playing with things he could not see. The unseen enemy dominated the quiet hours between explosions. Japanese torpedoes flew through the waters. British destroyers sent down depth charges and struck nothing. The men kept watch, and Hans stood rooted into his lookout position for hours.

Outlines of the gray ships dimmed in the twilight shades of evening when a sun bright fireball exploded behind them. There was no warning. The concussion of noise hit after they saw the flash. Spumes of water engulfed the ship, not the spray of a wild surf, but a violent white blast with the force of Niagara. The shutter clicked as Hans shot one exposure after another. Orange flames erupted against the violet blue sky, images that would be captured in black and white photos, the fireball appearing slightly gray.

Captain Schoonover's voice crackled over the speakers. "The VNS Gremer #51 has been struck. To stations for rescue operations." The convoy stalled to locate survivors. The Gremer was still a good half-mile back, but the waters began to stir. Fish and birds began to float by, their limp bodies resting on the waves and a few sharks circling in to harvest them. Crew kept watch for men in rafts or floating on pieces of debris.

Shadows disappeared as night fell. Japanese sonar did not distinguish night and day. It could spot ships in ink black waters. Men were ordered to their bunks for rest, while others remained on watch for the metal monsters. Hans closed his eyes but every muscle in his body tightened, ready to spring. In the narrow bunks there were no snores, and there were no audible breaths. He couldn't turn; he couldn't sit or stand. Even if he could walk around the ship, there would be nothing to see in the night fog.

At dawn a concussion shook the Westerveldt #41, and shattered the new day. Footsteps thundered through the ship as the crew ran toward the port side. The entire bow of the Amstelkerk #40 had been blown off in a single strike. The stench of smoke and burning fuel was close, and both ships were drenched from a hundred foot spume. The sailors' mouths gaped open, speechless. An ensign yelled, "You damn deck apes, get to the rails and get these men before the sharks do."

The Amstelkerk lurched sideways, with its exposed engine rooms facing the Westerveldt. Its belly shredded, the ship vomited parts of humans and machinery into the water. Hell on earth erupted as the sea boiled with flotsam whirling in the cauldron. Fires started as the fuel ignited, black smoke and flames obliterating the rising sun.

Through all this the sailors of the Westerveldt spotted yellow rafts and pieces of wood with Amstelkerk survivors. Hans's shutter clicked away at objects moving so quickly through his vision that he couldn't really understand what he was seeing. Expected to photograph heroic acts, he instead observed tragedies in the making. Orange-black light illuminated faces of the condemned crew of the Amstelkerk as their rubber rafts bounced to the side of the Westerveldt, exhausted eyes staring at the rails several meters above them. They were numb with shock. The realization that some of them would die silenced all his senses.

Turning to look at the commotion on the deck, Hans realized why Captain Schoonover had made sure that he knew how to tie knots. The shutter clicked one last time, and Hans ran to stow his camera. He joined the sailors at the rail, tying large slipknots to drop over the side, and draw across the chests of the victims. They lifted the first man. Releasing and retying knots, the men fished one sailor after another from the flaming sea. His arms went around each sailor that he pulled across the rails, holding the survivor tight until a stretcher was available or the man could walk on his own.

The debris began to thin. Even the sky began to brighten and they began to breathe in the sea air. Loudspeaker static broke the quiet, and the voice of the captain rang out with the next orders. "All available hands, report to sickbay." Hans joined the dozen or so men headed for the sick bay. The Amstelkerk survivors were covered in oil and smoke, some with terrible burns that needed to be cleaned and protected.

The chief medic instructed, "Scrub these men until they are as white as these sheets – as rosy as newborn babies." On the side of the bay were several stretchers with men who were not moving. The medic turned away to examine a man. He opened the eyelid of his patient, touched the eye itself, and signaled an orderly to remove the body.

A wave of nausea gripped Hans as he watched the medic. A sailor turned to him. "Mate, these guys need us. We gotta get to work."

Hans stripped his first man of his torn and waterlogged clothing, throwing the rags aside. As he began to wipe the young man's face, some freckles peeked out. The sponge began to reveal skin flecked with carbon from the smoke, and then pink burns. The dazed sailor winced with pain but let him go on to shampoo the black hair. When the soot was rinsed away, the man had red hair. Medics began to unroll their bandages and salves, binding one injury after another. Hans was awed by their power to change men from victims into patients, human beings who had reasons to live.

A second survivor was in worse shape, semiconscious and black from head to toe. He was a worker from the engine room, an oiler who had been in the belly of the boat. Although he worked right at the site of the impact, he had been blown clear. His wide eyes stared at Hans, but he could not respond or speak. He seemed to be totally deaf. Hans tried to wash him gently, but the oil, smoke, and dirt would not budge. Everything was burned black, even under his clothing. Only the palms of his hands and spaces under his fingernails were pink. A warm cloth was placed over the man's face to clear the oil from his eyes and ears. Hans picked up the rough sea sponge and began to scrub. The sailor moaned, but the stubborn dirt did not come away. Burn blisters rose as Hans worked to get the wounds clean.

He flinched when the medic yelled at him. "This guy's an African!" The man was black. Sailors were white, but some engine room workers were black Africans who were making the same contributions of life and fortune that every other sailor did. Hans set aside his sponge, queasy at his harshness and the damage that he had done to an injured man. Then he located soft flannel cloths and washed his patient once more, gently, like a baby. With tears of apology, his blue eyes met the man's brown ones and they shared a glance. Before his next patient, he stepped to a corner just long enough to wipe his eyes.

After #40 VNS Amstelkerk sank, the Commodore gave orders to re-form the convoy. The Westerveldt was to move from its current location into space #40. Instead, when the orders to shift position came through, Schoonover called for full steam ahead. His swift new vessel was leaving the fleet. For the first time its engines were brought to full power as they raced for the outside of the formation and charted a new course in the open ocean. The gamble was that the sub would not chase a lone ship when there was an entire convoy of valuable cargo. Schoonover had decided that his fast boat could outmaneuver any submarine, and he did not choose to be part of this carnival shooting game. There were no prizes on this ride except the load of scrap metal they were already carrying, materiel for bullets.

Schoonover made a decision that came with consequences. As the ship turned and sped away from the convoy every last sailor knew that they had disobeyed the English commodore's command. The captain was willing to face a tribunal to save them. Without further incident, the Westerveldt arrived in Sydney, ready to make steel. Hans met up with a few new shipmates, and set sail for New Caledonia.

CHAPTER 21

Amsterdam July 1942

"I herewith commission you to carry out all preparations with regard to... a final solution of the Jewish question in those territories of Europe which are under German influence."

– Hermann Göring To Reinhard Heydrich, July 1941

Sarah Goudberg was German born, but it didn't help her in the end. On every corner were Dutch boys practicing their Nazi salutes, imitating the German soldiers who filled the streets. Dutch citizens who cooperated with the Nazis had some privileges. Those who resisted simply did not exist in the eyes of the Reich. Beneath them were the Jews. For a year now Jews had been arrested on all sorts of pretexts, forced to leave their homes with a few belongings, and never returned.

The stoop of 94 Herengracht was unchanged, but it no longer welcomed clientele or visitors. Imposing wooden doors sealed off the offices. The ground floor hallway was lined in marble, but no maids kept the white stairs spotless, or the brass banisters polished. A dusty bicycle with a flat tire lay in the hall. Max was now the young man of the house. He had lost too much weight. During the wet spring he had so much fluid in his lungs that he sounded like a drowning victim, coughing until he vomited bloody phlegm. When there was food, he couldn't swallow it without choking. What he needed was a rich broth of chicken and that was nowhere to be found. Even a fragrant cup of tea would help, but it was not available on their rations.

Esther thrived in the harsh conditions. She was defiant. Her petulant complaints and temper had vanished under steady resolve. The family needed her, and she took charge of providing for them. She had charm and a knack for barter. With the flash of her smile she could get what was available.

On a morning in early March, Esther opened the windows and dug tulip bulbs from the window boxes and added them to a stew. The produce and meat from Dutch farms had been sent to Germany. The open market stalls were mostly empty, a wooden crate with a few spotted potatoes, empty shelves at the cheese store with only a few moldy pieces of gouda. Parsnips and carrots were gone. The translucent red currants that had graced every July table were nowhere to be found. Oh well. There wasn't any sugar either. Still, she went out into the streets each day, foraging what she could.

The visitors changed. No one asked questions of a young man in uniform who appeared after the evening meal one Saturday. Esther's shopping expeditions had ended when she encountered a Dutch policeman in the street. There was no yellow star on her jacket and her identification papers were smudged.

"A pretty girl like you shouldn't have to shop."

"It depends on what I am shopping for."

"What would you like?"

"Oh, maybe some cream …"

He laughed. There had been no cream in Amsterdam for months.

"And where would you keep the cream?"

"It depends on how much you have."

He liked the pretty girl. On late summer nights he acted the part of a gentleman, bringing gifts of wine or seized chocolate and cigarettes, but no meat or vegetables. Sarah wept, but she thanked him for the gifts. Her stepfather Sam sat in the library, opened a book, closed it, and opened it again, waiting for the intruder to leave. Max made himself scarce. The intruder's boots sounded on the stone stairs when he left late at night and doors in the upstairs hallway remained closed.

Another day had come to an end. Once again they went to bed not quite satisfied, but not starving either.

Their peace ended on July 22nd. Max heard the knocking first. He couldn't find his glasses in the dark, but he wanted to tell the drunks that they were at the wrong door before they woke up the entire household. He grabbed the railing and carefully picked his way down the first floor and to the ground floor.

The knocking became more insistent.

"Go away, you have made a mistake."

A voice responded in German. "Open up. Police."

"We haven't done anything."

"Open up. Police, or we open your door ourselves. "

He cracked the door open to face green uniforms. Lugers hung from their heavy leather belts, and hastily stitched swastikas decorated their collars. Six policemen barreled into the house, scattering through the ground floor hallways. Two ran for the stairs and the upstairs living quarters.

One tripped on an Oriental rug.

"*Scheisse!*"

"You don't have time to shit now."

"Maybe I do," and he started to drop his drawers before his comrade hurried him on. A small Japanese figurine was on a lamp table. One of the men commented, "At least they know enough to respect the Japanese," before he pocketed it.

Screaming from upstairs let them know that Sarah's room had been breached. She had not forgotten any of her childhood German. "You filthy pigs – get out of my bedroom." Her hair was undone, loose and hanging below her shoulders. Without her corsets, her body shook and swayed under the nightdress.

"Jew bitch. If you didn't resemble an old sow I would show you who is the boss of this bedroom." Her husband lowered his head as they got dressed. A policeman grabbed Sam's hands and tied them behind his back.

Sarah glared at her captor. "Where are we going? Why are we being arrested?"

"To the opera! Oh, and we might need these." He went through her dresser and grabbed a couple of gold bracelets, then shoved her roughly as she began to cry.

"I have new bracelets for you. See?" and he tied her hands behind her back as well. She felt something cold and hard pushed into her spine, and knew better than to turn around. As she was forced down the stairs, she looked through her tears into the public rooms and hesitated for a moment. The front door was wide open, and the brick steps to the street were faintly illuminated by the moon. "Get in the truck." A harsh command in German stopped her from thinking about the years in her home.

Esther glared at the man as he tied up her young brother, and shoved him down the stairs. A silent scream pushed against her throat. This policeman could hurt Max. She knew this bastard, this comrade of her recent boyfriend. They both patrolled her neighborhood and his hard jawline had contrasted with that of his partner. Max didn't stumble, but his footing was unstable; he couldn't use his arms to balance himself like he did when he skipped stairs or slid down banisters. Then it was her turn. A man grabbed her hands and bound them tightly. If she moved, the ropes would cut into her wrists. She stared through him and said nothing. Apparently the new love affair was over. Where was the bastard tonight? Coward.

They were thrown into an open wooden cart and taken to the Hollandsche Schouwburg, the national theatre that until recently had been reserved for Jewish entertainers. As soon as the wide doors opened, the stench poured out. Nearly 1,300 people were crammed into the 400 seat theatre, and the German soldiers had locked the doors. Two lavatories had broken down. Babies' diapers were filled, and children cried. Sweat and foul odors saturated the humid night air. Detainees had been there for as long as ten days, waiting. Esther recognized friends and neighbors, young people who had attended Hebrew school and elders who had prayed together their entire lives. She spotted her cousin Judith.

"Do you know why we are here?"

"Does anyone know?" Judith shrugged her shoulders.

"If they do, we are the last ones who will be informed. I'm not sure we even want to know."

Judith frowned. "We have been in this sty since yesterday. Do you have anything to eat?" Esther shook her head.

The two young women looked around at the throng of bewildered Jews. They both knew that once people had been taken, they never returned to their homes. Some had been allowed to bring a single suitcase or carpetbag, but these were now stacked together, inaccessible to all. People and bags would not be matched up for the next transport.

Old buses and trams came by daily and lists of names were called. By the third morning, Esther started vomiting. She stood in the shadows, unseen among hundreds of others who looked like her. Her fury rose as she thought of Franz, the pig who had lain on top of her night after night. She wiped her face, walked up to a guard, smiled, and ran past him into the street. He turned to block what he thought would be a rush of escaping young people, and didn't stop her. There were no others, and he couldn't see where she had gone.

Ripping the yellow star off of her sweater, Esther ran for the canal district, looking for alleyways and roof overhangs. Churches and their courtyards might provide some immediate shelter. Her leather shoes tapped on the cobblestones as she hurried, trying not to make any noise. Holland was vanquished but she was not. Think. She was squinting at house numbers - an address of a friend, a shop she knew, anyone who might help her. Turning the corner she recognized a corner home where her friend Cristina lived, a nice girl who had also worked in the stationery store. The steps had not been swept in days. She smacked the buzzer over and over until a head poked out of an upstairs window.

"Cristina, it's Esther."

"Shhh! I'll be down." In a moment the key turned. "Be quiet."

Cristina took her arm and walked her back to the dark courtyard. "Stay here." Her friend walked into the servant's entrance. In a few moments she reappeared with a roll and some tea. "Esther, you cannot stay." Esther looked at her puzzled. "If they catch you here, they will take my family too. I'm sorry."

"Why would they take you? You're not Jewish!"

"Esther, please go. Now."

Esther did not look back at Cristina. She sat down on a curb to cry, and to think. Hans had attained refugee status. How had he done it? In the morning she would try to visit some offices and see what she could do, claiming that she had an American brother. She hadn't really paid attention to some of the changes in the city. Dutch government offices were now German, and the Americans were no longer represented in Europe. Childhood friends whose parents had worked for the government were no longer residing in Amsterdam. Regret did not come easily to Esther, but on this night she shed her tears of remorse.

For two weeks Esther played hide and seek on the streets of Amsterdam, finding shelter from night to night, and food wherever she could. No one she knew occupied the familiar homes of her Jewish friends. There were ways to hide in dark protected crannies under bridges, or behind porch steps, even in courtyards when she got lucky. The summer evenings were warm and after ten days she began to move out of the heavily patrolled downtown neighborhoods.

Esther had fallen sound asleep near the river, a little south of the central city. Finally, she was at the marsh where she and Hans had spent countless summer days rowing a little skiff and playing in the fields. He had his camera, and she would draw birds and grasses in the breeze. The marsh grasses were soft, a wonderful nest for an exhausted girl, the only sounds being occasional rustlings of birds, or the honk of a swan. One whistle was particularly jarring – the voice of a human hunting other humans. The man shook her and ordered her to stand up. Her captor did not yell. He simply took her by her thin arms, pulled out his weapon, and told her to walk quickly. The barrel of the gun pressed into her back as he directed her forward.

"Get in the wagon."

She made no eye contact with the others in the canvas covered farm wagon. She did not utter a word during her return to the theatre. She stood absolutely still in the buzzing lines of people, waiting for her name to be located on the registers. Luck was on her side. Instead of being processed for the camps in the east, she would be deported to work in Germany. She was on the way to a place called Bergen Belsen. It did not sound like a vacation in the mountains.

The freight train drew close. Esther's future was crushed under the rumble and squeal of iron wheels. Within moments, police forced all the captives into the cattle cars. There were no destination signs on the cars or on the front of the German train.

Coal sparks and steam flew from the tenders of the train. The summer heat baked the cars stacked with hundreds of people. Urine and feces covered the floors of the car as the captives stood in place or collapsed. Esther willed herself to stand. Eighteen hours later she stepped out into the warm sunlight, blinking and trying to smooth her hair. She straightened her summer dress. Her shoes were gone. Standing barefoot in the dirt, her only thought was, "What next?" Soldiers inspected the girls. Once again, she boldly looked into the eyes of the officer, as he examined her full bosom and slim waist. "You are a pretty one. With those green eyes, why don't you have yourself declared Aryan?"

She laughed in astonishment, "It's a little late for that, don't you think?"

He walked on down the line. The women followed the guards toward their barracks and drudgery. This was a labor camp. As the line walked, the soldier accosted her once more.

"You there! Come with me." His harsh voice indicated that some special punishment was ahead. She followed him to another building, where a fat matron waited. "She needs to take a shower."

The matron grabbed her, stripped off her dress, and pushed her into a dark room. Without warning a spray of water came from the low ceiling. She scrubbed and wiped with no soap until the grime of the last three weeks was gone. When the spray stopped, the matron handed her an ugly pair of blue and white pajamas and told her to sit quietly.

At midday the soldier returned, pulled her hands behind her back, and marched her toward a row of small houses. When they stepped inside, he released her.

"Do you know how to iron?" She nodded. "I need you to take care of … my clothes."

He stepped forward and unbuttoned the top of the pajamas. Her full breasts were creamy white and he reached underneath them, holding them in his hands. Then he unbuttoned his pants and pushed her toward a chair. He sat down and asked her to come sit on his lap.

"You Jewish whores are all alike – don't be shy." She was terrified. An instinct told her to not follow his directions, and she began to shake. "Oh come on then, just kneel in front of me – touch it, you will like this." It was warm in her hand, and she inspected the uncircumcised flesh carefully – he asked her to touch him and showed her how to rub, so she went along with his request. She felt his hands grasp her around the neck as he said, "I don't need to see your pretty face." Yanking her hair, he pulled her head down.

Afterward, Esther realized that she had just come into some odd type of luck.

"I'm not a whore."

"What?"

In Dutch she replied, "I am not a whore. Whores take money for sex. I can give some comfort, but I won't take anything."

He laughed, "Not that it matters here." She had gotten him to say something.

"Also, my name is Esther."

He laughed. "I see. Now we are making formal introductions? I am Lutz, Georg Lutz." He spoke in German. She decided that she should pretend that she didn't understand the Germans, that she was maybe sweet and a little slow. Her survival was dependent on her choices. She might even be able to hide her pregnancy for a few more weeks, and become indispensable to him. She was returned to her barracks with his taste in her mouth, the only thing she had eaten in two days.

The women's dormitory was stifling. Even an afternoon rainstorm did not freshen the air. Three girls were assigned to each short bunk. Some were crying and others were praying to a deaf God. Esther pulled her knees up to her chest and buried her face. Hannah, a pianist from Amsterdam, had been carrying kettles of soup all day long. She nursed her blistered hands. A third girl in the bunk wheezed like Max did when they went out in the grass. She was too exhausted to even have a name any more. Their stomachs rumbled, but they were alive.

CHAPTER 22

Noumea, New Caledonia
August 1942

Battle of Guadalcanal begins.
"Australia and New Zealand are now threatened by the might of the Imperial Japanese forces, and both of them should know that any resistance is futile."

~ Hideki Tojo

HANK BURNS LOOKED INTO THE unfamiliar night sky. The Southern Cross blinked back at Hans Steen, his new identity.

Hans Steen, Dutch Civilian

They were truly on the underside of the world. The Westerveldt had landed in New Caledonia. The harbor was situated in a vast lagoon, surrounded by reefs that were visible in many places. The clear white sands, palm trees and brilliant blue waters were in stark contrast to the loading equipment, swearing men, and beehive of activity on the cargo docks. Was this heaven or hell?

The French island of New Caledonia was one of the few Pacific Islands that had not been seized by the Japanese. It was now a staging area for all services to be shipped north into the Pacific War. Troops were milling around in khakis with various insignia. Hans was one insignificant man, alone in a big war. Now a Dutch civilian, he no longer looked like one of them. He had grown a mustache, and an unruly mop of thick wavy hair had somehow altered his features.

A month ago in New York he had been called in front of his Commanding Officer to review his reassignment to Counter Intelligence.

"We're sending you to the islands. The Japs are taking everything, our boys are dying and the Allied troops can't even talk to each other. It's a mess." The Officer closed a file with a red label on it.

"Islands, sir?"

"The Pacific. There are two notes in your folder that say you are good at finding things. Are you familiar with CIC?"

"No, sir, not really."

"There are different types of combat and we need some guys who can fight a different kind of battle. Your two commendations indicate that you have presence of mind, and you are willing to take risks. Some battles are fought with will or wit."

"What about photography?"

"Oh, you'll be taking cameras with you. Thing is, you won't be carrying a gun. You'll have to figure out your own way to take care of your hide."

Now he was in a tent in New Caledonia, facing his new boss. Hans Steen was going undercover as a Dutch tourist in a French colony with a free pass to go anywhere and talk to anyone. He didn't know anybody. "Sir, I'm not sure exactly what I am supposed to find."

"Good question. We think some people are working for both sides of a conflict that is not two sided. This thing has more dimensions than a jigsaw puzzle."

Noumea was a busy international community. The sleepy island port was about to become the home for 150,000 soldiers from all over the English-speaking world. The closest civilization, if you could call it that, was New Zealand.

"With all the stakes in this war, we're having trouble making friends, even with the French. Who is a friend and who is an enemy? That changes by the hour as well. Most of them seem to be mercenaries. Get to know the locals. You are a businessman. Find out how the deals are made, and who is in it, for what."

Hank's steady gaze covered his confusion. He had never been a great listener, and now his life and others might depend on things he heard and remembered. The Captain spoke again. "Everyone is nervous because we are piling people and equipment in here, but the action is somewhere else. Drop off your written reports on Fridays. Stay away from the base unless it's urgent." With that advice Hans Steen was cut loose with no military ID and some cash.

It wasn't as if the Japanese officers were walking the street and posting their battle plans on storefront windows. Hans needed to start somewhere. Bars were a good choice for meeting people, but he was uncomfortable in them. Making friends had always been difficult, but drunken sailors do plenty of talking. Then it would be up to him to sort out the bragging and lies. He walked down the street until he saw the perfect venue. A pair of carved tikis stood 6 feet tall on either side of the entrance to a dark hole in the wall. Noise from within The Crocodile rolled out into the street in waves. Inside the open door he smelled stale sweat and beer, sweat that had rolled off the bodies of men who could not wash off the fear. Most of them worked on aircraft carriers and made all night and early morning runs to bomb whatever came their way. Each afternoon some returned, and some didn't.

Hans sat down at the bar and listened to a couple of background conversations. It had been a bad run this morning. "I don't know who was watching their coast, but it was like they expected us to come to their damn tea party." The speaker lit a cigarette, and continued. "Whose idea was it to get into that fly trap? Goddamn Japs seem to know where we're going before we even get our flight plans." Puffing like a smokestack, he blew smoke toward Hans and continued to talk to his buddy.

A filthy menu with a list of *boissons* – beverages – was thrust into his hand. What the heck was "Monkey Seed Monkey Screwed?" Turned out the viscous mixture involved coconut milk and bananas with various hard liquors. It looked disgusting. *Une bieré sil vous plait – Heineken*? A warm bottle was opened and placed into his hand. It tasted like rat piss.

The bartender was interested in repeat business, and wanted to make Hans feel at home.

"What's your outfit?"

"Pardon?"

"Your outfit, your unit – who are you with?"

"No one really, I came here on a Dutch Merchant Marine."

"What the hell, you a bloody tourist?"

"No, no – I came to settle up some business. My uncles have holdings in Jakarta and South Africa."

"Where are you from? You know there's a war on, right?"

He pondered his error. Had Hans Steen already provided too much information? He commented, "Amsterdam. But I'm just getting by like everyone else. Holland is a mess too… thank God for the British… and the Anzacs." He had noted the Australian accents. They were fighting on behalf of the Brits, and these rough men were warriors. Now he had presented himself as a profiteer, and hoped that he was on the right side this afternoon.

"Well, young man, there's plenty of opportunities here if you can fly right. The Yanks are buying everything in sight."

In the back corner sat another loner, with the brim of his sailor cap pulled down over his eyes. The top of the white cap peeked out into the dark room, but his hunched shoulders and clenched fists had no visible opponent. A wall of shot glasses separated him from the remainder of the men.

"That's Smythe. He got a letter today." What could a letter possibly say that would be worse than having a buddy crash into the sea? Hans looked toward the bartender. "You know the one, '*I've always been honest with you…You are one of the grandest people I've had the honor of meeting…. Blah, blah, blah.*'" Hank nodded knowingly, only he didn't.

"It's a real bitch. No gals around here at all." Another man offered the obvious. "We could have a real party if there were some gals. Stuck-up nurses are all 2nd Lieutenants. They can only dance with officers and most of the officers are married or they're gonna marry sweethearts that their parents picked out. Bloody shame."

"So how do you meet people here?"

"Here? You gotta be kidding. Hope you already have a gal at home, cuz you won't get one here. At least not a white one." Other men at bar began laughing, "... but, then again, if you go for dark meat...So which is it? You got a gal or you got a letter?"

"Oh, I have a girlfriend." Hans reached into his pocket and pulled out his wallet with a picture of his sister. Esther's photo would be pretty enough to shut them up for a bit. They passed the picture around.

"Damn, I'd like to climb into her pouch for a night!" Hans whipped his head around to the speaker, incensed. Esther was a loose cannon, but the assumption that she was a plaything infuriated him. Even if she were his girlfriend, he would have expected admiration and respect, not these jibes. "Hey, sorry buddy, didn't mean to insult her. She's a pretty one. What's her name?"

His fingernails bit into his palms. He had to keep cool. "Lilli." This was not the time or place for action. He turned to the bartender, ordered a Coca Cola and sat down, looking at Esther's picture once more before he put it away. God knows where she was, but hopefully it was away from roughnecks like these.

Across the room a silk Japanese Rising Sun was tacked to a dartboard on the bamboo paneling. There were some tears around the edges and a couple of the rays were barely holding together, but the red circle in the center of the image was intact. Except that it wasn't at the center. The sun itself was off-center – a captured naval ensign flag; the trick was to be able to hit it toward the left, which was tricky for a right-handed thrower.

In the crowd were several bombardiers from Australia and New Zealand, men who made a treacherous living climbing into the bay of an airplane, readying bombs, adjusting sights and hoping to hit Japanese ships. Others were gunners, trained for air battle. After a few drinks, they were taking shots at the Rising Sun. One didn't even get a dart onto the board. Darts nicked the wall and fell. Good thing there were no tables on that side of the room. Another player's three darts rang from the violence of the throw, but landed in the outer rays.

"Hey mate, let's toss a few!" Tattoos and a massive chest appeared above his line of sight. The sailor set the darts down on the little table. "Be a sport."

Hans looked up at his contender and smiled apprehensively. Oddly enough, others couldn't tell when he was nervous, because somehow under tension his entire body would go calm. He picked up the first dart, set it between his thumb and middle finger of his left hand, laid back his arm and threw. The dart veered a little off center, then punched right into the middle of the red sun. Dart two was about an inch away from the first, and dart three hit so closely that it deflected for a moment, then sank in. Hans sat back down quietly.

A burly arm appeared next to him, "H'lo mate. Name's Jaxton. Usually I throw darts for drinks, but let me save some time and just buy you one." Hans looked at Jaxton, a large man who had spent a lot of time outdoors recently. Jaxton's face was bright red, with scars from multiple sunburns.

"I'm Steen, Hans Steen. Thank you. Do they have anything besides beer and whiskey? Maybe gin?"

Jaxton smiled – this pigeon would be his soon enough, as soon as he had drunk enough so that they could start betting. "Sure they do. What do you want in it?"

"In it?"

"Yes mate, tonic? Lemonade? How do you like it mixed?"

"You mix gin?"

"Yeah, with anything."

"No, with nothing. Just a shot of gin and very cold please."

"I'll get you the gin, but there isn't anything cold here at all."

Jaxton picked up the next dart, and tore another hole in the flag. Hans still got two shots out of three into the rising sun. The gin steadied his nerves. Meanwhile, he was running out of things to say and do in his Dutch character. Continental manners were completely out of place here. These sheepherders were all brawn and brag. There was no information to get because they didn't have any. He wandered back out into the sunshine wondering what he should do next.

CHAPTER 23

Bergen Belsen
September 1942

"Everything human has its origin in human weakness."

– Franz Stangl, SS Captain

ESTHER HEARD THE FLIES BEFORE she opened her eyes. In the stillness of dawn inmates walked through the camp and stopped in front of each barracks to carry out the dead. Limp arms and legs in filthy striped rags slipped out of their hands or over the side of the occasional stretcher. Occasionally a body was stiffened in its final agonies. Flies buzzed, landing on the dead and the living.

She swung her legs over the edge of the bunk, and dropped to the floor. She scurried by the stacked corpses, eyes and mouths open but not seeing, not breathing. They no longer existed.

The latrines were evidence of the living, waste from bodies that still functioned. Overcome by the stench, hardly knowing which end to position over the hole in the bench, she retched. A whistle blew, and lines of people formed in the open areas between buildings. She ran to her group of 400 women lined up in rows of ten, an easy way for the guards to see if anyone was missing. The armed guards in their black uniforms walked down the lines hunting their daily prey – those hardly able to stand, and others too sick to work. On the morning that a woman could no longer walk, a ruddy-faced guard would enter the barracks and force the prisoner outside either to work or die.

Bergen Belsen was a labor camp. Outside of the shoe factory the footwear of barefoot prisoners was heaped up as high as the building, leather to be re-stitched into German boots. Iron ornaments from street lamps lay by the foundry to be recast as guns. Each camp had its own kitchen and the Germans had picked out ten of the prettiest girls for kitchen privileges. The kitchens were warm, lined by bread ovens down one long wall. Spelt and rye were ground into sour black bread. The coarse grain had to be kept dry so that that it would not rot. It was impossible to distinguish the spelt seeds from rat droppings.

Esther and Hannah were assigned to cook and serve meals. Long wooden tables were set up the length of the room so that guards could walk back and forth, patrolling and supervising the women's work. Rows of women were armed with kitchen knives, and stood by their vast steel pots as they sliced turnips into water for the midday meal. Berthe, the guard, was heavy set with greasy blonde hair that strayed from under her cap. She looked like a butcher's wife, but instead of a knife and apron she wore culottes and boots, carrying a riding crop to whip women who were not working fast enough.

She picked up an oversized turnip, toughened by too many days lying in the field. "Look, a sweet white potato. Won't it be delicious mashed? Gravy dripping onto the plate, a puddle of sauce to go with your roast beef." The prisoner looked up, and the whip came down. "Get your fat Jew ass to work!"

The guard stopped near Hannah and looked at her delicate hands, long tapered fingers that had spent their lifetime on an ivory keyboard. Hannah had already been in the kitchen for two days and she did not look up. Berthe had held her hands against boiling pots until the blisters rose. Hannah convulsed, gasping and coughing. She put her knife down and grabbed onto the edge of the table. Her body was racked with spasms as she tried to clear her lungs. Esther slapped her on the back, then ran for a dipper and some water.

"What are you doing?" barked Berthe.

"I need to get a little water for my friend."

"This is not a time to rest. You are not guests at a café."

Esther froze in her spot. "Sorry, I will get back to work immediately."

She turned back to the cutting board, picked up the next turnip and jammed her knife into the heart of the vegetable. Hannah blew her nose in the edge of her pajama top and then picked up a turnip as well. The two of them struck the vegetables with all the force that they could not use against their captors. The second guard came by, impressed with the speed at which the two girls were working.

"That is better. I was afraid that we would need to cut out your bread rations for three days until you were ready to work again."

Late in the afternoon a matron came to Esther and instructed her to follow. She was escorted outside, to stand before Lutz. He grabbed her hands and twisted them behind her back. "*Komm.*" She followed, head bent in submission. His eyes were hidden under the bill of his cap, his stern face meant for public observation.

She knew what he wanted. Inside of his quarters he sat in the only chair and stated, "I have a headache." She climbed on his lap facing him and began to rub his neck and shoulders. Even then he did not relax his jaw. Instead of pulling her to him, he peered at her intently. "You've lost weight. When is the last time you had a meal?"

She looked at him as if he had gone mad. The slight swell of her breasts and abdomen were hidden under the shapeless top. Hundreds of people were starving to death each week, and he wanted to talk about meals?

"On a good day we get three servings." She was puzzled that he didn't know this. He had seen the porridge and the boiled roots.

"I meant, when did you have a good meal?"

"Oh, but of course." She climbed off him and primly took her seat on the bed, unfolded imaginary linen and adjusted her napkin. Fingering a long string of make believe pearls she rolled her eyes upward at the waiter. "I would like Canard a la Orange. A soft white roll. Maybe a white Bordeaux with that?"

He watched her, amused. "Before this war, we used to say a good German cook is a French cook. But no French food now – just hearty German food, a meal with meat, potatoes and some vegetable." The words in German and Dutch were very similar and they understood each other well. He pulled out a crate from under his bed. In it were tinned food, tea, and even a bottle of wine. "Do you see this? If you do as I ask, you will have enough to eat."

A gag response came up in her mouth, but this was not a good time to heave. He saw the color of her face.

"I'm not hungry." She paused, eyeing the packets of foods she had not seen in months. "Besides, those rations are for men. I would be in trouble if I ate some."

He opened a packet of cheese and some biscuits. "Don't be a fool. The prisoners are starving to death. I don't want your lovely breasts to sag. You must eat to remain, umm, *saftig*." After she picked at the cheese, he pushed her down onto the bed, gently by the shoulders. "So, you are not a whore? But you would keep me comfortable for food?" He snickered, but then stopped abruptly. It was his decision to take a lover instead of visiting the brothels. He was a party to cruelty each day, and she knew it. If he wanted her, he could not treat her like a prisoner in his room. They were both hungry. He lay down beside her, and stroked her breasts, then like a hungry child, took one in his mouth.

Esther held him, stroking his neck and shoulders. Night after night he plundered her body. This man was savage and dangerous. She didn't love him, not like she had loved Peter. It wasn't the love of a girl. There were no expectations and no dreams. Even a beast had needs. If she could take care of him, he might take care of her. If he learned too much, it would cost her life.

Over the next weeks, he cared for her, his "little bird." At dinner he often did not finish his plate, and would sometimes take a bit of bread or meat with him "for later." Once he brought a sweet juicy apple. On a cool fall evening he had been hungry, but he only ate half the knackwurst on his plate, wrapping up the rest in his handkerchief with a piece of bread. He smiled as he brought the rich treat back to his quarters and set the prize down in front of Esther. She started to gag, but her eyes filled with tears and she began to cough, hoping to mask her revulsion at the greasy meal in front of her.

As she held her head down, crying and spluttering, he asked, "Why aren't you eating the meat? You are not sick are you?" He stood before her, his frustration evident.

"I have no hunger."

"Are you hungry for anything else?" She slipped into his arms, nodding. As he took her shirt off on that chilly fall evening, he looked at her body. She had lost weight, but her breasts were still firm. He placed his warm hands on her waist, and then embraced her, holding her close against him. "Esther, what is wrong with you tonight?"

"You can't tell, can you?" She had been trapped by her secret since the day they met, but nature would reveal it any day. Now she needed a partner to survive.

"Can't tell what?"

"That I'm pregnant."

He froze, and turned her around. Pregnant women were sent to the hospital for experiments. After the abortions, their ovaries were removed and, if they survived, they were placed in brothels until they died. Until that moment Lutz had always followed orders. Now there was one order that was even higher than the orders from Berlin. As a teen he had been told that he must never touch a woman until he was married. Women get pregnant and pregnancy was a kind of sacrament. You don't hurt pregnant women, and you must protect their innocent infants. But was a Jewish infant innocent? Could he father a child with a Jewish woman? Would it be a monster?

Abortion was a mortal sin. Lutz was an Austrian Catholic, and he knew his answer, but he did not know how to act on it.

CHAPTER 24

New Caledonia October 1942

"Jesus Christ and General Jackson, what a hot potato they have handed me!"

~ Admiral Halsey re. American Occupation of Noumea

There are millions of little men and little jobs in a big war. At a peak in the center of the island, drops of rain form rippled puddles and ponds. Lakes release the drops into streams and rivers. Eventually the drops become a force of nature, the ocean. Troops continued to pour into Noumea.

Hans's break appeared Sunday afternoon on a secluded beach. He walked down the path to a deep blue cove bordering the shaded lagoon. A little waterfall rushed down the hill into the lagoon, with well-worn rocks at its base.

Hans looked toward the waterfall, and saw a woman wading below the cascading water. Her back was bare. As she turned he saw her breasts, completely brown like the rest of her, hanging full like ripe fruit. Her long flowing hair draped into the small of her back. Only her dark coloring kept her from looking like a Venus from the sea.

He looked at her body, too startled to meet her eyes. The mist around the waterfall did nothing to cool him down. She came forward and touched him gently, then smiled. "Come with me – one dollah." Her pidgin language broke the spell. He looked out across the beach. Lying on towels and blankets were sailors with women. Uniforms had been tossed to the sides, and men were enjoying the day in their skivvies. Some showed the effects of too much alcohol and sunburn. Sarong clad women fetched drinks and simple snacks of fruit. There were dozens of couples on the beach.

Some women were still looking for partners for the day. Hans pulled out his little Leica pocket camera and began taking tourist photographs. He was ready for the next woman who approached him. He greeted her. "*Bonjour mademoiselle*! May I take your picture? You are so beautiful – here, you need to pose for me."

She grinned at him, revealing dark stained teeth. "Will you give me the picture?"

"Of course." Meanwhile Hans was already thinking about his need for a darkroom.

"Turn around, can you bend your arms this way – dance? My goodness you are graceful – have you ever seen a movie? Betty Grable or Rita Hayworth? You are as pretty as they are." The girl giggled, and then stood straight, like a stone statue, her huge grin revealing a couple of blackened teeth. "Here, stretch out your leg and turn away from me – there you go. Put your hand across your breast. It makes us wonder." After the "photo shoot" he asked for an address.

"You want to come with me?"

Hans glanced into her soft eyes, and smiled. The invitation was attractive, but he was very curious about the beach scene. It just looked a little too organized.

"I have an appointment. You know, it takes a few days to develop the pictures. Don't you want to see which pictures we should send to Hollywood?"

Her eyes lit up. She had been using her body to make a living, but acting in movies seemed too good to be true. "How do I see the pictures?"

"I will make a sheet of your poses and drop it off at your house next … What day are you free? Sunday … OK, I will be by next Sunday in the afternoon. Your address is?"

"34 Avenue Fontaine, Room 21. It's a big pink house, with balconies."

A short time after that girl had gone with a client, he approached another.

"Give me that beautiful smile – your eyes light up the sun itself."

"34 Avenue Fontaine, Room 26. The balconies are lacy. They paint them white."

And another, "You dance so beautifully. A real Ginger Rogers."

"34 Avenue Fontaine, Room 14. There are flowers in my windows."

"A friend will help me get your prints. It might take a week or so, so please be patient. I will come by to see you when I have them ready."

The girls lived in an old hotel. He had never been in one of these establishments before. Several tables were placed in the lobby, which was obviously the area for announcing your arrival and meeting friends. A polished mahogany bar was set across the archway into a receiving area, and behind it was an enormous carved French mirror, covered with gilt and decorated with nymphs and satyrs. The expansive lobby led off to several receiving rooms, each decorated with a gaudy screen and large wicker chairs. A double staircase wound up to the second and third stories of the building.

A young man and an older woman sat in the lobby. The houseboy rose to greet him. He looked up at the tall stranger. "You want a girl?"

"Oh, I'm here with something for Leila."

"You're here to see Leila? She busy right now. Come sit down."

The older woman inquired, "You buy me drink?"

"No thank you." He paused. "I'm not thirsty right now."

"You very handsome man. Girls like you. You want to buy me a drink?"

Her black dyed hair frizzed tightly near her forehead, and her wide nose was pierced. But she had warm eyes and he needed to kill some time. He might even need her to be his friend.

"You like this place? This place is mine. You like to buy me a drink?"

"OK, what do you have?"

"We have wine."

She reached below the bar and retrieved a bottle. "This is my special drink for man I like." The ancient bottle of Mogen David had a frayed and faded label. He was startled, but determined that she would not see his ears pull back as his jaw tensed. So he smiled. She poured two drinks. He lifted his glass and took a sip. The liquor burned though his nose, some sort of homemade berry infusion into god knows what. It was purple, and it was not Passover wine.

"So, you like Leila?"

"I have a little gift for her."

"Funny, we haven't seen you before."

"Oh, I'm not a client. I'm a photographer. She is very beautiful."

"You photograph me?"

He took a flower from the vase and stood her in a corner next to a bamboo screen. She took the bottle with her. "I don't think you should put the flower into the bottle. Why don't you put it in your hair? And here, let's pose you at a three quarter angle to show off your figure. Pull your muumuu like this. You should look back over your shoulder."

She flipped her frizzy hair toward her back, some of it straggling in various other locations. But she actually had an engaging smile and he was able to make her look presentable. He moved table lamps into position so that the light fell from above and cast a soft glow around her. For a middle aged native with bad teeth, she now looked her best. She probably had been quite attractive as a young girl.

As he photographed Madame Tutau, girls passed back and forth through the lobby. Leila's guest departed, and Madame Tutau pressed the button to her room. "She will be ready to see you very soon now."

Leila came down the stairs in a beautiful violet sarong tied up over her shoulders with fresh flowers in her hair. It was evident that she had nothing on underneath. Hank took a deep breath and pulled out the manila envelope from his camera bag.

"Here are your photographs. Please let me know which ones you like, and I will enlarge some for you." He turned and addressed the proprietor. "Madame Tutau, it has been a pleasure meeting you. I hope to see you again."

"No freebies."

"No, I am not expecting freebies."

Later that week, a battleship came in with British and Australian sailors. The French half-breed whores were already languishing on the beach. Pidgin French and English sounded everywhere as the sailors struck their bargains. Once again, Hans started taking pictures of the girls. His Leica pocket camera was a standard tourist model, but he was as convincing as a Hollywood talent agent, although he had never been to Hollywood.

Three girls were left over after the sailors had made their choices for the day. He photographed them - a childlike nymph arranged shells on the beach, soft pinks and lavender hues making delicate shadows against the sand. The forms hid among pebbles of similar colors as she laid out patterns, some symmetrical and some wandering. A bare breasted matron posed with her succulent fruits. She still had some refreshments for sale. A third woman swam nude in the brilliant blue lagoon. Although her shape was visible in the water, her skin wasn't. This was the best shot of the day by far, layers of transparency distorting light and ultimately obscuring the image. This photograph engaged the imagination of the viewer. He felt like a voyeur taking her pictures as she laughed and splashed water toward him. He wished he had color film to capture the aquamarine droplets lit by the sun.

The entire scene on the beach presented a puzzle. The girls were lovely, almost childlike, but everything on the beach seemed a little too planned. Hans's business experience indicated that he was looking at a fresh enterprise.

The Sunday morning quiet of Avenue Fontaine was a pleasant contrast to the normal wartime bustle of Noumea. There were no jeeps, no shouts, and no loudspeakers. Hans made his rounds to deliver prints to the girls. It was his understanding that they had a quiet late morning, with time for church or just relaxing. He also had a large portrait of Madame Tutau. He had carefully erased some lines and shadows, and even added a gentle color wash to the flowers, as well as lips and rosy cheeks. A final touch was a white cardboard frame. Madame Tutau was at her station behind the bar, washing up glasses from a busy Saturday night.

"Good morning! You buy me a drink?"

Hans laughed easily, "It's a little early for a drink. How about later?" He looked around the lounge. "Actually, I came here to see Mei."

"Oh so now you like Mei? Mei can't see you right now."

"I think I had better wait for her. She is expecting me." He pulled up a chair next to the coffee table.

"Mei can't see you. She has guest right now." He spotted the large open book, some sort of guest registry sitting on a coffee table next to the couch.

Hans walked across to the bar, winked at Madame and said, "It's morning here, but in Amsterdam I think it's still Saturday night. Do you happen to have a beer?" Madame laughed, and pulled a good liter of Australian beer into a glass. Hans carried the beer across the room.

The rattan couch had comfortable cotton cushions, a little frayed and out of shape, but comfortable. Hans studied the reception area. There were a few calendars on the wall, both Asian and European, the same kind he had seen inside of military lockers, drugstores, and Indonesian restaurants. He returned his attention to the coffee table. A large ledger covered more than half of the tabletop. The lines were all written in different hands. Some were neat and precise, some scrawled, some hasty and some crooked, but all were legible. The columns were headed in French and English:

1) Name and nationality
2) Ship you are on
3) How many on the ship
4) How long will you be here?
5) Where will you be going from Noumea?

Each horny sailor had dutifully filled out the columns with all the pertinent information. Hans reached into his satchel. He sure hoped Mei would not be available soon. He pulled out some picture postcards and a pen. First he carefully addressed a Postcard to Amsterdam, and then began to write in Dutch. A couple entries fit onto each postcard, and then he took another from the stack. By the time Mei came downstairs, he had completed a page of entries and turned to the previous page of the ledger.

After he gave Mei her proof sheet, he sauntered back across the lobby to Madame Tutau who had been watching the two of them closely.

"I also have something for you." He held out the carefully wrapped packet, with two layers of brown paper and string protecting additional layers of cardboard and the framed picture. Madame Tutau opened up the packet, one layer at a time – almost like a woman undressing in a film. The portrait peeked out from the last layer of brown paper. She picked it up, and then looked closely at the image – a face that looked like hers, only younger and fresher.

She took a deep breath, and closed her eyes, then pulled out a handkerchief. "Hans, you are artist. I buy you drink." She poured another beer.

"Thanks, but I have to go pretty soon." The postcards pulled at his trouser pocket.

"But wait, we have to put picture on wall." She walked around the room, trying one location after another. There was a wall between two doorways, a space with nothing else to detract from the photograph. The houseboy came out, and the picture was mounted so that it could rule the game room while the lady herself ruled the bar.

Out of uniform and smelling of beer, Hank showed his ID and entered the Armed Services compound. It might be urgent that he report what he had discovered at 34 Avenue Fontaine. After a shower and a change of clothes, he went to the Office of Naval Intelligence at Admiral Halsey's Headquarters. The only problem was that no one had notified the Admiral or the Naval Intelligence command of Army's plans to infiltrate the South Pacific with "civilians" acting as tourists. His credentials looked legitimate, but this skinny man with a foreign accent did not. He asked to see Admiral Halsey. An officer at the front desk laughed.

"Not in."

"Then I shall wait."

"Nope. He's out blowing up a bunch of yellow-bellied Japs. You could wait until eternity to catch him."

"I have orders."

"Tell you what. You can talk to Jenkins here. Hey Lieutenant, you got time to talk to some foreign tourist? What hell is that accent? You German?"

"Good God, no! I was born in Amsterdam and I'm an American soldier just like you."

Lieutenant Jenkins stepped to the counter.

"Hank Burns, Sergeant, U.S. Army, sir."

"Burns. We were beginning to wonder what you were up to. You AWOL or gone native? What's going on?"

"I need to talk to Admiral Halsey."

"Good luck with that one."

"Here let me show you what I have, and then you can see if the Admiral should have a look at it."

He drew out the first postcard. Jenkins took the first card, dropped it on the floor then picked it up. He began to read it, got confused by the Dutch address, then identified dates and names of ships in the messages. He looked back up at Hank, eyes narrowed, and handed the card to another officer who started to read. Jenkins shook his head and looked back up at Hank.

"You got any more of these?"

"I have three more cards. May I please see the Admiral?"

"Good God, man. Let me go see if he's available."

Within a moment, Hank stood at attention in front of the admiral. Halsey did not acknowledge his presence. His furrowed black brow, coupled with his sharp profile, enhanced his resemblance to that bird of prey. A downturned mouth, a slight squint and a total lack of movement in his face completed the image of the predator, ready to strike. There was no sound, no motion in the small office.

Silently, Hank placed his three postcards cards in a column on the desk, like a play in an Atlantic City poker game. Halsey picked up one, and then the next. Hank could not read any expression in the Admiral's face. Resolve and discipline had molded a portrait that did not move. Then Halsey placed both elbows on the desk and covered his face with his hands.

Just as Hank was about to ask what he should do next, Halsey announced, "Those three troop ships are lost. We have no idea where they are, and we have had no messages from survivors."

Jenkins touched Hank's elbow, jerked his head toward the door, and led him out of the office to initiate a detailed debriefing.

CHAPTER 25

Bergen Belsen
November 1942

"Axis in South France, France Is Overrun: Nazis Reach Marseille After Hitler Scraps Armistice Pact; Atlantic Fleet's Fate a Mystery"

– *New York Times Headlines*

Georg Lutz stared off into space, his gray eyes looking at everything and seeing nothing. Columns of prisoners stood waiting to be counted. The first frosts were on the ground, and the dark sky did not show a hint of sunlight. He shivered under his warm overcoat. The icy cold winds began to blow through the fences.

The prisoners had no overcoats or sweaters, no winter clothes at all. As the nights got chillier people were contracting diseases. Typhus, tuberculosis and dysentery were rampant. The stench was unbearable. Lice were everywhere. So many people were dying now that the German workers no longer removed the bodies. After roll call in the mornings prisoners had to pile the dead beside the barracks, first stripping off any clothing. Sometimes the pile of emaciated bodies was six feet high before a large truck would come and take them away to the crematorium or to one of the lye filled pits.

He had begun to care for Esther. She should have been just one more expendable whore, but he enjoyed her ability to make fun of the world around her. She was like a little cat, a bit temperamental, warm and cozy, and fun to watch. And she was carrying his child.

Could this child be born? Would it? If the father was a gentile.... No, specifically if the mother was Jewish the child was a Jew. Mortal sin was at the end of every path that he explored. Abortion was not possible and it could result in Esther's death. It was unlikely that she could carry the pregnancy to term. One option had not yet been explored.

A few days later the women were lined up for work. Lutz was supervising, counting out the rows of ten haggard women, lined up for their day's assignments. He pretended that he did not notice Esther and she ignored him. Then he turned around, smacking his riding crop, and came back through the line asking, "Who knows how to sew?" Esther and some others raised their hands and were selected to follow him. He took her to a large open room, where she met a matron in charge who handed her a large stack of uniform tunics. Some had holes in them that could be patched. Others had entire panels of fabric that needed to be replaced. They were not the black SS Uniforms. Instead they were varying shades of brown, gray and gray-green. Esther pulled a tunic out of her basket. The central panel over the chest was new fabric, machine stitched to a back and sleeves that still held an odd animal smell. *Whose were they? Where had they been? All had been washed clean, but the smells of conflict were everywhere. Had men died in these uniforms? Or had they lived?* Her task for the afternoon was to remove any insignia on the tunics and replace it with the SS

Insignia, a death's head to be sewn to the collar. First yellow stars, and now death's heads marked the garments of ordinary people who faced extraordinary fates.

That night Esther lay exhausted in bed with Lutz. He began to caress her, but stopped and instead rested his head on her breasts. His urgency faded away into something gentler, and he instead stroked her abdomen. "What do you think you have? A boy or a girl?"

"What does it matter? It won't even be ours."

"The reports from Berlin are good. Maybe Germany can win this war before our baby is born."

"And how will that solve this problem?"

Lutz pretended to sleep for a few moments, and then murmured, "Because I am Austrian…we could leave after the war."

Esther lay there silently. She was not asleep – her heart had not quieted down. It was beating like bird. Now there were actually two heartbeats, trilling against each other in her body.

She did not dare speak. She did not even dare to breathe. She could not cry. The man beside her was participating in unspeakable horrors. He had ordered Greek prisoners to stack Jewish bodies for the trucks; he had been on firing squads; he had cruelly looked up and down lines of filthy starving people as they got off the trains and decided on the punishments for each. If there was a devil, he was a minion in its legions.

If she could pray, she would pray that she not feel anything. Perhaps to be a corpse in the lime pits was not the worst thing that could happen.

He broke her silence.

"Esther, I have something to tell you, something very private and very dangerous. Can you keep a secret?"

A wry grimace crossed her face in the blackness of the room.

"I am forced to be here. You know that Germany annexed Austria, right? I was an engineering student at university. They marked the honors students for the SS – the elite."

She shuddered to think what the technical education might imply. The inner workings of the camp were a maze of pipes, some with water to sustain life, others with gases to guarantee a swift meeting with death. Everything was in a system, and the systems worked with the precision of an alternate universe, a black void of space and time. The stench from the furnaces was the only evidence of imperfection in the perfect world of the German exterminators.

"You were at University?"

"Esther, does it matter?"

"I guess not, except …"

"Except you didn't expect educated people to … treat other educated people like stock animals?"

"I know nothing of farm life."

Georg began to laugh. "Actually, neither do I. All farmers do is raise animals and then butcher them to feed other animals."

"They dig up turnips and roots. The sugar beet fields stink like pig shit." They began to laugh, and then Georg went completely silent. He rolled over and pushed her shoulders into the thin mattress.

"Esther, I must perform my duties or end up at the wrong end of a firing squad. I must salute and obey. After the war it will be different. We will go far away."

She wrestled her way out from under his grasp and sat up. "Lutz, how many happy families do you see around here? I don't think we will be allowed to have our child and explain all this to him."

"Or her, if she is a beautiful little girl like you. There are some children, and some of them will live to grow up I'm sure. Even some of the guards have children."

"And where do you think we will live?"

"Somewhere warm, and in a place where it will not matter that you were born a Jew. Far from Europe. Mallorca? Maybe the Canary Islands, where you can be an artist again. We will become a good Catholic family."

CHAPTER 26

New Caledonia December 1942

"Knowing is half the battle."

~ GI Joe, Guadalcanal

New Caledonia. This forgotten isle of France was its own land. The Pink House in Noumea and its fetching French girls traveled with unknown ghosts, men who had enjoyed a pleasant afternoon and then been sent to the bottom of the Pacific, their skeletons joining up with the millions of tiny bodies that comprised the coral reefs. Predators swam through the twisted darkness, seeking smaller prey. New Caledonia was one of the smallest fish in the war, a remote island far away from occupied France.

Hank Burns sat on his bunk and shuffled his thoughts. The guest registries from the Pink House raised new questions. Who used the registers? How did scribblings of drunken sailors become lost ships? Madame Tutau had not expressed any interest in the war except for the money to be made. Someone with money and purpose was in charge, and Hank would need to trap a lot of minnows before he could hunt a shark.

Someone on the island did not want the French allies to be successful. Was it a Japanese sympathizer, or a European with Nazi sympathies? Hans began on neutral ground. In the center of town was an office with a big seal over the door, "General Consulate of the Netherlands." Faded notices in the windows and graffiti on the sign indicated that the offices had closed suddenly. No one knew where the staff had gone. Holland had not been an independent nation for two years and no one had seen the Dutch Consul in months, but it was unlikely that he had returned to a German occupied home. This was going to pose a problem for a young man presenting himself as a Dutch businessman. There was no reason for Holland to be trading anything.

Javanese traders were appearing on the island, opening their stalls in the streets. Officially they were Dutch colonials. Hans joined their social club as a trader with lucrative American contracts. Everyone planned to make money off of the Americans. A first invitation was to the home of the Javanese Consul. His secluded compound in the hills overlooked the activities at the harbor. The surrounding dark island pines contrasted with the glittering water and the hues cast by the sunset.

Memories of the palate overtook him as aromas of open fires and freshly ground spices wafted through the air. It had been years since he had enjoyed a Rijstaffel. The traditional Javanese banquet offered every kind of delicacy that the tropics could yield. One at a time the servants brought out plates of curried eggs, wrapped rolls of meats and vegetables, a delicious dish of lightly steamed vegetables in peanut sauce, and some of the hottest chilies he had ever encountered, the heat washed away with cucumber and mint. Exotic pickled vegetables and iced melons alternated with the warm dishes.

A buzz of polite conversations began over beers, anything from golf to the problems of getting qualified laborers. Words began to pop out of the discussions in the room, "Pan Asian" "independence" "failed empires." These men were nervous. Hans looked over the head of a small Javanese man who lit an immense homemade cigar, and puffed on it until it glowed a brilliant red. Smoke drifted upward toward Hans's nose and he began to cough. The little man was tired of the small talk, and the gin had loosened his tongue. "There is no way in hell that Java will join a 'Pan Asian Empire.' Why would we flee from one set of rulers to another?"

Hans nodded, shocked that this islander thought that Dutch colonial support and Japanese domination could be compared. His companion sucked nervously on the cigar, gasping like a small child whose words come so fast that it is hard to talk. "But of course, the Japanese can force islanders to go peacefully or as a vanquished people." The little man stubbed out the cigar, and Hans continued to listen to him. "The Japanese talk of a great civilization, but they are savages. They make the damned Borneo headhunters look civilized. Just ask the Chinese."

This wasn't the gossip he sought. Men were losing their lives daily to keep Japan from controlling the South Pacific islands. Other men had determined that if the Japanese lost control of the East Indies, an independent nation could emerge. These people were treasonous subjects of the Dutch Queen. No wonder the former consul was not invited to this party. He must find the consul and get a more civilized point of view. Loyalty questions were getting confusing but he was now an American, no longer a Dutch royalist.

Henrik Susilo, the Javanese host, did not support or disapprove the proposed action. Susilo continued, "After all, Holland does not actually exist any more. If we accept ourselves as Dutch, then we are German subjects. We might as well have stayed behind and become Japanese." Hans picked up a skewer of meat and gnawed at it a little at a time, chewing all the pieces in silence and sucking on the stick to avoid grinding his teeth. With just a few comments the guests had upended his impression of the gentle Javanese who had hosted him as a teenager.

Susilo poured rich cordials – tastes that he had long since forgotten. Advocaat, cocoa and ginger liqueurs all gave a heady holiday aroma to the room. "Steen, is it? A Dutchman? Where are you from?"

"Amsterdam. We had a wholesaling business on the Herengracht."

"I noticed your eyes during the conversations. Your smile said one thing; your eyes said that you were somewhere else. So what do you think of their plan for independence from Holland?"

Hans took an audible breath and stared at Susilo. He didn't want to respond with an opinion, so instead he queried. "So much has changed. Do these people have what it takes to stand on their own? They did nothing with their land for generations, unless we gave it to them."

Susilo pondered for a moment, then looked up into the face of this Dutchman who was present and absent at the same time. "Good question. Are they just feeling some power because the Allies have laid down a few roads and put up a Red Cross tent? They certainly do not understand what is needed to maintain an independent state."

Hans continued, "French, Japanese – Do the islanders really care who is in charge?"

They stood silently while a waiter brought around another tray of cordials. Susilo took a deep breath and then continued. "It seems the Japanese are selling them a notion. The Pan Asian Empire is pure bunk. The Japanese empire has never approved of mixed races. The Germans certainly do not. Why would it be different here?"

Hans's gut clenched at the mention of racial mixing. His family had done business in Asia for generations. Attacks on Jewish businesses had set this phase of his life into motion. Beads of cold sweat began to slide down his neck, and he looked for a place to sit down. Susilo noted his pale face and looked across the room, fishing for a diversion. "Ah! Naomi, *ma Cherie*! Come and meet our new friend."

Everything Hans had ever thought about mixed races dissolved the moment he set eyes on Naomi.

"Naomi works over in the offices of the French governor. But she is also part Dutch, I believe." Naomi did not look French or Dutch. She was not pale and pink skinned like the sunburned Europeans and she wasn't squat and with the broadened features of the natives. She was like no one he had ever seen before – a sylph that should be rising out of the waves, not walking across the room at a party. Tall, slender with the grace of an island star pine, she was of the trees, of the waters, and of the brightly illuminated night skies. He gazed at her caramel complexion. Was she African or Asian? Her hair was tightly knotted like the Melanesian women, but her eyes… her eyes spoke of soft sea breezes, changing lights and colors, reflecting everything in his world.

Naomi laughed, "My mother is from here, but my father was from a coffee plantation on Sumatra." This was not the time for Hans to announce that he did not like coffee. He gulped. Naomi continued

"My mother was half French and my father was half Dutch, but the rest? Who knows what the rest is?"

Hans nodded. Her short skirt swirled around her knees. My God, where did her legs end? She was nearly as tall as he, but with absolutely splendid arms and legs, like an Amazon warrior. Was she a warrior? Hard to say, but Susilo made it clear that she worked in the war offices, and that she was on the right side. The young woman was almost mythical, and he wanted to learn her myth.

CHAPTER 27

December 1942
New Caledonia

"No one likes the Americans but they go along because they owe everything to them."

~ Governor Laigret

THE MORNING QUIET WAS UNNERVING. The base should have been buzzing with excitement. After weeks of waiting for engagement, dozens of small planes had been loaded yesterday morning, flying north into Japanese held islands. Hank was called into the Captain's office. He changed twice, discarding two sweat stained garments in favor of a neat khaki shirt that would hopefully hold for an hour. His hair was slicked back from his forehead and he prayed that it would stay in place.

Mitchell was at his desk, intent on his paperwork. A stack of black bordered stationery and envelopes sat to his right, typed letters to the left. He read one typed letter, signed it, and placed it with an envelope. Hank stood quietly and read the upside down text.

The Secretary of the Army deeply regrets to inform you that your husband, John Kenneth Lyell, Sergeant U.S. Army, was killed in action in the performance of his duty and in the service of his country. The department extends to you its sincerest sympathy in your great loss. On account of existing conditions the body if recovered cannot be returned at present. If further details are received you will be informed. To prevent possible aid to our enemies, please do not divulge the name of his station.

Hank stood at full attention, lost in thought. If something happened to him, who would get the letter? Who would know that he had ever served? He had no wife, and the Amsterdam address he had listed was probably not even where his mother lived now. Esther never had told anyone where she lived. He imagined a note like this, a dead letter for a dead loved one.

It is with deep regret that I am writing to confirm my telegram of December 6, 1942, in which it was my sad duty to inform you of the death of your son...

Mitchell looked up, pulled a packet of cigarettes from his pocket, and tapped on the bottom. "At ease, Burns. Care for a cigarette?" Hank did not extend his hand and Mitchell lit up, taking a deep breath and exhaling a cloud of smoke. "Have a seat."

Mitchell studied Hank's face.

"You seem to have made some interesting friends in Noumea. What can you tell us about Madame Tutau?"

Hank pressed his brows together, planning to state exactly what he had written in his report. "She says she owns the hotel where the girls live. Of course, she is doing some illegal things."

"What does she say about the war?"

Hank thought for a moment. Madame Tutau had never once mentioned the war. "Apparently it's good for business. Soldiers are her bread and butter, but …" He clasped his hand over his eyes, trying to remember something. "I don't think she cares where they're from. The girls seem to be from all over, too, maybe French mixed with … some dark types, and Asians, but I don't know what kind. I guess it takes all kinds."

"Sort of like a fully stocked bar? This is one twisted trail. Obviously Tutau has her register, but her business records are clean. How did she get the money to buy the old hotel? Not all on her back for sure. Who does she see?"

Hank turned away, thinking deeply. His brow furrowed, eyes narrowed. He turned back to his interrogator, but his glances kept shifting as he dredged up the details of his Sunday visits.

"I never saw anybody other than a couple of houseboys who work there."

"Anyone ever come in for drinks, socializing?"

"Heck, she even socialized with me – 'Wanna buy me a drink?' So I'm not sure who else is around other than clients." His hand went up to his cheek and he scratched his nose. "But I kind of distracted her."

"What do you mean?"

"Well I needed something to do so that she wouldn't ask me questions, so I had her sit for her portrait."

The captain began to laugh uproariously. "That's all you could think to do in a whorehouse?"

"I wasn't going to put my camera down. It could get stolen. We can't replace it here. It's a Leica."

"So, Hank, how did the portrait come out?"

"Actually, she likes it very much. It's hanging on the wall over the bar."

"OK, so we've got to figure out what to do next."

Mitchell was obviously bothered by much more than just the situation. He was trying to avoid scratching a mosquito bite, moving his back across the chair until Hank wanted to just tell him scratch the darn thing.

"Who don't you know in this stewpot? Are there other Dutchmen? I haven't met any. Of course, I've hardly seen the outside of this office."

Hank's wide-eyed gaze unnerved Mitchell even more. "I want to meet the Dutch consul. This is a French colony, but the former Dutch consul apparently still lives on the island."

"How long have you known this?"

Hank flinched. "A month or two maybe? When I was getting familiar with the island. The people in the office weren't even Dutch. I've met a bunch of Javanese, but they don't seem to be very interested in Holland. So where is he? He would have had access to a lot of information, and he doesn't have a country now. "

Mitchell stamped his cigarette into an ashtray, scrubbed it out and lit another. "Geez Hank, the French in this fight aren't even from France, they're outposts of an expired empire. I can't even keep up with the news, let alone all the gossip."

Sometimes it was hard for Hank to remember that Americans had blinders on when it came to colonial loyalties. They were great fighters but not particularly curious. The inbred instincts of the trader merged with his understandings of materiel needed for combat.

"Who controls the nickel mines and how are they selling it?"

Mitchell paused again. "Well, hard to say. These guys are all exporting metals. You know that. You came down here packed in with a load of steel. Natives work the nickel mines. Half of the French owners are descended from grandparents who were exiled from France, so they are all out for themselves."

"Somebody's making an awful lot of money in stainless steel. Rusty guns are no use to anybody." Hank thought about the immense spools of cable in the shipyard.

Mitchell dragged on the cigarette, then stubbed it out in the ashtray. He could hardly find room in the pile of butts and ashes that overflowed the little steel dish. He pulled out another one and started to light it, fished for his lighter and then set it aside. Hank did not carry matches. "Why don't you go and find out?"

A wry smile peeked out from under Hank Burns's serious expression. All that stuff must get smelted somewhere. The question was, who got the stainless steel after that? The merchants he had met as a kid were a bunch of salesmen who would trade their own mothers to make a profit. Their money would be God knows where, their goods would vary from day to day, and their houses would all be rented, that's for sure. On the island – off the island? Who knew? Hank decided to invite Naomi Batari to lunch.

He dialed the French Governor's office, hoping that she really did work there.

"Ah, it's good that I found you. This is Hans, or Hank as the Americans call me. We met at Henrik Susilo's Christmas party last week."

She paused, as if trying to remember him. "You are the Dutchman, yes? How can I help you?"

"Do you happen to know when the next supply ship is coming in? They are running out of coffee on the base, and I thought I might try to locate some for sale. Americans aren't going to fight a war without their morning coffee."

She laughed. "Ah yes, and they would prefer our French coffee if they can get it. I can ask Governor Laigret to see what we can do."

"Boy, I would owe you if you could arrange that." He began to get nervous as he remembered why he was calling her. "Naomi, it would be very nice to see you again. But I'd rather take you to lunch. So, do you think you can work up an appetite in the next couple hours?"

"I'm pretty sure that will be possible. Let's meet at Surya's, the little café down by the beach."

Hank arrived fifteen minutes early at a hut that didn't seem too promising. He looked around for someone to seat him at a table for two and finally just walked down the sidewall to the back and sat down. The sound of a muted trumpet reverberated into the air, a jazz tune winding its way through tinny speakers. It wasn't ideal, but it was dark and he didn't want to share his conversation with dozens of other people. As he studied the menu, a flash of white appeared by his side, a swinging pleated skirt with a middy top. The legs were unmistakable and he invited Naomi to sit down.

Her smile reminded him of his sister Esther, sly and mischievous, internal jokes playing in her silence. They spoke in French. She picked at her food delicately, cutting tiny bites and savoring the morsels. Then she put a mango on a fork, sliced just the skin into quarters, peeled it back like a flower and devoured the soft orange flesh. He wished he were a mango, consuming her attention in the same way, intent and sensuous at the same time.

He picked up his knife and fork and dove into his fruit plate, dicing the soft flesh into neat cubes. When they stood in the sunshine for their goodbyes he shook her hand. She grabbed him by the shoulders and kissed his cheek.

That afternoon he requested a short follow-up meeting with Mitchell. "Captain, sir, I have an idea." Mitchell looked across the desk. What was his boy up to now?

"Can you get me six sets of sharp household knives? Different kinds? Sheffield, Solingen, a couple of Laguiole hunting knives? Maybe some Japanese ones too? A cutlery dealer would be able to make friends with people living on these isolated plantations." He ran his fingers through his hair. "I also need a shave and a haircut, everything off, even the mustache. And I would like some tinted eyeglasses, just enough brown to cover my eye color, and a new business suit. Also cards, Hans Steen, International Dry Goods.... Here, let me give you an address in Amsterdam. And the suit needs to have inside pockets to hold my Leica without showing any bulge."

"What are you thinking?" Mitchell was intrigued by this man's ability to think on his feet.

They planned the mission. Who might he be meeting? What were their fears? The French locals who lived here were descended from criminals and communards with no particular loyalties to Free France, Vichy France, Occupied France, or otherwise. They would be out for themselves. Knives would be good, solid, household tools, Solingen steel. He would sell them as housewares, but they could be used for protection. He should be able to learn a lot with this ruse.

Mitchell listened intently, then put both elbows on his desk. He folded his hands and dropped his chin into the hammock of fingers. "You say the Indonesians may buy the Japanese idea of a Pan Asian empire? Sounds like they don't want to fight."

Hans asked, "With all due respect, sir, is anyone even left in Indonesia to make that decision? We've got more Indonesians here than up there. The ones I met out at Susilo's want to take back the islands, but not as colonies. Would we let that happen?"

"Do I look like some Swami fortuneteller?" Mitchell pulled out a white handkerchief and wiped his forehead. "The Japs look like they're ready to sweep the entire Pacific. We're here to stop them and not to save a bunch of European colonies. Boys are losing their lives on a bunch of damn floating rocks."

Two days later, with a tropical suit and a case full of knives and kitchen accessories, Hans Steen donned his new tinted glasses and set out for the interior. The former consul was believed to be on his farm, some 60 miles north on the lengthy island.

There was a detachment up in the area, all commanded by a U.S. Army Colonel. Hans was on his own now, with his sample case and his camera.

CHAPTER 28

New Caledonia, December 1942

"...the Free French colony of New Caledonia could avoid the horrors of war if the colony would return to neutrality and Vichy control."

~ Radio Saigon

Silence of the jungle contrasted with the pounding in Hanks' head and the constant juddering of the jeep. Like a high-speed film, tales of chaos and death had wound their way through barracks and bars. Thousands of young men who fell would never see home, laugh with a girl, or enjoy a cold beer again. Others would be maimed outside and in. Hank had not been in harm's way yet.

The Captain's orders were, "Somebody, somewhere knows something. Right now we know squat. Find out who is watching the coast." Coast watchers were all over the place, but their information could change by the minute, depending on how well they were paid. Hopefully, the ex-consul could help him learn more about the islanders.

Flickers of light between branches exacerbated the migraine and he squeezed his eyes shut. A lot was riding on his instincts and his ability to remember what he saw. Nausea from the migraine was getting worse. He pulled his arms across his narrow chest and grasped his gut.

How strange that this remote island would be the area to stage a war involving the fate of millions. The road through the jungle slashed through an undergrowth of unrecognizable vegetation. Hank began to take deep breaths. A canopy of trees reached a hundred feet high. Symmetrical branches and crooked trunks reminded him of people he had known, ones who appeared to be completely in control on the outside, while they concealed their inner mysteries. The stillness of this place contrasted sharply with the frenzied activity in Noumea.

As the jeep bumped along, Hank rehearsed behaviors that would make him appear calm and collected. The tinted glasses in his new disguise would help cover his eyes, especially the way they tended to dart as he observed his surroundings. He focused his gaze as if he were looking through a lens. What would this look like if he were hurrying the other direction? Some spots were particularly dense with distinctive branch patterns. A large rock stood alone in the path, forcing the road to curve toward a stream. Constant movement of the vegetation gave him a feeling not unlike being at sea.

December's mid-summer sun and suffocating humidity pulsed through the atmosphere. The road took on a diffused glow as they neared the sea on the other side of the island. Near the top of the ridge smaller clearings of bushes came alive with the sounds of birds. At another time this would be a fine spot to walk and reflect. With no time for photography, he would have to take away the pictures in his memory.

Sweat poured off the driver's neck, and Hank worried that his new tropical suit might show the patterns of sweat from where his back was sticking to the seat. On the other hand, a few wrinkles and stains might add a well-traveled authenticity to the traveling salesman. The borrowed display case had battered corners and scratches on the hardware. It would have to do.

The jeep pulled to an abrupt stop at a landscaped dirt road. There were no addresses, but area looked right. Apparently, the former consul lived on a coffee plantation somewhere around here and owned an interest in the nickel mines. The highway continued toward the harbor at Thio, where the mountain streams carved out a mooring place between the coral reefs. At the harbor the jeep would get lost in the maze of heavy equipment, turn around, and head back to Noumea.

The driver spoke, "It should be this turn. There's a plantation house about half a mile down the road. If you run into any problems, we have an army detachment just south and a little in from the road. It's just a pile of camouflaged tents." Hank nodded. "Hey buddy, you're looking pale. Are you sure you're going to be OK out here?"

"I'm fine. Good day – and thanks for the lift."

The driver looked at him once more. Fear does not make a man a coward. Doing a job under pressure takes courage, and Hank was eager underneath his pallor. "Come back in one piece, OK?"

Hank nodded and jumped out.

Walking down the road toward the house, he became Hans Steen, housewares merchant. A chunky Javanese woman squatted in the gardens, harvesting some greens.

"Selamat pagi! Good morning! Can you tell me where I might find the big boss?" Hopefully her explanations would not be too detailed. He couldn't remember much more Malay than that, the opening line of the sales pitches he had made with his father 10 years ago.

A broad smile and a gesture pointed him toward a white house with a large veranda, shaded by strange vines.

He climbed the wide steps and, clearing his throat, knocked on a massive teak door. Someone of importance lived here but it didn't look like a consulate.

The door pulled open slowly, revealing a stoop-shouldered man in the shadows. Hans addressed him in Dutch, "*Goedemorgen!* Good morning. I am looking for the Dutch consul. I need some help." Hans continued babbling away in Dutch, a long story about his being on a Dutch merchant ship that had left the Noumea harbor without everyone on board.

The man blinked and furrowed his dark eyebrows, peering at the figure silhouetted by the sun. "*Parlez vous Francais*?"

French. Oh God. It was going to be a long day. Hans began his story again in French, then broke it off and interrupted his narrative with an appeal for help. "*Voulez vous aidez-moi, s'il vous plais?* Can you help me?"

"Mon plaisir, entrez vous!" The shoulders straightened, and the eyebrows lifted to reveal a gracious smile. It was evident that European guests did not often appear at this door, and that he was welcome to come in.

Hans joined his host in the foyer, and an indoor servant brought a tray of coffee and fresh fruits. "*Bon jour Monsieur, Je suis Henri Chemin.* How can I help you?" Hans demurred, just long enough to rethink his story, changing some details to keep the pieces consistent. It was one thing to seek a consul who had left a town that was going to war, and quite another to barge in on an unknown planter. He looked around the room with its heavy carved teak furniture and Indian carpets. Perched near a window was a large black bird with a red tail and a fluffy crest. It was clearly not a raven or a crow. The cockatoo tilted its head and glared at him as he began to make up his story.

Chemin interrupted the tale. He lit a cigarette and placed it in an ivory holder. He offered Hans a cigarette, and Hans apologetically replied that he did not smoke. The bird flew over and perched on his shoulder, bending its neck for a scratch behind the crest. *"Ah, Pluton! Tch –tch–tch."* Pluton picked up a cigarette in his claw and tore it to pieces, bits of tobacco hanging off his beak.

"So, what kind of ship were you on?"

"Dutch Merchant Marine, the Amstelkerk." He deliberately gave the name of a ship that now lay on the bottom of the Indian Ocean. "I had some business in Jakarta and in South Africa. I'm so sorry – I only know French from school and I'm not sure I can explain everything." He patted the case. "I'm just a housewares salesman, but the war is making it difficult for us to do business. European shops are empty because so many of our trade routes are closed. I'm not finding the sources for new products."

Chemin set down his French china cup and saucer. "Dutch Merchant Marine you say? How interesting. I thought that Holland had forfeited her ships."

Hans spotted the red flag of conquest immediately, but Chemin continued, "Some come out of England, don't they?" He ran his hand through his hair. "Where was your ship headed?" Chemin picked up a few pieces of strange fruit, bit the ends off and began to tear out the succulent inner sections. Their red prickly skin covered a soft white inside. He spat out the large seeds. There was no way to eat the lychees politely with a fork and knife. Hans picked up a banana and removed his pocketknife to peel and slice it, carefully stripping off the tough skin.

He shrugged his shoulders. "You know, that is where it gets interesting. We were going to South Africa to pick up a load of steel. They have huge scrap yards there – every ship that has ever broken up on the reefs."

"So you were coming from Java toward South Africa, and...What were you doing on our beach anyway?"

Hans munched on a piece of banana, and recalled his days on the beaches. "They had a pick-up at Thio, and one over in Noumea. It was going to take them about six hours to unload supplies, so I thought I would take a little break. I met a pretty French girl on the beach." A guilty laugh was enough to set an impression on his host. He fixed his glance on a small statue behind his host, sitting on a table at the rear of the room. It was an exquisite bronze of a Japanese warrior, probably a souvenir from the opening of Japan to the West. Well, Japan wasn't open any more

"I was supervising a few crates of cargo for trade– you know, European housewares for South Africa. People still want feather beds and kitchen knives that cut something more solid than butter." He reflected on what he wanted Chemin to know. "But a lot of the cargo bays had been converted into bunks." The man was insatiably curious and the questions were on the wrong side of the conversation.

Chemin responded, "I never heard of the Amstelkerk. Is it a large ship?"

"No, I try and travel on the smaller boats. It's easier to get through customs; people aren't that interested in them." Obviously, Chemin knew how to interrogate. Hans would need to make sure his information was accurate.

"How large a crew does it take to run a cargo ship?" The simple question needed an ingenuous answer.

"When I was out here as a boy, there were only about a dozen crew members. But now there were soldiers on board, English or American. It seems like everybody wants to get into this damned war. Anyway, I was surprised that Dutch ships would be used to deliver men to the islands."

"Ah well, my friend, cargo is cargo. We shall see. I'm afraid we know nothing about ships here. We don't exactly have passenger lines coming back and forth through this harbor."

This was most definitely not a Dutch consulate. The man did not comment at all on the status of Holland, which was now annexed by Germany. The question was, what was he? Either war interfered with the quietude of plantation life, or he had some interests. So far, so good. Maybe this was just a coffee plantation. Hans commented on the coffee. Its mild flavor and exceptional aroma were very pleasing, a far cry from the bitter swill that the soldiers swallowed by the bucket each day.

"Oh that's right – in Holland they don't have tea or coffee, do they? Or sugar or bacon? Good thing we're out here where plenty of everything grows all year round. I would like to invite you to stay as my guest to dinner. You might enjoy some really excellent French cooking, and I would enjoy European company for a change." He called for a servant, and then spoke rapidly regarding a menu, wines and cheeses. Even if the visit were uneventful, Hans Steen would leave with a full stomach. Then Chemin suggested, "Shall we take a walk? You can accompany me on my duties and we will figure out how to get you off of this island. There aren't a lot of choices right now."

They stepped out behind the house and an enormous vista opened up, a river spilling out toward the ocean, and an isolated green cove sliced down between layers of rocks. The plateau extended until its vegetation slipped away and was replaced by sand and rock. There was not a footprint in sight. This contrasted sharply with the old hardware resting in the distance. Heavy industrial towers were rooted into the coral reefs by pylons, and ship-loading platforms extended out toward the sea. On the shore, Hans spotted roofs of mining shacks, and piles of ore. "What is that?"

"Oh, Société Le Nickel – a French mining company. Can you still get nickel steel for your housewares and knives? It doesn't rust you know." Chemin peered at him closely. "Do you carry stainless steel?"

Hans flinched, and hoped that it wasn't seen. He tried to continue smoothly. "I also carry fine Damascene knives, one of a kind items. Of course, those are carbon steel. Lagouile is probably my favorite for …" He had to think. He didn't know how to cook, he had never hunted, and he had never fought with a real blade.

Chemin spoke. "Ah yes, a fine French hunting knife. There is nothing like it for field dressing game meat. I used to have one. Killed a huge razorback with it. It is a challenging beast." Chemin's eyes brightened. "And the animal circled around, hunting me. A tiger will charge you, face to face, but the wild boar is the only animal I know of that will hunt the hunter. When the boar starts to hunt you, it is not for sport. He intends to kill. He was too close in for my rifle, so I used a Colt 45 to take him down. The Laguoile finished him." Chemin then expanded his chest, revealing a powerful back and shoulders. He grasped the imaginary dagger in his left fist and slashed downward. "That bastard must have weighed 100 kilos, and I had to carry him on my back after he was gutted."

Hans felt his blood run cold, and then continued his sales pitch. "Yes, each of the custom knives has to be certified by a Master Bladesmith. I can show you one if you would like." In his mind he reviewed the presentation that he had rehearsed.

"That would be very interesting I'm sure."

Hans looked at Chemin, and realized that he was much smaller and half the strength of a boar. He needed to keep focused on his sales presentation, or he could end up roasted with some yams.

"So, my young Dutchman, how is it that you can have German and French and English wares in the same case?"

Nerves made it hard to sustain a silence and the young Hans Steen began to babble. "Oh, we try to get what our customers ask for. It is private trade. Some of the families we work with date to my grandfather's time. We have known each other all our lives, and we will continue to do business after this war too."

"Ah, a profiteer!"

"Well, I haven't really paid attention to who is getting what, or from where. Obviously I need to." The response seemed acceptable to Chemin who could use this to decide that his young salesman wasn't very knowledgeable about the details. Ah well, Chemin had never actually operated a steam shovel and he owned a significant interest in excavating a nickel mine.

They took another path back toward a lovely pavilion, with its open sides covered by the branches of several large bushes. Tall pines formed the end wall, with coconut matting hung to shield the sun. Apparently there was electric lighting, because conduit pipe or something similar ran up the side of a tree. There weren't any light fixtures. Hank smelled chocolate, or did he? Something reminded him of chocolate. Large buds or pods hung from the branches, gold, green, red and even violet. Some were turning brown. What on earth was this? Chemin looked at him, "Ah yes, you are Dutch, and these are cacao trees. It is a delicious scent, *non*?"

As a child, Hans remembered weekend visits to a village of windmills. But the dried brown pods that were ground into Dutch cocoa? Of course. They had to come from somewhere. He had always assumed South America, but why not here as well? Chemin rang a bell, and a girl appeared with a bottle of white wine and two glasses. "The wine is from Australia. It's not French, but it is quite good. A little sweet perhaps, but still refreshing." He sniffed the wine and poured.

"Let me have a boy bring out your display." He clapped his hands, and gave rapid instructions in a dialect that Hans did not understand. The case appeared momentarily. Hans readied his memorized commentary on the Lagouile knives.

"The Damascus blade is handmade of carbon steel." Hans pulled a folding knife from the case. "I can demonstrate three of the tests that are used for the highest quality blades. First of all, the blade must be able to cut through a three-centimeter rope. May I show you with one of these vines?" He grasped a heavy vine and tried to pull it straight to slash the blade across.

"May I?" Chemin took the knife and cut through the vine in one immensely powerful swipe. "What else is this supposed to do?"

"The blade should be sharp enough to shave the hair off your arm."

Chemin laughed and grabbed Hans by the arm as he rolled up the younger man's shirtsleeve. But Hans had no body hair at all, except for the thick pelt on his head. Chemin held his arm tightly, and turned the wrist over, the soft white flesh an inch from the razor sharp blade. Chemin dropped his captive's wrist, took the knife and shaved a patch off his own arm.

"So, I can see you have brought the real items. Let's talk business after dinner. Don't plan on hitchhiking back tonight --- we have several rooms. I will even give you a lift tomorrow if you can wait until afternoon."

A servant escorted Hans up to a fresh guest room where he enjoyed a good washing up and a short nap before dinner. He could rest his aching feet and sore shoulder, but he must stay vigilant. He had brought no clothes to dress for dinner, but then again, this was an impromptu visit.

A grilled lobster was offered for the first course, and Hans struggled with the beast. He was highly motivated to extract it from the shell and dip into the real drawn butter on the table, but there weren't any tools. A platter of coconut rice appeared with a collection of fish, yams and chicken. Hans had almost no experience in eating with his hands. Chemin observed his discomfort, then picked up a claw and bit through the shell. This boy had not spent much time in the islands, no matter what his story. He certainly ate like a Dutchman, afraid to touch his food and lost without a knife and fork.

"We have come far, have we not?" The bushy eyebrows converged in the center of Chemin's face. "My grandparents were not traders. They were communards, prison laborers, and I am the son of prisoners. Do you see that stone bridge? I own that. It was built with the blood and sweat of my family. So now I have this lovely plantation, on an island that is overrun with uninvited guests. I have never even seen France."

Hans realized at that moment that he had not seen Holland in nearly four years. Europe was so far away that he could actually feel the earth spinning out of control. This island was supposed to be Free French, but known Vichy sympathizers, at least those who had not fled to Indochina, owned many of the large plantations.

"My dear friend, there is a little business to do tonight. I think we agree that we cannot let this war disrupt our trade. Do you need to get in touch with anyone? They must know you are missing by now. Hopefully, you haven't missed any important appointments in your misadventure. I have a short wave radio. We can let them know where you are."

Hans covered his mouth and then reflected. "I work for myself. Durban can wait."

Chemin commented, "Come on, young man. Bring your brandy and we'll go downstairs. I need to send a message to my brother. *Bâtard stupide* is in Tonkin." A simple den with a short wave radio was built into the foundation of the house. The short wave radio was large, more than twice the size of what he had seen in the army offices in Noumea. He wasn't sure if that meant anything.

The brandy burned a hole in Hans's stomach. At the same time, he felt a sense of exhilaration as the puzzle began revealing itself. Chemin pulled out a large sheet of paper – a ledger sheet – and began to type in code. "Beep, bip, bip, bitty, bitty, beep" ran in endless strings. Then more beeps and blips came into the receiver. Damn. Hank could only do code slowly and in English. But his eyes took over for what he could not memorize by ear. Hank was so stunned that he had to remember to keep breathing; the sheet that Chemin was transmitting from looked exactly like the pages from the ledger at Madame Tutau's establishment. The same drunken scrawls, the same number of columns, line after line of information from inebriated U.S., Anzac and French soldiers.

"*Merde!* Must get off this signal – The U.S. has some high powered coding equipment, and I really don't want them to know we are here." Chemin tapped furiously, and observed his guest. Hans let his eyelids droop and began to stretch and yawn. Good thing he had made this trip with no identification on him except the Dutch passport. He needed to keep his body at rest while he concentrated on the game. Should he spring and try to take Chemin, or might he be better off curling up and going to sleep? He had just awakened to the fact that he really didn't know much about operating a radio. It was time to end this convivial evening.

"That's right – you hitchhiked and walked many kilometers today looking for some help. Well, you have help. It may not be the kind you need, but it's what I have to offer. Sorry about the confusion over the consul. They left years ago."

"Look, I have a quick errand in the morning. Sleep in, and we will have an excellent café au lait after I get back." He faltered for an uncomfortable few seconds, as if he were trying to make some type of plan to hold Hans at bay until his interrogation was complete. "I'll even have the kitchen bake up some croissants."

The night was humid and Hans was sleepless. Wariness had turned into fear. A canopy of mosquito netting provided a small shelter, but in his nightmares it transformed first into a snarl of tangled fabric restricting his very breathing, and then became a series of ghosts, which thank God, he did not believe in. His goal now was to get out of here without turning into a ghost, or a piece of tiger bait in the jungle. He checked and rechecked the lock on the door, closing all windows tightly so that not so much as a breeze could enter his room.

Toward dawn the rustling and shrieks of small parrots disturbed his uneasy rest. Pluton would wake the household if he heard any unusual noise, and the last thing Hans wanted was a trip to the underworld. After dawn broke, he waited to hear Chemin's car start up. A hunting knife was already strapped into his ankle scabbard, the Leica in his pocket. He picked up his case and quietly stepped off the porch and onto the front path. Turning a corner away from the house, he was grateful for the perimeter walk the previous evening. Now to flee down the road.

The forest was dense, with vines on the ground, but it covered a lone man. His paces were fast and silent. However, the tan business suit did not camouflage well within the jungle and he made a point to move off the path and into the patterned light of the trees. This morning he wasn't sure if he was the predator or the prey. He was relieved when, within half an hour he spotted some camouflaged tents, stepped in toward the guard and asked to see the Captain.

"Who the hell are you?"

"Hank Burns with CIC, and I have instructions to return to Admiral Halsey's offices. The mission is classified, and I do need your assistance. "

"Hey Joe! We gotta guy with a foreign accent who wants to visit the Admiral!"

"That's a good one. What kind of accent?"

"Sounds like a German Schweinhund to me."

Hank interrupted. "Dutch."

"OK, Says he's Dutch. Are they even in this game?"

"What's he got for ID? "

"There's no ID. Says he is under cover."

"Then put him back undercover. That's what we got a jungle for."

"Wait a minute – says he knows Mark Mitchell. OK buddy – how do you know Mitchell?"

"He's my boss. I work for him."

"What's his rank?"

"Captain"

"You know his serial number?"

Hank panicked. He had never been told to memorize serial numbers. The soldiers laughed.

"Listen, you could be legit, but we have to radio up ahead and find out. It could take a while depending on what the action is today." Hank sat down on a metal chair outside of the camp. At least he hadn't been thrown back out into the jungle. He didn't want to be seen at all, especially not by Chemin. He tried to not tap his feet or indicate any type of anxiety. Pacing back and forth would be a bad idea too.

A soldier in full uniform came out to meet him. "Get in the jeep. We'll take you in."

CHAPTER 29

Bergen Belsen
February 1943

Response from the Pope following the murder of more than 200,000 Ukrainian Jews: "to bear adversity with serene patience"

~ Pius XII

Georg Lutz looked peacefully around his quarters. Within these walls he had everything he needed, a simple bed, warm clothing and a woman whose bright spirit gave him a smile or two each evening. A second bed was attached to the outside wall, and he did not currently have a bunkmate. Esther could stay with him through the harsh winter nights, and sleep in a warm featherbed. But tonight he had serious thoughts on his mind. He looked at her swollen belly. They had been living together for six months now and, at some point, there would not be just the two of them. His frayed vision of humans was to undergo still another transformation.

"Esther, when Jews pray, what language do they use to speak with God?"

She laughed, "Oh, I forget all those prayers. We went to Hebrew school. The prayers are in Hebrew."

"I was wondering about that. Jesus must have spoken Hebrew. So, when you pray, do you pray in Hebrew?"

"God and I are no longer on speaking terms. And I don't see any churches around here either." She looked at him intently. He had not flinched at her remark, but she knew she had said something harmful, even dangerous. "Lutz, in what language do you pray?"

"Funny you should ask that. We were taught to pray in Latin. I can recite all the prayers, but I don't think I have thought about their true meanings since I was a child."

He looked at her belly. "I want to live in a pretty town with a nice church, but I think our child should learn to pray … in some other way, not reciting verses in languages that are no longer spoken."

Esther stretched her back, arching it and extending her arms and legs. That was better. The chair pressed. She no longer had enough flesh on her thighs to sit comfortably. She lay down, and then stood up again. Finally she crouched in a squatting position to relieve some of the pain. Lutz removed his black uniform and pulled on a soft loden green sweater, one that had been with him all his life. The sweater reminded him of home in Tyrol, and quiet evenings under the stars. Evenings here in this cold living graveyard were another kind of quiet.

"Did your family worship together?"

"There is a very old synagogue in Amsterdam. We went there for special events and holiday services. My brothers' bar mitzvah services were there. The place was huge. A hundred guests did not even fill…." Her eyes began to shift around the room, and she blinked then wiped her face with her sleeve.

"I didn't know you had brothers. What happened to them?"

"You tell me. My parents and Max were picked up on July 22nd. Where did they go?" Lutz looked down, and rubbed his forehead. He began to fiddle with the buttons on his sweater vest. Out of reflex, but not empathy, Esther began to rub his temples. The bastards knew what they were doing, and he didn't even have the courage to say so. But she was an actress now, and acting was her path to freedom, if such a thing would ever exist again.

"How is it that you didn't come here until August?"

"I ran out of the theatre. I knew where to hide in the streets, but I got picked up again."

Lutz gently ignored her pointed query. "You said, 'brothers.' How many did you have?"

"My brother Hans left Amsterdam in July 1939. He was of age and decided to seek his fortune in America." She began to mentally check her facts, of why she had refused passage, and of her attachments to previous lovers. She did not want to continue this conversation, but Lutz was now curious.

"Hans was my best friend. He liked to be quiet and look at things. We used to play elaborate tricks on our governesses. But he spent more and more time with his stamps and his cameras. He hoped to go to New York and take pictures for magazines. He could see things that others couldn't, like patterns and shadows, things that are there and not there." Now the tears did begin to flow. Her last meeting with Hans had been anything but cordial and, on top of that, she had been wrong. The mirrors of the Café Americain began to flash through her mind, like some kind of Hollywood movie, but not a happy one with singing and dancing. She had made an awful error in judgment. Now she was paying the price. Sick that she couldn't justify her actions. How do people recover from mistakes? Were the tears sadness, regret or anger? She had no way of knowing.

Lutz looked at her. "You are so pale. Please don't get sick. Maybe we can find your brother after the war."

It was evident that she was dizzy, and she dropped onto the narrow bunk with its simple quilt. Lutz had a feather bed on his, bedding confiscated from arriving Jews. But she couldn't sleep. Where was Hans, and what was he doing now? The Americans were in the war. Maybe he came back to Europe to save his family, and then… and then what?

Confused images of Amsterdam, mostly red bricks and white patterns of window frames criss-crossed through her dreams. That and the waters of the canals flowing past her bedroom window. Then, she was in the canal, in a boat, all wet.

She awoke, "My God, I have wet the bed, and it's still coming, the waters will not stop." Water flowed from her body, but it didn't smell like urine. She shook Lutz, crying, "Something is wrong – water is coming." He reached around her to comfort her, and then felt it – her bed was drenched.

"I'm not peeing, but the water is coming everywhere." Then she began to shake uncontrollably. They got out of the bed, and he sat her in a chair. The cotton batting in the mattress was soaked through. They couldn't take it outside to dry in the mid-winter. It would freeze and thaw for days. There were no other sheets. She clenched her teeth with a groan. Grabbing her abdomen, she began to cry again. "I think the baby is coming."

Lutz looked at her in astonishment. "I thought babies didn't come for nine months."

"I have no idea, but sometimes they come early." She got up and began to pace the room frantically, cleaning the spotless table. A few minutes later, she doubled over with another groan. "It's the baby, I can feel it." They were both terrified of this moment. Lutz had asked a lot of questions about the camp hospital. There were no real doctors and nurses, just a few medical researchers who were investigating the physical abnormalities that made someone a Jew or a homosexual. They were working to perfect the human race, and here in Bergen Belsen they had an excellent laboratory.

On the farm in Austria Lutz had seen sheep deliver, and one time he had assisted his father with a horse that was struggling to deliver its colt. But he had no idea how it worked with human women. He placed the wool blankets on the wet mattress and suggested that they lie down again. He tried to rub her stomach as she groaned in pain. She got up to walk, but nothing relieved it. She could not miss the morning roll call, or she would be severely punished. Finally he put on his uniform jacket, went to the hospital and asked for a nurse to come with him. Someone was sick, and needed attention. The nurse walked with him back toward the barracks. When they turned on the light, Esther looked at them both, and then covered her mouth as she doubled over again. The nurse assessed the situation. "She is in labor. What we need to know is, how often are the pains coming? And has her water ruptured?"

Lutz stared at her. "The water?"

"Yes, the baby sits in a pouch of water in the woman's body. When the pouch breaks, labor begins and the baby comes."

Lutz pulled back the bedding. "Do you mean like this?"

"When did that happen?"

"A little after midnight, I think."

"Is this your baby? Or is she one of the whores?"

"Certainly it is my baby. We live together. She has never even visited the brothel."

"Keep her quiet, and I will go for a stretcher. We need to take her to the hospital. She is so thin, it is impossible to know if the baby is fully developed. Her belly looks awfully big for seven months, but we will see. Sir, do you want her back after she delivers, or shall we place her somewhere else?"

"I want them with me."

The nurse stared at him. Clearly he was out of his mind. But she was also not going to argue with an officer. He thought this Jewish infant would be going into the nursery. She would instead notify a commandant that he would need to be counseled. Georg's arm was drawn across Esther's swollen waist, now and then sensing the spasms that radiated up her back. He held her tightly while they were waiting for the stretcher. "This is not the place to talk of love, but we will be together." A second nurse followed the stretcher, and gave Esther a shot to quiet her down. Screams should not be heard outside. The SS Officer's quarters were a place of rest. The grounds of this place were silent as death, and not to be disturbed by the crying of women and children.

As the stretcher came into the brightly lit hospital hallway, a couple of thick-waisted women with flashlights examined Esther. A square jawed blonde with a nose like a potato glared at her sharply. "Well, Jew bitch, now you see what comes from your whoring." Esther glared at her, silent. They removed her trousers and then lifted her onto a table, with one of the women grasping her legs. "Gitta, can you examine her?" Birgitta's dirty hand reached inside, scraping her vitals. Esther screamed all the screams that had been packed inside her for the past year and cried all the tears that had not been shed in the barracks night after night. Gitta's hand was covered in blood. Great clots of dark flesh dropped out onto the table, and the blood poured from Esther. A dark haired nurse in a white cap gasped, then commented, "Gitta, be careful. *Leutnant* Lutz wants this one back."

Gitta laughed, "We have lots more where she came from."

Esther saw the open razor first, held out in the nurse Jutta's hand. If she died in this moment,…. The searing pain came again and, before she could breathe, Jutta lowered the knife into an area near her buttocks. "I'll take care of this one myself. We have to serve the officers even if one of them has a Jew baby. Girl, can you push now, very hard?" Esther screamed again as the pressure on her body exploded into a new spasms of energy. The infant shot out of her like a cannonball. "It's a little boy." Esther closed her eyes.

Jutta took a look at the baby - unfortunately it was not stillborn, even though Esther had arrived at the camp in August. It was perfect, and he cried as he entered the harsh lights of the cold room. Esther heard his cries, like those of a kitten, and tried to sit up. Jutta and Birgitta looked at each other. "What do we do? Lutz will want his son."

"Lutz doesn't have a son. That baby is the son of a Jewish bitch." Then she commented, "I will take him to the nursery," and wound him tightly into the dirty sheets, swaddled from head to toes until he went limp and silent.

Esther was carried back to her bunk where she lay for days, clouded by pain and fever. A restless sleep relieved some of the exhaustion, but it was not enough to obscure her memory of the brutal strangling of her infant son. Lutz did not come to see her, and he did not summon her. The nurses said that the baby was stillborn. Maybe they weren't even wrong, but it was terrifying how practiced they were at silencing a newborn whose eyes never opened to the cruelty of the world.

What could she possibly say to Lutz if she ever did see him again? Right now she was barely alive. Her fiction had worked. Maybe he was right and someday they would settle, have other babies, and become a good Catholic family. Why not?

The matron announced that she would be assigned to a brothel as soon as she was healed from the birth, and that was an optimal fate. Lutz was young, compassionate and had cared for her. There was no message from him. What did she expect? Flowers? Grinding under pigs did not appeal. She wasn't afraid of pain, but revulsion could say too much. The alternative would be that they would find no use for her.

Silence was her only defense, so for days she did not look up and she did not speak. Hannah thought she was praying, that the words were just packed up inside. Where was God now? No book existed to make this right. The empty myths only work when we are getting what we need. Then we can think of benevolence and fairness. Not in these days.

A bird built its nest in the rafters of the women's building. The huge wooden beams provided a platform for safety. Now the cheeps of babies came from the nest, and parents flew back and forth with tiny bugs for them. Soon little heads began to peek over, chirping bits of life. Even in hell, spring would come once again. Part of the earth might live.

A farm girl from Brabant began to complain about the birds, the bird shit and the early morning noises. She hated the sun peeking through cracks in the walls, threatening the arrival of still another day. The girl began to gather a small pile of pebbles, stacking them up on the rail of her upper bunk. One morning in the predawn darkness, she tore a strip of fabric to make a small sling, placed the rock in it and whirled it through the air. It clattered against the beam. Another rock flew. Naked and blind, the first baby bird fell out of the nest. Pelting the nest with rocks, Annaliese continued until all the birds had been killed.

Esther began to sob, at first gently then uncontrollably. Hannah tried to subdue her, first with a gentle rub to her back, and then taking her head and holding it to her own breast. Esther clawed at her dearest friend, screaming with rage. A second girl began to cry, as the perpetrator laughed. The wails increased to screams splitting the air, loud enough to bring a matron to the barracks.

The matron looked at the dead birds. "Savages, you are all savages, filthy… you never were human in the first place." She pulled the whip off her belt.

"Esther, stop crying. Immediately!

Anneliese, you will come with me."

CHAPTER 30

Flight Fishing
February 1943

Japs Hurled Back on Guadalcanal - Daily Mirror

After six months of desperation, disease, and brutal fighting, the U.S. declares Guadalcanal secure the day after the last Japanese soldier quietly evacuates the island.

COUNTER INTELLIGENCE IS ALL ABOUT weaving lies and truth into invisible webs. Information was available from every corner of the tropical universe. Sometimes he landed on a tasty morsel, and other times he landed in a pile of dung. Like a fly with compound eyes, Hank Burns was seeing many sides and none.

Which was Chemin? The cordial Frenchman had done nothing to him. Hans Steen, the Dutch wanderer, had been treated like a guest, but terror nearly overcame him during the long night at the plantation. The question was, "Why?" Chemin was physically powerful, and had displayed it openly. He also had made his Vichy loyalty clear and he really didn't care what his guest thought. Hans wondered whether the elaborate communications between colonials were a result of loyalty to

France, or a means to survival. Chemin was most likely a mercenary – an unknown element, someone who shifts loyalties for a price. Soldiers in Noumea had pledged to lay down their lives for far away homelands. Hank Burns had taken that same oath, but now he examined his own conscience for his loyalties. What, or where, was home?

Back at camp, Hank washed off streams of red jungle dust and made some brief notes. The events of the last twenty-four hours had been a jumble of evidence and languages. He strode rapidly toward Mitchell's office where the captain was waiting.

Mitchell looked up from his desk. "We hear you had an interesting trip into the jungle. How in blazes did you find that guy?"

"Remember sir, you sent me out to find the Consul, only there wasn't one. And the French are not as they seem to be."

"Gee, that's a surprise. You got Free French, Vichy French, French colonists, and descendants of prisoners all on some island that France could give a shit about."

Hans continued. "I think that some landowners may be loyal to the old Vichy governor. This man is only interested in the source of his next deal. As far as finding out that he was transmitting the information, well sir, that was just an accident."

Mitchell pulled a handkerchief across his neck, smashed a mosquito, and inspected the remains.

"Got him." A smile crossed his face. "Look, I'm not surprised. Laigret's been bitching about our foreign occupation of his damn island. We suspected that the French had all the loyalties of a weather vane. Looks like you were trying to ride this weather vane in a typhoon."

Figurative language with its crazy connections always confused Hank. It made his head spin.

"The weather was fine, but, sir, this man I visited has the ledgers from the Pink House, you know, that place on Avenue La Fontaine. He was transmitting pages in code to his brother in Tonkin."

"Are you sure?"

"Captain Mitchell, sir, I copied those ledgers onto postcards. I know the books."

Mitchell lit a cigarette. His ashtray hadn't been dumped in days. There were sweat rings on his uniform shirt, and ink stains on his hands. Was it even for certain that his body had left his chair since their last meeting? Mitchell commented, "Tonkin isn't Free French. Those Vichy sons of bitches have close ties to the Japanese. It's a wonder we didn't find you in pieces in the jungle." Hank stared, appalled.

"Glad you found Ringold's units out there. So tell me about your visit to the Frenchman. I hope he at least offered you dinner." Looking at Mitchell's haggard appearance, Hank decided to not go into details about the lobsters and drawn butter.

"You can't really see the plantation from the inland road. It's on a plateau overlooking the mouth of the river, not a big harbor like Noumea. Near the nickel mines. A lot of conveyor belts and tracks everywhere. Some of the hardware is really rusty, and other equipment looks like it could be used again." He paused. Mitchell's eyes were glassing over. "Do you want me to sketch that? I may not be sure of all the details, but I understand how it works."

"Please do put sketches in with your report," Mitchell commented. "So, tell me about the radio equipment."

Hank's long hands outlined the dimensions of the radio set. "His radio was the size of a large typewriter – much larger than what we are using in the field. But I didn't understand the signals. They were extremely rapid and, if he was talking to his brother, they were relaying in French. I'm sorry but I couldn't hear code and French at the same time."

"A radio system that size certainly indicates that he is communicating over a long distance, either Tonkin or the South Pole. Where was the antenna? It would have to be really large."

Hank froze. All those cable towers – can you run radio signals through hills? It should be closer in. A weather vane on the roof? By the time he knew about the radios, he was focused on how he would get away from the plantation. Looking back at the plantation in his mind's eye he thought of the house, the gardens and the pavilion. Oh, for heaven's sake – the conduit pipe in the pavilion! It ran up the side of the tree and he never thought to look and see how far it went. Hank began to draw. "There is a pavilion sir, over here…."

"We're going hunting and you're gonna be our scout. Let me think."

Mitchell tipped back his chair and stared at the ceiling. "You're going with them. You know who the target is, and we need to make sure we get him. Alive if possible, we want to know what he knows." He paused and looked at Hank's feet. "Oh God, I'd better call the Navy office for some back-up. We'll need a PT boat in the area tonight. They're gonna be pissed; takes them a week to do anything."

"Sir, why wouldn't they be willing to help out? Halsey said that we already lost three troop ships."

Mitchell's thoughts were elsewhere. To him this was more about red tape than expediency. "Dismissed. Get some sleep."

Hank's mind was whirring with information that might or might not be useful. A nap was out of the question. How did guys sleep in the middle of the day? Instead of sleeping, he drew detailed sketches and maps of Chemin's plantation.

After supper three jeeps were lined up by the gate and a dozen armed soldiers jumped in. "Bugs" the radio operator had his portable sets and antenna in case they ran into a problem. Hot rainy days left muddy ruts dried over into hard tracks. The jeeps bounced down the dirt road to the plantation and unloaded men in darkness. There was no moon, and stars did not offer enough light for them to see where they were going. An outline of the house was barely visible, only because it blocked out the field of stars.

Two soldiers strapped on their helmets and hurried silently toward the front door. The others began to sing and stagger through the jungle, spreading out around the property. The idea was to flush out Chemin, who seemed to live alone with a few servants. It was likely that they would be armed, but hopefully the ruse of drunken soldiers would keep the level of the confrontation down. The last thing they needed was yet another altercation with the French Governor.

Knocks on the door went unanswered. Strange. Servants answer doors, so they were expecting the intrusion of the soldiers or they were hiding. Hank and "Bugs" stood to the side, strangely calm, waiting to see what would happen next, fighting or an escape attempt. The heavy teak door would not budge. A rifle butt smashed through to open the front windowpanes and the soldier entered a foyer. Hank followed, but the main rooms were dark. It was certain that Chemin was not sleeping. Hank led them through the house and toward the kitchen stairs.

Downstairs in the radio room, Chemin finished tapping out an urgent message. He pushed a small button next to the radio. Then he grabbed a duffel bag, and slipped outside the house and down the path toward the cove. *Merde!* Who was that Dutchman that had accepted his hospitality and a bottle of excellent wine?

He ran through the sand in the cove, avoiding roots and tangles of kelp. A sea cave lay at the end of a jetty, and Chemin slithered inside feeling his way to a sandstone staircase. Thank God the tide was out, and the steps were not too wet. A small dark green launch hung on a simple lift, hidden in the shadows of trees. He had roused his boatman from a deep sleep, and they began to turn the crank handle, lowering the launch to the water. He threw keys to the throttle toward the boatman. Normally he would take the helm, but tonight he would pull off the hatch and open up the engine and a small radio room. The Japanese submarine was more than three hours away. Hopefully they had received his message and a landing barge would come and meet him. The launch could take cover in the night until they were in open seas.

Inside the house, the soldiers couldn't find Chemin. "Bugs" sent a message to headquarters, then cut the radio and began to pick up ledgers. Hank was examining the room, when he noticed a second door in the hall that opened to another staircase, one that smelled like the outside air. "Put those things down. He's gone somewhere." They clambered down the stairs and then stopped on a bluff, watching a launch depart toward the reefs. Dammit.

Racing back up the stairs, they grabbed the equipment and books, and ran to stow them. "Bugs" messaged again. Beep, blip, bip… "Subject has left Thio by water. Please advise." Oh crap. It was going to be another long night.

Captain Mitchell had stayed behind in Noumea. Someone needed to be on hand with knowledge of the operation in case there were any problems. He phoned the Naval Commander's offices. "We need some help on the water. There should be a PT boat over by Thio and we must activate him. "

"What kind of mess you guys get into?"

"One of our CIC guys found a Vichy spy and we were tracking him down."

"You knew he was on the water?"

"We found out about 10 minutes ago. Look, I called your CO this afternoon about this. The guy has been responsible for the loss of at least three troop ships. Those ships are yours, right? "

"Where's he going?"

"Goddamn it, we don't have time for storytelling. He didn't type out an itinerary for me. I don't know if he is meeting a ship or a Jap submarine. But he is going somewhere in a hurry, and he's not going to be crossing the Pacific in a 20 foot launch."

"I'll need to get back to you." The young naval lieutenant put down the phone, leaving Mitchell frustrated and anxious. He relayed Mitchell's concern to his commander.

A large contingent of PTs lay idle, patrolling waters circling the island and the small harbors near the mines. The little plywood boats were bristling with guns and torpedo tubes, able to wreak havoc throughout the thousands of islands. This particular mosquito was painted in green camouflage, nearly impossible to see against the waves.

Jack, the PT boat captain, relayed the message from his radio operator.

"We're going fishing!"

"Now? What are we supposed to be catching?"

"A bad guy. One hiding at night in a dark green fishing boat."

The engine turned over and headed into the Thio landing to pick up Hank and a sharpshooter. Then the PT roared to life, and they took off between the reefs.

A Patrol Torpedo boat is basically a flying arsenal. There is no safe place to sit, walk or stand. The deck is covered by a hard shell with a canopy and no guard rails. The sturdy wood boat could take off at short notice and high speed, its three powerful engines churning through the waters and able to turn on a dime. They could dive in and out of islands and between battleships. The only problem was that the compasses did not work well, so navigating at night was a game of chance.

A decision was made to operate no running lights. The three-engine PT boat makes a deafening sound and Chemin would hear them once they approached his small fishing launch.

Jack spotted the wake of the fishing launch, and heard it even though he couldn't quite see it.

"Cut the throttle!"

"Aye aye, sir. But I thought we needed to apprehend him."

"We also need to see where he is going."

"What if he is headed toward Jap ships? Or subs?"

"That's one way to learn where they are. He's not the only guy watching the coast."

They heard the roar of the fishing boat, sometimes to the starboard, sometimes port. It would disappear into a distance, then they would be slapped by wake that churned up nearby. The men could listen, and they could peer into the darkness, but they couldn't sight anything in the green black sea. The irregular movements of the fishing launch began to slow.

A gunner fired a warning shot into the air, enough to let the launch know that the fishing trip would soon be over. A second shot carried a flare, lighting up the sky so they could see the target, a dragon on the water, a Diahatsu landing barge with its distinctive pontoons. Its wings and tail were raised, a dragon ready to capture its prey. Now they would need to gamble on Chemin's survival instinct. Apparently the Japanese had purchased his very soul, a soul that might or might not fight through to death.

Chemin's fishing launch cut its motors and, evidently was planning to cast a line onto the Daihatsu barge. The bulky wooden craft was slow in the water, built for carrying large loads of supplies to the submarine fleet.

Jack gave the command. It didn't look like they could catch Chemin without a battle. "Wait until he gets on! We're gonna blow the barge."

Strangely, though, the crew of the Japanese craft was not throwing lines out to the fishing launch. Instead, they were tipping barrels and pouring something over the side. The distinct odor of petrol filtered through the night. A small flame lit and, like a firefly, it flew through the air, landing on the petrol glazed waves. The Japanese landing craft moved away without Chemin. Interesting. Someone had ordered them to pick up Chemin, and they were changing the plans. Probably a second set of orders that they were not to be captured. As the fuel surrounded Chemin's launch, the Japanese captain saluted him.

As soon as the barge began to move, the mortar crew fired. The oiled wood of the barge glowed for a second before it was engulfed in flames from the spilled petrol.

Chemin's launch also caught fire. In a split second, he dove over the side. Jack ordered the men to wait before making an effort to capture Chemin.

The water came alive with the flapping of fins. Blood had been spilled. Chemin was a strong swimmer, but he was no match for sharks. The animals poked and nuzzled him, waiting to surround him. From his movements it was apparent that they were bumping him, playing with their prey. Jack signaled for full power. The PT boat cut through the water, disturbing the school of sharks and pulling up alongside the exhausted swimmer. Hank threw a rope to him.

Two sailors pulled Chemin out of the water.

Henri Chemin was silent when he saw Hank's face. He wasn't quite able to place it, but he knew that he needed to negotiate for his life. He spoke to Jack in French.

"*Messieurs, Bonsoir!* Have we met?"

CHAPTER 31

Tonkin, French Indochina February 1943

Roosevelt and Stalin discuss the future of French rule in Indochina, a Vichy French stronghold.

~ *1943 Tehran Conference*

Jules Chemin wanted his visitors to leave. Merchants of war had gathered in his Tonkin courtyard for the evening, drinking Japanese Soju and German Schnapps – hard liquor that tasted like cough medicine to him. They laughed about the Americans and Anzacs, fools, lazy on the job and drunk on their nights off. Yes, Allies had taken Guadalcanal, but there were another 3,000 islands out there. What he would have given to pour an excellent cognac. His head hurt and he had indigestion.

Something felt very wrong. Jules had spent the evening brokering sales of supplies to the Japanese Navy, but he didn't have current information on the Allied movements. He waited near his radio, day after day. It had been two weeks since his brother, Henri, had last radioed him. It wasn't that operations in the Pacific were closing down.

In a recent report, Henri had commented on all the military equipment still being delivered to Noumea. Docks were full of crates and a steady stream of trucks ran back and forth to the harbor. Estimates were that tonnage had risen from 1,500 tons a day to nearly 10,000 tons daily in just a few weeks.

War signals good times for profiteers. Everyone wanted to make a deal and greed ruled the South Pacific. According to Henri, the Kanak natives were earning very good money as longshoremen in the Noumea harbor. Crews were still being added on. In fact, it was difficult to retain cheap labor on the New Caledonia plantations. Bars were full at night with salesmen, hucksters and supply sergeants all getting in on the action. Coveted candy and cigarettes, native souvenirs, and Chinese valuables passed through hands of traders.

Tonkin was bustling as well. The French colony was a solid Vichy stronghold and the Japanese had firmly established themselves with the Vichy French. The Germans were shipping in Panzer tanks. Jules was permitted to stay in his three-story mansion so long as he remained a gracious host. Guestrooms were often full and Jules' third floor radio room served as an Axis lifeline across the Pacific islands.

Henri Chemin of course was secured in a U.S. Army brig. His existence as a plantation owner with Vichy sympathies didn't surprise those who knew him. The big question was, how had his relays to Tonkin been identified as a matter of importance? Who had intercepted the powerful radio signals?

Jules and Henri had discussed plans in case one of them was ever captured. Self-preservation was their highest priority. Since Henri's disappearance, warships were crossing back and forth with fewer and fewer submarine attacks to stop them. The Vichy and the Free French walked across a tightrope stretched taut between the bays and harbors of southern Asia. Insignificant islands took on new importance as blood was shed by two warring sides; neither of which called the islands "home."

Germany and Japan may have held the keys to an idealized state and the future of mankind, but the brothers were mercenaries. The muscle-bound Allies might have infinite amounts of equipment and innumerable men, but they had no talent for intelligence. Their fresh-faced boys were just too simple, taking everything at face value. There had been no evidence of operatives or traders who could be clever enough to intercept high-level information. The Americans couldn't possibly understand the radio messages. They could barely order a beer in French, let alone Tonkinese or Japanese. The leaks had to be coming from Free French offices.

The question was how best to expose vulnerabilities in an ocean of personnel that grew by the hundreds each week. Naomi was a mixed race beauty who had helped them with several business transactions. Governor Laigret was very pleased with his multi-lingual secretary. She had come highly recommended. Now Jules needed access to files full of European correspondence, or at least the correspondence that filtered all the way out to the Free French. She had no loyalties other than earning enough money to afford a few luxuries, and her confident smile would attract all sorts of characters into the web.

CHAPTER 32

Venus Rising
February 1943

"How can you govern a country that has 246 varieties of cheese?"

~ *Charles de Gaulle*

At midday Hank locked his office door and headed for the showers. Why had he accepted Naomi's invitation to the beach? His pink and white complexion had never seen a day of sun. Whenever he had been out in the sun, he had burned up like a steamed lobster. She wanted to swim. He had no swimsuit. The guys just wore skivvies to go in swimming, no undershirts even. The entire project got more and more frustrating. But, eventually, he was clad in a plaid shirt and borrowed tennis shorts with his white legs nearly matching the bleached linen. A dark suit and a candlelit café would have been much more to his taste. The price for all the discomfort was that he was dating the most beautiful woman in Noumea.

The halter-top of Naomi's sundress showed off her shoulders and Hank forgot all about his worries for dinner. She waved and then called to him, "*Mon Cher!* Please help me with this." On the stoop beside her was an enormous picnic basket. Through its wood slats he smelled everything he had not eaten in five years. He lifted the basket and then picked up his map to the beach. Naomi looked at it and said, "That is a lovely beach, but I know of one where we will have more privacy. May I direct you there?"

"Of course, as long as you know how to get back out after dark. I'm not sure of the roads."

She laughed, "I will get you home safely. And don't worry about the road." They turned out of the main roads toward the beach at Anse Vata, which matched his directions. Then she directed him to a boat landing. "We are going over to a tiny island. Can those shoes go in the water? The coral is sharp." She called to the boatman. "Pierre! Please take us over to Isle aux Canards – and do you have some water sandals for my friend?" The picnic basket went into the boat, and they set out across the vast lagoon toward a tiny spot of land. He investigated the white pebbled beach, land out of a dream. Naomi unpacked tartare de ton, a rich sausage, cheeses, biscuits and wine. A selection of unfamiliar fruits lay in the basket, along with some French chocolates. As they began to eat, she nibbled at the treats, and he cut into his open faced sandwiches, voraciously consuming them as if he were a condemned man going into his last meal.

The last course was cheese – gruyere, camembert, brie, and a wonderful Roquefort. Naomi smiled at his naivete, as he whacked the ends off the wedges and piled the French cheeses onto his dessert plate.

"You haven't eaten cheese before?"

"The Dutch invented cheese – Gouda, Edam, Leidse…"

"Have you missed it much?"

"Actually, if I had to eat only two foods for the rest of my life, they would be *Roggebrod* and good cheeses. I suppose an apple and maybe a bit of ginger now and then would be perfect. And, of course, chocolates – Dutch chocolates."

She took a small piece of the Camembert and a bit of fruit, setting the two carefully into his mouth. "Is this too delicate?"

The absurd lecture stopped. He let the smooth cheese coat his palate and waft through his nostrils before he took a deep breath.

"It's delicious. You enjoy French food, yes?"

"Very much.... My mama was half French." Here she took a deep breath and then coughed into her napkin. Wiping her eyes, she set it back down on the table.

He took her hand. "What happened to your mama?"

"She died when I was twelve. My father's other women didn't want me, so I went to live with the nuns in the little French convent." She looked straight into his eyes. "So, how is it that you are a Dutchman working with the U.S. Army? Isn't Holland part of Germany?"

He smiled, expecting the question. "I'm a businessman and the army will buy supplies from anyone who can locate them."

That wasn't exactly what she wanted to know. "But why didn't you stay in Holland?" She paused, digging a little deeper. "Didn't you have a family?"

"My mother – I thought she loved us and would protect our inheritance, but she married again. My brother and sister – my sister is very...complicated."

"Women can be complicated." She smiled gently and reached over toward an unfamiliar orange fruit, placing her hand over the knife in his, "here, like this," and pulled off a perfect translucent slice of the mango. Cleaning up the edge a little herself, she licked the knife off. "I'm not sure we even understand ourselves." Then she placed the knife between her teeth and folded her napkin.

He watched her intently. "So, you work for the Free French. Why do you work?"

She examined the picnic basket, which now had been emptied of a week's salary. "My father did not acknowledge me in his will. He and my mother were never married. Their parents were not married. French laws do not acknowledge us. We have to make our own way."

"You and I are not so different. I was also disinherited when my mother remarried. My future was gone."

"Ah, but you are very talented. You speak many languages and you work hard. What do you do all day long?"

"I try to make some money – finding things people need. I enjoy the travel."

His answer left even bigger questions. He gazed out over the water watching the sun drop beneath the horizon. It was as if he hadn't heard her. She tried again.

"What do you like to do best?"

"Photography. I like pictures."

"And what do you like to photograph?"

"Women mostly. Beautiful places, and of course women in beautiful places."

"Will you take a picture of me?"

Hans flinched. She was not like the whores on the beach. "Yes, but not tonight. Tonight's pictures I wish to keep here." He tapped his heart.

She reached across and touched him, "Would you like to swim now?"

"I don't have a proper swimming suit."

"It's getting dark and the water is warm." She untied the halter to her dress and stepped out of it, slipped on a pair of water sandals and was gone, Venus sinking into the sea. He gasped for air, but there was none. Oh dear God, what was he to do now? If he undressed, she would surely see his prurient interest in her. He walked into the water in the borrowed shorts not feeling the cuts from the coral on his feet.

She moved like a dolphin, swimming out far into the bay with a graceful freestyle. He calmly splashed himself near the beach. She swam back and splashed water in his face. She followed him, wringing out her hair and leaving herself uncovered in the night air.

"When do you leave Noumea?"

"When this awful war ends. Who knows how long that will be? And you, how long have you worked in the French offices?"

He looked at her body, which was very unlike the experience of developing photos of nude women. He wanted to touch her, to smell her, and to seize her. He hardly heard her answer.

"Oh, about three months. I needed a job and the nuns educated me well enough to work."

He ached for her, but tried to keep himself under control. The wet white shorts were not much help.

Naomi spoke. "I think it is getting close to 10:00 and Pierre will be back with the boat. We need to get back in time for curfew."

"When can I see you again?" He didn't want to take her to the bars on Saturday night, and have her ogled by all the men from the bases. She was his now. He just needed to figure out how he could seal her heart. She knew the correct answer.

"How about Sunday afternoon? I can show you another wonderful place." She kissed him on the cheek. He turned her head and kissed her on the lips.

Naomi did not tell him that she had an appointment on Saturday night. First she had to pull together her personal notes from her workweek in the French Information and Propaganda Department. Her friend Jules Chemin was visiting from Tonkin. Jules' brother, Henri, had quit corresponding recently, and Jules had come to visit New Caledonia and learn more about his disappearance from the airwaves. What the hell? Henri Chemin had harmed no one. The two brothers had been very close, and radioed each other at least twice a week. Jules did not like the silence. She was to meet him at a small café a little bit up the coast from town, one that was only visited by locals.

———

Jules Chemin waited at a table for two. A few small orchids sat in a water glass, and the candle flickered. He avoided tapping his fingers or drawing any attention to his impatience. Instead, he lit a cigarette and took a slow drag, eyes focused in the distance, a man not to be disturbed. Naomi was an interesting tool, if he could control her. She sauntered in nearly half an hour late.

Chemin didn't look forward to this interrogation. The girl was French-Tonkinese on one side and some sort of Dutch-Afrikaner mix on the other. Her loyalties were to the next person who could put out a bowl of food. But she charmed men and could get them to do anything she asked.

Chemin would rather have stayed home in Tonkin. His home was filled with precious Chinese antiques, traded and purchased for safe passage as people fled one Chinese regime after another. A bevy of servants waited on his every need, and clients paid him well. Now he had to find Henri on an island full of Americans, Australians and

Free French – a stewpot of criminal elements that had inbred for some two hundred years. Peace would be possible if only the Vichy and the Japanese could work out the terms. There was no reason for all the disturbances with ragtag alliances across a bunch of islands populated with brown savages.

Chemin ordered dinner, then asked, "So, tell me the latest island gossip. How are you enjoying the governor's parties?"

Naomi thought quietly, and decided not to share any information about her private life with him. "I've actually been working a lot since I started the new job in Laigret's office. He hasn't held any parties. People are moving in and out so fast that I don't know if we even have time to get gossip started."

"Ah, the Americans are getting hit very hard in the islands. The Japanese are determined to send them home either in boxes or in pieces."

Naomi picked up her lobster and tore off the claw, played with it, then sucked out the insides. Jules admired his savage companion. "Why would a beauty like you be working so hard? There are certainly enough men around here willing to take care of you very nicely. There has to be more in their lives than tinned food and hospital supplies."

He had a point. Naomi was attractive enough to find a rich man in this sea of soldiers. She just didn't see herself as being a happy housewife – a nun who would still need to bed the same man every night, and raise children by day.

Jules continued to probe. "So, what have you heard from Henri recently?"

She startled. She was not assigned to keep tabs on Henri Chemin. She barely knew him. She had been to parties at his house along with several other girls, but their job was to just serve as hostesses.

"I need your help. Henri had a Dutch visitor about a week before his last message. We may be looking for a Dutchman." He pushed his food aside and lit a cigarette. "Or maybe a Gaullist."

She pondered his comment. "Jules, we are looking for a coconut flake in a bowl of rice. The Dutch aren't even in the war. But let's see, I was at a Javanese Christmas party with a good eighty people or so. I have a nice candidate."

"Have you slept with him?"

"I said he was a nice candidate. He is a Dutch trader who sells to the Americans. He gets us some little necessities now and then. I went out with him a few days ago."

"So, who does he know?"

"I'm not sure, he talked about his family in Holland. And church. He talked about church. He is too boring and innocent to be a spy."

"*Mon Dieu!* Church! What were you wearing?"

A sharp knife slit the lobster's tail, and this time she drew out the flesh and dipped it into a warm bath of sweet butter. "Mmmm… this is delicious!" She licked the butter off of her fingers. "I should be a mermaid so that I could eat lobsters every day." Jules stared at her.

"Oh, we went over to the island with a picnic. I went swimming; he was very uncomfortable."

"Are you seeing him again?"

"Tomorrow afternoon and no, I don't know where we will go. I will make sure we get time alone." Naomi paused to push the shells aside. Lost in thought, she pulled at the hem of the linen napkin and set it aside.

"Look Jules, I think this man is a virgin. I don't think I should seduce him. I need to keep him interested. There's definitely something under his honest grin. I don't know if he is the man you are looking for, but I could help you eliminate the question."

CHAPTER 33

Noumea
March 1943

TELL NOBODY – NOT EVEN HER

Careless talk costs lives

– Poster

She was the world to him. He no longer saw dark when he looked into her eyes. He saw a Pacific sunrise, the warmth of the colors bathing everything around her. Her scent, of flowers unknown to him, her dark skin untouched except by the clear waters of the lagoon, the jungle around them. Hunger struck in a new way. Hans was ravenous. He wanted her, to consume her, and to be beside her, reborn and intact at the same time. Flames of anticipation and danger flitted through his dreams – excruciating nights and distracted days until he could see her again. They say that passion is like death, and on this island he was surrounded by both. If he could die once, with her, he would have lived a full life.

Her mix of European perfection and Asian features blended into a unique beauty. Her smile lit rooms, and it lit him. The nights alone were almost unbearable as he lay in bed with his body on fire. Even the cotton sheets irritated his skin.

Then he pondered a second set of questions. What race was he? What if his race were a problem, one with real significance? He didn't want to throw away his future over a circumcision scar that had been set on him as an infant.

By now he knew that the Germans had gone through schoolrooms, having children list their grandparents' names on forms, to see if they qualified as Aryan. The existence of one Jewish grandparent cut a child off from the privileges of a society to come. Holland had been built on trade and its population was a three hundred year mix of people and languages. He had erased his past in a single afternoon in New York City. Was he a Jew even if he never set foot in a synagogue, not ever again? Then a new set of worries arose. What would he tell her? Would she know that another man might not … Had she seen other men? She did not tell him she was a virgin. She teased him, but he had never asked and she had never volunteered any information.

He decided to plan another picnic, one that would show his ability to provide and care for her. It was the hottest day yet, one where the sun and breezes stood still. So hot that it seemed as if steam would begin to rise from the harbor at any moment. The seas were supposed to boil when the world ended. Maybe this was the day. He looked out onto the docks at the Kanak laborers, lifting their heavy loads and managing the equipment. His mind could hardly follow the numbers on spreadsheets, and those men were actively working. The weekend was coming. He had received permission to take a jeep for an entire day.

He did not talk much as they drove the unfamiliar roads crossing the island. Rains had gouged deep ruts that dried in the sun, often derailing the vehicle. The men had told him that the Blue River was the perfect place for a date. They bounced on the hard seats in the hot sun, bugs snapping at them or splattering on the windshield. Finally she suggested a stop, a clearing in the woods at a bend in the river, a massive boulder facing a deep pool. There had never been so much blue. Blue was the color of life as he knew it, but the steely blue of the North Sea was replaced by a true azure, a jewel that had no boundaries.

He got out, but before he could open the door on her side of the car, she had jumped out and climbed the boulder, pulling off her sarong. Laughing, she dove off into the stream, her new American styled swimming suit gleaming in the afternoon sun. She was more beautiful than any pin-up girl he had ever seen in the calendars, the sun drenching her bare back and arms.

Hans had no idea how to dive. He stood on the rock, tugging on his new swimsuit, knitted navy blue wool with a white canvas belt. He had never confronted mountain streams and granite outcroppings. The North Sea dunes in Holland roll quietly toward a stormy sea, where danger is having a wave topple you. He might break every bone in his body on that rock. But if he could dive, he would be back in the womb of the earth. He took a deep breath and jumped. Water surrounded him completely. The luminescent bubbles, were they his breath? A flash of sunlight appeared above him, and he broke the surface, alive once more. She swam away, elusive as a fish escaping a predatory bird, and then raced toward him and splashed his face.

Breathless, they climbed out of the water and spread out an Army blanket. Trade winds curled through the trees as they kissed in silver sunlight. The Island pines were nothing like the stalwart trees of the American north woods. The crookedness of the trees wasn't apparent at first; but then he saw the straightness of the nearly horizontal branches, perfectly arrayed and symmetrical. When the winds blow, the branches still appeared straight, but the entire tree swayed in the breezes, and the trunks grew into a long waved form, bent by forces of nature. Naomi had the grace of an island pine, but he still didn't know where her center was. He wanted to possess her, not be blown over in some wild island typhoon.

Shortly after they finished their picnic, a gentle rainstorm began, suddenly and quietly announcing itself. She took his hand and they started down a walking path, following the signs toward the largest living thing on the island, a thousand year old Kaori tree. Suddenly she shivered, a little cool in the sudden breeze. He stopped and wrapped the picnic blanket around her, trembling as he kissed her softly, gently rubbing her back to warm her. She took the edge of the blanket and wrapped it around him. The earth was soft, and it was over much too quickly.

Some moments later, he spoke. "After we are married, we will swim without our suits, every day if you like."

"Pardon?"

"But we won't be able to marry until the end of the war, when we can return to the U.S. or Europe and get my business going again. I can't have a wife right now."

"Perhaps not, but we will have time to get to know each other."

Jules Chemin had given her a week to learn as much as possible. She and Hank spent each evening together. He took her out to dinner. He wanted to provide for her, but what sorts of things do husbands talk about?

He decided to impress her with his efforts at work. "You know, I am now in charge of an enterprise many times the size of my father's shops...and then I had to go to the Colonel's office for a signature... I understand that he's a very important man, but he kept me waiting for 45 minutes."

She sympathized with him, spending her days organizing paperwork for people who couldn't be bothered to pick up after themselves. "They treat me like a maid. I spent the whole day copying over notes that were scribbled on the backs of envelopes."

"Anyway, the colonel apologized for holding up the paperwork." He paused and smiled. "I have a lot to do."

Late nights found them on the beaches, in quiet secluded spaces where they could spend a few hours wrapped in each other's arms. On Thursday evening at dinner, he ordered champagne – warm fizzy drink, but pretty in the sunset. "I was thinking about, you know, the future." Out of his pocket he pulled the little ring box, the one that had been in his belongings for the past three years. "I'm afraid I don't know how to propose, but would you marry me after the war?"

Naomi took the ring. The tiny diamond lit in the sunset, and she put her arms around his neck.

On Saturday night she explained that the next day she would be going out with a few girlfriends, other island girls she had known since childhood. Her diamond gleamed in the torch lit café. He marveled at the bounties of the earth, this island, and his fiancée. His fortune had definitely improved.

"Go and enjoy some girl talk. Are you going to show off your ring?"

She laughed gently. "Well, I'm certainly not going to take it off. I may tease them and wait for it to be noticed."

Her Sunday morning walk out of town led her to the meeting place with Jules Chemin, an abandoned church. They sat down on the stone wall. A few birds and rodents pecked at odd bugs and crumbs that had been left by previous visitors.

She asked, "Have you found Henri yet?"

Jules Chemin remained silent. The trail had left off in a message that a Japanese barge was going to pick Henri up. "Oh, he'll turn up. He might just be out on a hunting trip." He halted his lie. "How is it going with your Dutch boyfriend?"

Naomi did not say a word. Instead she moved her left hand over onto his leg.

"So, you seduced him?" She groaned, and he noticed the little diamond. "What's that?"

"It's an engagement ring."

"Are you marrying this man?"

A broad teasing smile broke the silence. "You know, if I do marry him, he will take care of me. At least I wouldn't end up like the girls on the beach, or like some fat plantation mistress with a bunch of kids to take care of." Then she laughed at Jules. "There are no solid plans, but I'm his fiancée now and we can learn a lot about each other. For instance, we had dinner every night this week, and he told me about what supplies he counted. Every damn night. I worked all day and listened to more work for hours in the evenings."

"And what do you tell him?"

"Anything I can make up. Actually, I'm getting a lot of 'swell' American merchandise delivered to our offices now. He sends me anything I ask for, as long as the paperwork is filled out and signed by my boss."

"Speaking of that, what have you learned in your new job? Are the 'Free French' treating you well?"

"They squabble with the Americans a lot, don't they?"

"What do you mean?"

She rolled her eyes. "There seems to be a lot of contention. Sometimes they argue like schoolchildren. They even argue about the size of their barracks and who has more living space."

Jules stared at her as if she were a child. "The Americans are intruders. They need to just do their job and then leave. They do not need living spaces. We don't intend for them to settle here."

She was astounded by his ignorance. "Do you read the newspapers, the French ones? Vergès writes several articles about how our leaders have sold the island to the Americans. These common American soldiers act as if they were entitled to a colony."

Her expression metamorphosed into the stern and relentless countenance of an angry nun staring down at the infractions of schoolboys. She had learned well in the convent school.

Jules paused. "I like this."

"You like what?"

"I like this idea of the Allies not being so allied."

Naomi pondered his remarks. "The soldiers may be rogues, but my impression is that the Americans are very efficient. This war machine is huge, not that I even care. All Hank talks about are numbers."

Jules'eyes widened. "Interesting, *non*?" Naomi's boring fiancé had more to share than merchandise. She needed to hang onto him, but not to care too deeply.

"The Americans are invaders trespassing on the lands of French farmers. They bring military weapons on hunting trips, claiming that they will shoot the wild deer that are eating crops and then they 'accidentally' shoot a farmer's prized bull. They are treating us as if we were the hosts at a big barbeque. But I am intrigued by the idea of conflict between Governor Laigret and the American military. America is just a bunch of colonies itself."

He lit a cigarette, and then offered her one. She shook her head. "We got you a job to find things out. Try to remember some of those numbers. Get your fiancé to help us find Henri. Surely you can ask him some questions, yes?"

Chemin began to twist his hands and pulled off an elaborate ring, Imperial Jade with two golden dragons twisted around the bezel. "You need to give him a ring too, now that you are 'engaged.' We need to give him gifts that obligate him to us. I know you can't afford a nice ring on what I pay you. Take this one. Just bring it back when you return that diamond to him."

"Two dragons – how nice for two spies."

At dinner the next night she reached beneath the table, and tugged at her silk stocking. Hank stared at her and she laughed. "No, I am not disrobing! I have a surprise for you." She turned aside, undoing her garter and pulling out a tiny silk packet. "Close your eyes and open your hands." The gold ring with the two dragons was placed in his left hand. "It is our custom for the man also to wear a ring. This one was my father's, but it is a very good piece of jade. And tonight we are the two dragons swimming in the sea under a sky of fire." He looked up at the red sunset and slipped on the ring.

CHAPTER 34

Debriefing
July 1943

"Before Guadalcanal the enemy advanced at his pleasure – after Guadalcanal he retreated at ours."

~ ADMIRAL HALSEY

PEOPLE WERE DISAPPEARING, BUT THERE was no magic show. The fatal will of the Japanese claimed the lives of thousands in battle as campaigns to liberate the Salomon Islands consumed ships and men. Day after day, missions would return with incomplete cadres. Meanwhile, Hank continued to process orders for necessities. Some 200 Quonset huts were full of supplies to keep everything going – crates of paper here, ointments and bandages there, and always food for the mess.

"Burns, the captain needs to see you." Hank did not look up at the soldier. Instead, he carefully inked in a couple of numbers in the ledger, and then set his pen aside. There was no indication of what was needed as he followed the corporal down the corridor of partitions to the enclosed offices.

The captain had a visitor, a civilian. Hank entered the tight space and stood at attention. "At ease, Burns. Take a seat. I want you to meet Ted Knight. He works in Shanghai and wanted to get away to the islands for a few days. I think you know the territory as well as anyone, so you are to take him around, show him the lay of the land." Hank looked very confused. He wasn't going on leave, but he was supposed to drop his work and be a tour guide for three days? Who was Ted? A politician? A prospective governor?

Captain Mark Mitchell saw his confusion. "Ted is with the OSS, Office of Strategic Services. It's a brand new unit, okay, a brand new bureaucracy, because they think we need help figuring things out. Washington wants them to talk to our guys, and has sent him down here to take a peek. I want you to tell him about your adventures in the whorehouse." Hank looked like he had been smacked with a fish. "And the 'Dutch consul' out there in the jungle. Can you close up your books by midday, and then get the hell out of here? Lose the uniform, but keep your ID in a safe place. We'll have a jeep ready for you."

Hank was puzzled and a little frustrated. He had laid out his day's work and would have to rearrange his tasks. Hopefully, the Captain who assigned this excursion would remember why all the ledgers were not completely up to date. There would be even more work to do when he got back. He shook his head, staring at the neat stacks of orders and invoices on his desk, and picked up the telephone.

"Offices of the Governor."

"Naomi, it's Hank. ... No, I'm well, but they are sending me out for a few days."

He drummed his fingers on the desktop while his curious fiancée asked questions.

"No, I don't think it will be particularly dangerous, other than the usual hazards." He didn't want her to worry about him going into combat and never coming back. "Actually it's a visitor from Shanghai, and I'm supposed to drive him around to meet plantation people." A silence on the other end of the line let him know that his visitor was not welcome. "No, I don't know what he sells, but I'm sure I'll learn. I'm going to miss you doll, but yes, I'll call when I can." He paused, reflecting for a moment on still one more acquaintance who had not returned from battle.

Ted Knight wasn't like the soldiers at all, and Hank was tired of their constant pranks and fighting anyway. Knight had been educated at Columbia and was a practicing attorney in Syracuse, New York before the war. He had actually attended Lyceé in Strasbourg and spoke excellent French and pretty good German. The OSS was a new division of Counter Intelligence, and foreign languages were a part of the screening process. Hank stretched out his arms and stood as tall as possible. "Why haven't you guys been out here before? We have rats everywhere. I even found one or two myself."

Ted started to talk. "You know we are from separate divisions, right? The OSS is excluded from operating in the South Pacific. They have put us up in Shanghai, and no one speaks Chinese. Who knows what those buggers are thinking? Half our people can't tell a Chinaman from a Jap, or a Jap from a Korean." Hank couldn't tell the difference either, and was shocked to learn that some Korean spies went to great lengths to disguise themselves as Japanese.

Hank was aware of why the two organizations were not sharing information. Halsey's people were collecting their own intelligence and Halsey did not trust the mix of Ivy leaguers with no fighting experience and all kinds of odd political views. Full on spies were different characters. Ted was a nice guy, but one with a New York edge. They talked casually about Hank's interest as a photographer and

Ted suggested that they bring cameras along on their outing so that Hank could show him a few things.

There were still French girls picking up sailors on the beach. However, the pink "hotel" on Avenue Fontaine had changed owners. "That's the house. I still see some of the girls on the beach, but Tutau paid heavily for that ledger. I have no idea if she knew what she was doing, but hopefully Madame is enjoying a comfortable retirement somewhere. Depends on how she answered the questions. They probably still collect some information."

"Hey, I'm thirsty, wanna get a beer? I'll bet that place is Coney Island upstairs and downstairs."

Hank looked at Knight as if he were possibly suffering from sunstroke. "The bouncers have changed and, of course, we are holding Chemin in the brig. If I went in there, I'm afraid I…would not be welcome."

"Yeah, I guess you would have to be Harry Houdini to get out in one piece. Say, let's swing out to the beach and take some pictures of scenery, at least the landscape we haven't dug up for airstrips." The road above town led to spectacular views of the harbor. There was not even a cloud or haze to obstruct the view of what was being loaded, unloaded or deployed from the area. "What a place for an enemy coast watcher to collect information."

Hank looked across at Ted Knight. "Yes, it's a good harbor, but not everyone wants us here. Most of the plantation people don't care who wins."

Knight examined the scene. "Reminds me of my last assignment to Indochina. The French are a real mess, aren't they? They want us to support some guy, Ho Chi-Minh, in some cockamamie liberation thing. Not even sure what liberation the Viet Minh are looking for

– Japanese? French? It's a wonder that anyone can collaborate in this puzzle box."

Hank was astounded. Halsey's doubts about the OSS had just been confirmed in thirty seconds. These guys had no loyalties. They were smart, but they could make more problems than they solved. Thank God he worked where there was at least a chain of command, and where everyone had a tidy job to do. As sunset drew close, they headed back into town.

"So, what about a couple girls for us? You married yet?" Knight was certainly blunt. Hank had photographed hundreds of women, and not even gotten to know their names. He knew them as objects of beauty. Naomi was his first real companion and he was not about to drag her along on some soldier's adventure. He would tell Knight about Naomi once they settled down to dinner. Knight caught the light as Hank's gold ring flashed in the orange of the sunset.

Knight ordered two gins. He pushed one across to Hank. "Here's a good Dutch shot. Drink up, buddy. I'm afraid we don't have any herring out here to wash it down. Not sure that raw tilapia would quite cut it." Hank sniffed the gin, then tipped it back. Straight gin, or Genever, snorts back, right through the nose, unifying all the senses into one feeling of breathless existence. It had been a great day. Perhaps tomorrow he could requisition some color film for the two of them to get pictures out in the islands.

"So, you didn't answer. Can we get a couple girls tonight, or are we batching it? Shall we go to the officer's club and find a couple nurses?"

Hank blanched. "The officer's club?"

"Yeah, I can get us in."

"So you entered the OSS as an officer?"

"Sure, most of us have college degrees, more than one usually. So, do you have a girl?"

"I'm engaged. We will be marrying as soon as the war is over. She works for the French governor."

"Is she French?"

"Well, her mother was half French. She's actually mixed, but a beautiful girl."

"You're a lucky man. Sounds like she is smart too."

"Yes, she was raised by the nuns, but she also is very well connected to the wealthy planters. I'm sure lucky that she didn't choose one of them." Hank proudly showed off the Imperial Jade.

"So is that your engagement ring?" The light in the café was dimmer, but it highlighted the beautifully carved golden dragons on each side of the stone. Knight was staring intently at the ring so Hank pulled it off to let Knight admire the work.

The OSS agent turned the ring over and over in his hands, held it up to the light, and ran his thumbnail around the heavily carved dragons. Apparently the man was some sort of connoisseur, an odd hobby. Knight handed back the ring. He was familiar with gold work, and had recognized the inprimé of an Indochinese goldsmith. "Your fiancée Tonkinese?"

Hank looked puzzled, "I don't think so, but I only know that she is half European. Why?"

Knight commented. "It's very beautiful. What a precious engagement gift." But his mental landscape had changed completely. This ring could not possibly have been purchased on a secretary's salary. He had checked it for any working parts. The button on his own jacket concealed a tiny compass, and God knows what the Japs put into rings these days. It looked clean but it was too new to be an heirloom and too expensive to be from the girl.

Someone had given it to her, but why? He needed names, places and information and he had to get them carefully. Hank was not stupid.

Knight's ingenuous smile alternated with a wistful glance. "I don't have a serious girlfriend now. I was dating someone in New York, but she moved on. Life in China didn't appeal to her. There aren't a lot of American women in Shanghai, and I'm not really comfortable with foreigners. Too many twisted trails. So what's her name?"

"Whose name?"

"Your fiancée?"

"Naomi. She works for Governor Laigret and I met her at a Javanese Club banquet. She is part Javanese, but she is very tall. She was raised in a convent, so I don't know her parents." Somehow the tale of a dead mother and a father who rejected a little girl were just too delicate to share with a stranger. "I wasn't looking for anyone in particular, but when we were introduced, I knew she was the one."

"I know what you mean. Maybe I should be like you and look around a little more. I just never considered getting involved with a native. I was afraid of what I might find – or of what she might discover."

Hank looked down at his plate of fried fish and rice. His appetite was gone. He wasn't in the mood to counsel some lonely outsider and he didn't want to talk about Naomi.

Meanwhile, Knight stopped eating. He looked at his plate and moved his food back and forth with a knife and fork, lost in thought. He sat up in his chair in an effort to relieve the knot in his gut. This was serious. God, if the Vichy or Japs had their rats infiltrating all over this island, this would be one long damned war. He pushed his plate away.

Hank was tongue-tied. He didn't want to talk any more.

"You're looking a little fatigued buddy. The sun and the gin get to you?"

"I'm OK … "

Knight took the lead. "Let's call it an early night. And sleep in tomorrow morning. Shall we say a 10:00 pick up?" As soon as Burns dropped him off at his lodging, Knight went to work as a rat-catcher.

Relieved to have a little catch-up time, Hank got a good night's sleep and retreated to his desk in the morning. The orders and invoices had not disappeared, and there was comfort in knowing exactly where things were. Hank twisted his jade ring. He had called Naomi's office twice that morning.

An unfamiliar voice picked up the phone. "I'm sorry sir, she is not at work today."

He went by her rooming house. The attendant pushed a buzzer, then irritated, walked down the hall and returned.

"She is maybe visiting family?"

Naomi had vanished.

CHAPTER 35

Noumea
August 1944

"Russian Troops reach Concentration Camps in Poland"

– *News dispatch*

THE WHITE NOISE OF BUSYWORK filled days and weeks. Army bureaucracy was a scaffold of things that people used to construct their daily lives. Predictable routines and uniform American products offered a sense of comfort. All the chocolate bars were Hersheys, there were no truffle fillings here or variations in the grades of cacao. Firestone tires left the same distinctive tracks. The war was winding down.

Hank took just a moment to pick up a news dispatch before starting in on his first tasks. The Allies were winning in Europe. Only one outpost in France remained before the Nazis would be driven out. There were victories in the Pacific as well. The knockout blow was delivered in a small article near the bottom of the dispatch. It shattered any sense of an imminent victory for the "good guys." There were no details in this first report. No one knew what had happened in the concentration camps, only that the Germans had bulldozed them and hastily planted some trees, leaving the buildings behind.

Where were his mother, his brother? What had happened to Esther? He lay awake that night with his eyes wide open, avoiding dreams. This calamity was much larger than clan. It was a failure of the human race. Everything he had ever been taught about humanity was lost under the possibility that his family and his entire community had disappeared into the German ovens. No one deserved this. The Golden Rule that the Christians taught in their orientation services was obviously a flawed ideal. No country, rooted in any sort of belief in a God, could have done what the German monsters accomplished. That left only one possibility – that the idea of a God was a false one.

How could he find his family, if they survived? Or was he better off without them? Few kindnesses had been shared during their years together. He had loved his sister dearly, but when he gave everything he had to save her, she spurned him. Justice was absent from these scenarios. He resented the treatment from his family, but they had probably faced savage consequences. Letters and gifts were distributed to the men, but there was nothing for him in the mail calls. Then there were the girlfriends. Gentle Greta, with two thugs for brothers. What had become of her? Exotic Naomi, who had simply disappeared, would probably land on her feet with her intelligence and charisma. With luck, his clever sister Esther would use both brains and charm to see her way to safety. Women couldn't be trusted or else he would just need to get better at reading signposts on the roads to betrayal.

The orders on his desk required him to move to the Presidio at San Francisco. He had been recommended for officer's training school and, within a week, he would be joining those who were disappearing from Noumea. After that, who knew? Resting both elbows on his desk, he held his head between his hands, muffling sounds of the busy corridors.

His own mind was the loneliest place he could find, a place of dark dreams and odd silences in the midst of so much confusion. He would drink all day if he could do it without getting a migraine. How nice it would be to forget everything, just for an evening.

"Hey buddy, Congratulations! Hear you're leaving this hell-hole." A young corporal came by with a stack of papers, invoices to check and file. A troop ship was coming through, but they were not dropping off more men. They were picking up a stream of combatants who had been scattered all over the islands. The men were excited about a stay in Hawaii, and California was supposed to be some sort of a promised land. He didn't believe in promises. At their best, promises were weak links between human beings. There was no certainty even if the intentions were heartfelt.

Another harsh disappointment had impacted his ability to trust Americans. Hank was promised expedited citizenship in return for his service as a U.S. soldier. Unfortunately, there were a few snags in his paperwork. The time in Canada was deducted from his U.S. residency, and a new entry date was established after his return. The fact that he had provided important services to the U.S. did not help him, and he lost two years of his residency. The effective "Dutch" cover did not help him establish any credentials as a potential American either. As far as anyone was concerned, his five years of U.S. residency was now about two years. Buried in OSS archives were signed agreements that stated he would not disclose any operational details for fifty years, so he might well die as a man with no country. The knots and snarls of Army records were working against him when they should have been his ticket to a new life.

He was alone, but not the captain of his fate.

CHAPTER 36

Bergen Belsen
April 1945

"We have to go into the despair and go beyond it, by working and doing for somebody else, by using it for something else."

- Elie Wiesel

COLD RAIN PELTED THE WOMEN'S camp. Drips from leaks in the ceilings and walls were the only sounds in the night, time suspended in death. Bodies were everywhere, piled throughout the camp. During the past two months, transports of workers from Sobibur and Auschwitz had unloaded their cargo and the population of Belsen kept increasing. At the same time, typhus swept through the bunks, some of which were crowded with three or four girls. Esther had seen two sisters die already this week. Margot fell out of the bunk onto the stone floor and was too weak to get up. A day later her little sister died in their bed. They were now in the pile outside. The air in the room strangled her as she thought of her asthmatic little brother.

Esther had hoped that Lutz might take her to his warm quarters, but he had not asked for her in several days. She felt her thin body, and her oily hair – she was no longer a prize, and even her humor and teasing could not save her now. He probably had moved on to a fresher captive. Her arms went around Hannah, and the two young women nestled closer for warmth. Finally, drowsiness overcame them both and she fell asleep.

A gloved hand shook her awake. Lutz had wakened the guard and stood over the bunk, furious. "We will make an example of you! Thieving Jew bitch!" So, the time had come. She would be one more body in the alley between the buildings, rotting in the rain, unseeing and a part of oblivion. He grabbed her roughly around the neck, and dragged her outside, fired a shot and.... missed? She touched her arm, terrified to find that she was still alive. He seized her hand and threw a boy soldier's jacket over her. She remembered the pile of uniforms that she had encountered three years ago. She had cut out the bloodied patches, replaced them with new materials, and added Nazi decorations to one jacket after another, jackets like this one. She pulled on the trousers over her striped uniform. "Just walk. Not a word."

A Volkswagen was parked and idling at the edge of the women's quarters. An early April storm was at its height, pounding like heartbeats of the soon to be dead. "Get in the back and hide yourself. No, not the back seat. Get in the luggage well behind it. You are so small now, you can curl up like you are sleeping." Over her he placed a coat, and a nearly empty duffel bag. The engine started up, a deafening noise under her ear, and he drove down the central road of the camp and out the North Main Gate. A nod to the sentry; there were no official orders. "Supplies." There was no food left in Belsen, and he was prepared to raid farms for some root vegetables and anything that could be eaten. Pre-dawn raids on farms were the only way to get anything into the camp.

Rumors were that Germany was losing to the Allies. Lutz was not acting like a victor. He was very purposeful in his actions and demeanor, a soldier. They drove into Celle, and then stopped on a country road where he changed out of his uniform in the early light. The Volkswagen started up again, and they bumped along farm roads for the next four hours. Finally, he was willing to speak to her.

"Are you awake?"

"What are we doing?"

"You must be still. We are in danger."

She began to laugh. She had seen danger and this wasn't it. For the first time in three years she smelled fresh air, even if it was through mud and gas fumes.

"I can be still. But where are we going?"

"Hamburg. I will be meeting my friends there."

"Why did you take me?"

"I thought you might enjoy a holiday. Now, you must be quiet."

She thought of family holidays in August, days on the North Sea, smoked eel hanging on racks and *frieten* – French fries with golden yellow mayonnaise. This morning the thought of rich food didn't appeal. It was fine in dreams of the past. And, as of this morning, there seemed to be some sort of future. A blind misted future, but a future all the same.

The checkpoints were not orderly. Posts were abandoned and the inconspicuous tan Volkswagen threaded its way into the city of bombed out ruins. The car halted. Odors of fish and the sea were in the air, along with diesel oil and alcohol. Apparently, surrender included drinking all available German liquor before the Allies came through. The mid-morning quiet and bottles were evidence that this area was for nighttime entertainments. Lutz parked the car, and knocked on the door of a closed cabaret.

"You're early. We were not expecting you until 11:00."

"I had a chance to leave a little earlier. May I come in? I also have brought a guest with me." The dark haired proprietor looked out at the deserted street and the military car.

"Good morning, then. I am Juan Antonio. You may call me Johann if you prefer. Where is your guest?"

"We need to get him out of the car."

"I am not taking Nazi deserters."

"Please don't worry." He pulled down the back seat and removed the coat and the bag.

Esther looked up at them, "Are we there yet?" She smiled brightly. Even in a boy's uniform, she could flirt.

"My God, she stinks. We have beautiful girls here, ones with full breasts and shining blonde hair. Why did you bring another one?"

"She is not for you. I want to take her with me. The papers are for Herr and Frau Georg Lutz, *ja*?"

The agent laughed. "Let me wake one of the girls. She needs a bath." Turning back to Lutz he stated, "Also, we need to dispose of the car right away. Hand me the keys. We'll just take it down to the harbor and leave the keys in it. Someone will steal it soon enough."

Creaking stairs announced the presence of a sturdy young woman. She looked like the guards in Belsen. Esther looked around at the dusty furniture and the dark peeling wallpaper. What color had it been? My God, she didn't want to end up in a German brothel, but Irma seized her arm and led her away from the bar. When she faltered on the stairs, Irma grabbed her by the waist. "*Ach du lieber*, they have not been feeding you? Little boys sent out to lose this war, and they don't even feed them." Esther did not say a word. A warm bubble bath had been prepared, and it didn't look or smell like gas. She asked to bathe alone, and Irma said, "Of course, but let me know if you would like me to do your back or your hair. Please put the uniform outside the door. We will bring you clean clothes."

The tears came as Esther sank into the bubbles. Fear, relief, grief? Who knew? Then she began to sob. They mustn't hear her sobs, so she turned on the hot water to drown them out. A soft shampoo glided through her hair. She washed it three times. Maybe by washing her head she could wash away the dark and frightening thoughts. Her face would never be clean enough, not ever again. A smile played for a moment as she thought of childhood fights in the bathtub.

"Mama! I don't want water on my face! Ow! There is soap in my eyes."

The screaming child was dead inside her.

Irma knocked, "I have some clothes for you. They said you were to have these." Esther got out of the tub and opened the door, dripping and stark naked, the waters pouring off her emaciated body. "Here, use a towel." Irma began to briskly rub her back with the soft warm cloth. She handed her underwear. The long panties nearly fell off. "I'm sorry, those are the smallest we have." Irma surveyed her body. "Here is an undershirt. And I have a simple dress for you." A plain tailored navy and white polka dot dress with a demure white collar, just the sort of thing her mother would have picked out.

"What do you want me to do?"

"Get dressed of course."

"But then what?"

"I don't know. I was only ordered to dress you. I am following instructions. Here, you will also need a coat and a hat."

"Then I'm not staying here?"

Down at the bar Lutz had unpacked a small sack from his duffel and proffered it to Juan Antonio. He was now in a tweed suit with a proper hat and coat. He put his hand over the sack as Esther came toward him, and averted his eyes. The proprietor smiled at her. "Please go with Irma, she will get you some soup."

As the girls turned toward the kitchen, Juan emptied the sack of jewelry and several other small gold objects. He pulled out a scale and weighed it. "This will suffice. It is just a few grams short of a half-kilo." He pulled out blank documents. "So what do you call your 'wife'?"

Lutz thought a minute,"Zus. She is so sweet. Zus for Susani."

"So we will name her Susani Lutz?"

"I guess so."

"Wait a minute, you will need wedding rings. Let's find a couple in this. A gift from me. Good luck in your marriage. Now you need to get the hell out of here before the Americans come."

Esther sat down in the dining room with the soup. A newspaper on the table held headlines of Allied attacks on Hamburg and all of Germany. It did not tell of German officers fleeing. It did not tell of help from outside. Clearly, Juan Antonio was some of that outside help. Where was he from? Lutz came to join her and handed her the wedding band. She held it in the palm of her hand. Whose was it? This trinket that Lutz was holding out had been someone's dearest possession. She looked through it to see if there were any ghosts inside the circle. Lutz picked it back up and put in on her ring finger. "Where are we going?"

His worried eyes creased at the corners as the shadow of a smile crossed his face. "If you will have me as your husband, we will leave Europe immediately. Germany is expected to surrender within days. We leave this afternoon. Antonio will drive us down to the harbor and get us passage. By the way, your papers identify you as Susani Lutz, housewife."

Susani, Esther, what did it matter? She was now the captive of a captive. "Passage to where?"

"We can't ask too many questions. Argentina entered the war three weeks ago and they are willing to evacuate Germans and Jews in exchange for certain ... commodities. Gold, artworks, anything of value that has been stored for the new Reich."

She thought of the valuables in her Amsterdam house. No doubt it had been looted of everything. In her mind were images of the Art Nouveau furnishings and antiques, gifts from more than a hundred years of trading in Japan and China. Her mother had taken it all for granted, the lovely works of art and the task of making sure that the maids kept everything dusted properly. She wondered if they had found the safe that was built inside the wall? In it was a cache of diamonds, mother's large emerald ring, and silver that was used to set a formal table for twenty. All these possessions, and she had nearly died of starvation.

"Lutz, we need to go to New York."

"Juan Antonio can get us to Argentina easily." He looked at her, puzzled and a little shocked. If he remained in Germany, he would be captured as a deserter and executed. The Soviets were already advancing on Germany, threatening civilians. They could not wait. He hesitated. She always said things for a reason. Her calculating mind never stopped. He loved that about her, but was sometimes annoyed by her questions that had no good answers. "Zus, why New York.?"

"We need to find my brother. He went to New York."

What tales they would have to tell. No doubt Hans would be appalled that she had a German "husband." But, she had wanted to be an actress and she had survived as one. No lights, no cameras, just a daily life of pretending. What illusions she had performed. She looked like a wraith today, but after some food, who knew? Lutz apparently thought she could be beautiful again.

Of all the places on earth she had picked the largest and busiest city in human existence, in a country that would hate Germans. Who knew how they would respond to Jews? He had a good idea of how it would for Germans. Thank God he was Austrian. How ironic it would be if her race were their ticket.

"New York is a very large place, and who knows where your brother might be?"

"Lutz, what will happen to all the property – the homes and assets of the Jews? Of the Dutch, French and other people once the conquest is over?" His elbows had been on the table, with hands clasped, taking charge. Now one hand closed over his chin and jaw as he bit his lip. He peered at the 'helpless girl' that he had met three years ago.

Her questions kept coming. "Won't they allow families to make claims? Our home in Amsterdam is valuable, and my parents hid other assets before Holland surrendered to Germany. If there is a chance to reclaim ... anything... my brother and I will need to do it. Look at me. I have lost my name and my family. I don't have a chance to act alone, and I certainly can't file suits from Argentina under a name that was never known in Amsterdam."

Juan Antonio looked at the two of them. "Shall we try to get you on a train to Spain or Portugal? From there you may be able to board a ship for America."

Forty-eight hours later she looked up at the enormous steamship in the Lisbon harbor. What luck, she would finally be on her way to America! Over and over in her wildest dreams she had imagined escaping and finding her brother in New York. In 1941 she had heard an American speech about freedoms – freedom of religion, speech, freedom from want and freedom from fear. She had lived with the consequences of her awful mistake on her birthday six years ago, and had experienced the loss of each of these freedoms. Once they got to America she would be able to find Hans and her future.

CHAPTER 37

Upstate New York
May 1945

"U.S. Army Retrains Prisoners of War. *Handpicked prisoners are given a six-day course in U.S. style democracy and sent back to Germany or Austria as free men."*

- Christian Science Monitor

Lieutenant Burns looked up at the prisoner standing in front of him, a young German wearing a loose blackish jumpsuit with POW stenciled on the sleeves, chest and legs. The prisoner had no name, no rank and no home. A simple nametag read "Willi." He stood nervously in front of the officer, his steel-rimmed eyeglasses fogging up with nervous sweat. He did not stand at attention or salute. Military attitudes were forbidden to the prisoners.

Some eggheads had gotten together with the Department of State and decided that the army would now take on the process of making peace with enemy soldiers. Prisoners were coming by boatloads into San Francisco and shipping out to Camp Shoemaker in the East Bay. Used barracks were plopped down into Northern California, a short bus ride away from the San Francisco harbor. The eggheads' idea was that U.S. Army Intelligence would now determine the captives' loyalties, and craft democratic citizens who could be repatriated in a new Europe.

More than fifty countries had participated in the conflict, using young men who might have volunteered, might have been conscripted, or who might have been serving as prisoners all along. The process then was to separate European prisoners into groups of: Black – hostile and unrepentant, Gray – non-committal, and White – compliant listeners who might respond to reeducation. Former members of the SS and Gestapo were pre-determined to be "Blacks - *Schwarzen*" because of their proven loyalties to the Reich. They were sent to holding areas, where they would be reprocessed into work units. They would be trained for hard labor, and later sent to clean up the ruins of France. The rest would be sorted by a series of interviews. "Whites" would be given crash courses in English and the principles of American democracy before they were returned to Germany.

Burns looked at his prisoner, greeted him in German, and invited him to sit down. Willi stood with a stern, expressionless face, eyes not moving behind the glare of his spectacles. The Army Morale Officer pulled his chair around the corner of the desk and introduced himself. "I guess you know why you are here. It's a long way from Europe, isn't it?" The young prisoner startled at the friendly question, a quick short gasp, and turned toward his interrogator. This was not what he had expected. He had planned on being threatened, asked questions that he could not answer, and perhaps physically assaulted. He nodded his head. "Where are you from?" The prisoner looked confused. "Where did you live before the war?"

"Oh, we had a little farm in the Rhineland, but I went away to school. I was studying when I was called to serve."

"What were you studying?"

Burns waited through the long silence. Willi bit his lip, and looked around the room. He drew in his breath and puffed out a thick sigh, one that would convey his memories into words.

"Music, I was studying violin." Then silence, stillness so complete that not even air could escape. He removed his glasses and wiped them, keeping his head lowered and avoiding the scrutiny of the Morale Officer. He hadn't even heard a recording of a violin in three years, let alone touched one.

"Were you working as well?"

"I sometimes helped with repairs – fine woodworking, that sort of thing."

"Ah, so you are an artist and a woodworker." Burns paused. "I was an artist before the war as well – photography."

The captive became even more uncomfortable. Was this a conversation? Was he supposed to ask questions? Why were they talking about art?

"I want to ask you a few questions about your education. You must have been a kid in 1933. What did you learn about Hitler?"

"He was our leader, and we were supposed to.. to.. to organize our society around ideals?"

"Were you a member of the Nazi Party?"

"Everybody had to respect the Führer."

"I'm going to repeat the question." Hans looked directly into the eyes of his captive. "Were you a member of the Nazi Party?"

"We didn't actually join, but we were loyal."

"So you are a man of loyalties. By 'we' do you mean your family?"

"My papa tried to do what was best."

"When did you last write a letter to your family?"

Hank was already thinking about placing the young man into an intensive six-day course where he would study American Government and Principles of Democracy. The responses to these questions would need to match up under a polygraph interview. Some smart captives knew how to trick interviewers. Willi would also be assigned part time to the woodshop where he could practice his skills. It would be a long time before he saw a violin.

"Let's talk a little bit about your service to the Reich." The captive hesitated then explained the details of the recruiting officers coming to the conservatory and emptying it of able bodied young men. "So they sent you to the French front. Were you in Normandy?"

Willi hesitated. He was not a hero. He had been alone in the room of an abandoned hotel, his gun pointed out the window, when an American soldier walked into the room. Turning around, the soldier spoke, "*Hände hoch oder ich scheiss.*" "Hands up or I'll shit." The American had inverted the German ie/ei vowel combinations. He had meant to say: "*Hände hoch oder ich schiess.*" "Hands up or I'll shoot." The American had made a mistake, but he observed the young man's back shaking with laughter and the barrel of his gun bobbing in the open window. He was able to wrestle Willi to the ground and take him prisoner. As far as Willi knew, the consequences of laughing at the error might now result in his torture or death.

Burns smiled and quietly held in his laughter over the bizarre circumstances of Willi's capture. He had processed three other men that morning, including a defiant former officer, a sullen fifteen year-old kid, and a schoolteacher who possibly had communist sympathies. Willi was a good candidate for re-education, thoughtful and aware of how his life had been affected by the Nazi vision. Feeling pretty good about his efforts at making peace with just one German, Hank Burns stepped outside for a midday walk. At a local newsstand he looked at a couple of magazines, a San Francisco Chronicle, and city papers from all over the U.S. A news headline caught his eye:

Dachau captured by Americans who kill guards, liberate 32,000

DACHAU, Germany, April 30 – Dachau, Germany's most dreaded extermination camp, has been captured and its surviving 32,000 tortured inmates have been freed by outraged American troops who killed or captured its brutal garrison in a furious battle.

Prisoners with access to records said that 9,000 captives had died of hunger and disease or been shot in the past three months, and 14,000 more had perished during the winter. Typhus was prevalent in the camp and the city's water supply was reported to have been contaminated by drainage from 6,000 graves near the prison.

39 Cars Full of Bodies

A short time after the battle there was a train of thirty-nine coal cars on a siding. The cars were loaded with hundreds of bodies and from them was removed at least one pitiful human wreck that still clung to life. These victims were mostly Poles and most of them had starved to death as the train stood there idle for several days. Lying alongside a busy road nearby were the murdered bodies of those who had tried to escape.

Bavarian peasants – who traveled this road daily – ignored both the bodies and the horrors inside the camp to turn the American seizure of their city into an orgy of looting. Even German children rode by the bodies without a glance, carrying stolen clothing.

The camp held 32,000 emaciated, unshaven men and 350 women, jammed in the wooden barracks. Prisoners said that 7,000 others had been marched away on foot during the past few days. The survivors went wild with joy as the Americans broke open their pens, smothering their liberators with embraces.

Bodies were found in many places. Here also were the gas chambers – camouflaged as "showers" into which prisoners were herded under the pretext of bathing – and the cremation ovens. Huge stacks of clothing bore mute testimony to the fate of their owners.

Rescued by soldiers

When Lieut. Col. Will Cowling of Leavenworth, Kan. slipped the lock in the main gate, there was still no sign of life inside this area. He looked around for a few seconds and then a tremendous human cry roared forth. A flood of humanity poured across the flat yard – which would hold a half dozen baseball diamonds — Colonel Cowling was all but mobbed.

He was hoisted to the shoulders of the seething, swaying crowd of Russians, Poles, Frenchmen, Czechs, and Austrians, cheering the Americans in their native tongues. The American colonel was rescued by soldiers, but the din kept up.

Flags appeared and waved from the barracks. There was even an American flag, although only one American was held there. He is a major from Chicago captured behind the German lines when he was on special assignment for the Office of Strategic Services.

Reprint courtesy of New York Times

In a flash the feeling of satisfaction from his morning's work disappeared. There was no purpose in it. He had spent days asking young men about their families. Now he stood on a sunny corner reading the headlines. He and his family were part of a massive tragedy that had no purpose. There would be no peace. Desolation, despair, loneliness, yes. There was no meaning in reconciliation, no room for acceptance or forgiveness. He froze his face into a mask, one that would not reveal any thoughts or feelings.

There were no afternoon interviews. He closed his door and wrote up reports. Pain seized his chest, a squeezing and clawing in the area around the heart, but he didn't want to leave work to ponder the fate of his family. He wasn't sure if the liberation of the camps was good news, or if it revealed sorrows that could never be conquered. For one thing, who were these people and why had they been shipped from the east to Dachau? Six years after his last meeting with Esther he needed to think about fate – her fate and his. It was certain that she and Peter had not married and lived happily ever after. Had she been seized, and did she survive? He couldn't imagine his plump mother working or starving to death.

Resolve filled him. If Esther were a prisoner in the camps, there would be no bouquets of flowers on her upcoming birthday. Hopefully, she had found ways to survive. How did one find people who had been freed? That evening he pulled out his packet of blue stationery and decided to address a first letter to the family home in Amsterdam.

Dear Moeder,

It has been a long time since I have written, and we have all had experiences that perhaps are best not to share. I have been working for the U.S. Army since....

He broke off his sentence. What could he tell her? He had had three meals a day while Jewish families starved in camps. He was proud of his work, but he was under federal non-disclosure restrictions that would last most of his lifetime. He pondered the statements that bound his loyalties.

OSS NON-DISCLOSURE

I understand and accept that by being granted access to classified information, special confidence and trust shall be placed in me by the United States Government. ...

I have been advised that the unauthorized disclosure, unauthorized retention, or negligent handling of classified information by me could cause damage...

How could he let his mother know that he was a man now, that he had undertaken things that required great responsibility and judgment? He was not to disclose his accomplishments until sometime in the very distant future, if ever.

Unless and until I am released in writing by an authorized representative of the United Stated Government, I understand that all conditions and obligations imposed upon me by this agreement apply during the time I am granted access to classified information, and at all times thereafter.

Even though he had dispatched his duties with honor and received medals and promotions, he couldn't tell anyone what he had done. Heroes in bars would brag about tight moments in battle. What could he say? "I took pictures and counted supplies." "I shot the war with a camera, not a gun." He did not really belong to the brotherhood of returning soldiers. He was of no more consequence than when he inventoried shops for his stepfather.

Instead of writing up his exploits, he asked for information about his brother and sister. Where had they gone? Had Max survived? Either his asthma kept Max from being a good candidate for a work camp, or he had become stronger. It was also possible that there were no survivors, and the letters were an exercise in futility. Curiosity about his family prepared him for any answer and none. He folded the thin blue paper into thirds and carefully addressed the envelope to his mother. A new piece of paper was lifted from the tidy stack.

Dear Esther,

I am not sure that you will ever see this letter, but there are some things I want to put in writing. When we last saw each other, you were in love, and you were willing to give up your chances for life in America to be with your lover. I didn't understand why someone would do this. But I have also learned some things about love in these last five years.

Anyway, your birthday is coming soon and I hope that somewhere, somehow, you are celebrating it. I believe you would be 24 now, perhaps married? I have not been so lucky with love. We can talk about that when we next see each other.

I would like to hear from you, and also to hear news of mother and Max. Please let me know what you find out.

All the best,
Hans

Later that night Hank lay on his bed, his body rigid. Not a muscle moved, but inside he was trembling. Thoughts and worries flashed, nightmares with no images. He took stock of himself. A vast country far from Holland was now his home. Soon he would become an American citizen, but pride rang hollow. There was no one to celebrate his hard work, and his accomplishments were all in classified records. He sat up in the dark, eyes wide open, feeling nothing and everything. It was after ten o'clock.

He had seen men worn from battle, and he wasn't one of them. He didn't have scars that anyone could see. Some fighting men chased women. Hank's choices in women had proved disastrous. No wonder people drank. It had its merits. He dressed, looked at the neatly stacked letters on his desk, and left his room. Maybe a shot or two of gin at the officer's club would numb the worries and help him sleep.

The club was quiet, a few couples were sitting in banquettes, some single men perched on stools, and a couple of card games were in progress. He took a stool and ordered a shot of gin. Tipped it up, set the glass down.

"Refill, sir?"

"Please."

He lifted the second shot, a silent toast to Holland running through his mind. The shot of gin burned. In just a moment he should be able to relax. The chest pain came again, a brutal squeeze that took his breath away. Officers don't faint, but the next thing he knew he was lying on the carpet. The room twisted around him. There were a few peanut shucks right in his line of vision. He could hear garbled talking, as if he were under water, but he couldn't speak. There just wasn't enough air in the room. More talking, and hands grasping him. He didn't like the jostling – the movement on the stretcher made him queasy. Seasick. He hadn't been seasick a day in his life. Why didn't things stop moving?

The night went on and on, like a scene out of purgatory. The ambulance pulled up to the Army hospital. The glass doors opened into white glare and noise. People rushed toward the gurney, dragging boxes, attaching stickers to his chest and legs, trying to make him talk. He wanted to close his eyes and sleep.

By now he knew he was in the hospital, a place where some would be saved, and some would not. He was pretty sure it didn't matter much in his case. A bed, some sleep – that mattered. Near dawn a nurse came into the darkened ward, looked at his chart and took his wrist. She turned her watch around and began to count the seconds. The touch seemed so familiar. It wasn't his mother's touch. She checked his wristband. "Hank Burns, Lt."

"Hank Burns?" She dropped his wrist and hurried to the end of the long room with its two rows of beds. He looked out toward the nurse's station at the far end, and saw that she was tall, blonde hair rolled up under her starched white cap. She spoke rapidly to another nurse, pointing toward his cot. The second nurse shook her head, took the blonde by the shoulders and steered her back into the ward.

"Mr. Burns, I have to take your pulse again." She took his wrist, breathing slowly as she concentrated on her counts for one minute. Sixty-three. The bartender said he had only taken two shots. Clearly he had been sick, but it was not life threatening. "Sir, can you tell me what happened?"

His voice was weak, but the Dutch accent was unmistakable. She asked a different question.

"Do you know who I am?"

Obviously, he was supposed to know. Her touch was so…

"Greta?" Good God, she had the right to kill him. "Greta, I'm so sorry."

She cleared her throat and took a deep breath.

"Why are you sorry? Drinking too much, or seeing me again?"

"Not – sorry … to see you again."

"Never mind. It was a long time ago. I waited days for you to call, but I also knew why you didn't. You just left."

The combination of a hangover and tranquilizers had stolen his wits. He had to say something. "I decided to join the army." Hopefully that would suffice.

His eyes came into focus on her face. "So, you work here now? At this hospital?"

"Yes, I joined the army as well. Once I got my nursing degree, I went to Ohio with my husband."

"You are married then." She certainly didn't act like a married woman.

"I'm widowed. Ron died in Normandy."

Hank grasped her wrist. They sat quietly in the ward holding hands as the sun began to rise through the windows. Her co-worker rushed through the open room, waking patients, and getting breakfast trays ready. Greta straightened her cap, and began to help men move from their beds. Her duty would be ending very soon. He wasn't sure if she had just been nice to him, or if there could ever be a way to repair all the damages that had been caused by others. A new nurse brought Hank a breakfast tray. On the tray was a slip of paper with a telephone number. The note said "Do you still like meatloaf?" He recognized the writing.

The doctor came by and moved the stethoscope around Hank's chest and abdomen. "Breathe."

"You did not have a heart attack. Sometimes we can have anxiety attacks. They are very real, and they can be dangerous."

"It's important that you don't work for three days. I'm going to notify your C.O. You need to get away and relax a little."

Those were words that Hank did not want to hear. He had been fleeing for six years – from Amsterdam to New York, to Noumea, and back. Wherever he had gone, he had brought his own thoughts, his own desires, his successes and disappointments. The idea that someone would "get away" for relaxation seemed like a false promise. He couldn't imagine a day without work, a day where he didn't know what to do. He put her note in his wallet as he dressed.

CHAPTER 38

Upstate New York
May 1945

"In an old Dutch Garden where the tulips grow
That's where I first whispered that I love you so."

~ *Glenn Miller song*

Hans paced the hall at the rooming house. At the end sat a small telephone table with a lamp, beckoning him. He never called anyone. If he did talk to Greta what could he possibly say? He wouldn't lie to her, but he certainly couldn't tell her everything he knew. The pacing and worrying made him feel weak again. He sat down on the chair by the table. After a few deep breaths he pulled out her note and dialed. Maybe she wouldn't be home anyway. He would give it five rings, and then go outside.

She picked up the receiver on the second ring.

"Greta, it's Hank."

"I thought it might be. How are you doing?"

"I'll live. It wasn't a heart attack. And, yes, I still like meatloaf."

Two nights later he showed up at her door with a large bouquet of red tulips. She kissed him on the cheek and put the flowers into a coffeepot filled with water. A saucepan with ice in it held a bottle of White Niagara. She handed him the corkscrew. He opened the wine and poured two glasses of the chilled New York sunshine. A plate of Dutch cheese and German Rye crackers sat on her coffee table.

"Greta, how did you end up in the U.S. Army?" He had been debriefing Germans for weeks, and none of them had been as dangerous as her brothers.

"I married about a year after I finished nursing school, and when Ron joined, I decided to go with him. He was a regular American boy." A soft smile contrasted with the sadness in her eyes. "An engineer. We had gone to high school together. And you?"

"Hard to say. I was in the Pacific." He had nothing more to say. His hand froze around the stem of the glass, and he set it down.

"Hank, you have to tell me the truth."

He hadn't thought of it quite that way, but he would want an honest wife.

She continued. "I went to your home. Your landlady didn't know where you had gone. You even left your clothes. I went to Rosenbaum's. He said that you had not come in to work, ever again. What happened?"

His head was down, trying to sort the information. She was right. He had to share something, and it had to be true. Yet, if he told all the truth, he would lose her again.

"Greta, you asked me something yesterday, something about worry. What happened to your family?"

"If you mean my parents, they bought a farm in Pennsylvania. Papa talks to his cows, raises a few pigs for meat, and mother sells eggs to the grocers. She has a couple hundred chickens. It is a busy, good life for them both. I talk to her every month, but I only see papa at Christmas."

"What about your brothers?"

"My brothers are both drunks. Mean drunks. They hate everybody, but they don't visit at all. We don't speak."

Hank was in the midst of a wrestling match with his conscience and his desires, angry about her brothers, jealous that she had already known love, and frustrated by his need to keep secrets.

"I don't know what to say about your brothers, but I can tell you this. I was an immigrant, and they had Nazi sympathies. Do you realize that if I were caught around any of you, I could have been deported?" He left out the fact that if he had been deported, he would have ended up in the work camps as a Jewish prisoner.

When their eyes met, both saw hurt and regret. He took her hand, immaculate and smooth. There were no long nails to scratch; nothing was chewed or bitten, she did not use lacquer to cover imagined flaws. She was strength and beauty, warmth and comfort. He lifted her hand to his face and kissed it. She startled, and stood up, quickly wrapped an apron around her dress and retrieved the meatloaf from the oven. They were both ravenous. He watched her as she sliced the meatloaf, and scooped the mashed potatoes onto his plate.

"Do you still like to dance?" He couldn't think of a future, only of things they had known together. She picked up the dishes, and pirouetted toward the sink. A bowl of fresh strawberries appeared. He arranged the two wine glasses and the tulips on her coffee table. Just as he poured, she dropped a strawberry into his glass and smiled. He fished it out, and popped it into her mouth, a little juice dripping toward her chin. He started to grab a napkin to wipe it away, then leaned in and kissed her instead. She was moist, sweet, and ripe.

CHAPTER 39

Brooklyn, New York
July 1947

"Four of the world's great powers sit in judgment today on twenty top Germans whom the democratic nations charge with major responsibility for plunging the world into World War II."

~ *Nuremberg Trials, New York Times*

Esther, now Susani Lutz, regarded the little cat in her open window. Warm summer sun streamed into the room, and the orange tabby seemed to be playing with the rays of light speckling the balcony. The tiger was hunting once more. She was fascinated by the actions, some quiet and stealthy and some bold and larger than life. How does the cat know which strategy to employ?

The little kitten had located its prey, a small butterfly. At first it carried the beautiful creature in its mouth, and then it decided to seize the wings as a toy. Once the butterfly stopped moving, it was no longer of interest to the kitten, which went on to find another creature. The young woman smiled and remembered looking out of her bedroom window in Amsterdam. As she went to pick up the dead butterfly from its place in the corner, it moved slightly in her hand. Setting it down on the windowsill, she watched the butterfly take off into the air. Playing dead had given it one more chance at life.

Susani and Georg Lutz lived in Brooklyn, in a cheery apartment with flowered drapes and carpets, a heavy cushioned sofa and a leather easy chair, all purchased on installment plans. She had picked it because the building on the corner of Prospect Place was yellow, and she wanted to spend the rest of her life in the sun. A grocer's and a baker's window were across the street, displaying their wares. Sometimes she would go to the Jewish delicatessen for the makings of a cold supper, or perhaps a piece of poppy seed cake. There, customers sat at little round tables speaking Yiddish and German. She did not sit with the women for long conversations. They were talking of their new appliances and their children. Babies with bottles and pacifiers firmly attached to their faces wandered around the shop and occasionally opened up their mouths for a piece of zwieback to chew on. Mornings were best. After lunch, noisy school aged children in the shop begged their mothers for cookies or sweets to take home.

The European environment of the deli was the closest thing she could find to the dairy and meat markets of Amsterdam, the Kosher bakery and the greengrocer. Holland had disappeared into the flood of news about America's uncomfortable rivalry with Russia and U.S. efforts to repair Germany and Japan. German and Dutch collaborators were seizing property all over Europe. If the home at 94 Herengracht was still standing, it was a valuable property. The diamonds and silver hidden inside the walls could sell for a small fortune. The problem was that she saw this as property that was rightly hers, and Lutz saw it as war booty.

Sometimes new acquaintances were curious about the young couple – the silent woman and her self-possessed husband. People would ask how they met, and she would smirk and respond, "In prison." Nobody asked anything more than that. Her green eyes often gazed off into a distance, far removed from the noise and energy of New York. The American dream was all over the magazines that Susani loved to look at, but it was far away from their Brooklyn neighborhood. She was picking up English quickly, but Georg was struggling with the language.

After he had drunk a couple beers at the German club, Susani occasionally heard his voice spouting old propaganda. He lacked the courage to mention that he had not planned to join the German Army in the first place. No one had planned to join any of the armies, so that was a moot point. It would be reprehensible to mention that he had been an SS officer, and he did not wish to end up hanging like a broken puppet at Nuremberg. In his mind it wasn't wrong to act against personal will, in the service of a greater cause. *It wasn't as if he had had a choice.* She hated him for his cowardice. *If you don't see a choice, make one!*

Lutz might have earned a hydraulic engineering degree in Austria, but with his German accent he was one of thousands of immigrants looking for work. He had finally found a position with a plumbing supplies manufacturer, and spent his days putting toilets together. The laborer's daily pay barely covered their rent and groceries and there had been countless arguments over money.

Now Georg had a second job. He had befriended the superintendent of this apartment building, offering his mechanical expertise to make antique radiators simmer with new energy. When the superintendent left to buy a farm upstate, Lutz was recommended for the job. People trusted him, his easy smile and his attention to their problems. Both of Georg's employers were Jewish, at least two generations away from Eastern Europe. He did not grasp the idea that his employers were now Americans. They left one foot in the immigrant world of the last century, and were not particularly aware of the recent efforts to destroy the Jewish people. In their rational world it was possible to hire a German mechanic.

In private discussions he would share his concerns about money, and about his employers. "The capitalists started the whole war. It was all about their greed." His tirade was one of dreams not realized and bitterness with no bottom. A sympathetic ear would get more than it bargained for. "Jew Capitalists caused the depression. Even the English knew that. Roosevelt knew it, but then he let them ride roughshod over our countries." If the conversation didn't halt at those comments, the bigger ideas would come out. "Hitler was our only chance against the capitalists and against the communists. We could have shown the world an ideal society."

He knew his wife was the daughter of "Jew capitalists" but she remained quiet during these comments. She was not rich. Due to his efforts, she was alive. It was enough that his wife's family had been sacrificed on the flaming altars of commerce and war.

Susani was learning to type, and to write simple inquiry letters in English. There was a Dutch consul in New York. She would need to persuade Lutz that a claim on the Herengracht home would be worth pursuing. Either they would be happy together, or she would be independent. At the consulate she stood in line and filled out several stacks of papers. An efficient clerk suggested that she stay updated on developments in Europe and the status of Dutch assets. Jewish homes were being seized as "abandoned property" and were now sold for pennies on the guilder. European families were starving, and a particularly cold winter had covered the Northern Hemisphere in ice that disappeared into floods. No one would want a four-story house to heat. The downstairs marble ballroom alone would consume fuel rations for the entire winter.

November 1947

Weeks later, in Amsterdam, Dinah Engels was filing letters for the Red Cross. Stacks of filing cards with names of senders and recipients were on her desk. The shards of families were scattered around the world like thousands of broken clay pipes, delicate, fragmented and too minute to reassemble. It was not possible to fill in the blanks. In front of her was a stack of cards tied to the valuable houses along the old canals. They had been occupied by Germans, the British and by every type of relief worker. Squatters filled in the spare rooms and attics. The street had escaped significant damages. She was to open each inquiry and to file the information on persons of interest.

Hans Bernsteen (Hank Burns) Rochester New York, USA. Mr. Bernsteen appeared to be quite industrious. He had written every three months since 1945. Like so many others, there were no other Bernsteens who had written to this address. A few blocks away in a legal office lay a letter and forms inquiring about the same address. A Mrs. Susani Lutz from Brooklyn, New York had formerly been known as Esther Bernsteen, or so she said. This would not be the first time that someone with dubious credentials was claiming title to an estate. The legal secretary checked with the Red Cross to see if there were any other family members who might have rights to the intact property.

Miss Engels rolled two sheets of paper and a sheet of carbon into her typewriter. "Dear Mr. Bernsteen (Burns): We have been unable to locate any of the persons you describe. Titles to the property are held in trust. We are in receipt of correspondence from a Susani Lutz, who claims to be Esther Bernsteen. Enclosed please find her documents from the Royal Dutch Embassy in Washington, D.C."

Hans sat in the red leather easy chair in his Rochester apartment. It was his one luxury, a place to read and relax after workdays. After three years of writing letters, Hans held onto the thin sheet of paper, staring at it in disbelief. His sister would not have married a Nazi. By now he knew that Nazis and Dutch collaborators were seizing any unclaimed property, hoping to turn fast profits. He consulted an attorney in order to prevent Susani Lutz from claiming the property in Amsterdam. He also decided that he would make contact for identification purposes only. "Please do pass my forwarding information on to Mrs. Lutz. It is imperative that she not be identified as Esther Bernsteen until I meet with her myself."

Susani received the official notification from the Red Cross about six weeks later. That evening she set down a plate of potatoes and cutlets, as well as an excellent beer. Lutz complimented her on her clever bargaining with the grocers. She smiled, and brought out a piece of warm apple tart.

Then she commented, "I may need to go to Amsterdam."

"Susani, you do not need to go anywhere." He wiped his napkin across his face, and dropped it beside his plate. "There is nothing in Holland. The war is over."

"Would you like some cream?" He looked at her in amazement, and took the pitcher from her hand. "Georg, I need to meet someone, a Mr. Bernsteen, who claims to be my brother. Our parents' house in Amsterdam is worth hundreds of thousands of guilders."

He looked up, spoon in mid-air dripping the cream onto his dessert plate. "Did you say 'hundreds of thousands'? What do you need to do to claim the estate?"

She sat down, appealing to her satiated man. "If my brother is alive, he and I need to file the claim together. Otherwise, both of our claims go to the state and we get nothing. Surely you want me to have what is mine?"

His mistrustful look covered the silent space between them.

"When did you know this?"

"I received a letter yesterday and had to have it translated. It is in English."

Lutz thought for a moment. He needed money and his Jewish wife might be able to provide it. Then he could invest in a business.

"An agent can sell your house and wire us the money."

Esther looked at her husband. She had concealed her identity – marriages had been destroyed when a husband or wife found out that his mate had been born as a Jew. Lutz had evaded the tribunals. She now attended Catholic mass with him. God knows what he said at his confessions. She would never confess anything, and she had never hurt anyone.

"Mr. Bernsteen does not even believe that I am alive. He had been writing the Red Cross in Amsterdam for two years looking for me. Now he has retained a lawyer and blocked all action on our property until I identify myself. Hans and I must present ourselves in the New York courts, and possibly in Amsterdam as well."

CHAPTER 40

Rochester, New York
July 1948

"We are going to have peace even if we have to fight for it."

~ *Dwight D. Eisenhower*

Hank looked at his lioness, stretched out languidly on the beach blanket, her mane of long hair moving gently in the breeze. Greta's long legs were bent to fit into the space, and her swelling abdomen moved slightly as she lay on her side. Hank was wide awake, alert and anxious. His import-export company was not doing well. It was a modest living, but not enough. People didn't want imports. Americans had come back home and there were more than enough men to make things the people didn't even know they needed. Like all women, Greta loved pretty things, a necklace here and there, maybe a set of inlaid steak knives or something for her attractive supper tables. But now she was seven months pregnant and a third person would soon be entering their lives.

Hank had not told her about the difficulties with his business. Instead, he had written checks and deliberately placed them into misaddressed envelopes so that nothing would be cashed too quickly. It wasn't actually cheating, just a little delay, no explanations needed. Explanations crowd the things that people want to believe about you. But now he would have to come up with some explanation. He promised Greta that, when his claim in Amsterdam had been processed, there would be plenty of money, enough even for them to purchase a small home of their own. Yes, it would have a washing machine.

The letter sat on his desk. A woman claiming to be Esther Bernsteen had filed a duplicate claim to the house in Amsterdam. When the Dutch letters arrived, he told Greta that they were for his business, and in a way they were. He wasn't lying; he just wasn't saying anything. He had protected himself with silences his entire life. Silence never hurt anyone. In the quiet of the August afternoon, he looked up into the sky, where a few white fluffy clouds moved along overhead. Would thunderheads be forming? He hoped not, and anyway, there was time before it would be necessary to pack up their picnic.

A trail of ants led from the picnic basket to a bare spot of ground, marching like soldiers in a column, bearing food and occasionally dragging the body of one who had fallen. Where were they going? He followed the trail with his eyes, and saw the small rise indicating an anthill. With the gleeful smile of a young boy he took a stick and poked it in, just to see what was inside.

The ants scrambled every which way, some digging into the hill, and some exiting with their possessions. My God, is that all we have done for the past ten years, run around an anthill? He had left Holland with a camera, keeping a sharp lookout for his safety. His sister had dug further in. With the stick he began to examine the anthill for tunnels, supplies of food and other creatures.

What if Susani Lutz really was his sister? How would that change things? Did he want to meet her and learn what had happened? Probably not. Were other family members alive? He wasn't interested in ghosts. In some ways, they made their own graves when they… what? What choices had they really had?

He would have to meet Mrs. Lutz if he wanted to claim property in Amsterdam. Who knew what it was worth now? He had avoided looking at the newspapers and at the modest shops of displaced Jews, or the paths that Jewish properties took through the maws of mixed currencies and uneasy new alliances. Oh, and one last detail. Greta must never know that he had been born a Jew.

He scheduled a business trip to New York City.

The Brooklyn address was in a noisy neighborhood. The houses looked like Amsterdam row houses, but instead of quiet canals, tires screeched, horns honked and children were running everywhere. Once Hank was on Prospect Place, he had no need to look at the addresses to identify the apartment. If Susani Lutz was indeed his sister, she lived in the yellow brick building with the sunny bay windows.

The drab hallway with its dark woodwork was not inviting. Old-fashioned wallpaper covered the space in muted patterns, and a dirty mirror kept the visitor from looking too closely at himself. The doorman, busy accepting deliveries and buzzing apartments, finally noticed Hank and pointed him to the elevator. A door was cracked open on the fourth floor, and he knocked. A strange man opened it and looked him up and down.

"You must be Hans? I am Georg Lutz. You have come to see my wife, I believe."

"Yes, if she is originally from Amsterdam." Hank twisted the wedding ring on his finger. An entire life had been deconstructed and rebuilt since he last saw Amsterdam.

"Please come in."

A vase full of roses and Queen Anne's lace stood in the hallway, strangely reminiscent of the trailing vines and wildflowers that his mother used to arrange. He stepped into the sunny living room, tears beginning to form in his eyes. A pretty brunette came toward him.

She was Esther, and not Esther. There was no laughter in the green eyes. They were haunted, fearful and submissive. Her high cheekbones were translucent, not rosy. Her proud shoulders and bosom were covered by a loose housedress. Then she laughed, "My God Hans, I wouldn't recognize you – tall, mustached, come here."

He was very wary of the strange woman in front of him, a ghost of his sister. Her arms went around him, and she kissed him on both cheeks, then pinched his elbow, a warning gesture from their childhood, an alert that secrets should not be shared.

The pinch dissolved his suspicion. He choked on the tears, and she began to sob into his white shirtfront. He handed his camera to Lutz. "Could you take a picture of us together?" then took a fresh handkerchief from his pocket and wiped her smeared mascara as the two of them faced the camera.

Lutz looked at the shining new camera with its elaborate system of dials for focus and light, snapped the picture and wondered who would want this photo. He was the only family Susani had. As for the strange man with the intense blue eyes, was he a Jew too? A brother would want to know that his sister was an obedient wife, well cared for

"Come, Zus, may we eat a little something? Hank, would you like a beer?"

Hank demurred. "Not right now, but thank you."

"I have bought my Susani a new refrigerator. Now she does not need to go to the market every day. She is turning into a real American housewife." Lutz said nothing about how they had met.

Susani held her tongue, taking in every feature of the man who was a stranger and a brother at the same time. The eyes and the high forehead were the same. His mouth and jaw were now resolute. The slouch was replaced with a square shouldered stance. Where had he been for nine years? She stepped into the kitchen and prepared a tray of light sandwiches and cake. A pitcher of iced tea would have to do, and Lutz could complain about beer later. The three of them discussed grocery stores and shops – funny soft American bread, cheese with no flavor, and no butter or cream to make a proper cake. They laughed about the mushy fruits and vegetables in cans and complained about the lack of greengrocers and butchers. They were unified in their criticisms of the country they had chosen.

An awkward silence fell as Hank tried to open the discussion about Amsterdam. Had Susani/Esther been successful in locating mother? Max? She wept and, by a glance, they decided to not discuss where each had been for the past several years. She couldn't tell him about captivity, and he couldn't tell of his specialized tasks. Lutz broke the ice. "I say live and let live. I'm not so sure we even needed the war."

Hank strangled in his own silence. The Germans had been defeated, and only then did they decide that the war was a bad idea? News of Russian attacks on German civilians was reaching American papers. Hank had heard one story after another in his work with the POWs. An agreeable comment would make it possible for him to visit with his sister. "Let's face it, our common enemy is Russia, and we have not solved the problem. Stalin could make Hitler look like a schoolboy."

Lutz continued with his friend's story, passing it off as his own. "In 1941 we were on a march, an awful cold march, along the Moscow to Vladivostok line... the Russians were marching toward us... no one could shoot because you would end up shooting the guys in front of you. Both columns stopped, it was bitter, very bitter cold. We shared our flasks of schnapps and vodka. I asked for the red star from his uniform, and he gave it to me. I gave him a patch from mine. That was our great victory, our battle with no bullets. We liked each other, a bunch of 18 year-old boys, and that morning we didn't even know why we were marching in columns to fight each other. Then we marched on. They were nice. We were embarrassed. I often think of them."

Here was one of the "Black Ones – *die Schwarzen"* alive and well, with a nice apartment and a wife in the United States. The bastard had escaped against all odds. Hank knew his sister. She was alive, with a new name and in a new country, and that was enough. If Lutz could accept friendship from anonymous Russians, he would accept Lutz as her husband. He was American now, and Americans were fair in conquest. It would be necessary to win the peace.

The doorman's buzzer rang incessantly and Lutz went to respond to a call, changing into his overalls and picking up his toolbox. He didn't want to be seen as a manual laborer, but there was no choice. An elderly lady on the first floor was certain that she smelled gas. She smelled gas all the time, afraid that she would die like her mother and sisters in Sobibur. She was terrified by his German accent, but he was extremely kind to her. She didn't trust him, but she liked him, often baking little treats for him and his pretty wife.

As soon as he left the apartment, Hans nervously explained to Esther that their past could not be disclosed. It was as dead as the family. She laughed.

"You think I don't know this? Look at me, married to a captor and making dinner for him each night. He's hardly a movie star. There is no Clark Gable at this tea party."

"Are we still Jews?"

"I'm not sure. I'm an atheist now, but my Catholic husband does not need to know that. I tried to become a good Catholic wife. I have even been pregnant twice."

He looked around. "You have children then?"

"No, no children."

"My wife and I are expecting a child."

They began to discuss the Herengracht property, agreeing to use Dutch for all their written communications. Greta did not understand Dutch, and Lutz was not a reader. They would conspire as they once had when they were children, wheedling things from their parents. Esther's cat slept on the windowsill.

Cats have nine lives, and they were only on their third.

54414904R00194

Made in the USA
San Bernardino, CA
16 October 2017